BY THE SAME AUTHOR

NO COWARD SOUL

by
NORMAN TUCKER

---

*'No coward soul is mine,
No trembler in the world's
storm-troubled sphere'*
EMILY BRONTË

JOHN LONG

LIMITED

LONDON   NEW YORK   MELBOURNE   SYDNEY   CAPE TOWN

DEDICATED TO

A. M. G.

Printed in Great Britain at
The Fleet Street Press
East Harding St., EC4
1947

FOREWORD

THIS is the fifth historical novel with North Wales as a background. The setting was chosen because this is a land I love. As an Englishman I feel that I can write impartially, dispassionately, without national bias or prejudice. To many people North Wales is still an unknown country—or at least unexplored. I should like to feel that my books have at least helped to make its charms more widely known. I want to convey to those who have not sojourned here a hint of the majesty of the mountains, the tranquillity of the vales, the romance of the castles.

Above all I should dearly like to see a closer understanding between near neighbours—English and Welsh. The days of border warfare are long past. Among my prized friends are many who are Welsh—their warm-hearted sincerity has meant much to me.

Perhaps I am unwarrantably presumptuous in using the term "historical novel." I think I am. *No Coward Soul* does not merit so imposing a designation. No research has gone into its fashioning as was the case with earlier books. Yet one incident is worthy of comment. This is the tragedy of the Conway River ferry. In his *History of Aberconwy*, published in 1835, the Rev. P. B. Williams says: "On Christmas day 1806, owing to a heavy swell in the river, the boat conveying the Irish mail with eight passengers, the coachman, guard, and a boy, in all fifteen in number, including the boatmen, was upset, and only two escaped with their lives."

It is said that the disaster was so shocking that it set afoot an agitation for a bridge. This resulted in the erection of Telford's stately structure which enhances the scene to this day.

A Conway sailor, Griffith Owen, did fight at Trafalgar on board H.M.S. *Conqueror*. His grave is to be seen hard by the porch of Conway's ancient parish church. Save for the fact that smuggling appears to have thrived between Anglesey and the Isle of Man, most of what remains in the book is mere fiction. Yet so long as humans are beset by life's perplexities and problems, fictitious characters can sometimes speak as forcefully as men and women of flesh and blood.

NORMAN TUCKER

"Penshurst,"
    Colwyn Bay,
        North Wales

WHEN, upon a morning in spring, the sun shines upon the Menai Straits, there can surely be no fairer scene anywhere in the world. The landscape is bathed in a green tranquillity which breathes peace. The very waters have a jade translucency which reproduces not merely the image but the tints of the trees which grow verdantly upon the banks. If there is any motion it comes from the drowsily moving current, the wing of a passing gull, or the prow of a cutter gliding hopefully out to the fishing grounds, or returning laden at eventide to its anchorage. Like some hoary watchman, grey with age, who placidly spends his declining years in nominal occupation, venerable Beaumaris Castle poses as protector of the peaceful scene. Peace seemed to spread abroad its comforting wings on a May morning in the year 1803. The throstles and blackbirds put peace in their notes. The boys romping on the shingle at Gallows Point laughed instead of wrangling. Gossips near the Shire Hall smoked their matutinal pipes in complete content. The very corvette which had dropped anchor in the roads the evening before had her ports closed, and lay "as idle as a painted ship upon a painted ocean." There was peace, peace everywhere. But it was the calm before the storm. Europe's stormy petrel, France's First Consul, was fluttering his wings preparatory to another flight over ambition's restless waves. If the men of the ancient borough were aware of the war clouds they did not reveal their anxiety. Beaumaris might be too far distant from the capitals to be troubled by the foibles and follies of mankind. It almost seemed so. And yet it was not entirely so. The strife of nations had not passed the borough by. Enoch Hughes had left for Wrexham to enlist in the Twenty-Third Foot—the celebrated Royal Welch Fusiliers. Danny Parry had gone to sea. This was less surprising for Beaumaris had been a port since the days of Edward the First—perhaps even farther back than that. Danny, a foretopman aboard H.M.S. *Majestic* had been at the battle of the Nile. He came home two years after with such stories of that great fight that it was the means of providing him with free ale so long as he remained on leave. Folk still talked about it. It was something to be proud of that Danny Parry of Beaumaris, and Nelson had given the Frenchmen such a drubbing.

"But that damned Boney ain't licked yet," grumbled Madoc

Morris as he settled his shoulders more comfortably against the sun-warmed wall of the inn, and spat meditatively into the roadway. "There's trouble brewing, I'm telling you. Listen to what I says, lads, and don't go saying I never told yer."

He looked about him defiantly, daring anyone to contradict him. No one did.

"What can we do about it?" ventured a little fisherman who specialized in the catching of lobsters. His tone was mild but he embarrassed the burly Madoc Morris.

"What can we do, Tom Lobsters?" he remarked. "We can fight, of course, fight Boney and keep on fighting him."

"Are you going to fight him, Madoc?"

"Huh! Not unless the press-gang get me. Still, what I says is, we ain't going to lie down and let Frenchies walk over us. That Boney's ambitious. That's what he is, ambitious." The word pleased him. He looked from face to face to note the impression he had made. "He's as ambitious as Nigel Preece."

"Is Nigel Preece ambitious, Madoc?" inquired Tom mildly.

"He talks so that no man knows what he says."

"That's not being ambitious, Madoc; that's being learned."

"He's ambitious," said Madoc darkly. "Mark my words. No good'll come of it."

"Well, Madoc, he's been to college. And he's a schoolmaster."

"All the same he's no right to be ambitious, man."

"Why not?" asked Tom. He had a way of disconcerting his powerful comrade.

"Why not? It's wrong. *Duw anwyl*, man, did you ever hear of a schoolmaster being ambitious?"

Apparently no one had. There was no response until Madoc removed his pipe and pointed with the stem. "There he goes now. Owns all Beaumaris by the looks of him. Ambitious. That's what he is."

All heads were leisurely turned towards a figure crossing the road. The man was worth looking at. Despite his sober clothing he had an air of distinction. There was haughtiness about his cultured, intellectual features which might well have evoked Madoc's damning condemnation. Yet, when a curly-headed boy came running from an open door and collided with his legs he caught the child under the arms and swung him high in the air in a manner which betokened good-nature as well as strength.

Then Nigel Preece strode rapidly on his lonely way, and the houses hid him from view. There was silence until the stillness was broken by the regular clatter of a horse's hoofs.

"Here comes Squire," observed Tom. The remark was superfluous.

The Squire was as well known as Beaumaris Castle or the Shire Hall, and it was his custom to ride to the town at this hour of the day. No other horse walked with such firm assurance down the old street. The sturdy roan seemed conscious that he bore on his back a person of consequence. He placed each hoof loudly and deliberately as though to say—thus shall you be trampled underfoot if you dispute our progress.

Yet the face of Hugh Vaughan of Castell, Esquire, was not an entirely brutal face. It was hard, arrogant, accustomed to command, proud, glowing with bodily health. There was a certain sparkle in the blue eyes as he nodded to the folk touching their forelocks as he passed by. He greeted them with a familiar uplifting of his riding-crop, but many an urchin knew well that, had he failed to touch his cap, the lash would have flicked his legs as a sharp reminder. Manners maketh man.

The clop-clop of the deliberate hoof-beats cut the silence of the quiet street. There was an awkward hush until the well-built horseman in his snug-fitting coat of green, his cord breeches and riding-boots, his glossy beaver hat, was out of sight.

"Well," observed Madoc ponderously to the vanishing shoulders, "he dunno wot I know, else he wouldn't sit so proud like."

"What do you know, Madoc?" Tom inquired, almost anxiously.

"I seen his daughter talking to Nigel Preece."

"And then wot?"

"Just that, Tom. Ain't that enough?"

"Why shouldn't Miss Bronwen talk to Nigel Preece?"

"I dunno, quite, why not. But he's ambitious, is Nigel Preece. Mark my words." His brow was furrowed in thought. He spat into the roadway. It was a signal for departure. The men sauntered to the shore, crossing the broad strip of grass which stretched like a pleasant lawn between the houses and the water. The diminutive Tom sought his lobster-pots, Madoc with the other men returned to the upturned boat which they were repairing.

Along the Penmon road Nigel Preece was standing stiffly on the grass verge as the squire reined in his mount. There was no hat-touching. It was an exchange of formalities; platitudes. One could almost sense a veiled hostility. On a cold and cloudy day this might have been more pronounced, but how could one be anything but civil on a morning as blithe as this?

" 'Morning, Preece. Fine day. No school, eh?"

"Good morning, Mr. Vaughan. It is a delightful day; typical of the approach of summer. The school is closed to-day. I should hardly be walking here during lesson hours."

"Just so. Well, you've picked a good day for your holiday. Chose wisely."

"I endeavour to choose wisely, so far as my fallible nature permits me. I have given the children a whole holiday to-day in honour of young Bevan, my senior scholar, who has secured a scholarship for Jesus College, Oxford."

"Ha! Nick Bevan's son, eh? The rascal must have brains. And—where did you say? Jesus College? That's quite a good place, I've heard say."

"I am naturally biased in its favour, Mr. Vaughan. It happens to be my *alma mater*."

"Demme, yes, I'd forgotten you were a college fellow, though you don't hesitate to proclaim the fact."

"I have no recollection of ever having referred to the matter before. Might I remind you, Mr. Vaughan, that the topic was of your own choosing?"

"Whatever else they may not cram into a man at Jesus, I'll say this: they teach him a proper sense of his own importance. Well, I hope young Bevan does well. What's he going in for? The Church?"

"His father has not yet determined upon his boy's career."

"Army could do with him. They need fine, upstanding young fellows like Bevan. This upstart Napoleon Bonaparte is going to cause more trouble, I hear. I had no faith in a patched-up peace."

"I am afraid that there is no limit to Bonaparte's ambitions, sir, since he became First Consul. The invasion of our country is not beyond the bounds of possibility."

"By gad it isn't, Preece. Well, he'll have a hard nut to crack. If it comes to that I've a mind to turn out with the yeomanry. Not too old yet to sit a horse, you know."

"No one would doubt your spirit, sir."

"Never let a Frenchie beat me, anyhow, Preece. Quiet, there!" The latter was addressed to the roan, which shifted impatiently. The squire tightened the reins in his left hand, paused staring straight ahead, then turned quickly with his right hand on the crupper.

"Heard my daughter was at the school yesterday, Preece."

"Yes, Mr. Vaughan. It is correct. Miss Vaughan did call at the school yesterday afternoon."

"What does she want ?"

"Miss Vaughan wished to show me some verses she had been composing. She was flattering enough to think that my criticism might prove helpful!"

"Verses? You mean the girl's writing poetry? Huh! What's the stuff like?"

"It holds promise, Mr. Vaughan. Her delicacy of thought is obvious. There are structural weaknesses such as one might reasonably expect from one who tries her 'prentice hand."

"Seems harmless. Good enough for girls as like as not, though I fail to see how a vigorous young fellow like you should tamper with such rot. Don't get like this fellow Wordsworth."

"I understand that Mr. Wordsworth walks as vigorously as he talks, sir. So far as I am concerned my ideal has always been *mens sana in corpore sano.*"

"What the devil might that be?"

"A sound mind in a sound body. I imagined everyone knew that."

"Well, I didn't, and I'm not above admitting it. English or Welsh is good enough for me, without raking up that jargon. But you wouldn't be a pedagogue if you did not like airing your knowledge. I suppose that's what we pay you for. Good day, Preece."

"Good morning, Mr. Vaughan."

The clatter of the roan's hoofs again sounded on the dusty road. Nigel Preece walked across the grass. His head was high, his expression calm. There was a faint flush on his cheeks.

The grass stretched seawards almost without interruption; it was surprisingly open country for a strip of land which was so densely wooded farther up the straits. Here the ground was smooth and unbroken. Its edge was fretted by the persistent attention of the waves, its low green bank an impudently frail barrier to mark the limits of the mighty deep. At this point the estuary widened perceptibly. The Caernarvonshire shore seemed far away. So did the smooth hills which rose precipitously. So did the mighty mass of Penmaenmawr's majestic headland. It always made Nigel think of Gibraltar. He wondered if the Fusiliers garrisoned at the Rock ever detected the likeness; whether it made them nostalgic. Probably their minds did not dwell on anything higher than beer and Bonaparte. He glanced down. The pollen of buttercups was gilding his shoes. It pleased him. He loved nature. Did the flowers and the bees know more about the secret of the source of life than mortals did?

A hail from seaward cut in on his reverie. A boat was out there, pulled by two oars, moving easily with the flow of the ebb-tide. At the oars were two figures, bare of head, tanned, healthy, happy, buoyant. They waved. Nigel Preece's face brightened as he responded. His steps quickened. There was eagerness in his stride. Who, in Beaumaris, did not know the Penryn twins—merry, mischievous, roving, reckless? They had passed their twenty-first birthday but somehow they refused to grow up. Swarthy as foreigners from the sunny south, dark brown eyes which sparkled with animation, teeth which gleamed particularly white, hair which curled black and glossy as a raven's wing, they seemed in their right setting when afloat. Local legend had it that they were descended from old Piers Griffith of Penrhyn who built ships in the Aber Cegin and sailed to fight the Spaniards, and whose piratical exploits subsequently caused his sovereign such embarrassment that the predatory Piers had to dispose of his estate to pay the fines imposed upon him for deeds committed when he roved the Spanish Main. This ancestry was but gossip, yet it savoured of fact, for if ever a youth was bred true to type it was young Piers Penryn whose conduct seemed to proclaim that the wild, reckless blood of the long-dead sea-dog ran in his veins. The twins wore home-knitted blue guernseys. They looked, in the distance, alike, but Nigel knew them well enough to appreciate that it was Puah who pulled the bow oar, and that the snug-fitting guernsey moulded a form which Aphrodite might well have envied. Piers wore a broad leather belt in which he carried a gully made fast to a soiled white lanyard. It seemed his badge of office, his token of authority. Piers backed water as they neared the shore.

"Come aboard, you lubber," he shouted.

"Yes," called Puah over her shoulder, "do come out with us in the boat, Nigel. Are you playing truant, to-day?"

"And why, pray, should not an overworked dominie have a day off as well as two indolent buccaneers?"

"Piers, did you hear that? Splash him with your oar. He pretends we don't do any work."

"I'll make him work," said Piers grimly as he ran the boat's prow close to the bank. "Off with your coat, my fine schoolmaster. You shall pull my oar until your hands are blistered."

"Very well," said Nigel, rolling up his sleeves and cautiously descending to the water's edge. "Is this a confession of lassitude or incompetence, Piers?"

"What on earth does all that mean, Nigel? You do love big words," objected Puah.

"I mean, is Piers lazy or doesn't he know how to row? Anyhow, I will not join you unless I can row bow oar."

"Why?" demanded Puah.

"Never you mind. Get on to that next thwart."

Piers took the tiller as the boat was pushed off. Nigel dipped his oar with an ease which showed that he was at least no novice where boat work was concerned.

"Where are you heading for?" he inquired.

"Priestholme," explained Piers, "after guillemots' eggs."

"After gulls' eggs, razor-bills' eggs, puffins' eggs, any eggs," added Puah.

"There must be some reason for this sudden outburst of enthusiasm."

"There is, Nigel. A man arrived at Bangor on the coach yesterday. He came to collect birds' eggs. Piers was there and offered to get them. Only, Nigel, I'm ashamed of him——"

"Now, shut up, Puah. No telling." Piers looked fierce.

"I shall tell. He said he would get the eggs—if he was paid."

"Why shouldn't I be paid?" Piers grinned. "I never miss an opportunity to plunder my fellow-men. Blame my ancestor. It's in my blood."

Nigel, noting the gold ear-rings which gleamed as the young man moved his head, could not help feeling that he spoke more truly than he realized. He loved Piers as a brother yet he had to confess that there was something wild and untamed and uncontrolled about him which at times was almost frightening.

"And already he has so much money that he does not know what to do with it," added Puah with simulated sadness.

"Yes, Piers, where do you get all your wealth?" asked Nigel. "Is it some pirate hoard you have discovered, concealed by your long-dead ancestor? I suppose he must have buried his ill-gotten gains somewhere."

"Oh, I'm not rich," observed Piers casually. "I have a guinea or two to throw about. It is because I am thrifty, really, and have no woman in tow to waste it for me."

"If your woman did not get more out of you than I do, Piers, she would throw you over," remarked Puah.

"You greedy minx, you drain me of all my hard-earned cash!"

he shouted with mock ferocity. "Nigel, in spite of her prating, I'll wager she claims half of what I get for the gulls' eggs."

"Why should I not? I shall have earned it."

"You see, Nigel. And this is the jade who criticizes me! Nigel, what the deuce did you want to sit so far for'd for? You'd have done better to have left Puah where she was. The boat's not trimmed properly. She's down at the bows and rides like a log. If we're going to cross to the island safely we ought to get her more shipshape."

Nigel did not reply. He was wearing one of those slightly haughty looks which came naturally to his features.

"Yes, tell us why, Nigel," added Puah.

"If I sat on the after thwart I could not see Puah," explained Nigel. "As it is I have a wonderful view of those saucy curls at the nape of her neck."

"I'll slay you," cried Puah as she dropped her oar and turned with upraised fist.

"Look out, you mad fools! You'll have us over!" yelled Piers. "We're getting into the tide-race. Sit still, or we'll upset."

CHAPTER II

O N the top of Puffin Island—Priestholme, to give the isle its more ancient name—Nigel Preece and Puah sprawled side by side with their toes and elbows embedded in the soft, short turf. They had chosen their vantage point well; a high place where the cliffs sloped abruptly, and the bracken had not encroached to spoil their view. They had turned their backs on the Caernarvonshire coast. It limited their vision. Here they could look seawards, out to the distant horizon; a prospect as wide and uninterrupted and limitless as their visions and their dreams. A sable cormorant, its ungainly neck outstretched, flapped awkwardly over the wave-crests. The gulls were clamorous. Guillemots swept past in anxious, hurrying flocks, like aerial cavalry at manœuvres. Half-way down the cliff-face the watchers could see the dark blue figure of Piers clinging to crevices by fingers and toes.

"He'll be breaking his neck if he isn't careful," observed Nigel anxiously. "Hadn't we better fling him a rope?"

"He'd scorn it," said Puah, unmoved. "Piers will never break his neck; don't worry. I often tell him that it is left for the hangman to do that."

"But need he bother about more nests? Surely we have eggs enough." Nigel glanced towards the basket in which the brown mottled eggs made a colourful pattern.

"Yes, we have eggs enough and to spare. It is not that. He must be doing something. And he must take risks. Life would be tame to Piers if there were no risks. Let's talk of something else."

"What shall we talk about, Puah? Shall I tell you what a little fool you were, nearly upsetting the boat in the tide-race?"

"Pah! We can all swim, and the weather's mild. Anyhow, you should not have made fun of my back hair. I'll not put up with it, Nigel, so now you know."

"I did not make fun of it. I meant what I said."

"That makes it all the worse. I will pull bow oar on the way home. Then I'll be able to say rude things about you behind your back."

"My remarks were not rude."

"They were. But I shall not argue with you. Talk of something else. What was Squire Vaughan saying to you? No. I beg your pardon. I had no right to ask that. That really *was* rude. I ask your forgiveness. I don't know what made me say it—just for something to talk about, I suppose."

"My dear girl, I don't mind telling you; not in the least."

"But I don't want to know, Nigel. I just wondered whether he was scolding you for not touching your hat. He's fussy about such things. I could see you standing up to him, straight and haughty, as though you defied him."

"Did I look like that? I am sorry. I was unaware of it."

"Oh, don't say that. I just lov—admired you for it. He gets too much of his own way. All the townsfolk give in to him; all save Piers. It is not right. Who made him a little god to rule over us?"

Nigel was plucking at a grass stem. "I can tolerate almost anything but patronage, Puah."

"I know you are proud, Nigel."

"Damnably proud, God help me! Isn't pride categoried as one of the seven deadly sins, Puah? If so, I am to be counted among the damned. I cannot help it. It is in my blood, just as wildness runs in Piers' veins. Merely because we do not know our ancestors we have no right to assume that their traits do not manifest themselves in us. Sometimes I fancy that many of our so-called weaknesses are not of our own devising at all but are legacies from those who are dead and gone."

"I always think that is a bit unfair. I suppose that's what the parson means when he talks about the sins of the fathers being visited on the children."

"To the third and fourth generation, Puah. So if you and I can withstand the devil, our grandchildren may be free of the curse."

"That's not very cheerful for you and me, Nigel. Anyhow, Piers' ancestor goes a long way farther back than four generations, but from what folks tell me old Piers Griffith must have had an extra big dose of the devil in him, so maybe it hasn't got properly diluted yet."

"My ancestor goes a long way farther back than the days of Elizabeth."

"Your ancestor, Nigel? I don't know what you mean."

"Do you know how I came by my name?"

"Nigel? No, but I like it. It suits you. And it flows as smooth as the tide."

"My mother's maiden name was Loring. The spelling has been altered, but her father was descended from the same Sir Nigel de Loryinge who was given a grant of land at Pwllheli and Nevin by the Black Prince for his services at Poictiers. I have never mentioned it to a soul before, Puah, and I ask you not to. But that is why I, with the blood of a knight of the Black Prince in my veins, will never bow the head to a man like Squire Vaughan who does not know the name of his great-grandfather."

"You look a thoroughbred, Nigel. I—I wonder how you can stand to waste your time on poor fisherfolk like Piers and me."

"Puah!" Nigel sat up, flushed, upset, almost angry. "You shall not talk like that. How dare you! You know that you and Piers are the best, no, the only friends I possess in this forsaken place. If it comes to ancestry wasn't your Piers Griffith of the oldest blood in North Wales? And as for you calling yourselves poor fisherfolk——" He broke off abruptly. His mood changed. He picked up Puah's small, sunburnt hand and held it gently. "You will not talk like that again? Promise me. It hurts."

"Does it hurt, Nigel? Then I won't. I—I am glad that our friendship means so much to you."

"It means more than you realize. When I am occupied in the school I am reasonably content. Once the hours of the day are over I have no companionship but yours. There is no one to whom I can turn but you and Piers."

"But we are not good enough, Nigel. You are so clever. You have a college degree. You have so much that I lack."

"You have much that I lack. So we will exchange. We will help each other."

"Yes. Let's share." She gave a little laugh; a happy laugh. "Now, tell me all the squire said."

"Let me see. Why were the boys having a holiday? I told him about young Bevan gaining a scholarship for Jesus College. Said, inadvertently, that I had been there. Whereupon he observed that Oxford gave its graduates a proper opinion of themselves."

"Oh, good!" cried Puah, her dark eyes dancing with delight. "That's when I caught sight of you looking so haughty. As if you had thrown down your gauntlet and were challenging him to a duel. Go on."

"Not much else. We spoke of the possibility of war breaking out; the likelihood of an invasion."

"And just as he was about to move off he turned and asked you something."

"Ha! Yes. Said he had heard that his daughter had called at the school."

"And had she?"

"As a matter of fact she had—to show me some poetry she had written."

Puah was silent. She rose to her feet and stood staring out to sea. "Is—is it difficult to write poetry, Nigel?" she asked dreamily. There was a slight breeze. It ruffled the dark waves of her hair. It moulded her figure. She stood statuesque, blue-garbed, some tutelary spirit of the sea.

"Hard to write poetry? My dear girl, either you do or you do not. If you cannot write poetry it is not hard to learn—it is impossible. If you can write poetry, you cannot help yourself. Almost it writes itself. At any rate it gives you no peace of mind until the words are recorded."

Puah sighed. "I have never felt like that. Is Miss Vaughan's poetry good?"

"It would scarcely be seemly for me to offer criticism."

"Then it isn't! I'm glad. Glad!" Her expression changed. It was animated now. "Let us fetch Piers. There won't be a nest left on Puffin Island. And I am sure it is time we had something to eat."

They went down to the boat which had been hauled on the shingle at the only spot where a landing was possible. They fetched the provisions, Nigel carrying the hamper. Together they lit a fire of driftwood. The man stood idle while Puah prepared a meal. With the wood-smoke curling upward, and her black hair tossed about her sunburnt face, she looked more gipsy-like than ever. A true child of the wild. So thought Nigel who stood regarding her, finding a certain æsthetic pleasure in the natural grace of her movements. Puah glanced up and noticed the intensity of his gaze.

"Off with you and find that brother of mine. He ought to be here by now. It isn't like Piers to be missing when there's food about. Take a rope with you just in case——"

Nigel picked up the coil and started to climb the cliff, pausing once to hurl a stone at a rabbit which disappeared into the bracken with a flourish of white tail. There were many of them on the island, as the close-cropped turf indicated. Nigel wondered idly how they managed to get there.

Once on the cliff-tops he shouted. Presently he saw the head and shoulders of Piers appearing over the edge. Piers scrambled on to the grass and bent to dust his knees.

"Where have you been, Piers? The meal's ready and we are tired of waiting for you."

"Well, I'm damned! There's gratitude for you."

"Gratitude? For what?"

"Well, haven't I made myself scarce? Two's company, three's a crowd, so they say. I've left you with Puah all to yourself all afternoon."

"Oh!" Nigel spoke sharply. "Well, thank you, but it was quite unnecessary, you know."

"No?" Piers was busy disentangling his lanyard which had become twisted during his perilous ascent. "No? Sorry, Nigel. Meant well—for once in my sinful life. Let's go back along this path. I left some eggs in my cap. There it is. Right! Now for a bite and sup."

It was a quiet meal. For some reason an unexpected silence settled on the group as they sat around the fire. The three who had chatted so cheerily as they came down the straits now found no topic for conversation. There was nothing amiss with Puah's cooking. The fish she grilled was tasty. When they finished eating Piers filled a pipe. Puah sat clasping her knees and gazing across to the Caernarvonshire mainland. Nigel lay back on the shingle and watched the gulls gliding against the cloudless heavens. It was Piers who broke the stillness.

"I wonder what that damned sloop is doing at the anchorage," he said. "The Navy don't often favour us with their presence."

"Maybe she's bound for the Isle of Man," suggested Nigel. "A day or two ago a man was telling me that there's a lot of smuggling going on there."

"Huh!" Piers sucked vigorously at his pipe, which did not seem to be drawing well. "I'd give her a wide berth if I were you, Nigel."

"What? The corvette? How does she concern me?"

"Press-gang." Piers was succinct.

"But there's no war on—yet."

"No, there's no war on—yet."

"What makes you talk like that, Piers?" asked his sister. "Do you think war is likely?"

He nodded. "This new First Consul is the very devil. Boney means to invade England. The French are building huts at Boulogne by the hundred. By the thousand, I should say. There will be the very deuce of an army waiting to cross the Channel before long—that is, if our Navy will give 'em leave."

"Are you sure, Piers?" Nigel sat up, interested. "How do you know all this?"

"Oh, a man told me."

"But was he rightly informed?"

"I should say so. Give me a hand with this hamper. It's time we got to the boat. The tide is on the turn. Ay, the Navy'll be in need of men, all right. Take my tip, Nigel. Keep off the streets at night, so long as the corvette is here."

"That will not be difficult. I rarely go out. But what of you? Is there no risk?"

"They'd never catch Piers." It was Puah who spoke. "I wish they'd have a try. It would be fun—watching."

"Your idea of a joke is feeble, Puah. I should be led like a lamb to the slaughter."

"There would be slaughter, but the lamb would do the slaughtering! Come on! Let's get the boat launched, Piers. And you take an oar this time. I'll steer."

She stepped lightly into the stern-sheets and caught hold of the tiller. The two men ran the boat off the shingle and stepped in. A few strokes bore them into the run of the tide.

The sun was getting low when they drew near to Beaumaris. There was a hush over the straits. The corvette had swung at her anchor. They could see her graceful outline, broadside on, the black gun-ports picked out sharply in the yellow band which bisected her black hull.

"Twenty guns," counted Piers.

"I wonder what her name is?" surmised Nigel.

"She's the *Unique*. I read the name last night when I pulled out and lay right under her counter."

"What on earth for?"

"Just to see if the marine sentries were awake."

"You might have had a musket-shot for your pains."

"Bah! They couldn't hit a barn door, those lads. And they were asleep anyway. See, they are lowering a boat. Someone's coming ashore. See here, Nigel. I'll run in and land you on the bank. Go back by road—it will be safer. They may overhaul us. They're pulling four oars. We can't compete with them for speed. Hard a-port, Puah."

There was no further word spoken until Nigel stepped ashore.

"Thanks for the picnic, twins," he said. He looked at Puah who sat in the stern-sheets fingering the tiller. She smiled gently.

"Good night, Nigel. Thank you for coming."

"But what about you folk?" added Nigel, pausing. "Suppose they overtake you. They might impress you, Piers. You run as great a risk as I do."

The young man's teeth showed white. "They won't catch this bird, Nigel. Never you fear. Take the other oar, Puah.

A bit of pulling will warm you up. Sweet dreams, Nigel. Keep clear of the roads."

The schoolmaster stood motionless for a while, watching his friends rowing towards the town landing-place. He noticed that they hugged the shore. The corvette's boat was ahead of them. Two officers had stepped ashore. He could tell they were officers by their neat blue and white uniforms. He wondered who they were; what they wanted. He saw Puah wave her hand. He responded.

Nigel walked, a solitary figure, towards the cottage where he lodged.

CHAPTER III

NIGEL PREECE showed no hurry to go home—if one could apply that cherished word to the comfortable cottage where he lodged. Perhaps he had come under the spell of the evening. He was in a contemplative mood. He wanted to be alone with his thoughts though he could scarcely have defined what those thoughts might be. Certainly they were not objective; only abstract, vague. He was conscious of a restlessness of mind, a yearning for something so far unattainable. Something as intangible as a drifting cloud, hazy as mist.

He leant against a low wall of dry stone, weathered by age. The world was still. The fresh green leaves of the sycamore above him were unstirred. The water was placid, an unruffled mirror. He wondered why it was that this hush so frequently came at the going down of the sun. Was there some scientific reason for it, or did it indicate that nature was settling the world to sleep? Of course there were occasions when the wind blew and the rain descended at the close of day, but mostly it seemed that this was a silent hour; a time of tranquillity, of rest, of repose.

There was no repose in his mind. But did he desire repose? Too much stillness might indicate stagnation! It was not repose he sought; it was attainment. He felt that he had been sent into life for a purpose; he had a sense of vocation; a belief in his own destiny. And assuredly he was not fulfilling it at Beaumaris. Not that he was idle. No man could have been more conscientious in his duties at the school; no student ever crowded more hours of study into candle-lit evenings. But it took him nowhere. It was like unwholesome food which filled without satisfying.

He was proud and he was ambitious. Not in any vain or unworthy fashion. It was as though some instinct within him, something in his blood, persisted in reminding him that he was cut out for better things. He was not consciously aware of it and yet the urge was for ever there; a slow fever which left him never, day or night. He glanced down at his attire and his lip curled scornfully. The sombre cloth was faded, worn, and ill-cut. He would have dressed fastidiously had his purse permitted. Why was it, he mused, that he who scorned money was perpetually handicapped for lack of it? It was as though money was personified and, knowing his contempt, resented being treated with contumely.

A passer-by would not have found anything base in his appearance. The fading light had softened sartorial defects. All one would have discerned would have been an erect figure with the haughty mien of an aristocrat, a broad, intellectual brow, calm, fearless eyes, and a proudly poised head as clearly chiselled as a cameo. Perhaps the original de Loryinge looked thus while he awaited the accolade.

Weary of inaction Preece began to walk towards the town. As he passed the castle moat he heard voices. Men's voices, one cool, cynical; the other loud, raucous, as though its possessor was not too sober. He saw the neat blue and white uniforms of the two officers who had landed from the corvette, and caught a glimpse of gold braid. One officer was dark, saturnine. The vociferous one, he of the carroty hair, had features reddened by rain and rum. He was a sturdy, stocky man, a trifle unsteady. At the sight of Preece he broke off his conversation and stepped into the roadway.

"Hi, you! What's the course to Squire Vaughan's?"

Nigel's eyebrows were slightly elevated. He looked through the man as though he had been a wraith.

"Damnation!" bellowed the sailor. "I'm addressing you, fellow. Which is the way to Vaughan's house?"

"Ask civilly and I may tell you, fellow!"

"Damn your impertinence. D'y' realize I'm a King's officer?"

"Yes. Do you?"

"Demme, Pink!" interposed the dark man. "He's hit you there between wind and water. Come on, you fool, and don't make a scene. You're drunk."

"He's 'sulted me!" argued the red man, endeavouring to pull his sleeve from his companion's grasp. "You, fellow, d'y' hear? You're damned insolent."

"So are you."

"By the flaming devils of hell, I'll——"

"You'll shut up and conduct yourself in public with decorum," said the dark officer firmly. His grasp tightened on the struggling man. 'See here, Pink, stop making a fool of yourself. 'Pon my oath, you strain the bonds of friendship. Sir!" He turned to Preece. "I ask you to accept my apologies for the discourteous treatment accorded you. You may perceive that my friend is hardly himself. Might I trouble you to indicate the way to Mr. Vaughan's house?"

"Certainly, sir. This road will lead you direct to his gates."

"I thank you, sir."

"Pleased to be of assistance, sir." Nigel Preece gave a slight bow and proceeded on his way, his ears apparently oblivious of the nautical expletives which the drunken officer volleyed at his haughty back.

Outwardly he was unruffled but there was a slight flush on his cheeks. How difficult it was to control one's temper! It would have been so much more satisfying to have lashed out. His fingers clenched at the thought. To have sent his fist crashing into that coarse mouth. . . . Preece shrugged his shoulders. How primitive the best of us were! Was civilization nothing but a veneer which could be chipped by a few stinging words?

There was a small garden to the house in which he stayed. At the green-painted wicket gate he paused as though reluctant to forsake the satisfying calm of the wide out-of-doors for the cramped confines of his parlour. A short path led to the front porch, a walk of shingle, edged with round sea-stones over which London Pride thrust its feathery fronds in a pink spray.

In the low, dark hall he was met by the owner of the cottage, Mrs. Evans, a comfortable person in a spotless white apron. She addressed her erudite lodger in motherly tones.

"A lady is waiting to see you, sir. I showed her to your room. I hope it is the right thing I did."

"It could not possibly be otherwise, Mrs. Evans. A lady to see me? I wonder—what it can be!"

Nigel Preece tripped over the word "what." He was almost saying "who" when, like a flash, intuition suggested the identity of the unknown caller. He was not surprised to see Bronwen Vaughan seated in the wing-backed chair; the cosy, cretonne-covered chair beside the hearth where he so frequently sat. His books were on a small table at its side. Miss Vaughan had one of them in her hand.

As she rose to her feet it fell to the floor. She stooped to recover it but Nigel, lithe of movement, forestalled her. Their heads almost collided. Miss Vaughan's face was flushed and her eyes unnaturally bright when they straightened up. Nigel was calm. He placed the book on a table with studied deliberation.

"I am sorry. How foolish of me, Mr. Preece. Perhaps I ought not to have touched your books."

"My books are always at your disposal, Miss Vaughan."

"I suppose you are wondering why I am here. You are too courteous to ask me."

"I am satisfied to await your explanation."

"I—I have been writing some more poetry, Mr. Preece."

"I compliment you."

"There seems to be some magic in the spring which prompts one to give expression to one's emotions in verse. You understand that?"

"I understand. Your experience is by no means unusual among those possessed of a desire to write."

"The desire. I have the desire, Mr. Preece, but alas, not the ability! How could I possess that, living as I do amid such worldly surroundings? And to-day! It is the harbinger of summer. The whole world breathes peace and poetry. Were you not conscious of it? You must have been. And I—I had to find some medium to express the thoughts which surged within me. Tell me, do you like what I have written? Is it not typical of the sunset sky at which you have just looked?"

Somewhat shyly she handed him a slip of paper. Preece concentrated his gaze upon it. He read aloud with deliberation:

> *"It is a beauteous evening, calm and free,*
> *The holy time is quiet as a Nun*
> *Breathless with adoration; the broad sun*
> *Is sinking down in its tranquillity;*
> *The gentleness of heaven broods o'er the Sea."*

For a moment he did not speak. His face was set like some classical mask. Bronwen Vaughan, looking fixedly at it, thought that she had never seen such beauty in a man. But cold. So cold. Expressionless. Devoid of emotion. Enigmatical. What was he thinking? She would have given much to know.

"Is it good, Mr. Preece?"

"Flawless."

"The best I have written?"

"Better than you have ever written." The words were spoken quietly but they made Bronwen Vaughan catch her breath. She looked almost startled. "What do you mean? Oh, Mr. Preece, don't look at me like that. You frighten me. What have I done?"

"I do not wish to frighten you, Miss Vaughan. It is not any expression on my face which causes you disquietude. Tell me, candidly, why did you do it?"

She hung her head, looking so like a child, conscience-stricken, repentant, that Nigel felt an irresistible desire to stroke the lovely hair. Stroke it soothingly as one would comfort an infant in trouble. Instead, he walked across to a cupboard, sorted some papers, and returning laid them on the table. His forefinger, long, pointed, artistic, indicated a written poem. Miss Vaughan read only the first words:

"It is a beauteous evening, calm and free. . . ."

She sat down suddenly in the arm-chair and covered her face with her hands. "I am wicked! I ought not to have tried to deceive you, Mr. Preece. It is true. The poem is not mine. I—I only copied it. But I did so want to please you; and you found fault with my other verses."

"Could you please me by deceiving me? Can I take pleasure in duplicity?"

"Oh, no. No! I will never attempt to deceive you again. I never have done so before and I never will again. All the other verses I have written were my own. I might have known that you, who are so clever, would have detected my subterfuge. Though I do not know now how you came to know."

"My dear Miss Vaughan, Mr. Wordsworth wrote that beautiful sonnet last year. It has not, as yet, appeared in print, but it has been circulated amongst acquaintances and lovers of poetry, all of whom speak most highly in praise of it. I happen to be one who keeps in touch with a literary circle in London and a copy was sent me by a friend. There is nothing unusual in this. What amazes me is that the poem should have reached you."

Miss Vaughan touched her eyes with a handkerchief before she looked up. "I will tell you," she confessed. "My father has a correspondent in London who sends him news-letters each week. Without father's knowledge I wrote to his correspondent and engaged him to collect the most recent poems for me. I hoped that my style might profit thereby. And this one was so beautiful that I copied it hoping that you would consider that your pupil had improved by your tuition. I thought to please you; instead I have displeased you. How you must despise me! How I despise myself!"

A slight smile crossed his features. "The crime, my dear Miss Vaughan, is not so heinous. Let us laugh at your folly. You see, it has brought its own punishment."

She sighed, but looked relieved. "Yes, I suppose it is always so. When one does wrong one is punished for so doing."

"There was a time when I thought so; now, I believe that there is no greater fallacy."

"Indeed?" Miss Vaughan looked surprised.

"I am inclined to the belief that the person who gets punished is not the one who does wrong but the one who makes a mistake."

There was a look almost of mischief in Bronwen's face as she glanced up. "Then I have not done wrong; I have only made a mistake?"

"Undoubtedly you made a mistake."

"If you had not received the poem from your friend in London would my attempt have deceived you?"

"This is positively embarrassing, Miss Vaughan. Have I to be courteous or candid?"

"Be candid, please."

"Then let me say that I should have found it difficult to believe that my inadequate tuition could have wrought so great an improvement in so short a time."

She smiled ruefully. "How gently you deal your blows, Mr. Preece!"

This time it was Nigel who smiled. He wondered whether a certain naval lieutenant would have endorsed her opinion. The smile faded from his face, leaving his expression grave.

"Miss Vaughan, I beg you to forgive me for mentioning it, but are you discreet in visiting me—unchaperoned?"

"No!" She shrugged her shoulders. "I know that I am not."

"Then, why do it? For myself I care nothing, but I am jealous of your good name. Your father spoke to me this morning, intimating that he had heard of your visits to the school."

"My father hears too much. I suppose someone has gossiped."

"Someone invariably will gossip. Such is my experience in life."

"Was my respected parent unpleasant?"

"Oh, no. But his words set me thinking. The most innocent actions are apt to be misconstrued. Remember what I just told you—we get punished not for doing wrong but for making a mistake. Why do you come to see me?"

Her eyes told him. But her lips replied: "I get so terribly bored at home. Every night the menfolk sit drinking. Every day they are absorbed in sport. Father considers himself the domestic sun and we lesser luminaries must bow down and worship. There is no conversation worth listening to. They never open a book. To speak of literature, of art, of culture, is to brand oneself as a nincompoop. My brother Rhys does what he likes—why should not I?"

"Because, Miss Vaughan, you are not your brother Rhys."

"They regard me as if I were a piece of furniture. But I will not tolerate it for ever. I will have my own interests, my own friends. I will come to see you—if you will allow me. I must. Only I will remember your words. I will not make a mistake."

"You are making one now. You are staying too long. You will be missed."

"Must I go?"

Instead of answering he drew back the corner of the blind. "It is as black as the pit. I had better escort you home."

"I would like you to," she said softly.

CHAPTER IV

NIGHT. Soft darkness. Stillness. Shadowy outline of gable and tree against a starry sky. On the water, ripples of light from the lanterns of the anchored corvette. Cottage windows with candle points. Murmur of distant voices.

Nigel Preece and Bronwen Vaughan paused as the door closed behind them, paused close together until their eyes grew accustomed to the night.

"How dark!" whispered Bronwen. She could not have told why it was she whispered save that the world seemed wrapped in silence, and speaking seemed sacrilege. She laid her hand timidly on Nigel's arm. Her fingers touched the sleeve lightly at first but when he moved towards the gate she followed, crowding closer because of the narrowness of the path. Her hand took a tighter grasp as they moved down the road. She was conscious of the firm, muscular strength beneath the cloth. The roadway was deserted. The hush of eve had given place to the silence of the night. They walked without speaking, treading softly, they knew not why, and yet their footfalls seemed loud, so still was the world. As they passed an alley they heard a subdued: "Hist!" Both turned their heads quickly, Nigel inquiringly, Bronwen nervously. A small shambling form detached itself from the gloom.

"Mr. Preece, sir?" The whisper was low. "I was just making my way to your house, sir, when I see you come out of the light of the open door."

"Why, it's Tom Lobsters," observed Bronwen with relief in her tone.

"No names, miss. Not to-night at all events. Mr. Preece, sir, I was sent to carry you a warning."

"A warning? From whom? About what?"

"Never you mind who sent it. Let's say as it were a friend. About what, you asks? The man-o'-war's company is planning a raid on the town to-night. They wants likely lads for the King's Navy. He! He! Reckon I'm safe. That's the best of being a little 'un. So I was sent to tell ye to keep off the streets."

"I thank you for your kindness but, as you see, I must escort this lady home."

"Bit awk'ard, that be. I got no instructions about no lady.

Well, I've delivered my message, fair and square, as you might say, and I dunno as there's any more as I can do about it."

"There isn't, Tom. I thank you."

The man touched his forelock and shuffled back to the darkness of the alley.

"What are you going to do?" asked Bronwen as they moved forward. For a moment her companion did not speak. She glanced up, noticing the clear-cut lines of his features. He seemed more handsome then ever in that dim light: like the reincarnation of some Greek god. Her fingers, almost imperceptibly, tightened on his arm.

"Do? Why, I shall see you home, of course, Miss Vaughan. When I set out to accomplish a thing I am not easily deterred." He spoke quietly but there was firmness in his tone. He seemed to fling defiance at fate. "Those fellows dare not lay their hands on me."

"Are you sure, Mr. Preece?" Her tone was anxious.

He laughed. "No," he confessed. "I am not at all sure."

She stopped suddenly. "Then we will not go along the road. The castle approach is an ideal place for an ambush. Come, let's go by way of the Castle Meadows; over the fields. I know the way."

"But the dew is on the grass. You will get soaked."

She laughed. "Much I care!" There was a touch of bravado in her tone. Different, thought Nigel, from the demure miss who consulted him about her poetry. "Come!" she said firmly, and her fingers slid from his arm and tightened about his wrist. They turned into a side road, but before they had gone many paces, Nigel pulled up. His arm went instinctively about her shoulders bringing her to a standstill. "Hush!" he breathed.

From out of the darkness came the steady, methodical, orderly tread of marching feet; feet marching down the road they had vacated but a moment before.

"The press-gang!" whispered Bronwen. "Quick!" She darted into a cottage gateway, pulling Nigel after her. They crouched below the level of the low stone wall. It was whitewashed and had irregular stones along the crest; a rustic attempt at an embattlement. A large fuchsia bush thrust itself over the top, and from behind this they peered cautiously forth.

It was strange, thought Nigel, as they waited with fast-beating hearts, to be crouching in a stranger's garden with the cool earth damping his knees, and the daughter of the proud squire close beside his elbow. He was conscious of the gentle pressure of her body; his nostrils caught the fragile fragrance of some exotic perfume she favoured; a scent which he ever more associated with Bronwen Vaughan.

Against the pale outline of the road they could see a body of men pass by; men in dark clothing. From their hips thrust the awkward outline of cutlasses. There was no speaking. They marched in silence intent on their mission. The watchers waited until the moving mass melted into the gloom of night. Bronwen sighed her relief, and straightened herself. Then she gave a low laugh of excitement. "Wasn't it wonderful?" she whispered gleefully. "I was terrified for a moment but now it's over I realize I haven't experienced such a thrilling moment for years. We were only just in time."

"I owe my escape to you, Miss Vaughan. Accept my thanks. What made you think of it?"

"Womanly intuition, I suppose! What would you have done had they caught you?"

"Alone, I should have fought my way through; with you—candidly, I do not know what I should have done. But thanks to your perspicacity I am spared that dilemma. It looks as though we should have to cross the Castle Meadows. Unless you wait here while I get someone from Price's livery stables to drive you home in a dog-cart."

"What? And have all the household hear my approach? No, thank you. I shall slip in by the servants' entrance and change out of my wet clothing before I am noticed. Don't talk. Follow me."

It was Bronwen Vaughan who led the way now, moving with the sureness of one born and bred in a district. More than once she stretched back her hand, taking Nigel's fingers in hers as she guided him past a difficult piece of country. Once, in the midst of a meadow, they paused as the night carried shouts and sounds of strife. They waited until the noise had died down. Then they resumed their way without speaking. Comment was superfluous.

Finally they reached a low stone wall which marked the boundary of the Vaughan estate. Bronwen seated herself on this but instead of making any endeavour to cross she ruefully examined her sodden shoes.

"My feet are soaking," she commented.

"I warned you!"

"But what could we do? You are not sorry we came this way, surely?"

"No, I am not sorry. But hadn't you better get in and change."

"There's no hurry," said the girl, clasping her hands about her knees.

"No hurry? Will you not be missed?"

"Oh, they don't trouble their heads about me. There will be a drinking bout to-night. Rhys has invited two officers from the warship over for a spree."

"I know. I saw them."

"Really? One dark, and the other all carroty?"

"The man they call Pink?"

"You have his name. Yes, he'll be there. That's why I want to keep out of the way. He's a loathsome beast, really, always trying to paw me."

"I was not prepossessed by the little I saw of him, Miss Vaughan."

"Miss Vaughan! Call me Bronwen."

"It would be presumption on my part."

"It would not. I want you to call me Bronwen when we are alone at all events. You must call me Bronwen. You shall call me Bronwen."

She slipped from the wall with agile grace and caught the lapels of his coat. "Please call me Bronwen, Nigel, please! I've no one in the world to turn to but you. No one I can trust. No one on whom I can rely. Please, Nigel."

"You are in trouble? You are not dissembling? You are really and truly as distressed as you appear?"

"Really and truly, Nigel. You think me forward, I know, but I'm desperate. I am alone. Trapped. I must have a friend to stand by me or I shall collapse. You are wholesome, upright, honourable. It is written all over you. I turned to you from the moment I set eyes on you, like a flower turns to the sun. Poetry—what do I care for poetry! No, I don't mean that. I—I like it, in its way, but I had to make some excuse to get to know you better. You understand? And do you think me quite shameless?"

"I think you must be in very real need of protection," he paused, and added gently, "Bronwen."

"Thank you, Nigel." She held out her hand. He took it in a firm grasp. Her fingers were as cold as stone.

"Tell me," he commanded. "You must tell me. And tell me everything. If we share, we share utterly or not at all. There can be no half-measures. Either you trust me or you don't. I won't have half-confidence. Is that clear?"

"I understand. I will tell you everything. First, about that beast Pink. He wants to marry me—so he says."

"Marry you! What does your father think of the proposal? Or does he not know of it?"

"Know? He has arranged it. He wants me off his hands. And it is what is called a good match. That's all that matters in holy matrimony, Nigel. Make a good match. Love, honour, tenderness, understanding, kindred interests—silly rot not worthy of serious consideration! What's wanted is a good match. Get the girl married into a good family, by gad! Plenty of money; heir to a title and all that!"

"And is this—Pink—a good match?"

"The Honourable Hubert Kirby, my dear Nigel, is heir of Lord Aldergate, with every prospect of a speedy inheritance as his noble father is a four-bottle man and is crippled by gout."

"And the other man—the dark officer?"

"I don't know him so well. Lieutenant Moir. Only met him once before."

"What does your brother think? Does he sympathize with you?"

"Sympathize? Rhys? It's a colossal joke to him. He's betting on the issue with anyone who'll take him on. The odds are all on Pink. If you want a flutter, just suggest it to Rhys and he'll accept your bets."

Nigel drew in his breath. He had been taught to reverence women. "And your mother is dead?"

"Dead these seven years, thank heaven. I believe father's coldness hastened her end. I cannot understand my revered papa. I see no indications of his being vicious, but he's as cold as a tombstone. I could picture him standing at the side of a dying man and clearing up some ambiguity in the will with the utmost thoroughness. He thinks no more of disposing of me than he would of a litter of spaniel puppies."

"There's no one to whom you can turn?"

"A couple of servants are loyal to me—otherwise there is no one, Nigel."

"Yes," he said slowly, "there is! I am a person without influence. A man of no consequence. I have neither position nor wealth. Nor have I prospects for the future. But if, in your extremity, you feel in need of a friend, Bronwen, I will never fail you so far as my endeavours will serve."

He spoke quietly but with subdued fervour. The girl made no answer. She stood motionless as a statue, her face turned to the sky. A crescent moon had crept above the distant hill-tops. By its faint illumination Nigel could see her features. She was, (as she had observed) not unprepossessing. He would not dispute that statement. Her eyes were lustrous, unnaturally large. A glistening tear rolled down her cheek. The sight of it embarrassed him. He had not seen a woman weep before. Was she going to make a scene? But she stood silent, stoical. When she spoke her voice was restrained, subdued. Perhaps she had been fighting to overcome emotion.

"Thank you, Nigel. You give me fresh hope. This is one of those immortal hours which impresses itself on the memory; on the heart. God knows what the future holds, but—I shall not forget."

She caught up her skirt and clambered over the wall with surprising agility. Nigel watched her running across the grass. She did not look back. He was sure of that for he watched until her form vanished from sight. A dog barked once, but only once. Then there was silence.

Nigel suddenly became aware of the coldness of his feet. He turned his sodden shoes in the direction of Beaumaris. An eventful day, he mused.

He sighed. The morrow's school was going to be unendurable.

CHAPTER V

I T was an unusual experience to be in school again. To Nigel Preece it savoured of unreality. His class-room seemed a strange place, and he a stranger within it. He kept looking over the tousled heads bent industriously over the knife-hacked desks and wondering whether these really were his scholars. They seemed more difficult than usual, more restless, more aggravating. Perhaps they sensed his abstracted mood. He kept staring out of the dusty windows, noticing a tree against the blue sky. It was a focal point on which he directed his gaze while his thoughts strayed by devious paths. Mostly they crossed a dewy meadow in the dark. He had discovered a new Bronwen Vaughan and the discovery pleased and puzzled him. It intrigued and fascinated him. He had come upon an open door and his eyes beheld strange sights. The skeleton in the family cupboard of the Vaughans had been briefly revealed to his wondering eyes. And the girl who had called at the school with her attempts at poetry was not the vapid, insipid society woman he had imagined her. His judgment had been at fault. She was a woman of spirit. A woman in trouble. A desperate woman. A woman who appealed to his sense of chivalry and who, mutely, called upon him for aid. How could he aid her? He, who was without influence—without money! That was the devil of it. Money was power. He must get money if he was to aid her in an emergency. And how could he get money? Assuredly not as a schoolmaster. A feeling of frustration swept over him, infuriating him at the thought of his impotence. His fingers tightened spasmodically on a quill with which he had been toying. As it snapped, the faint crack brought his thoughts back to earth. He glanced up quickly to find a score of curious eyes turned in his direction, wonderingly. It was almost as though the boys were trying to read his thoughts. Preece felt the colour rising to his cheeks and he endeavoured to cloak his confusion.

"Keep your eyes on your books. Any more of this inattention and I will keep the whole school in for an hour!"

Down went the heads like those of marionettes when a string is pulled. There was an atmosphere of studied concentration as though each boy was resolved to outdo his neighbour. Their lips moved inaudibly. Preece knew that this was to give the impression that they were drinking in every word they read.

He also knew that their minds were far from the printed page.

For the first time in his life he found himself completely indifferent to their studies. Instead of their being citizens in the making they had become encumbrances, annoyances. He wished vainly that he could send them away on another holiday. But that could hardly be. Bevan could not keep on winning scholarships. And Bevan was holding up his hand, sitting bolt upright, his gaze turning from the master to the window, from the window to the master.

"Please, sir, there are two bluejackets coming to the school." Simple words, yet they sent an uncomfortable feeling down Nigel Preece's spine. The schoolmaster glanced with apparent unconcern through the window. He saw two middle-aged men with tarry pigtails, bell-bottomed white canvas trousers, short blue jackets and striped vests. Each wore a cutlass at his brass-buckled belt. They came with deliberation towards the door. Their footsteps sounded outside. There was a sharp tap on the panel and the door swung open. Mr. Preece was calm and self-contained.

"Well, my men, what do you want?" He spoke crisply.

"It's a school, Jack," said the taller man. "I said as how it was a school."

"Ay. It's a school right enough, Jim." The second man turned to the master. "Begging your pardon, sir. We're just having a look round, as it were. Sorry to interrupt the young lads in their lessons."

"Do you want me? Is there anything you require?"

"No, sir. Not at all. Give you good day."

The man gave a careless salute. The door closed. The seamen vanished from sight. But something of their presence remained. The boys seemed more restless. Nigel Preece assumed a more stoical expression, which was a sure sign that beneath the placid surface he was agitated. He was thankful when the bell tolled the hour of noon. At his curt dismissal the boys scrambled for the door. The class-room was empty. Preece walked thoughtfully to the cottage where his meal awaited him. It was a substantial meal, well cooked, but for once he had no appetite.

"Nothing wrong with my cooking, I hope, sir?" Mrs. Evans was concerned as she cleared away the plates.

"How could there be?" asked Nigel with one of those rare smiles which women found irresistible. "No, Mrs. Evans, I am just not hungry to-day."

"Maybe it's the spring," she suggested hopefully.

"I should not be surprised," agreed Nigel courteously.

School again. Another interminable period. What could he give the boys to do? Something which kept them occupied and yet left him free to his thoughts. His mind kept going back to the visit of the bluejackets. Why had they called? There must have been some reason. They had not looked in to see if it was a school when it was so palpably a school. They were looking for him. He was sure of that. They could not intend to impress him! It was unthinkable. Yet stranger things had been known. And once in the Navy it was not easy to get out again . . . unless one deserted! What a life a deserter would lead! Always looking over his shoulder. He would sooner volunteer than be pressed. It was a matter which required thinking out carefully. He was not averse to fighting the French, but it seemed such a waste of good time. Had he taken a degree for no better purpose than to holystone a frigate's maindeck? He beckoned Bevan and took him outside the door.

"I am taking you into my confidence, Bevan. I don't like the visit of those bluejackets this morning."

"You think that they are after you, sir?" Bevan's dark eyes were shrewd.

"It is not beyond the bounds of possibility."

"Would you like me to keep watch, sir?"

"I was going to suggest it. You could possibly take your Latin book with you and improve the shining hour."

The boy fetched his book and Preece returned to his desk in an easier frame of mind. It was with a feeling of relief that the hour for dismissal was reached. The boys ran off shouting to the Castle Meadows for a game before tea.

Nigel Preece was left in a deserted school, alone with his thoughts. They were, it must be confessed, almost entirely of Bronwen Vaughan. Why had she come into his life like this? Twenty-four hours ago he was content—or reasonably content— to live the life of a scholar. Now he was restless, ill at ease. His ability to concentrate had forsaken him. The country was on the eve of a great war and he was barely interested. Was he falling in love? The thought came to him as a shock. He weighed the matter carefully. Not having been in love he decided that he could not be sure but was inclined to doubt it. There seemed to be no appeal to the emotions, and from what he had read that was the primary quality of love. Rather the situation appeared to be a claim on his chivalry. In his inexperience he did not appreciate that the two experiences were not poles apart.

He did know that the realization that this girl was unhappy, troubled and harassed, touched and stimulated him; aroused in him a desire to hasten to her succour. Something of the long-dead de Lorynge stirred in his veins. He must enter the lists on her behalf. But how? As he sat behind his desk meditating he heard a light step and Bronwen walked into his thoughts.

"Good afternoon, Mr. Preece. What a lovely day!"

"It is indeed, Miss Vaughan. Too nice to be indoors."

"I have brought another poem for your criticism," she remarked casually, as she spread a paper on his desk. "And have all your scholars departed?"

"Every one. Do you want me to—comment on this verse now?"

"No." She spoke shortly. "I want to talk to you. Are we alone?"

"Yes."

"Shut the door."

She toyed with her gloves nervously, staring out of the window. Nigel returned to the desk and waited for her to speak.

"It was horrible last night."

"Did they know where you had been?"

"No. But they had missed me and had been looking for me. Fortunately they accepted my story that I had been out with the dog. Lieutenant Kirby was there."

There was an inflection in her voice which conveyed more than her words.

"I take it that he was objectionable."

"More so than usual. He insisted on kissing me. You see how candid I am with you?"

"It was agreed. Thank you for telling me. When I understand I can decide how to act. I will see to it that he is duly chastised."

"No, Nigel, that is the last thing which must happen. You see, my father insisted that we should be betrothed. They were all pretty much in their cups."

"And you?"

"I consented."

"I congratulate you, Miss Vaughan." Nigel gave a formal bow.

"Don't be a fool. What else could I do? We must play for time, Nigel. The corvette sails at sundown. I do know that. And it may be a long time before she returns. Perhaps—it is sinful of me to think it—perhaps Pink Kirby may be killed in action."

"What a predicament! I still feel that I should like to give that rascal a good drubbing."

"No. No. For my sake. He has already got his knife into you. I heard him saying that you had insulted him. Somehow he has found out who it was he spoke to. And he swears he will be revenged on you."

"I am not averse to meeting him."

"Please keep out of his way until the ship sails. Please, for my sake!" She came close to him, pleading. At the look in her eloquent eyes, he crushed down his pride, and answered gently: "Very well. I will not seek him out."

Perhaps there is a fate which decrees that a man's best intentions sometimes come to naught. Nigel Preece felt virtuous in his resolve not to seek out the man whom he had come to regard as his enemy. There seemed to have been aversion at sight. It so happens at times, just as there is attraction at sight.

A silence fell upon the room. Nigel idly touched the paper on which the poem was written. It was, he noticed idly, about daffodils and so Bronwen must have written it some time ago—if she had written it. He read the lines casually, not being in the mood for verse. His brain was puzzling itself over the problems which had so unexpectedly descended upon it. The sound of steps approaching at a run caused them both to turn. The upper part of a face appeared at the window and a grimy finger tapped vigorously. The window opened. Nigel strode towards it and flung it wide. Tom Lobsters' diminutive form was outside.

"Squire's a-coming!" he panted, and ran away.

Nigel turned towards the girl, biting his lip.

"What is it?" she inquired anxiously.

"You did not hear? He said your father was coming."

"Here?"

"Obviously. What will you do? Escape while you can?"

"No. Why should I? I am not ashamed of being here!" she looked defiant.

So they stood in the silent room waiting. They heard a horse's hoofs and the rattle of wheels; a curt "Whoa!" . . . the sound of footsteps . . . two sets of footsteps. Squire Vaughan stood framed in the doorway; behind him showed the blue and white of a naval uniform.

"What are you doing here, Bronwen?" The voice was cold.

"I am consulting Mr. Preece about a poem, Papa."

"Ha! Is that it?" Mr. Vaughan strode to the desk and snatched up the verse. Perhaps he had anticipated something more sentimental. When he read the words slowly there was disappointment as well as disgust in his tone.

> *"When apple trees have burgeoned red*
> *Despite the March winds blowing,*
> *I like to walk with stealthy tread*
> *Where daffodils are growing,*
> *Half listening lest a trumpet note*
> *Should issue from a golden throat."*

"Is this all? Don't tell me you have come here to consult this man about such rubbish! And March, eh? You're a bit out of date, girl. What else is there?" His broad fingers impatiently sorted the papers on the desk. His search was not revealing. A few puerile attempts at Euclid; a sum or two. An imposition.

"Well, sir? Is this your idea? These clandestine meetings?" The squire stared coldly into the schoolmaster's face.

"Clandestine is incorrect, Mr. Vaughan. I must ask you to withdraw it."

"Damnation, sir, I do no such thing! Do you deny that you are getting on friendly terms with my daughter? Bear your station in mind. I give you warning. I have other plans which I do not intend to have spoiled by your interference. Take warning, sir. Come, girl. Home."

He took Bronwen's reluctant arm and led, almost forced, her towards the open door. Lieutenant Kirby who stood a silent spectator stepped aside with a bow to let them pass. As father and daughter walked towards the waiting dog-cart the lieutenant turned to Nigel Preece who stood in haughty silence in the centre of the open space.

The sailor took a slow step forward. "I have something for you, my fine fellow," he said. Nigel glanced disdainfully into the furious face. Something in the steely blue eyes warned him. His hands moved instinctively. Too late! A great red fist, coarsened by sea life, crashed into the point of his jaw. Preece staggered and fell against the desk, catching the back of his head a cruel blow on the corner. He thudded to the ground and lay with outspread arms. A thin trickle of blood traced its pattern slowly across the boards of the schoolroom floor.

CHAPTER VI

T H E group of loungers on Beaumaris main street turned curious heads as the sound of hoofs and wheels came to their ears. A trap was coming down the road. They knew that it would be the mail cart which usually made its appearance at that hour with the mail bags collected from the coach which ran to Holyhead on its way from England with the post for Ireland. Tom Mails— so called to distinguish him from Tom Lobsters—was so regular that a man might almost set his watch by his arrival. But to-day he was ahead of time. They had not expected him for five minutes at least. And his speed was in excess of the methodical pace at which his chestnut mare was accustomed to trot from the ferry.

Madoc Morris removed his pipe and spoke like the town oracle. "Big news, lads. Tom Mails only whips up the mare when there's news. And I bet I know what it is!"

"War's broke out?" asked Seth Price.

Instead of replying Madoc stepped into the roadway. The day was drawing to a close and the streets were quiet. Against the flush in the western sky they could see the silhouette of Tom Mails flicking his whip. It was an unnecessary gesture as the mare was doing her best. Obviously it was intended to create an impression. Tom liked to be the centre of attraction. The bearer of tidings. The purveyor of news. The chestnut was foam-flecked.

"Hi, Tom Mails, what news have you to-night?" shouted Madoc. "Is it war?"

"My news is for His Worship the Mayor!" shouted Tom over his shoulder as the red wheels rattled past the group.

"Grr—drat his swelled head," muttered Madoc as he returned to the sidewalk. "But it's war, lads. Take my word for it. Come along to the Shire Hall. It's sure to be posted and proclaimed. Let's not be missing nothing. Any of you seen Tom Lobsters? He's up to something, is Tom. Well, he'll miss the news this night, and serve him right."

The diminutive Tom, at that moment, was not troubling his head about the declaration of war against France. He was on tiptoe staring through a window of the old grammar school, staring wide-eyed into the rapidly darkening room. On the floor sprawled a figure, arms outstretched, its head in a pool of darkness which could only be blood. Tom hastened to the door, glanced

down at the still, white face of Nigel Preece, and began to run
as fast as his short legs would carry him, not to his boon companion, the burly Madoc, but to the home of Piers Penryn.
Without the formality of a knock he burst into the kitchen
where Puah and her brother sat. He gasped his news.

"Preece School is murdered! He's lying dead on the floor of
his class-room with his head bashed in."

Piers was on his feet. His chair crashed to the floor. It was
typical of him to act and not to ask questions. He shot through
the door so fast that Tom was brushed off his balance. Puah
followed her brother so rapidly that the two were almost out
of sight by the time Tom was in the roadway again. Sturdily
he set forth in the wake of the lithe, long-limbed runners.

Tom came upon them bending over the stricken schoolmaster. Piers was parting the hair with fingers as practised as
those of a surgeon. As Tom panted into the room Piers glanced
up. "He's not dead," he said crisply, "though he's mighty near
it by the look of things. The bleeding's stopped now but he's
lost a lot of blood."

The remark was superfluous.

"*Anwyl!* What happened?"

"Somebody's knocked him out." Piers gently touched Nigel's
left jaw. It was swollen and discoloured. A thin thread of blood
had trickled from one corner of his mouth. Puah moistened her
handkerchief with saliva and gently cleaned it away. It seemed
to mar the beauty of that marble face.

"Never you mind that, Puah. Give me a scarf or something to
bind his jaw. It's dislocated. And get me a bandage for his head.
And a pad. Run home for a pillow-slip or something. The blood
has caked over the wound but it may reopen when we move him.
Tom, run across to Price's livery and get a light wagon. And
chuck in as many rugs as you can lay hands on. Say it's for me,
but keep your mouth shut about what's happened. Understand?"

Tom nodded and disappeared. Puah had already run off. She
was back first, ripping a pillow-slip into bandages as her brother
deftly applied them.

"You'd make a good surgeon, Piers," she said admiringly
as she sat back on her heels. While she spoke she was automatically chafing one of the cold hands which lay listlessly in hers.

"Had plenty of practice." Piers was concise. "Wonder who
struck him."

"I'd like to know," said Puah with emphasis.

"So should I. And it won't be long before I do find out. They must have taken him by surprise. He's pretty slick with his fists, is Nigel."

"Perhaps they clubbed him," suggested Puah.

"No. Knock-out on the jaw. He hit his head on the desk, see?"

Puah moved restlessly to the door and after a few minutes came back to say that Tom was leading a livery nag attached to a light wagon down the road.

"Take the horse's head, Puah, and send Tom to fetch Madoc and two or three others. We'll need to lift Nigel carefully."

They waited. It could not have been long but it seemed long. Puah, with her hand at the horse's bit, never took her eyes off the road. Piers, squatting beside his friend, never took his eyes off the still face.

"The lads are here," said Puah, entering the quiet room. "Where shall we take him?"

"To the rendezvous." When Piers spoke in a quiet, firm voice, it meant that he must not be contradicted.

"Not home?" ventured his sister.

"No. Press-gang. They're after him. This may be their work. I'm not sure, yet. But we must get him out of town."

"But surely——"

"Don't argue. We'll take him to the rendezvous. There's something queer at the back of all this."

Madoc and three other men came in, walking gently in their heavy boots. They carried a tarpaulin. No word was spoken. They moved as though in the presence of the dead. They paused until, at a motion from Piers from whom they took their orders as though from a superior officer, two gently raised the unconscious man a few inches from the schoolroom floor while the other two rolled the tarpaulin under him so that it formed a flexible stretcher.

"Are you taking him home?" asked Madoc softly.

"No." Piers was quiet, too, but emphatic. "To the rendezvous."

"Hell!" breathed Madoc. "And why?"

"Why? Because, you fool, the press-gang are after him."

Madoc did not reply. He chewed his tobacco quid as though ruminating. Then he walked to the schoolroom grate, rubbed his hands against the chimney's soot and blackened his face. The other three men, of deliberation and without comment, followed suit. Their action occasioned not the faintest surprise to either Piers or Puah. Then they returned to the four corners of the tarpaulin. It was fortunate that Nigel Preece did not recover consciousness at that moment for as the sooty-visaged bearers bent over him they might well have appeared as denizens of the nether regions.

Puah tenderly supported the bandaged head as the men slowly bore their burden to the waiting wagon where the diminutive Tom held the horse's head. A few neighbours came out, mostly women. There were a few whispered questions, compassionate looks.

"Pity, too," said one robust dame who carried a broom. "And him so gentle like. Wonder who done it."

It was no easy task lifting Nigel Preece into the wagon. Puah superintended the operation, looking as concerned as though the patient was her only child. Tom had not merely obtained a pile of horse-blankets and rugs but, with commendable forethought, had thrust a few armfuls of hay beneath, so that Preece would lie in comfort. Piers examined the head bandage anxiously and then gave a nod of satisfaction. The bleeding had not restarted. Absorbed in their mission of mercy no one paid heed to what was happening in the street. Even the sturdy boatmen started with surprise when a woman's voice shrilled:

"Look out! 'Ware the press-gang!"

The stillness of the evening was broken by the sound of running feet; a shout or two; a hoarse command. There were bluejackets in the road, approaching from both directions at a lumbering run. Burly men with cudgels in their hands and sheathed cutlasses in their belts were under the charge of a warrant officer, a bos'n.

Burly Madoc Morris, unrecognizable save for his size, knocked down a seaman with his mighty fist. The naval men closed in on all sides. Puah, squatting on her heels at the side of the unconscious Nigel, looked about her, bright-eyed. Her brother was not to be seen. The black-faced boatmen were struggling with the men in blue. The odds were all against them but the movements of the press-gang were hampered by an ever-increasing body of women who ran from the houses, belabouring their heads with mops and brooms, flinging buckets of water into their faces, while urchins joined in with volleys of stones. Shouts! Curses! Commands! Confusion!

Only Tom Lobsters stood his ground. The horse, terrified by the commotion, plunged and backed. Tom, possibly feeling secure from arrest on account of his stature, grabbed the reins and quickly swung himself into the driver's seat.

Puah turned as the vehicle swayed with the pressure of his body. "Oh, good for you, Tom *bach!* Drive like the devil. Let's get out of this."

A bluejacket sprang for the horse's head. Puah snatched the whip and cut him across the face. A comrade wrenched the whip out of her hands and leaping on to the shaft began to wrestle with Tom who, despite his smallness, was tough. The horse moved forward and broke into a frightened run. Puah lost her balance and fell back into the vehicle. They were drawing away from the surging crowd. She was conscious of a bluejacket in the roadway behind raising his arm threateningly as they moved off. His cudgel came flying through the air. Puah flung herself in front of the prostrate Nigel, and gasped with pain as the missile struck her shoulder a shrewd blow. She bore the bruise for weeks, a proud memento of the encounter. Her concern was for Nigel. The horse was galloping now. The vehicle was swaying. She tried to hold Nigel's head. The bleeding had started afresh.

"Tom! Tom! Pull up!" she yelled as she rocked with the swaying wagon. There was no response. Puah looked up to see the bluejacket hurl Tom into the ditch. Then the sailor groped for the reins which were slipping on to the horse's heaving flanks. His burly fist retrieved them.

"Whoa, there, you mad devil!" he yelled, throwing his weight on to the tightened reins, but the animal had the bit in its teeth and, terrified by the commotion, was bolting. They were heading for the open country, up a long hill which would have deterred the exertions of a less frightened horse. The sailor, still tugging at the lines, flung a reckless glance over his shoulder to where Puah, flushed but beautiful, vainly struggled to support the wounded man's head.

"Hell for leather!" shouted the tar. "Hey, lass! come aboard with me. I'll see you are stowed away for the voyage!"

Puah looked grim. A roll of the wagon sent something against her leg. It was the cudgel which had been flung at her. She picked it up with the ease of one not wholly unfamiliar with such weapons.

"You'd better join Tom Lobsters in the ditch, my lad," she said grimly, and brought the stick against the side of the man's head with a force which sent him sagging in the seat.

Puah added her weight to the roll of the vehicle, and snatched at the reins as the sailor tumbled into the roadway. Puah felt the front wheel bump, but she had no time to see what had become of the man. The galloping horse occupied her entire attention. Fortunately the severity of the incline was slowing down the animal's pace. Presently she brought it to a trot, then a walk, and finally, with heaving sides and sweating, foam-flecked coat, the horse came to a standstill.

Puah guided him gently into a farm-yard.

In this spectacular if unceremonious fashion, the scholarly and ambitious Nigel Preece took his departure from school.

CHAPTER VII

T w o days later Nigel Preece, pale, bandaged, but convalescent, sat in a rocking-chair on the blue stone flags of a farm-house path. He looked out across an expanse of ocean, stretching beyond green meadows which sloped from the farm to a sandy bay. He felt curiously weak and listless. A faint breeze tempered the warmth of the May sun. It ruffled the surface of the sea pleasantly. It set the white spray flying with each surge of a wave against the rocky headland on his left. Idly his eyes rested on graceful gulls, on the brown sails of a fishing cutter, and most of all on the white sail pyramid of a ship of war. That she was the *Unique* he had no doubt. He could see the yellow band along her black side; could see, too, the dark gun-ports though she was too far off for him to count their number, and straining his eyes made them ache. How graceful she looked with the squaresails set on each of her three raking masts, and the trysails on her thrusting bowsprit! A thing of beauty. It savoured of irony that she was designed for war. She was sailing away and her course seemed to be north-west but he felt far too great a lassitude to figure it out by the position of the sun. The main thing was that she was leaving, bearing on her decks, doubtless, that execrable Pink . . . what was his name? He could not remember the name. It would come back to him in time . . . in time for the day of reckoning. The very thought of the naval officer set his heart racing at a speed which frightened him in his weakened condition. By an effort of concentration he switched his mind off the subject. What should he think about? The lark carolling in the blue sky? The sheepdog stretched on the flags? The tabby cat on the wall? The black cattle somnolently ruminating in the buttercup-gilded meadow? Anything except the author of that cowardly blow! He owed his life to Puah . . . Puah and Piers! What staunch friends they were! He did not know where Piers was: neither, for that matter, did Puah. All Nigel knew was the account which Puah had given him of the skirmish with the corvette's landing party. She had remained with him at the farm. The people were friends of hers, she assured him. Puah and Piers seemed to have friends in all parts of the island.

Her light step caused him to open his eyes which had closed while musing. His pulse had steadied now but there was a flush on his cheeks. Puah was bending over him anxiously. Her tanned fingers touched his face.

"You look a little feverish," she said. "Or is it the sunshine which is too hot? Wait, I'll rig up an awning."

"No, no, Puah. I am all right. The breeze tempers the heat. I got excited, that was all!"

"Well, stop getting excited. After that crack on the head you must not get excited. At any rate there seems to be nothing much the matter with your jaw by the way you are talking."

"It feels tender still."

"I was afraid it was fractured, but when I fetched Dr. Pritchard to you he assured me it was only dislocated, and he soon had it back in place. There's not a great deal the matter with you, he says, save for the loss of blood. But, Nigel, you did give me a fright."

"Unintentional, I assure you." He patted her hand. "You have been very good to me, Puah. But for you I might be aboard that warship this very moment. I shall always be in your debt. I shall never forget how you have cared for me."

"Oh, that's nothing." Puah looked embarrassed. "I—I like nursing. An outlet for my motherly instinct, I suppose. Tell me, Nigel, was it the sight of the *Unique* which disturbed you?"

"In a sense it was, Puah. At first I admired her beauty, and then I started to think of that fellow being aboard her and . . ."

"That's enough. Keep your mind off him, if you please."

"Very well—nurse. I assume that is the *Unique?* There could not be two such craft here off this coast at the same time, surely. But I thought she was to weigh anchor the night I was struck down."

"No wind," said Puah succinctly. "She's been waiting for a breeze. Beaumaris will be glad to see the last of her."

"I wonder what made her put in. We don't often get a warship in the roads."

"Recruiting her crew, of course. I wish she had run aground on the Dutchman's Bank. They've got four of our lads—Peter Hughes and three others. Confound 'em!"

"Why should they select Beaumaris?"

"That's easy to tell. Seafaring folk dwell here. They prefer fishermen to farmers' lads if they can get 'em. Don't require so much licking into shape. Matter of fact our boys very often prove to be better sailors than the tars themselves, at least when it comes to sailing."

"They didn't capture Piers, did they?"

Puah laughed. "Not likely. He's too spry for them, Nigel. I don't know where he may be but he's gone to earth somewhere. He'll be turning up like a bad penny one of these days. I never worry about Piers."

It was obvious that she never did. But she worried about Nigel Preece. Her cool hand was on his forehead. A glass of water had to be fetched for him to sip. "And now you have talked enough. Close your eyes and go to sleep."

"I don't want to. I prefer to talk to you."

"Do what you're told, Nigel, and don't argue. I shall not remain, so you cannot talk to me."

She reminded him of Piers in the emphatic, crisp manner she had of delivering her statements. She was resolute, too. Rousing the sheepdog as she passed, she made her way along a field-path towards the cliff edge. Nigel watched her. Her ways might remind him of Piers but as she walked she looked very much a woman. Stooping quickly she picked up a stick and flung it for the dog to retrieve. No, not a woman. A girl. An ingenuous, impetuous girl, but one verging on womanhood.

When she passed beyond a hawthorn hedge Nigel closed his eyes. The landscape no longer interested him. The sun was warmly pleasant; his thoughts, too, were pleasant. He slept.

The next day was wet and he stayed indoors. Almost he resented the restriction of the small parlour with its tiny window piercing the old house's thirty-inch wall. Puah did her best to dissipate boredom. She read to him, read patiently, frequently stumbling over long words. Nigel helped her, gently, as one would a child. She did her best to read what would please him. But not poetry. Never poetry. Not under any circumstances.

"But why not, Puah?"

"Because I won't. You'd laugh at me."

"Puah!" His tone was reproachful. "When you have been so good to me? I would never laugh at you. Never."

"You won't get the chance. Listen! The thrushes are singing. The rain has stopped, I think. I will look."

She went to the porch and returned to say that the day was clearing but she thought it too damp underfoot for him to venture out.

"There's nothing wrong with my feet, Miss Tyrant. It's my head which was cracked."

"Never mind, Nigel. Stay where you are. I'm not having you catching a chill just when I'm getting you better."

She sat staring out of the window. "Nigel, what made Squire Vaughan come to the school with the navy officer?"

"I believe Mr. Vaughan came in search of his daughter."

"I believe he did. From what I heard when I was in town fetching Dr. Pritchard he marched her off in fine style. Why does she come pestering you, Nigel?"

"She wished me to see some more of her poetry, Puah."

"Bosh! She's setting her cap at you. She can't write poetry any more than I can."

"You have concealed from me your attempts at writing poetry, Puah, so I cannot judge."

"Now you're being high and mighty. You know perfectly well I have never written a line—and never will either. Not even to please you!"

"My dear Puah! You sound almost savage."

"I feel savage. What does that woman want to come disturbing you for? What can't she mind her own business?"

"I assure you, Puah, you misunderstand her motives."

"No, I don't. I can read that madam like a book."

"Puah, you're unreasonable. She, Miss Vaughan, is, so I understand, betrothed to Lieutenant—Lieutenant Kirby. That's the name! Yes, Kirby."

"The coward who struck you down? Huh! They'll make a good pair, I'll be bound. Birds of a feather."

"Now, look here, Puah——"

"Now, don't get excited——"

"I'm not——"

"You are. You'll get all worked up again, and you'll be ill, and—and——"

Puah jumped to her feet and hurried out of the door. Nigel heard her calling Pero, the dog. From the window he saw her running across the field. He sighed. He looked a little troubled. And very mystified. . . .

*   *   *   *   *

The farm kitchen was large. It was the most used room in the house. When night fell a lamp, which hung suspended from a beam, was lit, but as its light was insufficient two candles in brass candlesticks were also lit and placed at either end of the high, black-painted mantelpiece on which copper and brass gleamed like precious metal. There was a fire in the hearth, partly because the air was chill once the sun had gone down, but more particularly because of the cooking which had to be done. A kettle was always singing on the hob, for there was no other source of hot water. Evan Tudor, the farmer, was attending to the cows in the shippon. His wife was busy preparing supper, cutting slices off a huge, farm-baked loaf with a crisp crust. Nigel Preece sat beside the hearth in a Windsor chair over the back of which Puah had spread a rug lest there should be a draught. The tabby cat had removed from the sunny wall to the rag hearth-rug and sat staring drowsily into the glowing coals. Its purring blended with the singing of the kettle and gave an atmosphere of homely comfort which was emphasized by the musical tinkle of teaspoons in saucers as Puah set the table. A tap on the window caused Nigel to glance up quickly. Puah seemed unconcerned though he noticed her mouth twitched in a gentle smile. The dog growled softly, pricked his ears, and then his tail thumped the floor. The wooden door-latch clicked and Piers walked in.

"Well, Nigel, how goes it?" he inquired cheerily. "Puah been looking after you properly? Any complaints?"

"The only complaint is that she has tried to kill me by kindness."

"You're looking better than I expected. Head still sore? And how's the jaw? Not fractured, I see. I thought it was only a dislocation but with that swelling I could not be sure."

"Both jaw and head are a trifle sore, Piers, but nothing to complain about. Where have you been? Just come from Beaumaris?"

"No. I haven't been to Beaumaris." Piers was off-hand.

"We've missed you. Have you been anywhere in particular? I was concerned lest the corvette's crew had laid their hands on you but Puah thought otherwise."

"Puah knows me. I've been out in the ketch, Nigel. Just landed at the cove. We can get about a bit more freely now that damned warship is over the horizon."

"Been fishing?"

"Oh, I suppose so. What's for supper, Mrs. Tudor? You don't mean to say you haven't got me a slice of your home-cured ham?"

"Never knew you was coming, Piers. I'll put some in the pan this very minute, lad. It's hungry you must be."

By way of answer Piers hacked a corner off the loaf and commenced to munch with his back to the blaze.

After supper they sat and talked. Evan Tudor lit a pipe;

so, to Nigel's surprise, did Piers. The tobacco-jar was nearly full: a large jar of dark blue glaze.

"You keep a plentiful supply of tobacco, Mr. Tudor," observed Preece.

Tudor looked across at Piers, puffed thoughtfully, and gave a non-committal grunt.

"Just as well," commented Piers. "Some distance from the source of supply. Won't you try some?"

"It is a habit I have not cultivated, Piers."

"We'll teach you. What do you intend to do when your pate heals, Nigel?"

"Go back to the school, of course."

Piers smoked thoughtfully. "I wouldn't," he said.

"Why not?"

"Hell of a life for a man. That big frame of yours was never intended for a desk. And what about your future, Nigel? You'll never make your fortune there, my lad."

"What would you suggest?"

Again Piers smoked thoughtfully. "Why not cast in your lot with us, Nigel? Your university degree would not help you much, but your brawny arms would. There's more money to be made at it than in schoolmastering."

"What—in fishing?"

"What nonsense you talk, Piers," interposed Puah. "Of course Nigel must go back to the school. He is clever; far too clever for the likes of us."

"Huh! There'll be some explanations needed when he does turn up. That pompous ass, Vaughan, will stir up trouble, mark my words. Or his daughter will."

Puah picked up a teapot and held it thoughtfully. "Piers!"

"Well?"

"If—if Nigel did not go back to the school, do you think. . . ." She looked at her brother who looked at her.

"I'll see what I can do. Have to talk it over first. Leave it at that. I must be going. Get to bed early, Nigel. You're still mighty pale. Good-night. Coming to the end of the lane with me, Evan Tudor?"

The door closed behind them. Puah resumed the clearing of the supper table. Mrs. Tudor was in the scullery washing up. They could hear the clatter of the dishes.

"Let me help you," said Nigel suddenly, standing up.

"No, sit where you are. This is nothing. Do—do you really want to go back to the school, Nigel?"

"Now you mention it, I am not sure that I do. But I shall have to earn a livelihood somewhere. It was in the back of my mind to apply for a better post next year. My real reason for coming to Beaumaris——"

"Yes, Nigel, what was it?"

"I was preparing a thesis for my Master of Arts degree, and chose the Plantagenet castles of Gwynedd. This seemed a most suitable place. But I have sufficient material now. I could finish it elsewhere."

"Oh, but you mustn't leave Anglesey. It's not to be thought of."

"I must get a livelihood somehow, Puah."

"Ye-es. I suppose so. I'll talk to Piers again to-morrow."

"By the way, does he make much money out of fishing?"

"I—I suppose so. I've never really asked how much."

"Is fishing lucrative?"

Puah did not answer. Glancing at her Nigel saw she was hanging her head. He repeated the question. "Is it lucrative, Puah?"

"I—I don't know what that word means, Nigel." Her voice was subdued.

"Lucrative! Is there much money in it? Why, Puah, there are tears in your eyes."

"There are not. Don't be such a fool Nigel! Only I wish you wouldn't use such big words. I'm not—not clever like you."

"My dear, I did not intend to appear erudite. What a fool I am, Puah, I—I never realized. My dear friend, I—I did not do it purposely. I suppose one gets in the habit of thinking thus and the words slip out. As a matter of fact it is far, far harder to talk in simple Saxon words. A man who could talk in words of one syllable would be a genius. I'm sorry, Puah, if I hurt you. It was unintentional I assure you. Damnation! That's the worst of being a pedant."

"What's a pedant, Nigel?"

He looked so dumbfounded, so miserable, that Puah burst nto a peal of laughter. It broke the tension.

"Go to bed, Nigel," she said. "I agree with Piers. It's time you stopped being a schoolmaster and learned to talk sense. We'll have to make a moonraker of you."

"A—a what, Puah?"

"Go to bed. Pleasant dreams!"

CHAPTER VIII

PUAH had gone to Beaumaris to shop and to collect some clothing from home. This was not surprising considering the nature of her arrival at the Tudor's farm. It was not the rendezvous of which Piers had spoken. In view of the raid by the press-gang Puah had, of her own initiative, decided that it was advisable to take the unconscious man to the first friendly roof she could find.

The day was fine. Nigel was able to walk about the garden quietly, with the aid of a stick. It was pleasant in the sunshine with the marvellous sweep of the bay stretching out to the blue skyline. He saw the sheepdog prick his ears and stand staring across the meadows. Nigel looked too. A rider on a spirited horse was coming at a gallop. From the side-saddle Nigel could tell that the rider was a woman, a woman in a blue riding-habit. The animal was a bay. Its glossy coat shone in the sun, rippling with the animal's easy movement. A pretty picture, thought Nigel. How gracefully the animal placed its feet. How rhythmical was its pacing. How erect in the saddle was the rider. The horse rose to a low stone wall and then came thundering up the hill towards the farm. It was only then that Nigel recognized the rider.

He moved to the garden gate as Bronwen Vaughan slowed her mount to a canter and then walked him towards the spot where Nigel, his head still bandaged, awaited her.

As the panting, snorting horse came to a standstill, Bronwen, her face flushed from her exertions, bent from the saddle.

"Nigel, how are you? It was only an hour ago that I learned of your mishap. Are you better? I am more sorry than I can say. It does not look like you—so bandaged and pale. Go and sit down on that seat. I will take Brownie to the stables and rejoin you."

She guided her horse across the yard with the assurance of the daughter of the owner of the estate. Nigel was glad to sit down. The encounter, brief though it was, had tired him. He was trembling slightly which annoyed him. He had to confess that he was glad to see his visitor. She made a charming picture as she came through the gateway into the garden with her long, blue skirt looped over her arm so that her riding-boots glistened as the sun struck their polished surface. Nigel struggled to his feet, but she waved him back.

"Don't move, please. Sit still, I beg you. You must still feel shaky."

"I could hardly sit and leave you standing."

"Very well, then, I will fetch another chair. No, you shall not exert yourself. I will see to it."

She brought a kitchen chair and placed it on the flags of the path, tossed her riding-crop on the grass, and clasped a knee with her hands as she stared out across the bay.

"What an amazing affair, Nigel. I had to come over to find out more, and to see whether you were still alive."

"But your father? He will object."

She shrugged her shoulders. "He has gone to Conway and will not be back for a couple of days. I am tired of playing the dutiful daughter, anyhow! If he tries me too much he will wake up one day to find me missing."

"How did you hear of . . ." Nigel paused, "my accident?"

"The whole town's talking about the raid. I heard a dozen garbled accounts. But it was something which Rhys told me this morning which brought me over here as fast as Brownie could carry me. He came home with some cock and bull story about——"

"Yes, go on."

"I don't wish to hurt your feelings, Nigel. I do not know what to say."

"You must tell me everything—even if it hurts. I cannot understand unless I know everything. That was the basis of our friendship, wasn't it?"

"Very well. He told me that after I left—huh!—after I was escorted from—the school, Pink stayed behind and gave you such a thrashing—because of your attentions to me—that—that he left you unconscious, and he was half-afraid he had killed you. He had asked Rhys to make sure you were alive. Rhys found out you were still alive, and were being taken care of at this farm . . so I came. . . . I don't know how true it is, of course, but it is obvious something pretty serious has happened. Did Pink fight you on my account?"

Nigel gave a mirthless laugh. "It would be nearer the truth if the valiant sea-warrior had said that he took me unawares and struck me down before I could lift a finger to defend myself."

"Nigel!" Bronwen was on her feet. "He didn't! He couldn't! Oh, Nigel, of course it is true because you are incapable of saying anything that isn't. But it . . . it seems incredible. I have no illusions about Pink's code of morals. They are as degraded as it is possible for a man's to be, but I did give him credit for being sporting. He . . . he . . . took you unawares?"

Nigel nodded.

"Oh, the brute, the coward! Nigel, I loathe him fiercely as it is, but I shall hate him worse than ever now. The bully . . . !"

"Do not excite yourself, Bronwen. He will not take me unawares when next we encounter."

"You must not fight on my account. Promise me."

"On your account? My dear Bronwen, this fellow requires a few lessons in manners. I should be failing in my duty to society if I did not instruct him. Believe me, it will be purely for personal reasons that I shall call him to account when next we meet."

He endeavoured to appear dignified. The effort strained him, and he sank back in the chair with his eyes closed. The world seemed swirling around, slipping away from him. . . . He became aware of a cold touch on his brow, the thick glass of a cottage tumbler moistening his lips. A sip of cold water revived him. Bronwen was bending over him, a look of the utmost concern in her eyes.

"Are you feeling better? You must not excite yourself. Please be calm. Forget about it. Forget about everything except that you have to rest and recover your strength."

He gave a faint smile. "I apologize for my weakness." He said.

"Hush. Just lie back and be quiet. Close your eyes. I will stay beside you."

He rested for a while and then opened his eyes to find Bronwen's gaze fixed on him intently, anxiously.

"I feel better now." He sat more upright in the chair. "I never thought a crack on the head could make a man such a fool. Really, I am ashamed of myself."

"I am ashamed of myself for disturbing you like this. I ought to have known better. But I felt so concerned. I have done the wrong thing, as I usually appear to do! But I meant well."

"No! No! It was nice of you to come."

"Nigel, let me say this while I think of it. Whatever lies ahead, if I appear strange, or inconsiderate, or thoughtless, remember that I say to you now that I am grateful for the sympathy and understanding you have shown me. I will always

cherish it, come what may. And say—if ever I am to be judged—
she meant well."

Nigel smiled. "How serious you sound. I fear I have upset
you with my folly."

"Now I must go or I shall tire you. You will remember my
words? I will come to see you some other time, when you are
stronger."

"Better not. It may cause unpleasantness for you at home.
Suppose you are missed to-day? Your father is away, but your
brother Rhys. . . ."

"Rhys is out in the yawl. He will not be back before dark.
I'm safe enough—to-day."

"I shall be about again, soon. I must get back to the school.
I don't know how they are managing without me."

"I should not worry about that. Your first task is to get
better."

She held out her hand and took his in a firm grasp. She
smiled. "Get well soon, Nigel. Remember you are my friend.
I look to you. I need you. Get well and keep happy."

At the wicket gate she turned to wave farewell. A few minutes
later he heard the hoofs of her mount crossing the yard. He
watched her ride down the sloping meadows. Once she turned
to wave her riding-crop in the direction of the farm. Then trees
hid her from his sight.

Nigel lay back with eyes closed, resting, ruminating. He
had enjoyed seeing Bronwen even though the pleasure had to
be paid for. He was annoyed with himself. How humiliating
it was to be ill! He had never had an experience like it before.
Vigorous and healthy, he had hardly known the meaning of
frailty all his life, and it was a blow to his pride to be sitting
half-fainting in a chair like an ailing girl. He vowed that he would
make Kirby pay for the humiliation when next they met. . . .
The very thought of the encounter set his heart racing again.
He bit his lip, leaned back and endeavoured to regain his
composure.

He was feeling shaken when he heard the latch click and saw
Puah entering the garden with a laden basket on her arm.

"Hello, Puah!" His attempt at a cheerful welcome was not
a success. Puah glanced at him.

"Hello!" she said shortly and walked to the house. She
came out presently without basket or hat.

"What's the matter with you, Puah?" he asked.

"What's the matter with you? When I went away you were

looking well. I come back and find you white and shaken and looking half-dead. Has that hussy been plaguing you again?"

"Puah!"

"Oh, don't try to deceive me. A farm boy told me that a woman on a bay horse galloped across to the farm. It could only be her. I know! What's she been saying to upset you like this."

"Nothing!"

"Then why are you upset? Come. Tell me."

"It was only that her brother said that this fellow, Pink Kirby, had the effrontery to say he had given me a thrashing. . . ."

"That's the ridiculous sort of thing she *would* say to a man who was suffering from loss of blood. The woman's a fool. Does she think I'm going to waste my time nursing you just for her to come and undo all the good I've done . . . ?"

"Really, Puah, it was most kind of her to inquire about me. . . ."

"Oh, very kind indeed! Well, she can just keep her kindness for other folk. If I find her hanging around here again I'll set the dog on her. Tell her that!"

Puah turned on her heel and stalked haughtily towards the house!

This unexpected ebullition did not improve Nigel's feelings. Tact, or weakness, caused him to make no retort. He did not see Puah for the remainder of the day. He was not sorry. He went to bed early and laid an aching head upon a welcome pillow. But sleep was not instantly to be coaxed. Snatches of conversation, mental images, persisted in intruding. Puah, he felt, was unreasonable. Bronwen had been kind and considerate to inquire after his health. Puah had no right to speak as she had done. It showed lack of breeding.

Nigel was inclined to be critical. He wondered whether Bronwen would have acted like that under similar circumstances. He thought not. But he was not sure. He was beginning to discover that one could never be quite sure of anything. The unexpected had a trick of happening. It was going to be awkward if Bronwen called again. Ought he to ask her not to? Puah might snub her! But he did not wish to offend Bronwen. Neither, for that matter did he want to hurt Puah. She had been so kind to him. No one could have cared for him more tenderly. And she was one of his best friends. But Bronwen was a friend, now. He had not known her long, of course, but he was glad of her friendship. Perhaps—he endeavoured to be candid with himself—

perhaps it flattered his vanity to think that the squire's daughter sought his companionship. He admitted it. But there was, after all, something deeper than that. Some quality more substantial; more abiding. He felt that Bronwen was sincere. That all her instincts were wholesome and straightforward but that her home atmosphere militated against them continually. It was almost as if he had been sent into her life to supply some known want.

Then he wondered whether people met casually or whether they were brought together by some invisible Puppet-Master who pulled the strings of destiny. If so, was it all worked out beforehand? Or was it just a gigantic experiment to see how people would react? And what happened if one reacted the wrong way? He was inclined to think that there was some definite purpose at the back of life just as there was a law running through nature. But he wasn't sure. No one was sure. So what was the use of bothering about it . . . and his head was too sore to puzzle with such stupid problems . . . and he was feeling really drowsy now . . . and he did hope Bronwen would not call again . . . at least not until he felt better able to cope with women's vagaries . . . because Puah was sure to show her resentment . . . and then there'd be the devil to pay . . . he did wish women would be more reasonable or logical . . . or something . . . he didn't quite know what . . . and he didn't care, so long as he could get to sleep!

CHAPTER IX

I T was one of those May mornings when the world was at its best, when it was hard to think evil, when the wild flowers and bird song, sunshine and gently rippling waves, betokened the spirit of the day. Nigel was feeling stronger, almost himself. He intended to return on the morrow to the school where the curate was making valiant if unsuccessful efforts to fill his place. Puah insisted on his walking to the shore. He must regain strength by exercise. Her jealous mood had departed. She was kind. She was attentive, if somewhat possessive. Nigel, who was gaining experience faster than he realized, was tactful. He did not once mention poetry or Miss Bronwen Vaughan, and all went well.

They made their way down the grassy cliffs by means of a narrow path, scrambled over some surf-smoothed boulders, and crunched across the soft shingle. Thus far Nigel had been assisted, but once on the beach Puah appeared to consider that her duties were ended and she went roving, searching among the sea-pools with the avidity of a child, taking a delight in coloured seaweed or shells. Turning over a stone she found a crab and her quick fingers plucked him from the water before he could burrow into the sand. She brought her prize to Nigel.

"Too small to eat," he commented. "What are you going to do with it?"

"Put it back where I got it from."

"Then why catch it?"

"Because I wanted to."

As there was no refuting this, Nigel held his peace. They walked on to the sands of the bay, soft sand at first, then harder sand, ridged and furrowed by the rippling tide. He glanced back. Their tracks stretched clearly across the otherwise unbroken surface; his large, heavy imprints alongside the outlines of her small feet. Their way was written across the page of sand. Symbolical, perhaps? He wondered. The next tide would obliterate the marks which showed they had passed that way. . . .

"Look!" Puah was pointing to the headland. From beyond it there glided the head-sails of a small vessel. It had a familiar look. A gentle breeze kept the sails sufficiently taut to give the vessel headway. It was Piers' brown-sailed ketch.

"It is the *Four Winds*," observed Nigel. "Did you know that Piers would be coming this way?"

"I thought that he might."

"Was that why you brought me down here?"

"Perhaps. We might as well be here as anywhere else. Has it tired you?"

"No. Not much."

They stood on the sands and watched the ketch. It was a pleasing sight; the blue-grey sea slightly ruffled, the clean-cut black prow of the boat, the ruddy sails, Piers, swarthy and bareheaded, standing with the tiller in his sunburnt hand. They saw him put the tiller over, the sails quivered in the breeze, the vessel lost headway. A man moved forward and the foresail came crinkling down. An anchor splashed over the bows with a spurt of white spray.

"Piers is coming ashore," said Puah.

Nigel glanced aft and saw that Piers had loosened the painter attached to the dinghy which was towed astern and was hauling it alongside. There was a calm deliberation about everything done aboard the ketch. The crew seemed more like toy figures than real men. No sound was carried ashore. It was like watching a moving picture. The two men forward were leisurely stowing the foresail, their blue guernseys showing dark against the tan of the canvas. Piers stepped into the stern of the dinghy with a light sureness of foot which betokened familiarity with the manœuvre. He did not seat himself on the thwart. Instead, he picked up one of the oars and thrusting it out astern began to scull the little craft shorewards. The bows were well out of the water and Piers stood, moving his arm rhythmically with an indolent indifference.

"Looks precarious," commented Nigel. A less experienced man would, he felt sure, have lost his balance and plunged overboard.

"What's 'precarious' mean, Nigel?"

"Oh, Lord!" sighed the pedagogue. "I shall be afraid to open my mouth soon, Puah."

"It's because I am so ignorant, Nigel. If you tell me, I shall remember. I shall not have to ask a second time." There was a quiet ingenuousness about her which Nigel found appealing.

"It looks a bit risky, Puah," he said.

"If you keep on trying, Nigel, you may make me clever."

"If you keep on trying, Puah, you may make me forget I am a scholar and talk like a human being. My dear, I believe you are doing me good. You have opened my eyes. I can see I had the makings of a first-class prig, and I was blissfully unconscious of the fact."

Piers ran the bows of the dinghy on to the sand and stepped out.

"How's the head, Nigel? No, I don't need to ask. You look a new man, and not so ghastly now the bandage is off. I never thought to call you thick-head, but you must have a pretty thick skull to stand a crack like that. Well, good-luck to Nigel Thickhead."

"Let's hope it has knocked some sense into me, Piers. I hope to go back to the school to-morrow."

"Then you belie your own words."

"How so?"

"It can't have knocked sense into you if you are going back there. Now you are away, why not stay away?"

"Because, my impetuous buccaneer, I have to earn my living."

"Huh!" Piers was contemptuous. "What a way!"

"Be quiet, Piers. Nigel is clever and he is going to get his new degree while he is here by writing a—a treaty—isn't that it, Nigel?"

"Something like it."

"Come and sit down," said Piers curtly.

"It won't do you any harm to have a rest, Nigel," said Puah. "I think you've been on your feet long enough."

They sat themselves on a sloping bank of sun-warmed shingle, Nigel and Puah with their shoulders against a smooth boulder, Piers flat on his back with his hands clasped behind his dark, curly head. He seemed completely absorbed watching the antics of some black-headed gulls.

"I've been thinking," he said.

"About what?" asked Nigel.

"About you. I wanted to have a talk with you when you were well enough."

"Is that why Puah brought me down here?"

"Well, partly, I did suggest I might be cruising about here to-day."

Piers spoke casually, still watching the gulls. Nigel, who knew his ways, appreciated there was something on the boy's mind. (He always regarded Piers as a boy though he had come of age—he was so impetuous). Puah sat very still, her knees clasped, staring out at the anchored ketch. There was the slight creak of a rope in a block: the men aboard were lowering the mainsail. Piers had something to say. She must wait until he had spoken.

There was just a faint, soothing, rippling sound as the wavelets washed the sand. The gulls were calling in the distance: that sound of the sea without which no coastline seems complete. Then Piers spoke.

"You were never intended for a schoolmaster, Nigel. Lord, it's like putting a gull in a wicker-cage to shut you within doors. All you think of is your silly mind: bothering your brain about words. As if they matter. So long as I make my men know what I want, what do I care if I speak right? And all the while you have a body which shouts for the out of doors. Man, I wish I had your frame. I'd knock the stuffing out of. . . ."

"Who, Piers?" Puah spoke for the first time.

"I don't know, quite. Somebody. Anybody. Just for the fun of it."

Nigel permitted himself to smile. "I believe you would, Piers. That was typical of you. But unfortunately I am not built that way. And my silly mind enjoys playing with words."

"All the same you're a fool to go back to the school. This mishap is a heaven-sent chance to cut your cable."

"But, my dear fellow, I must have a means of a livelihood. I hope when my thesis is accepted that I shall be able to get a more lucrat—— a more profitable post."

"I'll mighty soon put you into a more profitable job if you'll cut loose from your school-teaching, Nigel."

"Really? Our worst enemies could not accuse us of being over-paid. What occupation would you suggest, Piers? Not fishing, surely?"

Piers did not answer. He might have been deaf. He lay watching the gulls against the blue sky as though they absorbed his complete attention. Puah still gazed at the boat. The mainsail was stowed, now. One of the men was lighting a pipe. Piers sat up with a jerk and stared hard with his bright, dark, penetrating eyes into Nigel's calm blue ones and said, almost fiercely.

"Swear that you'll never tell a soul of what I'm going to say?"

"No, Piers!" Puah spoke sharply. "No! Nigel must not swear. You must not make him."

"He must. He shall. The secret is not mine. There are other men concerned. I will never play them false. Nigel shall swear or I'll never open my lips."

"He shall not, Piers. It is an insult to him. Cannot you see— do not you know your friend well enough—to know that an oath is not needed. You know his sense of honour. Would Nigel ever betray you? Never. He'd die first." She spoke vehemently.

"He takes an oath or I'll keep my mouth shut," said Piers, almost sullenly. "I'll not say another word."

"Then I shall. Nigel, Piers wants you to join the Free Traders."

"Damn!" ejaculated Piers.

"The Free Traders, Puah?" Nigel's tone was puzzled.

"The smugglers. We're in it. That's where the money comes from."

Nigel said nothing. He looked blankly from Piers to his sister. There was an awkward silence.

"You're a fool, Puah!" Piers turned almost fiercely on his sister. "The cat's out of the bag now, with a vengeance. And he hasn't sworn. Can't you see you've shocked him?"

Puah glanced, a little timidly, at Nigel's set face. "Are you shocked, Nigel?"

"Not shocked, Puah. Just a little surprised."

"You don't think bad of us?"

"How could I? You are my friends."

"Then swear now!" It was Piers who interrupted, almost harshly. "Swear now before it is too late. Swear you will never divulge."

"He shall not, Piers. Never. You do not understand that Nigel's sense of honour is bigger than any of your Free Traders' oaths."

Nigel patted her sunburnt hand. "That was gracious of you, Puah. A compliment which I appreciate. A trust which shall never be betrayed. *Noblesse oblige*. Oh, I'm sorry, Puah. That means . . ."

"I know," said Piers picking up a stone and hurling it into the sea. He watched the tiny fountain of spray. It might have been a roundshot falling in the distance. "I often hear it in Brittany. There's a broken down count there who is one of us. The revolution ruined him but he's still high and mighty in his poverty. Whenever he undertakes anything he reminds us— *Noblesse oblige*. He's a bit of a dirty dog for all that."

"Well, Nigel isn't, Piers, and you can trust *him*."

"What about it, Nigel? Now you know, we may as well thrash the matter out. Will you join us?"

"Piers, I respect your secret, but I hardly think that I was destined to be a—what's your quaint expression?—Free Trader."

"You'd have plenty of time, between runs, to write this thing that you're so anxious to finish to get your M.A."

"My thesis?

"And I said, 'treaty,' Nigel. I wasn't sure I had it right." Puah sighed. "What's a thesis, Nigel?"

"It is a—dissertation——"

Piers roared. "Now you know, Puah! Jove, man, come to sea and learn to talk sense. If someone yelled at you to let go the jib halliard in a squall you won't find your damned dissertation much use. Well, so you won't join us?"

"Many, many thanks, Piers. I'd rather not consider it. I know that the motive which prompted your offer was generous in the extreme, but I'd rather not."

"Truly, Nigel?" The girl's tone was wistful.

"Truly, Puah."

"And—and you don't think less of us?"

"I think more of you, rather, for this fresh proof of your belief in me."

"Then join us, Nigel, for my sake."

"No, Puah. I won't join the Free Traders."

Piers picked up another pebble; a larger one and hurled it at an inoffensive ocean. They heard it plop.

"You will," he prophesied darkly. "You will one day."

CHAPTER X

I T is hard to concentrate when there is something on the mind; something which intrudes, which aggravates, persists, niggles. So Nigel Preece found when he resumed his duties at the school. He was given to periods of abstraction. He became absent-minded. At first the boys attributed this to his accident and were sympathetic. This soon wore off and one by one they commenced to take advantage of the listlessness of their master. Several trains of thought assailed his mind. There was this suggestion of Piers'—that he should join in running contraband. In moments when the school with its irritating infants and petty restrictions grew intolerable, Nigel contemplated the idea. He felt wild and restless enough to attempt anything. Then the sight of his books within reach of his armchair of an evening scattered these dreams of the open sea. His books meant so much to him. They provided a world of his own. A world of thought. A world of fantasy. More real than reality. The words of long-dead Greeks spoke more forcefully than the voices in the street.

Then there was Bronwen Vaughan. He wanted to help her in her quandary. He wanted to prove her loyal friend. But it meant falling foul of the squire, that intolerable autocrat. And if that was not sufficient complication there was this sudden, unconcealed, bitter animosity on the part of Puah. Puah whom he would never willingly hurt. He would never willingly hurt Bronwen for that matter. But he was in a position where he was almost sure to hurt one or the other—or both. Unless he walked very delicately. That seemed the only solution. But could he do it?

The very schoolroom was, in itself, a reminder of yet another problem; another and greater course of irritation. The blue and white figure of Lieutenant Kirby, R.N., persistently intruded. A voice seemed to echo through the classroom—"*I've something for you, my fine fellow. . . .*" And a surge of hatred would sweep over Nigel Preece so that he could feel the blood rush to his head, setting it throbbing, making him dizzy. More than once he staggered and had to sit down. Then Bevan would fetch him water in a beaker, and several other boys would rush to open the window with unnecessary zeal. It was humiliating.

The evenings were not much better. He tried to work on his thesis. In vain. His ardour had left him. Who cared about

Plantagenet castles in North Wales? If Cromwell had slighted the whole lot, what would it have mattered? That's how he felt. Very different from the eager student who delved for facts in ancient manuscripts with the eagerness of a miner seeking gold. What had changed him?

He endured the school until Saturday and then went to Bangor. The crossing of the Straits made him feel better. There was a sailing wind and the ferry-boat cut across briskly with the water lapping musically against her timbers. Once in Bangor, Preece went in search of a gunsmith's. He had put some of his scanty sovereigns in his breeches pocket. To his surprise he found himself examining pistols while a courteous shopman expounded their merits. One pair of neat target pistols in a polished wood case pleased Nigel greatly. He tested their balance as though familiar with firearms. They had a homely feel. Perhaps there was something in his blood which responded to the touch. He paid for them and left the shop with the case tucked under his arm and a parcel containing powder and shot in his coat pocket. Back on the Anglesey shore he made his way into the woods. It was tea time but he was in no mood for tea. He came upon a deserted quarry, almost surrounded by trees. It seemed ideal for his purpose.

The quarry had not been used for a long time. That was obvious. The rockface was dark with weathering and moss. Ivy trailed its tendrils across broad surfaces and grass grew in the crevices. He sat himself down on a flat boulder and laid his purchases beside him. Then he paused and listened. There was silence in the woodland save for the twittering of some small birds. Little sleepy notes. Bluetits, perhaps. He wasn't sure, and it did not matter. He took out a pistol carefully and tested the hammer. The pouring in of a charge of powder occupied his attention. It was not as easy as it looked. He spilled some. Then the wad was rammed in. Hard, so the shopman had said. Now the bullet. And another wad. He stood up, holding the loaded weapon gingerly. He looked about him for a mark. As he stood facing the quarry face a vision in blue and white appeared to rise before him. There was no need for a mark. He must fire at his enemy's heart. Slowly he brought up the pistol and sighted. The explosion was so sharp and sudden that it brought him back to earth. He stared almost unbelievingly before him. So real had it seemed that it came as something of a surprise to find that no body lay there. There was no result from his firing save a faint haze of powder in the air, a smell of powder in his nostrils, a twittering—vigorous this time—of disturbed birds, and a tiny white chip of stone on the rock face. Nigel permitted himself to smile. The ice was broken. He had fired his first shot.

He laid his pistol down and kicked amid the dead leaves and bracken until he found a length of wood, part of a decaying bough. He set this against the rock wall and reloaded his pistol. This time he fought no imaginary duel. He pointed at the log and saw a splinter fly. It was a foot from the place where he had aimed but at least he had hit the wood. He felt encouraged to persevere.

Three more shots he fired with varying results. The loading took longer than he expected. It was quite interesting, though. Better than teaching in a school. . . .

"What do you think you are doing?"

The voice startled him, so engrossed was he in his occupation. He wheeled, pistol in hand, tense, alert. Bronwen Vaughan stood in the path. A patch of westering sunlight fell upon her like a spotlight, showing up the tints in her hair. She looked more attractive than usual. Her eyes were grave.

"Ah, Miss Vaughan. Bronwen. You took me by surprise." He made a formal bow, inwardly feeling a little foolish.

"I have been watching you," said Bronwen coolly. "Your pistol is throwing high. Have you had it tested?"

Nigel shook his head. The girl took the weapon out of his hand with the ease of one familiar with their handling. She looked at it critically. "Not bad," she said. "That foresight needs a little attention. Better let the gunsmith adjust it."

She picked up the case which lay on the rock and seated herself with the pistols in her lap. She motioned to Nigel to take a seat beside her.

"Sit down," she said. "Now, Nigel, what's the meaning of this?"

"I thought it was time I did a little practising—particularly if there is to be fighting with France."

"That's not your reason, Nigel. And you are a novice. Have you fired before?"

"No. I am afraid I haven't."

"I will give you some lessons, but not now. I am considered a fair shot. Even Rhys admits that—though he usually mocks me."

"Thank you." He spoke lamely.

Bronwen turned sharply. "Now tell me. Why are you doing this?"

He coloured and made no reply.

"It is obvious to me, Nigel. Have done with such folly." She spoke sharply.

"What folly?"

"You know perfectly well. You intend to challenge Lieutenant Kirby."

"I do not deny it."

"My dear Nigel, he is a professional fighting man, and already has three duels to his credit—or discredit. Don't be so ridiculous. You can hardly hit a log. What chance would you have?"

"I am not afraid of him."

"Oh, I know that. But it's beside the point. What use your throwing away your life needlessly?"

"It concerns my honour."

"I cannot see it at all. It will merely mean that you will be killed."

"If I do not call him out I shall have to live with myself and that will be worse than death for I should never cease to call myself a coward. Besides, what matter if I am killed? I have no one dependent on me."

"Are you sure, Nigel?"

"Quite sure. My parents have been dead years. I am not married. I have few friends."

"I am dependent on you, Nigel."

"You?"

"To whom else can I turn? I have explained all to you. But perhaps you have forgotten."

"No, Bronwen. I have not forgotten your dilemma."

"Perhaps you have ceased to care?"

"That was unkind, Bronwen."

"You cannot care greatly or you would not put your honour before mine."

"Before yours? I do not understand."

"If this wretch returns it will be to claim me as his bride. I will not suffer it, Nigel. And I shall not know what to do, or where to go, or to whom I can turn."

Nigel was silent. He picked up the empty pistol he had been using and began to finger it abstractedly. Bronwen firmly removed it from his hand. "Don't play with weapons, Nigel. You're too absent-minded. Pay attention to me. What would you do if Pink Kirby insulted me in your presence?"

"Thrash the blackguard."

"Without my permission?" Bronwen's eyebrows were raised and there was a smile, a slightly mocking smile, on her lips.

"Yes," said Nigel vehemently. "I should knock him down, and beg your leave later."

"Good!" Her eyes were bright with laughter now. "Nigel, let's make a bargain. If you will not fight Pink Kirby with pistols, I will give you my full approval to strike him, thrash him, flog him, kill him if you like, the moment he insults me."

"You mean it?"

"I do, Nigel. I'm not the milk-and-water miss you appear to think me. I don't mind you fighting Pink, but I want you to win. It would only make matters worse if you fought him with the odds against you."

"It's time I got into training," said Nigel. He thrust the pistol into the mahogany case and clicked down the lid. "Bronwen, I believe Piers was right. I'm not at all sure now that I was intended to be a schoolmaster."

*   *   *   *   *

They walked slowly along the mossy ride through the woods as the light from the setting sun was beginning to fail. The birds were drowsily singing their hymn to departing day. Footsteps made no noise on the sward. Afar off a brook made a murmuring sound. Few words were spoken. It was one of those moments when nearness meant more than words. Nigel felt that he had grown more familiar with this companion who had come so unexpectedly into his life. He was not used to women's company. Save for an inherent sense of chivalry he had shown little interest in them. His first feeling towards Bronwen Vaughan had been purely that of compassion. She was in difficulty and turned to him for aid. That was sufficient. But now, with each meeting, he felt that new links were forged. There was a sincerity about her, a candour which pleased him. There was no dissembling—or, at any rate, there had been none since she had forsaken the role of poetaster. He liked her better as he found her to-day. Though, even so, he felt just a little strange in her company. He could never wholly forget that she was the daughter of Squire Vaughan. His conduct had been irreproachable: he knew that. Yet he recalled the very maxim he had proffered not many days before—"We are punished not for doing wrong but for making a mistake." He was making a mistake in walking through the woods with Miss Vaughan of Castell. He knew it. Yet what

was he to do? He could not forsake her without discourtesy.
And in any case, why should he? He was as good a man as
Squire Vaughan. The only difference between them was the barrier
of wealth—that, and the contrast between arrogance and breeding.

Nigel Preece felt resentful. Fate, he considered, had been
ungenerous to him, placing him in a subservient position where
he had to submit to the whims of the neighbouring gentry.

"Why are you so silent, Nigel? Is anything on your mind?"
Bronwen glanced up at him anxiously.

"Many things."

"Tell me?"

"They are far too numerous to enumerate. And why should
I burden you with my cares?"

"You were willing enough to accept the burden of mine.
Let me share yours. A burden shared is lightened. Already you
have proved that to me."

"Well, then, you are one of them."

"I can well believe that. But in what way?"

"If we continue to meet it must, sooner or later, lead to
unpleasantness at your home. For myself I do not mind; for you
I mind very much."

"Don't trouble about me. There is so frequently trouble at
home that I am accustomed to it."

"It would be wiser if we did not meet."

"Far wiser. But why be wise?"

"Folly brings its own punishment."

"So does wisdom."

Nigel laughed. Her repartee pleased him. He had not crossed
verbal swords with anyone for so long. He acknowledged himself
vanquished but felt no rancour. Instead, he saluted his
adversary.

"You have me worsted there, Bronwen. It will be punishment
to me not to see you now that I am growing to appreciate the
value of your friendship."

"I shall miss you, too, Nigel."

"You agree we must not meet?"

"I agree it would be wiser not to meet—openly."

The last word was spoken softly, but it set his heart racing.
He stared ahead, not knowing what to say.

"Do you not want to see me again, Nigel?"

Nigel Preece wrestled within himself. "Yes!" he said, almost
savagely.

They both stopped and looked at each other. Nigel was biting his lip. "Go home," he said unsteadily. "I will not come farther with you. It is—is inadvisable."

Bronwen nodded her head. He saw that she was flushed and that she was breathing noticeably. "Yes, Nigel. I—I think you are right. I will go." She turned, took a couple of steps, then paused.

"If we must meet—where shall it be?"

He paused and then in a carefully modulated voice replied: "It was my intention to practise shooting at the old quarry every evening at this hour."

Bronwen did not reply. Nigel waited a trifle anxiously. She was so still he wondered whether he had offended her. Yet all he had done was to answer her question.

She turned with unexpected suddenness and began to walk briskly down the curving path. She did not look back. Nigel watched her form until the tree boles hid her from sight. He sighed, took a firmer grip on his case of duelling pistols, and turned to make his way homeward through the gloom of the darkening woods. Somewhere in the distance an owl hooted. The path which he had trodden with Bronwen now seemed long, interminably long. And lonely. And all about him the woods were eerily silent.

CHAPTER XI

THESE visits to the disused quarry became an evening pilgrimage. It was a new experience for Nigel Preece. He went a trifle apprehensively, feeling self-conscious, imagining that all the town watched him and speculated whither he went. Later he realized that no one paid any attention. By that time he had reached the stage where he did not care if they did. He was defiant. It was none of their business. He always took the flat mahogany case with him. At first he persuaded himself that he went solely to practise his shooting. Of course, Bronwen might possibly make an appearance. If so, he would be glad to see her. And Bronwen did appear. The first evening he found himself shooting badly. It annoyed him, until he realized that his mind was not on what he was doing. He was listening for the rustle of her approaching steps. It was no good pretending he came for the purpose of shooting. He was disgusted at his casuistry. By the end of the first week, during which time Bronwen never once failed to disturb his shooting and destroy his aim, he admitted to himself that he came to meet her. It was no good trying to evade the obvious truth. One evening he forgot to take his case of pistols.

Bronwen was waiting for him. The sight of her beside the flat, lichen-coated rock on which they first sat, made him think of Maid Marian. There was something about the greenwood which frequently brought to mind Robin Hood and his merry men—Robin who had defied law and convention and had built him a house in the forest glade.

"Where are your pistols, Nigel?" Bronwen was observant. He had noticed that. It pleased him.

"I fear I have forgotten them to-day."

"How annoying. To walk all this way to practise shooting and then to find you have forgotten your pistols! What a wasted journey. You *do* come here to practise shooting?"

"Of course. And you come to watch me; to give me advice?"

"Of course, Nigel."

"Yes," he agreed, "of course."

"Are you speaking the truth, the whole truth and nothing but the truth?"

She saw him colour. "Well, it's hardly an untruth. Let's call it sophistry."

"Mine's an untruth and nothing else. I have not the least interest in your shooting. I came solely to see you and you know it."

"I did not leave my pistols behind, to-day, Bronwen. I really forgot all about them. Evidently they were of no consequence. There is something in what you say. The shooting obviously does not occupy the first place in my mind."

"You came to see me?"

"Yes."

They sat very still, so still that a squirrel ran up the bark of a nearby ash and then paused on a branch to gaze down inquiringly at the human intruders he had not noticed in passing. They watched him intently, noting his bright beady eyes and his bushy tail. They seemed at one with these woodland folk.

"Do you think we are falling in love, Nigel?"

"I begin to wonder. I have never been in love. It used to appear to be a foolish business."

"Do you still think so?"

"I suppose it all depends on whether it happens to you or to someone else."

"Yes. One appears absurdly prejudiced in one's own favour. Things which appear nonsensical in another seem eminently sensible when they concern oneself. If another woman came to meet a man day after day at a woodland quarry I should frown with disapproval."

"I should certainly consider it reprehensible."

"And yet I come. I know it is not sensible. Yet if I do not see you my day seems pointless and purposeless. How does it effect you?"

"I cannot concentrate. I do not care whether I get my thesis completed or not. I do not care what happens to those confounded ruffians I teach. I no longer regard them as young citizens in the making. They have become pests who interrupt my reverie. When I stare at a printed page I see your eyes looking at me. I behold the invisible. The unreal becomes more real than the real."

"I know. The symptoms seem identical."

"And irrefutable. It would appear that undoubtedly we have fallen in love. But how ridiculous, Bronwen. How illogical."

"Is love logical?"

"I haven't the remotest idea. I should say not."

"Why should you want it to be logical?"

"I hardly know. But it is illogical that I, an impecunious schoolmaster, should have the temerity to fall in love with a squire's daughter."

"And it is illogical that I, brought up among inebriated

barbarians should fall in love with a man who is cultured, and chivalrous, and noble. . . ."

"Bronwen, please, you must not talk like that."

"Why not?"

Nigel sprang to his feet and stood staring before him into the green depths of the woodland. Then he crossed and leaned his back against the broad bole of a beech. He stood with one foot on a raised root. He might have been posing. Bronwen, watching him, knew that he was oblivious of what he did or what he looked like. She could see by the intense, concentrated look in his eyes that he was thinking deeply. She knew that expression. Loved it. That broad, smooth brow of his bespoke intellectual power.

"We must stop!" His voice was low, tense, emphatic.

"Stop what, Nigel?"

"Stop this. Stop everything. Stop seeing each other. Stop falling in love before it is too late."

"It is too late."

"But we must stop, I tell you. It will only mean trouble for you and I could not bear that. I could hurt myself, freely, willingly, but I could not hurt you. It's impossible."

"Not impossible. Inevitable."

He looked at her appealingly. "Don't make it harder for me. Do you think I want to talk like this? I have myself under control. Reason must rule emotion."

Bronwen laughed. "Reason can never rule emotion. Never has done and never will. Life itself is just one terrific emotional urge. So is every great action, every noble thought."

He looked at her in amazement. He had not expected her to talk thus; think thus. He had underrated her mentality. There was something about her way of thinking which seemed akin to his own.

"I want my reason to rule," he said, and he spoke with difficulty. "I am not without emotion. Since I have known you I have discovered sources hitherto unsuspected and unrevealed. But where is all this going to lead us? I am endeavouring to look ahead. I cannot afford to marry you. I could not take you from your luxurious home to offer you the humble life I have to lead."

"I do not care for my home. I escape from it whenever I can. I am, this moment, here in a woodland with you, and I am happy and well content."

"Your father would not give his consent."

"Much I care. I do not love my father. I do not even respect him. He brought me into the world but he considers that if he feeds and clothes me he has done his duty. If he takes his obligation to me so lightly, I will treat with equal lightness my obligation to him."

"He will be furious when he hears."

"Does that trouble you?"

"For myself, no. I am no coward. But I worry to think of what the consequences might be to you."

"They would be worse if I married the man he would force me to wed."

"Lord! I had forgotten that. The fellow had gone clean out of my mind."

Bronwen laughed suddenly. "I believe you would marry me for no other reason than to despite Pink Kirby, Nigel. I like you for it."

"The other reason weighs with me more, believe me. But what you say indubitably makes me harden my heart."

He still looked troubled. His brow was furrowed. "Bronwen, I must get money. Never before have I realized its need. I shall have to acquire it, and acquire it quickly, for you. Fortunately I know it can be done."

"You know? Have you a new post in view?"

"Nothing half so commendable. No, if I am to get money quickly I must set scruples aside."

"And you—a man of honour—would do that for me?"

"Yes!" He spoke savagely. "To serve you I would let nothing stand in my way. Not even my code of honour. Do you despise me?"

"I adore you."

She came close to him and laid a hand upon his arm. It trembled slightly. Nigel looked fixedly over her head.

"How will you do it?"

"I shall. . . ." He paused, suddenly.

"Well?"

"I can't tell you."

"Nigel!" Her voice was shocked. Pained. "I want to know."

"I am sorry, my dear, I cannot tell you."

"Is it too terrible? I promise not to be scandalized. After all, you are doing it for me."

"No, I don't think it is terrible. Irregular, perhaps. A defiance of law, but after all laws are made by man and can be broken by man, provided one is prepared to accept the penalties."

"Lud, Nigel, how exciting. You sound as though you intended to become a knight of the road."

"I don't ride well enough!" He permitted himself a slight smile.

"Then tell me." Bronwen was coaxing now.

"Please don't press me. It is a secret."

"But you have no secrets from me! You can trust me."

"Oh, I know that, Bronwen. I would with anything and everything—except this."

"Why not this?"

"Because it is not mine to share."

"Have you sworn an oath or something?"

"No. That's what makes it so binding. They trust me—implicitly. I could not break faith with them."

"What a man of honour you are, Nigel. It's hardly fair of me to plague you."

A silence fell upon them. It was Bronwen now who stood staring into the green depths of the woods with thoughtful, unobservant eyes.

"Nigel?"

"Yes, dear."

"Is—is it anything to do with a woman?"

He started. "Why, what on earth made you ask that?"

"But has it? You always tell me the truth."

"In a sense, yes."

She drew back from him and her eyes seemed to grow larger. "Oh, Nigel!"

"Oh, not that way, Bronwen. For heaven's sake don't put a wrong interpretation on it. I have given you a direct answer. It so happens that there is a woman involved in—what shall I say?—the transaction. That is all. There's nothing deep or sinister about it. Nothing which can possibly affect you, my dear.'

"Then tell me?"

"I can't."

"I—wonder—who—she—can—be?"

"It doesn't matter in the slightest."

"It matters to me."

"You know I cannot tell you. Really, Bronwen, you are rather exasperating. There is no sentiment involved. It is merely point of honour. Of keeping troth. Of not being false to those who trust me."

"You prefer to keep faith with her to keeping faith with me?

"Please do not be absurd. There is no comparison. I must say you are very illogical."

"Love is illogical. Nigel, can't you see I'm jealous. I can't

help myself. Dearest, take me in your arms and tell me everything.
I shall never betray your confidence. Never! Never! Never!
But until I know I shall have no peace of mind. I shall be torn
asunder. Tell me, Nigel, please, please tell me, dear. Please,
please tell me."

"I cannot." His face showed his distress.

Bronwen laid her face against his shoulder. He imagined she
was crying and his fingers softly stroked the bowed head. She
had been crying. When she looked up her eyes were somewhat
red. And later, as he walked home, he discovered that the cloth
of his coat was wet from her tears.

"I ask you for the last time, Nigel," she said speaking with
forced deliberation. "Will you tell me?"

"God help me, I cannot."

Without a word she turned on her heel and walked away
from him. He started in pursuit and she quickened her pace.
She did not want him! He paused, staring at the receding form.
Her head was bowed. Nigel walked miserably home. At times
he felt almost vicious. It was all stupid. Unnecessary. Why were
not women logical? He stalked moodily up the street, hating the
place, the houses, the inane people who walked about, the fatuous
idiots who stood in groups and looked at him as he passed on his
dejected way. He hated them all. Hated life. He wanted to be
alone. No, he didn't; he wanted company. He would get drunk.
Anything to forget. He wanted—— Curses! He wanted Bronwen.
And now perhaps he could never have her. And all because of
a stupid ridiculous whim. Or a sense of loyalty. It was the very
devil when loyalties clashed. Puah was nothing to him. Not in
that sense. Just a dear friend. But he could not break faith with
her. She had been so loyal, so amazingly loyal, and understanding about Piers not making him take the oath. She did not
mean to him what Bronwen meant. There was no comparison.
But he would keep faith. Had he put her before Bronwen?
No, that wasn't a fair question. And yet, obviously, he had.
So he argued with himself as with brain in a turmoil he strode
up the main street.

A hail from across the road arrested him. Piers was swinging
down the roadway with a fishing-net over his shoulder. And
Puah was at his side. Both were sunburned and smiling.

Puah ran across with the impulsiveness of a child. "Where
on earth have you been, Nigel, all this time? Piers and I were
just talking about you. Come fishing with us to-morrow!"

CHAPTER XII

IF it was contrast Nigel needed he received it in full measure. In place of a woodland glade, there was the tossing sea; instead of a lichen-coated rock there was a brown-sailed ketch; instead of elegantly dressed Bronwen Vaughan, Puah stood, hand on the tiller, peering ahead, her curls tossed by the wind, her face moistened by the spray which came with each wave which slapped against the thrusting bows of the *Four Winds*. Once clear of land, Puah had discarded her encumbering dress for a man's ancient worsted boat-skirt which she had somehow procured; and there she stood, bare of leg to the knee, her shapely feet gripping the boards firmly as she steadied herself against the slant of the deck.

Nigel, his arms locked in the mizzen shrouds, was close at hand, his eyes sometimes resting on Puah's lithe but sturdy figure, sometimes gazing seawards towards the fretted horizon, staring at nothing in particular but deriving a certain exhilaration from this freedom to look wide.

The *Four Winds* was decked, having a forecastle where the three members of the crew slept, and a small cabin, specially constructed in the stern. Small though she was she was stoutly built and a good sailer.

"We could not have picked a better day," observed Nigel, "This breeze freshens, the sun is glorious. Where are we heading, Puah? Don't forget that I must be back at the school by Monday morning. I don't want to be stranded miles from home if the wind fails."

"Stop fidgeting and enjoy yourself while you can," ordered Puah.

"But where are we heading for?" Nigel glanced astern across the foaming wake to where the Anglesey bays and cliffs showed low and distant. Penmaenmawr Headland and the Great Orme seemed little more than mountains of mist.

"Better ask the skipper," retorted Puah, succinctly.

"Hi, there, Piers! Where are we heading for?"

Piers, sprawling in the sun on the deck forward in a manner highly undignified for a skipper, raised his head. Nigel saw his teeth gleam white in a smile. "Never you mind, Nigel. I'll know better myself when we get there."

"But we must be going somewhere."

"Hear that, Puah? There's wisdom for you. That's what comes of being a scholar."

Nigel smiled and desisted. If Piers did not mean to tell him, questioning was not going to advance matters. There is something about life aboard a vessel (when all goes well) which makes a man content to do nothing. Perhaps the easy rise and fall of the craft beneath his feet is soporific. There is no need to hurry. There is no possibility of hurrying. Ship and wind and ocean dictate the terms. On shore one is nearly always going somewhere; at sea it is the ship which does the going. So Nigel took a firmer hold on the weather shrouds and resumed his daydreaming. He wondered whether Bronwen would visit the quarry during his absence; whether she was so offended with him that she would never see him again; whether it was a woman's caprice which had sent her away. A lover's tiff, perhaps. He had read of them. So this was what was meant. A silly business. He shrugged his shoulders.

"What was that for, Nigel?" He saw Puah regarding him intently.

The wind and the sea and the spray had whipped so much colour into his face that she did not see him blush. Nigel felt uncomfortable. It was as though she had read his thoughts. What could he say? He temporized. "What do you mean, Puah?"

"That shrug of your shoulders. It meant something."

"Oh, I was just thinking."

"Of course, but of what?"

"I don't know what to do." No sooner had he spoken than he felt that it was the remark of a lost child. "What would you do, Puah, if you were in a strange country and came to some crossroads and did not know which to take because you did not know whither any one of them led?"

"I'd look at the signpost." Puah was always inclined to be practical.

"But there is no signpost at my cross-roads, Puah," he said sadly, "metaphorically speaking."

"What does that mean, Nigel?"

He sighed. "There are times, Puah, when I get positively annoyed with myself for talking as I do!" He took a sudden dislike to the mizzen shrouds and forsaking them he sat himself down with his back against the weather bulwarks, his feet at no great distance, now, from Puah's bare toes.

"I'm trying to explain that I feel lost and don't know which way to go; don't know what to do. I think and think about things until I get bewildered. I want to do what is right but I don't know what is right."

"That's a bit awkward, Nigel."

"It's deucedly awkward. So I tried to liken my predicament—my awkward position—to that of a traveller who had lost his way. He does not know where to go, and there is no one he could ask."

"You could ask me, Nigel."

(And that, mused Nigel, is precisely what I can't do!) But he said: "Thank you, Puah, but a man must find things out for himself. Still, a signpost would be useful."

Puah turned to him and her eyes danced with a sudden mischief.

"This is your signpost, Nigel. You're sitting on it."

"I'm sitting on the deck of the *Four Winds*."

"That's just it, Nigel. The *Four Winds* is the signpost you seek."

"Ah!" said he. "Now that, my dear girl, is what is meant by metaphorically speaking."

"Oh, Nigel, you are funny. You can't help being a schoolmaster and wanting to instruct. We would have made far more progress if we had just talked sense, don't you think? Sailor language. Good solid Saxon! All the same you can see what I mean. The *Four Winds* is pointing the way you should go. Finish with your silly school. Throw in your lot with us. You will make money. You will have freedom. And—and—we'll all be together."

All at once Nigel felt an irresistible desire to curse life for being so complicated. Had this happened a couple of weeks before he would not have hesitated. He would have been happy with Piers and Puah; happy as they had been when they went to Puffin Island after gulls eggs. But now Bronwen had come into his life. She had confused everything; befogged the issue. To make matters worse there was nothing definite about his relationship with Bronwen. After the words which had passed, was he in honour bound to her? He felt that he was. And his affections were with her. But how did she regard him? That was the crux of the matter! She had seemed so fond of him. So devoted. So anxious to seek his company. But after all she had chosen to walk off!

Some pride in his blood caused him suddenly to harden his heart. His mouth set firmly. There was a defiant look in his eyes. His head went up proudly. He glanced at Puah. Her dark eyes were fixed on him shrewdly. She was watching him. She was waiting. With her womanly intuition she was not interrupting.

"Yes, Puah," he said quickly. "You are right. The *Four Winds* points the way. The life I lead becomes intolerable. I will cast in my lot with you and Piers."

"You mean it?"

"I mean it!" Nigel hurled defiance at Fate.

"You mean it? Come wind, come weather? You're in this venture with us? Sink or swim? Neck or nothing?"

"I am."

"Piers! Piers! Come here quick."

"What's wrong?" Piers looked up lazily. The sun was striking the foredeck most pleasantly. He had been half-asleep.

"I've something to tell you."

"It will keep."

"It won't keep. Come aft or I'll let go the tiller." As though to emphasize her words she allowed the boat to come into the wind. As the sails flapped, the skipper sat up angrily. Piers always prided himself on the set of his sails.

"Don't be a fool, Puah. She was drawing beautifully."

"Well, come here when I call you."

He came aft, grumbling. "What a pest you girls can be."

"He's coming in with us. He's just said so."

"Confound you, Puah. What did you tell him for?"

"I didn't tell him. He said so of his own accord. You volunteered to be a smuggler, didn't you, Nigel?"

"I am afraid I was misguided enough to do so," said Nigel with a grave smile. Piers did not smile. "Damn!" he said, and kicked at an unoffending rope fender. "Damn!"

Nigel was on his feet now, holding on to the mizzen shrouds, and he looked down at the scowling face of his young friend.

"Why, Piers, I imagined you *wanted* me to join you? Why this change? It was you who put the idea into my head. Truly I imagined you wanted me."

"So I did. But you've gone and spoiled the best bit of fun we have planned for a long time. Oh, damn, again!"

"But what have I done?" protested Nigel.

"Tell him, Puah. Come on. Give me that tiller. You're not paying attention. She is yawing like a derelict."

He took the tiller almost angrily out of his sister's hands. Puah seemed quite unperturbed. She walked up to Nigel and slipped her arm through his. There was something saucy in the sunburnt face which looked up into his. "Shall I let you into a secret?"

"Please do. I'm all at sea—literally."

"You may not know it but—you're being kidnapped."

"What? Kidnapped? I don't understand."

"It was Piers' idea. We could see you could not make up your mind and that you were unhappy at the school, so we decided to force you to decide. We enticed you on board and—and—you're not going back to your stupid schoolhouse again. It's a smuggler's life for you whether you want it or not."

"As it happens I have resolved that I do want it. So what's Piers so annoyed about?"

"Why? Because if you come of your own free will it's all so tame. Think how furious you would have been when you found yourself aboard a French lugger and realized that you had been tricked!"

Nigel permitted himself to smile. He knew their regard for his welfare; their manner of seeing to it was typical of Piers. "If working myself into a frenzy of indignation would gratify your brother I will endeavour to do my best," he observed gravely. Piers, who must have overheard the conversation, paid no heed. He was watching one of the sailors—the burly Madoc Morris—who, holding on to the forestay, was staring at the horizon.

"What do you make of her, Madoc?" called Piers.

"Dunno!" Madoc shook his head. "Don't quite like the looks of her; better see for yourself, isn't it?"

"Take the tiller, Puah," ordered Piers. His tone was crisp. He stepped to a locker and drew out a telescope in a leather case to which a shoulder strap was attached. He slung this over his head and walking forward, grasped the main shrouds and went swarming aloft. At the cross-trees he carefully seated himself and locked his ankles to make sure of his balance. Then, drawing out the glass, he carefully adjusted it. Puah kept the vessel steady, her eyes never moving from the motionless figure in the cross-trees. Nigel watched, too. The very silence which reigned was ominous. He could feel the tension in the air. Piers lowered the glass, polished it meticulously with his silken neckcloth, and raised it again.

"He's not quite sure," murmured Puah. Though her voice would not have carried down the wind, she spoke softly, as if anxious not to interrupt her brother's deliberations.

Piers thrust the telescope back into its case and came sliding down a stay.

"It looks infernally like her," he muttered. "Hugh Jones told me on Wednesday he was sure she was still cruising off the

Island. Nigel, how'd you like to see your friends in the *Unique* again?"

"Under the circumstances I am not hungering to renew their acquaintance."

"Neither am I, by the lord. She's on the same tack, providentially, and drawing away. Down sails, lads, we'll lie easy until she's out of sight. There's no hurry. The *Marie* won't put in an appearance so long as that devil is hanging about to spoil sport."

*   *   *   *   *

It was growing cool. Nigel was glad to put on the thick coat which Puah brought for him. She, too, was more warmly clad. The *Four Winds* seemed alone in a world of water. No longer was it possible to see the Anglesey coast. The wind had almost failed. It was just the even, leisurely movement of the tide which set the blocks creaking. Piers was at the tiller, his eyes fixed on the stars which were showing faintly. He did not seem in the least impatient, or perturbed. Nigel assumed that Piers knew where he was but to the landsman's sense there appeared no possible means of telling. The *Four Winds* seemed a perilously small craft to be out in the waste of waters. It made Nigel think of a small child lost on the moors in the darkness. Madoc and the other men did not appear the least concerned. They sucked their pipes with stoical indifference and—waited. It seemed that life had become a period of waiting.

It was a different *Four Winds* from the one which Nigel was accustomed to see gliding along the placid waters of the Straits. When the corvette was hull-down on the horizon a burst of energy overtook Piers. The mists of evening had all but hidden the land from sight. Down came every sail and spar. The ruddy-brown sails with which Nigel was familiar were folded and stowed. The gaffs were unshipped and lashed securely. In their place came two spars on which were bent sails of dirty white canvas. These were hoisted lug fashion. Foresail and jib gave place to a staysail. To a casual observer the *Four Winds* had become a lugger.

Nigel unable to restrain a pardonable curiosity asked Puah the reason for the change.

"In case we are seen," she explained. "There is no reason why the *Four Winds* should be recognized. The coastguard might sight us, or we might get close enough to land for the riding officers to see us. There's no point in asking for trouble, is there?"

Nigel smiled grimly. He seemed to be asking for trouble. Yet he could not help but experience a certain thrill of anticipation, he scarcely knew why. At any rate there was a sense of freedom such as he had never known in Beaumaris school.

They did not do much talking and what words were spoken were uttered in a subdued voice. It seemed ridiculous to be so quiet for there was no one within hearing. Yet there was something eerie about this waiting in a vessel almost becalmed at night in a lonely sea. For it was night now. The last streak of evening had vanished from the west. The stars grew brighter. They seemed more friendly than when seen from the shore. Puah picked up the end of a halliard and began winding it about a cleat. No sooner had she completed the operation than she unwound it and started to wind it again. She did not speak but her fingers seemed to betray nervousness.

"Nigel!"

"Yes, Puah?"

"Why is it that we have not seen you for days?"

Nigel stared out into the wall of night which surrounded them. "Why? Does it matter?"

"Of course it matters. I wondered if your head was bad again."

"No. There has been nothing wrong with my head."

"Madoc said he saw you coming out of the woods twice. Late in the evening."

"Yes. He might have done. I have been practising shooting."

"He did not say you had a gun."

"I shot with pistols."

"Why did you go in the woods? You could have come out in the boat if you wanted to fire at a mark. Now, couldn't you?"

"I suppose I could."

"Then why didn't you?"

"I did not think of it. The woods seemed better suited."

"You went there so that you could see that woman again!"

"Puah! I did not. Not the first time."

"But you did see her?"

"As you press me, I did see Miss Vaughan, if that is to whom you refer."

"You know I mean her and you need not talk so dignified."

Puah unwound the hailiard vigorously. It called forth an admonition from her brother.

"Make fast that rope, Puah. What do you think you're doing? And stop talking, you two, and listen. We would have met the

Marie by now if the wind hadn't dropped. She's out there, some-where—or should be. Keep your eyes open—and listen."

So that was it, thought Nigel. They were waiting for the French vessel. He had no idea the French would have ventured so far from their home port. But he did not ask any more questions. Instead he obeyed his instructions, stared into the night, and listened. There was no sound but the creak of the timbers as the ship rode the swell. The minutes dragged on. Piers swore softly.

"Puah, get down to the cabin and light the lanterns. We must risk a signal. I did not wish to flash one but we can't loaf about here all night."

Puah vanished into the cabin and Nigel could hear the click of the flint and steel. There was a subdued glow. The girl came on deck with two lanterns concealed beneath her coat. Nigel could see the red glow reflected on her bare ankles.

Madoc came shuffling aft. "Shall I run 'em to the main truck?" he inquired.

"Try showing 'em over the starboard side," suggested Piers. "Keep the hull between the light and the land. If the *Marie's* close ahead, it may do the trick."

The two lanterns were lowered over the side of the ketch, one a yard above the other. They hung there, casting red ripples on the black water.

As they looked about them, Nigel caught a flash of light in the darkness.

"Light on the port bow," came a subdued hail from the look-out in the *Four Winds'* bows. Two green lanterns showed in the darkness. They vanished and the night appeared to have swallowed them up. Piers called Madoc to him and the two lowered themselves into the dinghy. Nigel felt the vessel give a light jerk. She moved.

"Are they towing us?" he inquired.

"Yes, lower your voice. I don't know how far we are from land."

They stood silent, waiting. Puah was close beside him, touching his arm. She might have been cold, or excited, or interested in what was going on. A darker shape showed against the sky: the angular outline of sails. They were close upon a three-masted lugger. In another instant the *Four Winds* was alongside. The moment the vessels were lashed together they became a scene of bustling activity. Few words were spoken. Men panted as they heaved on corded bales, or curved their arms to receive heavy kegs. Tubs, they called them. "Come on," said Puah, briskly. "Lend a hand. Pass them down to me and I will stow them."

Nigel worked methodically, mechanically, handing down the tubs to Puah who, in the ketch's hold, stacked them with the skill of one well used to the task. As he worked Nigel experienced a sense of unreality. He was breaking the law. He was helping to run contraband. He was, in very truth, a smuggler.

CHAPTER XIII

N I G E L was looking better than he had done for many a long day. He was back at the school. Despite Piers' threat to put him aboard the French lugger, they had decided to let him enter his new life by easy stages. Nigel felt better. His eyes were brighter. Young Bevan noticed it on the Monday morning and, being the senior scholar and privileged, commented upon it. "You're looking a better colour, sir," he ventured. "I hope that you have quite recovered from the effects of your accident."

"Thank you, Bevan, I spent the week-end in a fishing-boat. That probably accounts for the colour."

"It's done you the world of good, sir. I should go again."

Yes, thought Nigel, it had done him good. It had been a tonic mentally as well as physically. Possibly spiritually, too. He wondered whether a purist would have accepted smuggling as a source of spiritual power! It appealed to his sense of humour. From the results which had accrued it evidently did possess some such attribute. His lips twitched at the thought. He might contend that the spirit was manifest—tubs of it! He saw the boys looking at him curiously and realized that he was smiling to himself. He must cure himself of this trick of allowing his mind to stray during school hours. There were times when he wondered whether mental telepathy could be within the scope of humans— under the circumstances it was, perhaps, as well it were not. It would be decidedly awkward if the Excise officer, or some of the more reputable townsfolk, could read his thoughts. What would they have done had they known that he, their respected schoolmaster, their pattern of probity for the young, had been engaged in landing contraband; consorting with Frenchmen, his country's enemies. Never in his life had he been guilty of so great a dereliction. Yet he not only felt unashamed; he felt positively elated. He felt that he had redeemed his manhood in his own eyes. There had been a certain risk, especially when they knew that the *Unique* was not many leagues away— fortunately to leeward. The most exciting part was on the Sunday when, throughout the day, they had cruised along the coast fishing with every appearance of innocence when all the while the brandy-kegs and the bales of silk were underneath their very feet. Piers had chosen his fishing-ground well. He knew the banks. The ketch was never in really deep water, and had any

Customs boat put out to investigate, the goods would have been quietly slipped overboard. He had taken cross-bearings, and in addition there was a float to mark the spot. The procedure had all been explained to him by Puah with the charming, disarming innocence of a child. To her, outwitting the Revenue officers was something commendable like earning one's living. But it had not been necessary. There had been no untoward interest shown, and the *Four Winds*, restored during the night to her original rig, drifted openly along the coast as far as Prestatyn. They caught some fish, enough to serve their purpose, though there was no undue interest in the operation. All felt that they were fishing in deeper waters than those which spread along the North Wales coast that sunny Sunday afternoon. It was not until night had fallen that the real activity commenced. Down came the sails. The wind had dropped. Piers produced two powerful sweeps and these, double banked, were manned by the crew while Puah took the tiller. Across the still night water they pulled, Nigel putting his back into it with the rest. They rowed with muffled oars, dipping carefully to ensure that no splash should rise above the gentle breaking of the waves. Off the Little Orme they dropped anchor. Boats came alongside. There was no talking. Just a certain panting and straining as men wrestled with the corded packages to ensure that nothing fell overboard. Then the boats vanished into the night to deposit—so Puah assured him—the smuggled goods inside the White Chapel cave, that commodious cavern so conveniently situated that it could only be approached from the sea. If the coast was clear a pack-horse train would be waiting beside the marsh. The goods would be rowed to the near-by creek and landed there for transportation inland during the hours of darkness. But that was the affair of the gang ashore. The *Four Winds* had fulfilled her purpose once she had met the French lugger and brought the contraband to the cave. When the vessel was empty—save for fish—they pulled well out to sea, dropped anchor, and waited for the dawn. Nigel, wrapped in his greatcoat, was glad to roll himself in a spare try-sail and rest his aching muscles. He felt positively virtuous when, early next morning, the *Four Winds* put in to Beaumaris with its catch of fish. The nocturnal adventure seemed a product of his imagination. It was only the feel of a wash-leather purse in his breeches pocket which convinced Nigel that it was no dream but a blessed reality. The little bag contained his share of the enterprise; more guineas than it had ever been his lot to handle. His downfall was complete. He had taken the wages of sin. He had broken the law, which, to a Briton's eyes, was far more heinous. Nigel Preece, the impeccable scholar, had burnt his boats.

These and similar thoughts passed through his mind during the hours of lessons. Periodically he took himself to task and deliberately turned to the blackboard, talking and working with more than usual intensity as though to recover lost ground. But as soon as the tousled heads were bent over their slates again he would revert to his world of fantasy. The one matter which troubled him was not that he had abandoned his principles and had become a law-breaker but that Puah was so plainly jealous of Bronwen. The girl made no secret of it. This was on Nigel's mind. While he did not trouble greatly about becoming a breaker of the law it did disturb him to think that he might be a breaker of hearts. He was so fond of Puah. She was so wholesome—all fresh and breezy and sunny, like being aboard the *Four Winds* on a summer's day. He did not want to hurt her. He would go to great lengths to prevent her being hurt. But he could not love her to order. Nature, apparently, did not arrange things that way. One did not sit down in coolly calculating mood and say—It is more desirable that I should marry so-and-so; I will arrange to fall in love with her. Usually the attraction was quite outside control. It just happened. Sometimes most illogically and inconveniently. It was as though an unseen power, instead of helping matters along, resolved to make them as difficult as possible. There was, for example, no logical reason why he should be attracted by Bronwen Vaughan—it was a stupid business and was bound to cause trouble. He knew it. She knew it. And yet they were drawn together. He had never taken her in his arms; never kissed her. For some reason he felt that it would not be honourable. He could control his feelings to that extent. But he had to admit that he could not control his desire to do so. There was about her some magnetism of the flesh which continually attracted him; some invisible power which made impossible things appear possible, and ridiculous things seem sensible, and wrong things look right. He imagined that when he went roving with the smugglers the excitement would have driven her out of his mind. It might have done—temporarily. He made the astounding discovery that you cannot run away from love. It follows wheresoever you go. It takes no heed of time or distance. A person can be absent in the body but present in the spirit. Nigel was learning many things which had not been included in the curriculum at an Oxford college, or, so far as he knew, any college outside the University of Life.

And then, as the afternoon school was drawing to its close, the conviction came over him that he must see Bronwen again. It came with such a surge of emotion that it set him trembling. He was consumed by restlessness. He glanced at the clock. There was still ten minutes to go. Ten interminable minutes before he could move from his desk. Ten more minutes wherein those urchins could try to read his secret thoughts.

"Put your slates and books away," he heard himself saying. "It is too nice an afternoon for you to be shut indoors. You may go."

The pandemonium seemed more pronounced than ever. Would the boys never get out of the door? What was young Owen lingering for? Trying to be tidy! The young idiot! Whoever expected a boy to be tidy, neat, and methodical? Why couldn't the little fool fling the things anywhere like the others had done and get out . . . get out!

Nigel locked his desk when the room was empty. Nigel locked the schoolhouse door. Nigel took the way which led to the woods. He strode with long, impatient strides. Of course, Bronwen might not be there. She might never come to see him again. He might be going on a fool's errand, but well he knew that he would have no peace of mind until he had been. And all the while he kept resolving that he would steel himself against disappointment. Bronwen might not be there. Bronwen would not be there. He was positive of it. Bronwen could not possibly be there . . . but she was!

His footfalls were deadened by the sward of the woodland path, and he came upon her unawares. She was seated on the rock, the lichen-coated boulder on which they had sat together, and all about her was the green silence of the forest trees. Her head was bowed. She looked listless, depressed. No, not depressed. That was not an appropriate word. Forlorn!

A dry twig snapped under his foot. She turned her head quickly; rose to her feet. He noticed that she was agitated. He was conscious that his own heart-beat had increased. It was racing so fast that when he attempted to speak his words came in jerks.

"Good—afternoon—Bronwen," he said formally, as he raised his hat.

"Oh, good afternoon. Fancy seeing you!" She endeavoured to speak calmly. Suddenly it came to Nigel that she, too, was experiencing difficulty in finding her words. "Would you care—to sit down—Nigel?"

"Why, thank you, I will."

There was an awkward silence. Nigel leant forward with his elbows on his knees and stared at the ground. Some little insect was climbing a grass stem. He watched its progress intently. Fancy a creature as small as that having legs, and muscles, and apparently a respiratory system. He wondered whether such insects ever fell in love. He supposed there must be some sort of process. Quaint idea making love when you were as small as that! Probably it simplified matters. No social position to consider. . . .

Bronwen was industriously digging a hole in the turf with the point of her shoe. She worked conscientiously, obviously as intent on the occupation as Nigel had been in watching his insect. It had disappeared now. Gone home, most likely. And Bronwen was taking the polish off the glossy leather of her shoe by her persistence.

"It's—quite nice to see you again!" she ventured.

"It's nice to see you again. I hardly expected . . . I wondered . . ."

"Wondered what, Nigel?"

"Well, I wondered if you would ever see me again; whether you would ever want to."

"Oh, Nigel! And I wondered, too. When you did not appear yesterday or the day before . . . I almost stayed away to-day, only I did not know what to do, and I was so restless."

"You came here yesterday? To meet me?"

"Of course, Nigel."

"But after the way you acted! After what you said! When you went away without a word. . . ."

"Silly! You didn't pay any attention to that, surely?"

"But I thought you were annoyed . . . upset."

"So I was. Furious. I was never going to speak to you again! But it didn't last. That mood!" She turned on him almost angrily. "You ought to have known that mood wouldn't last. You ought to have known I should have come back to meet you. And you stayed away."

"But, Bronwen, how was I to know?"

"I thought you cared for me."

"I do. I was so miserable and restless this afternoon I simply had to come in search of you, though I did not expect to find you here. How was I to know you would change your mind?"

"Your common sense ought to have told you. Your heart ought to have told you. What is the use of your knowledge?"

"Truly, Bronwen, I am beginning to wonder. In some matters my ignorance is abysmal."

"That's because you seek to be guided by your reason, Nigel. You should trust to your emotions. They are far more reliable."

"They may be in a woman, Bronwen. I have heard of a woman's intuition. But a man is more logical. Reason must control emotion."

"That is like a Latin motto. It sounds impressive but I don't believe it. Every good and noble act springs not from the mind but from the heart."

Nigel turned and looked at her a little wonderingly. "I suppose that the mistake that most of us make is to believe that knowledge is the same thing as wisdom. Yet between the two there can be a great gulf fixed. I may have knowledge but I lack your wisdom."

"My dear, a woman in love is always wise."

"I heard it said that she was always—unwise!"

"But her lack of wisdom is the greater wisdom!"

"Bronwen, you are a joy. You draw out my mind into by-ways where it never rambled before. When I talk to you I want to go on and on. One thought leads to another. When I leave you it is with sentences unspoken; thoughts unexpressed."

"That is how I feel when I have been with you. So much has been left unsaid—for the next time. It is like putting down a fascinating book with the knowledge that there are chapters still unread."

They sat silent awhile.

"Nigel."

"Yes?"

"I think it was a good thing you did not come to the rendezvous for some days. It has taught me many things."

"It has taught me much, too, Bronwen. It taught me how much I miss when I miss seeing you."

"Sometimes it is necessary not to see in order to see more clearly."

"I see more clearly now, Bronwen. I see with perfect clarity that life without your companionship is purposeless. It is life without an objective. When I am with you I am content, happy. tranquil; away from you I am restless. I cannot concentrate. I spend my time either in thinking of what you said, or else in imagining what I shall say when next I see you. It's all very complicated. I cannot see how I can have you and I cannot see how I can manage without you."

"Oh, Nigel, how dispassionately you talk, as though you were endeavouring to find the solution to a problem."

"I am. Does it not strike you that way?"

"It strikes me, but not that way. The problem of the future is so bewildering that I cannot face up to it, and so I am well content with the present. Or I should be if you were more prepared to make the most of it. I never could remember my Latin but there was one tag which has stuck—*Carpe diem!*"

"So you think I should embrace the opportunity?"

"I should prefer you to embrace me! No, no! I should not have said that. It sounds appallingly forward!"

Nigel put his arm about her gently, wonderingly. Never before had he known the slenderness of a woman's waist. He looked at her shyly. She half drew away.

"My dear. I do not want to appear shameless but you do— require a little encouragement, don't you? Do you really love me?"

"You know I do."

"Well?" She looked into his eyes. "Still letting reason rule emotion?"

Nigel laughed slightly. "Yes, I am afraid so. If I followed my inclinations I should take you in my arms and kiss those soft lips——"

"Then why don't you?"

"I feel that I ought to ask your father first whether I have his permission to marry you."

Bronwen drew back with a laugh so unexpected that it frightened a blue-tit on a near-by bough. It was an amused laugh, a cynical laugh, a bitter laugh. "If you wait for that, Nigel, I shall die unkissed."

"But it seems the only proper and honourable thing to do."

"Don't be so absurd. You know perfectly well that my father would never give his consent. Never! He would scorn you; mock you. If you are to love me, Nigel, it must be despite my father."

"It may make matters difficult for you."

"That is for me to face. If I, who take most risk, choose to run the risk, is it for you to weigh the cost?"

Nigel was breathing hard; so hard that he could not speak. He could only shake his head. And then suddenly all his good resolutions vanished; all his carefully conceived code; all his coolly calculated reasoning. All he knew was that the woman he loved was near him, very near, warm, inviting, and alluring.

Something within him surged; something primitive. The next instant his arms were about her. He crushed her to him and she came so readily that he was almost taken by surprise. And then his lips found hers.

*   *   *   *   *

Time had ceased to matter. They were content; more than content. The light was beginning to fail. It was Bronwen who moved. She straightened up and looked about her. "What was that?" she asked softly. Nigel, too, raised his head.

"I heard nothing."

"I thought I heard a rustling; a movement." The girl was looking about her, a trifle apprehensively.

They sat motionless. All about them was a wall of tree boles, leafy branches, bracken. But no movement. No living thing.

"I must have been mistaken. The woods are so still they make one a bit jumpy. But it is time we moved. It's time to part."

"To part. I do not like the sound of those words, even from your lips. God knows I wish that I might claim you so that we should never part, until death us do part."

"Even if that parted us. My dear!" She stood up and looked down at him with a wealth of feeling in her eyes. "Good night, Nigel." She bent and kissed his brow. "Good night, my dear one. God keep you. I shall be here again to-morrow. You will come to me?"

"Need you ask?"

"I shall count every minute until we meet again. No, don't accompany me this time. I must hurry. I am late. I shall have to run or I shall be missed."

He watched her graceful figure as she ran with the ease of a child. Not until the curve in the woodland path hid her from sight did he turn to go home. The woods seemed more silent than ever before. But never before had he known such gladness of heart.

CHAPTER XIV

THEY met again the next evening, and then for two days they did not set eyes on each other, for it rained. Such rain that no one, not even a lover, would care to venture forth. Nigel braved the deluge and waited a while under the dripping boughs. He was not surprised when Bronwen made no appearance. He went back feeling that at least he had done what he ought. He had not broken faith. That, to Nigel, was one of the pillars of his creed. There were certain things the right and wrong of which were debatable; there were others which were beyond dispute. To keep faith was one of these. It was something more than a conviction; it was an inner urge. It permeated all he did and said and thought. Another of his guiding precepts was never to cause pain if he could avoid it. To the autocrat or the bully he could be completely callous, but to his friends, the aged, the infirm, those weaker than himself, those less able to bear life's buffets, he was as tender as a woman with her first-born child. Because of this Nigel felt that he had to walk meticulously. He had, that evening, encountered Puah as he made his way up the street.

"Wherever have you been, Nigel? You are soaked to the skin." Puah was always refreshingly outspoken.

"For a walk," he had replied.

"People do not go for walks in rain like this for nothing," was Puah's comment. That was all. Had she asked him outright where he had been he would have told her. There was no dissembling about Nigel. But she had not spoken another word. Instead she turned away. He felt he had hurt her. But how could he have avoided it? The thought troubled him. He did not want to hurt Puah. He was so fond of her. But what could he do?

It proved an exceptional day. A wind had driven the rain in squally gusts. When these passed, the sky would momentarily clear. The respite was brief. If any man imagined the rain had stopped he was soon disillusioned. During one of these spells of calm, Nigel ventured forth from his rooms. He was too restless to stay long indoors. His thesis, spread over the table, was practically complete. The research work had been done. The draft, in his neat calligraphy, testified to his labours. All that remained was to have it fair copied for dispatch to the University. But he could not get on with this. Its very simplicity was a deterrent. It occupied his time but not his mind. That went roving. He was aboard the *Four Winds* or at the quarry in the woods, anywhere but at the paper-strewn table.

On the broad grass strip which stretched between the street and the strait Nigel could see a group of men, fishermen mostly by their garb, burly Madoc among them. They were staring seaward at something which engrossed their attention. Nigel walked closer and he, too, looked. The *Unique* had dropped anchor in the roads. She could not have been there long. Nigel could see the topmen on the yards making snug the canvas. There was a heavy swell and the masts were swaying. He could not say why, but the presence of the warship brought with it a sense of uneasiness; foreboding. Would there be another raid by the press-gang? Possibly the men grouped on the grass were wondering the same thing. It might be well to take Piers' advice and stay indoors. The town was quiet. The streets were almost deserted. Nigel returned to his rooms, drew the curtains, lit the candles, and settled down to his writing. Periodically he would lay down his pen and listen. The night was quiet. It was long past midnight when he went to bed.

The following morning the sun was shining. He breakfasted early. Before turning towards the school curiosity drove him to the water-front. The anchorage was empty. The corvette had departed with the turn of the tide. Nigel breathed a sigh of relief. But why had she been there? Her appearance was ominous. Or so he thought. She might merely have sought a haven because of the squalls. But that brief glimpse of her yellow-banded side filled him with apprehension. It was like the shadow of a passing hawk.

The boys were chattering about the warship's brief visit when he arrived at the school. Instead of silencing them their master allowed them to talk for a while. He listened. There had been no raid. Nothing untoward or suspicious. Just a brief coming and going. With his mind more at rest Nigel took up the day's tasks.

When he went home for his tea he found Bronwen seated in the wing-backed chair. He thought she looked paler than usual. She had his manuscript in her hand.

"Is this your thesis that you have spoken about?" she asked, and there was a studied indifference about her tone as though she deliberately avoided a formal salutation. "I have been reading it I hope you do not mind. I do not usually pry into

D

another person's papers but this seemed to be—almost—public property. And you had told me about it. I was interested."

"Yes. That is the thesis. It only requires copying."

"And then you will become a Master of Arts? How wonderful! Can I assist with the copying, Nigel? I have time on my hands."

"Thank you, Bronwen, but I can manage it myself. It was kind of you to offer. Did you come to talk about the thesis?"

"You know I did not. Shut the door."

"What is it? Has something gone wrong?" He took her by the shoulders and glanced into her face. She kissed him lightly and went back to the chair. He could tell that she was disturbed. The uneasy feeling which had taken possession of him the previous evening returned in all its potency.

"We must not meet in the woods again, Nigel! Don't ask me why. I could not tell you! It is scarcely more than a womanly intuition. I believe that we have been spied upon. The first day it rained I was starting out when Rhys came up to see me. He remarked that it was a wet day for walking. Just that. But there was a smirk upon his face which I did not like. It made me ill at ease. So I did not venture out. I agreed quietly that it was not fit to go and took off my things. But he went. He came in later, soaking, his boots mired. Did you go to the woods?"

Nigel nodded.

"He must have seen you," the girl resumed. "The next day I stayed home deliberately. Again he went out into the woods and came back saturated. Now Rhys likes his creature comforts and nothing but a woman or the chance of sport would make him stir on such a day. We must meet elsewhere."

"If we continue to meet."

"Nigel? What are you saying? Have you tired of me already?"

"It is not that. How could such a thought enter your head, Bronwen? My concern is solely for your safety; for your good name."

"Never heed that. I shall continue to see you. I must. I have no other interest in life. You remember what you said—people are punished not for doing wrong but for making mistakes. Let us plot and plan carefully; make no mistakes."

Nigel was silent. His was a nature which loathed subterfuge. He liked to be transparent in all his dealings. Plotting and scheming were not for him. He preferred the open challenge; the throwing down of the gauntlet.

"Bronwen, you know that I wish to marry you. Would it not be better for me to ask your father's consent?"

Bronwen laughed; it was a hard, mirthless laugh. "You do not know my father. You might anger him; you might amuse him. He would not take it seriously. All that your nobility would achieve would be to make him take good care that you did not see me again. No, we must outwit them. It is no good your regarding father and Rhys as men of honour. They do not know the meaning of the term; to them honour is conceit, pride. And, Nigel . . . I had to come to tell you . . . Pink Kirby was at our place last night."

"Ah!" The presence of the *Unique* was explained. Or had the naval lieutenant merely taken advantage of the situation to pay a hurried visit ashore. "He has distressed you, Bronwen? Has he been particularly objectionable? I wish it could be my good fortune to meet the fellow on something like equal terms. He requires a lesson."

"Do not quarrel with him, Nigel. It will do no good. In fact, it will only make matters worse. He was more drunk and more objectionable than ever, but I do not want to discuss it. Nothing can be done about it. Father supports him because he regards the marriage as a good match; Rhys, because he likes Pink, who drinks with him and tells him coarse stories of a vintage not to be obtained ashore."

"The mystery is that such a creature is regarded as a gentleman! God save the expression!"

"I felt polluted by the touch of his thick lips. Nigel, could you ever kiss me again? I struggled, wrestled, but all to no purpose. Rhys was there and laughed at my unavailing attempts. Offered to bet odds. My father told me not to be a fool and to submit as a woman was in duty bound to do. And they call that love! If I were forced into marriage with that man I should have no more rights than a slave wench, yet it would be termed holy matrimony. If I see you—you who are the soul of honour; you who are kind and tender and chivalrous; you who revere and cherish me in a manner I have never before known—if I see you, I am doing wrong and people are scandalized. Why is it?"

"It is not a question of right or wrong. It is a question of custom and convention."

"Then we shall defy both."

"And as for my not wishing to kiss you again. . . ." Nigel took her in his arms. "Set your mind at ease, dear one. I will wipe away his presence with an absolving kiss."

A heavy step in the hall caused Bronwen to slip quickly from Nigel's embrace. A boisterous voice shouted:

"Hi, there, Nigel! Are you at home, man? I've news for you." The door was flung open and Piers, his curly head bare, his eyes bright, pulled up abruptly on the threshold. His gaze rested not on Nigel but on Bronwen. He stared so fixedly that Nigel, too, turned to look. A pretty sight Bronwen made, her hair slightly disordered, her cheeks flushed, her eyes large and sparkling.

"Sorry, Nigel! I did not know you had company. I . . . I thought you might like to come fishing again."

"Thank you, Piers." Nigel's voice was quiet, carefully modulated. He spoke without fluster, with dignity. "I believe that you know Miss Vaughan?"

"Very well, by sight. All Beaumaris knows the beautiful Miss Vaughan."

"I think all Beaumaris knows Piers Penryn," observed Bronwen. "If we have not spoken before it cannot be because we are unaware of each other's existence. I often see you putting off in that trim ketch of yours, Piers. You and your sister. And how is your sister?"

"Puah? Nothing ever ails her. Well, I won't stay under the circumstances. See you again, Nigel. Miss Vaughan, I bid you good day."

He made what was, for Piers, a bow of some pretensions. The door shut. They heard him whistling down the street.

Nigel and Bronwen looked at each other. Bronwen's fingers strayed to her hair. She consulted a gilt-edged mirror. "I must have looked a fright, Nigel. My hair is all over the place."

"You looked particularly attractive, Bronwen. I could not help noticing it. Piers noticed, too. The lad seemed to be almost struck dumb by your loveliness."

"I hope he did not see . . .   I hope he did not suspect . . ."

"Of course not. And we can trust Piers not to divulge. He is one of my best friends. Only I wish he had not come."

"Our luck seems to be changing, Nigel."

"Bronwen, this cannot go on. You must run away with me and we will get married. I am only waiting until I can get enough money. I must get money. I will get money. Quickly. At once."

"Is that why you cast in your lot with the Free Traders, Nigel?"

"Yes." The word was out before he knew it. He could have bitten his tongue off, so chagrined was he.

"My dear, don't look so conscience-stricken!" pleaded Bronwen. "It was unfair of me to take you unawares. I know you, Nigel. You are worrying because you feel you have broken faith, even though it was unwittingly. But, my dear, I had guessed as much. Especially when you went out for a couple of days with Piers in the *Four Winds*. Everybody knows how that reckless young villain gets all his money."

"They . . . know?"

"Perhaps I should say, suspect. They don't inquire too closely. I soon put two and two together. Only I should have preferred you to tell me . . . and yet I admired you for not telling. It gives me confidence, in a way. If you are so loyal to others you will be equally loyal to me."

"More so, I hope."

"Was it only because of earning the money quickly that you went, Nigel?"

"Of course."

"No other reason whatsoever?"

"None, Bronwen. What other reason could there be?"

"That young Penryn girl is attractive in her bold way."

"I never gave her a thought, in that sense, Bronwen. Bold she may be, if you mean reckless. Bold she never is, if you mean brazen. I count her and Piers as my best friends. But tell me, Bronwen, are you ashamed of me for becoming a smuggler?"

"Ashamed? How little you know me, Nigel. You did it to get money so that you could marry me and I adore you for it. I fear I have not your high sense of honour, Nigel. My principles are flexible where you are concerned. So long as you do not seek the company of that girl, I care not how often you go smuggling, provided you do not get caught. Tell me, why did you require the money?"

Nigel looked puzzled. "I thought I had already explained."

"You did."

"Then why do you want me to tell you a second time?"

"Why was it?"

"Because I wanted to afford to make a home for you. I wanted money so that I could marry you."

"Don't you think a woman is justified in wanting to hear that a second time?"

Nigel laughed and unbent. As his arms went round her he said: "You are quite fascinating, Bronwen. I believe, under your tuition, I may become a lover yet."

CHAPTER XV

FRIDAY remained in Nigel's memory ever after. It was one of those days which stand out in life; never to be forgotten. It was a day of decisions. It was, he later admitted, a day of wrong decisions. But like most good things that turn out ill all were actuated by the best intentions. He got up early, for the sun was beckoning. As he dressed he resolved, first, that he would not go on any more smuggling runs with Piers and Puah; secondly, that he would call on Squire Vaughan and formally ask for the hand of his daughter in marriage. Nigel had his own way of looking upon life and the ordering of it. That the ways of others were not his ways did not occur to him. Neither, for that matter, did it strike him that his motives would be misunderstood. If going out in the *Four Winds* was going to complicate a situation which was already sufficiently involved, the sooner it ended the better it would be. It would mean a loss of revenue; it would mean a loss of sentiment. But he felt that it was the right thing to do—in fairness to Bronwen; in fairness, for that matter, to Puah also.

He meant to marry Bronwen. She stirred him as he had never been stirred before. Reason had ceased to rule emotion so far as the conceiver of that admirable axiom was concerned. It offended his pride to meet Bronwen surreptitiously. Stealth and secrecy did not commend themselves to him. He wanted to come out in the open, every act ready for inspection, everything he thought and said and did impeccable, beyond reproach. It was his duty as a man of honour to speak to Bronwen's father. That the squire would not give his consent was apparent even to so sublime an idealist as Nigel Preece. But having told him candidly of his intentions, Nigel would then feel free to act despite the squire. The buttons, as it were, were off the foils. To do Nigel justice the thought of the possible repercussions on Bronwen did not enter his lofty mind. He would treat the squire as a man of honour. That the squire would not react as a man of honour never occurred to him. Which showed that Nigel's knowledge of classical literature was more profound than his knowledge of humanity, squires in particular.

Because he liked to exercise in the sunshine before incarcerating himself in the small and not too salubrious schoolroom, Nigel strode along the grassy sward which stretched so pleasantly beside the strait. There were others astir, one of them Piers.

"Hello, Nigel! Sorry I burst into your room as I did. No idea you were not alone."

"I'm sure you were unaware that I had a visitor, Piers."

"And a damned pretty one, too. As trim a little craft as sails these waters. Is she still bothering about poetry, Nigel?"

"Yes, I believe so."

"Take my advice and sheer off. You are in shoal water. The squire's a touchy old boy, and as proud as they make 'em. My own private opinion is that he set his bully on you to lay you out because he did not approve of his daughter seeing you."

"I think you do him an injustice there, Piers. The sea-bully acted on his own initiative, I am convinced. You see, he spoke discourteously to me on a previous occasion, and I reproved him."

"You would, Nigel! I can picture you reproving him! I wish I had heard it. Well, as friend to friend, I wouldn't poach on that particular preserve."

"Poaching is hardly an apt expression, Piers."

"That's probably how old Vaughan would regard it. And he's the vindictive sort of devil who'd set spring-guns for poachers. Anyhow, Nigel, I'd give that pretty little lady a wide berth, if only for Puah's sake. She would not like it if she knew."

"She does know, Piers. I do not conceal anything from my friends."

"You're either a better man than I am, Nigel, or a bigger fool. The latter, I think. Women are jealous creatures. If you must play with more than one take my advice and keep it dark."

"I am not playing, as you term it, with anyone." Nigel was dignified. "I believe in being candid; it simplifies matters."

"Does it? I should say it complicated 'em like the deuce. I've wondered what's come over Puah of late. It's plain, now, if you tell me she knows about Bronwen Vaughan. Stop it, Nigel. I don't want Puah hurt. She's a good kid."

"The last thing I desire is to hurt Puah."

"Well, you are doing. Take that from me."

"But not intentionally, Piers; unavoidably."

"The devil! What difference does it make provided she *is* hurt? You've a bit of a lawyer about you, Nigel. Splitting hairs. If you won't leave that pretty bit of goods alone for fear of the squire, cut adrift out of loyalty to Puah."

"I am not disloyal to Puah. Nothing has ever passed between

us. I regard her as a very dear friend. But Bronwen, I speak in
confidence, is more to me than that. I intend to marry her."

"Marry her? Why, you fool . . ." Piers could only give
vent to his surprise by resorting to language usually reserved for
his crew during a gale.

Nigel flushed. "Your words are uncalled for, Piers. I overlook
the expressions because I believe that at the back of them is
concern for my welfare. But please be more discreet in future,
or it may strain the bonds of our friendship."

Pier's quick temper set his eyes blazing, but with an effort at
self-restraint he turned away and gave vent to his feelings by
hurling stones into the water.

"We are going out to-night, Nigel," he said in a voice which
was carefully under control. "You will join us?"

"Thank you, Piers. Not to-night."

"I mean . . . it's one of the special trips. Money in it.
Guineas. Wind's in the right quarter. We're expecting a cargo
from the Isle of Man."

"Sorry, Piers. I . . . I have decided not to accompany you
any more."

"Hell! Turned respectable? Or are you scared of the risk?"

"Neither. I mean to call on the squire this evening."

Piers gave a laugh and flung another stone into the sea.
"You'll come away with a flea in your ear," he said. "See here.
There's the *Four Winds*, and there's her dinghy drawn up on
the shingle at Gallows Point. If you change your mind join us
at sunset. But don't leave it too late."

Without another word Piers walked away. Nigel could
tell he was upset. In a temper. And when his blood was roused
Piers was volcanic. Nigel knew that never had Piers' regard
for him been more truly revealed than in his recent restraint.

The day dragged. The hours of lessons seemed interminable.
The thought came to Nigel that he was never intended to be
a schoolmaster. He was in his wrong niche.

When school was over Nigel went to his room and changed
into his best clothes. He bathed and shaved and combed his
hair until its thick waves were set. So far as he could recollect
this was the first occasion for him to pay the slightest heed to
his personal appearance. Though he would not see Bronwen he
felt that it was done for her sake. He wished to look his best.
As he took a final glance at himself in the mirror he was forced
to admit that he did not look unbecoming. There was a quiet
hauteur about his intellectual, aristocratic features which was

undoubtedly impressive. That was the one thing which he was resolved to impress upon Squire Vaughan. That so far as intelligence and ancestry were concerned he was his equal. It was only the lack of money which was the barrier, and this could be overcome. He might as well have aspired to convincing a Hereford bullock.

His face was paler than usual as he took the road to the hall. His shoulders were straighter, his head held higher, his lips set with a determined line which might well have characterized his long-dead ancestor ere he rode into the press at Poictiers. The day was glorious, the sun still bright, though beginning to slope to the west. The wild flowers in the hedgerows held Nigel's eye as he walked the road of destiny. More than once he paused to pluck a bloom but the fragile stalks soon wilted in his hot fingers and he threw them regretfully away. For how many centuries, he wondered, had those delicate little blossoms starred the hedge banks? How many generations had beheld their beauty before they fulfilled their task and faded into seed and so attained their immortality? A hart's-tongue fern caught his eye. There was a cool corner under his window where it would flourish.

He paused, his fingers fondled the fronds, out came his knife and he delicately cut the turf about its roots so that it came away from the bank well protected. He slipped his knife back into his pocket and moulded the soil firmly about the fibres, wrapping long grasses to form a protective nest. Engrossed in his task, he was surprised when his ears caught the sound of approaching hoofs. He looked up. Nigel was to be spared the journey to the hall. Squire Vaughan was approaching, his proud roan walking almost silently along the grass verge of the lane.

"What have you got there?" The squire's salutation was crisp.

"A fern for my garden. I think it will live though this is not a good time to move them."

"Put it back where you got it."

Nigel's face revealed his amazement. "I beg your pardon."

"I spoke plainly enough. Put that fern back where you got it from. This land is mine. I do not tolerate stealing."

Nigel's eyes narrowed. His breath came quickly and he fought to control it.

"You regard it as stealing?"

"I do. The land is mine and all that is on it."

"Then I will replace the fern." Nigel walked to the hedge and thrust the plant into the hole. The squire shook his rein. His horse had not taken a pace before he was surprised by a sudden "Stop!"

It was so peremptory that the horseman instinctively obeyed.

"You are not to go yet," said Nigel, coming closer and brushing the soil from his fingers. "I have an explanation to offer. I did not put the plant back because you ordered me to do so, Mr. Vaughan. I put it back because you implied that I was stealing. I want that made clear." Nigel's voice was ominously calm. "I was under a misapprehension when I took the fern. In my ignorance I imagined it belonged to the Almighty."

"It belongs to me."

"Perhaps that is synonymous."

"You have an insolent way of speaking."

"Did you imagine you held the prerogative?"

For a moment the squire did not speak. His heavy face was frowning as though he wrestled with a mental problem.

"Why, damn you! You are insulting." He rose in his stirrups and uncoiled the thong of his whip.

"Be careful!" Nigel's eyes were fixed on his with an intensity which made the squire pause. "If you touch me with your whip, I shall kill you."

The two men faced each other, both breathing hard. There was that in Nigel's eyes which made the older man, mounted though he was, lower his whip. He still fingered the thong.

"Ah!" he said, and his voice was now calm. "And what right have you to threaten me with murder?"

"As much right as you have to threaten me with assault. As much right as you have to accuse a man of honour of stealing. As much right as you have to insult one who is, at least, your equal."

"Ah!" said the squire, and then "Ah!" again. He seemed at a loss for words. Or perhaps his thoughts were too tumultuous to find expression in words.

"I endeavour to treat with courtesy every person I meet," said Nigel evenly. He was cooler now. "I expect equal courtesy in return."

"So you consider that . . . I . . . overstepped the mark, eh?"

"You accused me of theft. You knew that was unwarrantable."

"Hum! A legal point. I must get advice." The squire sat silent, thinking. He, too, was cooler now. The flush had passed from his face. Nothing remained but a cold, callous look.

"So you criticize my conduct, Mr. Schoolmaster. I see. Let

NO COWARD SOUL 107

me observe that you appear to set considerable store on your dignity, your so-called honour."

"You never spoke a truer word."

"And I appear to have transgressed. I was under the impression that as a landowner of some standing I was a person of some consequence in this district. It takes an impecunious schoolmaster to put me in my place."

"I would like to have you know, sir, that though my position may appear insignificant in your eyes, I am not despised by scholars of consequence in this country. And if it comes to breeding I consider that on my mother's side I have in my veins blood which is as illustrious as any in North Wales."

"Doubtless on the sinister side, Mr. Schoolmaster."

"That is an insult, sir, which cannot be overlooked. I have a brace of pistols at my house. Allow me time and I will fetch them, and then I shall be entirely at your service."

The squire's answer was unexpected. He burst into a loud guffaw which wounded Nigel's pride more than any blow could have done. The roan tossed its head at the unexpected touch of a spur. Nigel found himself gazing at a broad back which rose and fell as the horse trotted down the roadway.

Nigel retraced his steps. He walked briskly. His face was set hard. He went upstairs to his bedchamber and changed into his oldest clothes. As he came downstairs the sun was low in the heavens. He hastened shorewards with impatient strides. The sails of the *Four Winds* were creaking into position. The dinghy had vanished from Gallows Point. Nigel broke into a run. At his hail he saw Puah step on to the bulwarks. She waved a cheery greeting.

"Just in time, Nigel! Are you coming?"

"Yes. Send the dinghy ashore. I have changed my mind!"

CHAPTER XVI

I F Nigel wished to escape from surroundings which had suddenly become distasteful to him he could have chosen no more efficacious way. Light was failing and the ketch, alone on the vast expanse of water, had become a world of her own, detached, self-contained. It took a little while for Nigel to recover his composure. He sought occupation, busying himself with rope and sail in a manner which brought forth a grin of approval from Piers, who stood, hand on tiller, an unlit pipe between his teeth.

"Here, take hold of the tiller while I light my pipe. You may as well have a shot at steering. You are not likely to run into anything on this course unless you strike the Isle of Man."

"Are we going there?" asked Nigel, curiously.

"Not this voyage, though we are meeting a cutter from that island. There is more trade done with the Isle of Man than any place along the West Coast. Did you know that? They've all manner of jealously guarded privileges there which makes 'em a happy hunting-ground for the Free Trader. Keep the sheet taut, Nigel. That's better."

Piers, whose pipe was now alight, adjusted the sail to his liking, and thrusting his hands into his pockets, resumed his conversation. He was in a genial mood. Nigel could tell that.

"We'll make a seaman of you yet, Nigel. You must come out with us more often. Nothing like practice, my buck. I'm damn glad you changed your mind. I could tell Puah did not like it when you sent word you were not coming to-night." He glanced forward to where his sister was standing beside the look-out in the bows.

"I encountered Vaughan. Our conversation, though brief, was acrimonious."

Piers burst into a laugh. "Hell, man, what did you expect? Well, I for one am not sorry it has happened. It has brought you to your senses. Forget it, Nigel. You were never intended for folks like that. They give themselves high and mighty airs but they're low for all that. You stick by me, Nigel. I'm bad, but you know the worst of my badness. I don't conceal it from any-one—but the Excise officer. All's square and above-board in the *Four Winds*."

He puffed contentedly at his pipe. Things were evidently going to his liking. Nigel was less content. He stood, conscious of the pull of the tiller, staring at the drawing sail. His thoughts were far away.

What an impossible man Vaughan was! It was a good thing he had not used the whip. Nigel verily believed that in the passion of the moment he would have killed him as he had said. He gave a little shudder at the thought! How different Bronwen was—the girl must take after her mother. Probably her horsemanship, her love of the open, were inherited from her father. The way she handled the pistol was more like a man than a woman. He did not mind her inheriting those traits, so long as she was free from the contaminating strain.

"I'm going forrard for a bit," interrupted Piers. "Keep her on this course. We ought to be picking up a signal shortly. If you should see a green light showing, sing out."

Hands in pockets he sauntered towards the bows. A whiff of French tobacco came to Nigel's nostrils as he moved away. It was not long before Puah came aft. She was wearing, Nigel noticed, the short worsted boat-skirt she adopted when at sea. It was a good many years since mariners wore that garb. He wondered where she had picked it up. It was undoubtedly useful. Became her, too. Gave her a sort of nautical swagger.

"How is the fair and fascinating buccaneer?" inquired Nigel with a quiet smile as she leant against the weather bulwarks.

"If you mean me, I'm happier now you have joined us. It just spoilt the whole trip when I heard you were not coming. Piers is glad, too. He's fond of you, Nigel."

"And I'm fond of Piers."

"Did he tell you of the kindness he did you?"

"No. I do not recall his mentioning anything."

"You remember the squally night that horrid corvette anchored in the roads? Two officers came ashore. They were evidently on some spree for they put off in their jollyboat and rowed themselves. One of them was the beast who nearly killed you. Piers watched them land down the coast, haul up their boat, and make their way to Squire Vaughan's place. Piers was thinking of setting their boat adrift when he had a better idea. But perhaps I had better not tell you. You might not approve."

"Probably I would not. I know Piers' deplorable sense of humour. But having gone so far you may as well continue."

"He fetched a brace and bit and bored several holes in the bottom. He plugged these with corks, thrust in far enough so that they would not work loose until the boat was well afloat. The men would be too drunk to notice until the boat was half full of water I have no doubt."

"But Puah. It might have sunk under them. It might have drowned them both."

"Yes. It might."

"Did it?"

"I don't know."

"But Puah, you should not have let him do it."

"I helped him."

"Puah!" Nigel shook his head.

"Nigel, I hate anyone who is cruel to you. After the way you were treated I don't care if they were drowned. They nearly killed you. I shall never forget the first sight I had of you sprawled on the floor with your face so white and your head resting in a pool of blood. I thought you were dead. And I hate that man. Hate him. Hate him! I'd kill him if I could."

"Puah, my dear. I . . . I don't like to hear you talk like that."

"I don't care. I'm bad and wild like Piers. I hate my enemies. But I love my friends. And I won't have anyone hurting you . . . whatever way they do it."

Nigel bit his lip. He sensed a fresh hostility in her tone.

"It's generous of you, Puah, but you know I really am big enough to take care of myself."

"You're big enough but you're not sensible enough. You let people deceive you. You believe good of everybody. You are too honourable, too noble."

She turned her head away. There was silence for a moment broken only by the creak of a block or the slap of a wave. When Puah spoke her voice was casual.

"You are keeping your eyes open for a signal, Nigel? Piers told you to watch for a green light."

"Yes."

"The Isle of Man boat is to show one. She ought to be due any time now. I hope she hasn't overshot the place in the dark. Let's do something, Nigel. I hate this waiting; this doing nothing. Piers will be altering the rig soon, I expect. How do you like the *Four Winds* when she's lug-rigged? She's the *Moonraker*, then. Did you know? We always alter her name, just in case someone should steal up close enough to read . . . let me show you."

She fumbled in a locker for some tools and bending over the taffrail unfastened the name which was painted on to a strip of wood. She placed the name-board on a seat and picked up another strip of identical size and showed it to Nigel before she fastened it on to the stern. In the dim light he could read the name—*Moonraker*.

"You said I should become a moonraker," he said with a smile. "The name conveys nothing to me."

"Oh, it's an old joke. I forget which county it comes from. Some Free Traders were chased and had to hide their tubs in a pond. The next night they went to recover them and a yokel saw them fishing in the water and asked what they were doing. They told him they were raking for the moon."

"And so I am expected to rake for the moon? A novel thought, Puah. Perhaps it is symbolical. I find that I have been crying for the moon."

"I don't know what you mean."

"I don't mean anything, really. It is just my stupid way of talking."

"Well, talk sense. Here comes Piers. We shall have to get the sails down now."

They worked in silence until the vessel had lug sails substituted. They remained hove to, riding idly on the swell. Every eye peered into the night. It was Puah who broke the silence. "There she is. Port bow."

Piers emerged from the cabin with a green light which he flashed. There was an answering flash out of the blackness and the two vessels drew together.

Nigel saw the sharp outline of a large cutter; a bigger craft than the *Four Winds* despite her single mast. An exchange of passwords sounded over the black waters. The vessels were alongside. Nigel saw Piers place a heavy pistol on the locker before him. All the crew had picked up arms until the newcomer's identity had been established. There was no time for talking. The moment the vessels were lashed together they became a scene of bustling activity. Package after package was heaved over the cutter's side and into the *Four Winds'* hold. Puah worked with a will, handing bales down to Nigel.

"That's the lot." The skipper of the Manx boat spoke curtly. The lashings were cast off. The vessels drifted apart. The *Four Winds'* sails creaked into place. There was no formality of farewell. It might be novelty to Nigel; to the crews of the two vessels it was routine work to be accomplished with as little fuss as possible.

Piers took the helm. The *Four Winds* came about and headed for the Anglesey coast.

"I did not know you carried arms, Puah," said Nigel when the two stood side by side, still heated from their exertions.

"We always do. We have not had to use them—yet."

"Is there risk?"

"There's always some risk. That's what makes it so exciting. Don't you like risk?"

"I am inclined to think I do."

"There may be more risk than usual this time. Don't you think so, Piers?"

"Maybe, Puah. We've had a long run of good luck. It's time it changed."

"What makes you think it may change to-night?" inquired Nigel.

"Piers heard from one of our spies that the departure of the *Unique* was a hoax. They have left a boat behind concealed in one of the bays."

"Is that likely? I thought it was left to the Revenue people to put down smuggling. The Navy would not concern itself surely?"

"Not unless there was a reason," said Piers. "If that drunken sot had the ducking I imagined he had, it is quite likely he has been trying to find out who was responsible for it."

"But nobody knows, do they?"

"Nobody knows, but there are people who could make a damn good guess. That slimy swine, Rhys Vaughan, for instance."

"Ah!"

"And then the Navy are always glad to impress Free Traders. We are better seamen than they are, and they know it, though they'd never admit it."

Puah, who had gone into the cabin, came out with her face blackened and a pot of some dark grease in her hand.

"We'll take precautions," she said, and Piers, in a matter-of-fact way, blackened his face.

Nigel demurred. "No, Puah. I should look ridiculous."

Her hot hands were drawn across his face. "Well, you are ridiculous at times, Nigel, so you should not mind."

"You little fiend," he said clutching her wrists, half-amused, half-annoyed.

"Shut up, you two!" Piers was curt. "Tell Madoc to get the cudgels out, Puah. And see that the pistols have dry primings. Now, no more talking. Keep your eyes open—and listen for all you're worth."

The men stood silent, each at his respective post. All eyes

stared ahead. Each man had a brace of pistols in his belt. Cudgels were ranged along the side where they could be snatched at a moment's notice. There was no talking. There was a sense of expectancy; of apprehension in the air. Nigel was conscious of it. He had known it on the previous trip. This time its potency impressed him. There seemed some premonition that all was not well.

"We are not far from the shore, now," whispered Puah, coming close to him.

"How do you know?"

"Cannot you hear the gulls calling about the cliffs?"

Nigel had noticed the sound but its significance had not struck him. The vessel moved forward in silence.

Suddenly Puah clutched Nigel's arm. An orange light broke the darkness of the sky ahead. It rose like a flame, flickering, increasing in volume. "What is it?" whispered Nigel. "It looks volcanic!"

"The furze," said Puah. "Some one has fired the furze. It is a warning signal."

"Get ready to put about!" Piers' voice was crisp but low.

The sails were dipping-lugs and it took time to get the boat on a new course. The men jumped to the halliards and the sails came creaking down. Nigel looked about him. A flash of white between the ship and the shore caught his eyes. There was foam, the sparkle of phosphorus. Was it a breaking wave? It seemed to move; it seemed to move outwards. Towards him. He stretched his finger to point, intending to ask Puah what it signified when her voice rang out clear but low.

"Boat on the port quarter!"

"Stand to your halliards, lads. Heave! With a will now. Get those sails up. The boat can wait!"

Nigel glanced at the straining crew. The yards were creeping up the masts again. The men worked with a will. He glanced towards the land. The white was more visible. He could see the splash of oars. It seemed a race; it was a race. He was conscious of a thrill of excitement, not without a certain curiosity, entirely devoid of apprehension. The white shape grew larger. It was a ship's boat, four oars aside.

The sails were up. He could feel the *Four Winds* quiver and move. He staggered slightly at the slant of the deck, recovered himself, and reached for one of the cudgels. Puah was coming from the cabin with pistols in her belt and pistols in her hand.

She took the latter to her brother and thrust them into his broad belt.

A hail came across the dark waters. "Heave-to, there! In the King's name."

Piers might have been deaf. With one hand on the tiller and the other holding the sheet, he coaxed more wind into the hesitant sails. "Heave to, or I fire!" came the voice astern. The man-o'-war's boat was gaining rapidly now, hand over fist.

"Make fast those halliards and come aft to repel boarders." Piers spoke coolly, giving orders as succinctly as a naval officer would. Nigel formed the impression that he was enjoying himself. From his blackened face Piers' eyes sparkled brightly. "Cudgels, first, lads. Don't use firearms except as a last resort."

From the pursuing boat a pistol cracked and a bullet embedded itself in the mizzen mast. The boat was level with the *Four Winds'* stern. It was opposite her quarter, gaining, drawing close. Nigel saw the oars lifted out of the water and he heard the thud and clatter as they were shipped. He saw a man in the bows balancing with a boathook in his hand; saw the oarsmen, men in striped singlets, brawny-armed, tugging out cutlasses. Saw in the stern, upright, hand on tiller, his fierce red face set in a determined scowl, Lieutenant Pink Kirby, R.N., masterful, ferocious, bringing his boat up for boarding. The boat was alongside, the boathook was fast in the main shrouds. There was a rush of black-faced smugglers to the side, the sound of cudgels thudding against cutlasses. Shouts, orders, curses, a groan, a shriek. A man, cutlass between his teeth came swarming over the bulwarks. Instinctively Nigel leaped forward and brought his club a thwack on the exposed head. The seaman let go and toppled backwards into the boat. Nigel was in the thick of it now. A spectator no more. A participant. An outlaw. Fighting against the forces of the Crown.

"Keep 'em off a moment longer, lads. We've got the wind. She's drawing away. Keep 'em off." Piers, his teeth gleaming white, was obviously excited. In his element. Madoc, picking up a cutlass dropped by the seaman Nigel had knocked out, delivered a sweeping cut which shore off the head of the boathook. The boat fell away.

"Damnation!" yelled the lieutenant. "Can't you lubbers get aboard? Follow me."

There was a gleam of white as his breeched leg came over the taffrail. He balanced on one foot, striving to grasp a shroud overhead, plainly outlined against the sky. Nigel could see his coarse, red face flushed with the lust of battle. He heard a catch of breath from Puah, saw her whip a pistol from her belt. He sprang forward and struck up her arm. The flash of flame stabbed the night as the ball soared high.

He heard Puah give an exclamation, half sob, half curse. Dropping his cudgel Nigel stepped forward and as the naval officer bent to leap aboard his fist caught Kirby full in the face. The man's head went back with a jerk, he swayed and fell back. They heard his body splash in the water; saw a couple of tars stoop to grab him under the armpits. Nigel, as he watched, realized that the boat was no longer alongside. It was tossing, its crew confused, yards away . . . yards away . . . they were free! He heard Piers laugh as the sails did their work. Nigel realized he was trembling. He looked back. The white boat was a tossing shape astern, dim in the darkness.

CHAPTER XVII

I T seemed strange to tread the Beaumaris streets again, unreal, unnatural. Nigel felt that he lived in two worlds, led two lives, as, indeed, was the case. Puah had passed him a moment since, going shopping, a basket on her arm. Puah who, not forty-eight hours before, had levelled a murdering pistol at a King's officer. It had taken Nigel a long time to remove the last trace of the incriminating black grease from his face and hair. It would take longer to erase the recollection of that night from his memory. In his mind he relived the exciting hours which followed the escape from the man-of-war's boat.

Piers, balked at the first landing place, had coolly set off to search for an alternative spot. "They can't possibly be watching both beaches," he argued, as he flashed his signal ashore and then ran in to the anchorage. He was correct. In perfect security they rowed their bales ashore, stored them in a cave, received payment, and vanished into the night. The following morning the *Four Winds*, her fore-and-aft sails restored, her name replaced, came in to Beaumaris Bay with the early morning tide. There was a good catch of fish to show for their labours. Nothing else, save, perhaps, a bruise or two, and eyes somewhat red for lack of sleep.

And also the little bag of guineas in Nigel's trouser pocket, but only he knew about its comforting touch. He could not recollect having had so much money before. What amazed him was the quiescence of his conscience. He, the most scrupulous of men, had become unscrupulous. He could not account for it. Or rather, he could account for it. His new code of conduct was dictated by his love for Bronwen. Never before had he realized how true was the old saying: "All's fair in love or war." Circumstances removed barriers. If Squire Vaughan had been amenable, Nigel would have been proud to have married Bronwen with every circumstance which convention demanded. This was denied him. He had been repulsed with contumely. He was placed outside the pale. Very well then, he would act as those outside the pale are driven to act. He would act not as he wished to act but as circumstances forced him to act. He began to reason that every law was qualified: there were exceptions to every rule. That different circumstances called for different applications; that it was impossible to generalize in life. Yet that was what most communities tended to do. Things he once thought were wrong no longer seemed wrong. He viewed them from a different angle. He wondered how one was to determine what was right and what was not. It was, apparently, right for Squire Vaughan to make his only daughter miserable. It was wrong for him (Nigel Preece) to wish to make her happy. He could not understand. So much he did not know. What, then, did he know? What fact stood out unchallenged?

The one fact about which he had no doubt was that he loved Bronwen Vaughan and was prepared to undertake anything to make her happy. Even smuggling! Even to resisting a King's officer!

It was not at all how he would have ordered his life. He would have been a paragon of respectability had he been permitted. But life had not gone as he had wanted it to go. He must either bow his head in tame submission, spiritless, cowed, broken—or else hurl defiance.

So Nigel, the scholar, chose to fling down the gauntlet at Fate. As yet he did not send out heralds to proclaim his challenge to the world. He must still move by stealth. With a quiet smile of satisfaction he passed down the street. His pupils found him in a mood unbelievably tolerant.

The mood did not last long. Thoughts of Squire Vaughan were sufficient to put thunder clouds in his sky. He became anxious about Bronwen, wondering how he could get word to her, wondering when he could see her again. There seemed to be nothing that he could do except wait. He waited. He waited several days. Then a note was left at his rooms by a manservant. It was from Bronwen. Her father, she said, had been unusually objectionable and she had not been allowed to leave the house. He was going to Bangor the following day and she intended to go out. It would be risky to meet at the old rendezvous at the quarry in the woods. She would be in the ruins of Castell Aber Lleinawg. Did he know the place?

The student of castles in North Wales did know it—the quaint Norman keep on its motte amid the trees which stood back from the shore on the way to Penmon. It was a good distance to walk. Nigel allowed himself plenty of time. He arrived hot, dusty, curious. Bronwen was there before him.

Amid the silent, grey, ivy-covered walls she stood near a tangle of brambles and bracken. He noticed she looked paler.

"Ours must be true love, Nigel," she said.

"Why?"

"The course does not run smooth." She smiled.

"I am afraid that I am the cause of it," said Nigel, and told her of the encounter with her father.

"I am glad you stood up to him. But it has left him coldly furious. I do not know what is to happen to us. I cannot see a step ahead. If things get more intolerable I shall run away."

Nigel dived into his pocket and brought out two small bags of guineas. "I feel like a highwayman," he confessed with a grim smile. "I want you to have this gold. You may need it. It is yours."

"Not mine, Nigel. Ours."

"Very well then. Ours. I earned it because of you. Do with it as you will. If it brings you comfort, freedom, or happiness, the winning of it will have been well worth while."

"But I cannot take it home."

"I confess I, likewise, do not like having it about the house."

"I have an idea; let's hide it here. People hardly ever visit this place."

Nigel looked about him. At the north-east corner a battlemented tower rose against the sky. He forced his way through the undergrowth and paused at the base. Drawing out his knife he began to dig, scooping out the soil with his hands. Bronwen handed him a thin stone to serve as a trowel. The hole went deeper. Nigel looked at it with a smile of satisfaction, selected several small flat stones with which to line it, and placed his smugglers' gold within. Then he filled in the hole, smoothed the surface, and sprinkled it with leaves. There was hardly a trace to indicate that the wilderness had been disturbed. He chipped a stone on the face of the wall above to indicate the spot. "Some day you may require it," he said. "It is there for you; for you alone. You must not hesitate. It is yours."

"Ours."

"If you use it, I use it. Never forget. Never hesitate. If I get more, I will add to it."

As soon as he had spoken Nigel noticed that he did not say, "*When* I get more." Bronwen apparently did not notice. She was staring ahead, dreamily.

"Nigel," she turned, and putting her hands on his shoulders stared into his face. "I wish you had not encountered my father that day."

"I intended to call on him to ask his permission to marry you."

"Nigel! You are mad. But you didn't, surely?"

"I did not get the chance."

"I am glad of it. Matters are bad enough as it is. You must face up to the fact that any day I may be prevented from seeing you again. I cannot understand what is going on in the house. There is an atmosphere. I can sense it but I cannot fathom it. There is scheming, plotting, of some sort. By the way, Pink made his appearance a couple of nights ago. He was wet and bleeding and in a vile temper. I gather that there had been a brush with some smugglers and that he had got the worst of it."

She spoke casually but suddenly her eyebrows arched and she looked inquiringly into Nigel's eyes. He nodded his head.

"He did not recognize you?" she asked anxiously.

"We all had our faces blacked."

"But the vessel?"

"That, too, was disguised."

"I feel he knows something. Did you—encounter?"

"I had the pleasure of knocking him overboard."

"Oh, good, Nigel! How good! I'm glad. I wish the sea had claimed him. But no such luck! Tell me, you are sure he did not recognize you?"

"How can I be sure, my dear? I can only surmise that he did not. It was highly improbable."

Bronwen walked slowly away from the grey walls against which they stood. She passed through the ruined gateway.

At the edge of the fosse she paused beside a fallen tree and seated herself with her hands clasped in her lap. All about them stretched encircling trees, shutting in the Norman ruin, making it a fairy castle in an enchanted glade. There sounded the faint twitterings of small birds as they hopped industriously among the branches. Bronwen sat staring before her, a look of unutterable sadness in her eyes.

It touched Nigel more profoundly than words. He dropped on one knee beside her and took one of her hands in his. "My dear, what is it? What troubles you?"

"Oh, Nigel, why should it be? We ask so little of life. Just a home of our own, and to be together. It seems so little, and yet that little is so much."

"It does not seem much to ask of life," he agreed. "Yet if it were granted it would make a human heaven for me."

"Perhaps that is why it is withheld. We should be so happy, my dear, so blissfully happy, that a celestial heaven would hold no attraction. Dreams! Dreams!"

"The dreams will come true, beloved."

She shook her head, slowly, sadly. "Not our dreams, Nigel. I know it. I feel it."

"Why should they not? I am young. I am strong. I will not always be unknown. When that thesis of mine is accepted, when I get my degree, I shall apply for some higher post."

She smiled gently upon him. He seemed so boyish. So much in earnest. "It is nearly finished, isn't it?"

"Nothing remains but to complete the copying and send it to the University at Oxford."

"How good, Nigel. I do want your worth recognized. You must hasten to finish it lest some mischance should befall."

"It shall be completed soon, Bronwen. But no mischance is going to befall, my dear."

Bronwen shuddered. "I do not know what it is, but I am frightened, Nigel. Frightened." She looked about her. The trees of the wood were green and silent. Not a leaf moved. "The very stillness here disturbs me. It seems as if some evil influence was at work, as though someone was lurking behind every trunk."

Nigel slid on to the log and pulled her head against his shoulder. "This isn't like you, Bronwen. You have always shown such spirit. What has made you like this?"

"I cannot say. Intuition, perhaps. My dear, my dear. If we should be separated—if you are taken from me—you will always be with me in spirit. Tell me that!"

"Always, Bronwen. You have opened up a new world for me. I ask for nothing but to be near you. To serve you. Care for you. Watch over you. Cherish you."

"I know. Nothing but good could come from all the loving-kindness you have bestowed upon me. But there are other influences at work. Evil powers. Do you believe that evil is stronger than good, Nigel?"

"Light is always more powerful than darkness, Bronwen. But I sometimes think that evil is more active than good, more pertinacious, more subtle, more scheming."

"You believe in good and evil?"

"I must do. Their works are manifest. One can tell a good man from a bad."

The sadness passed, temporarily, from her eyes. They were thoughtful.

"But men are not merely good or bad. Some men are. That beast Pink is bad—all bad. But so many are good and bad intermingled. How can they be judged? It is so complicated."

"So complicated that it becomes simple. We judge ourselves

as we go through life. Reward ourselves. Punish ourselves. Reap what we sow, whether it be good, bad, or indifferent."

"But you talk, Nigel, as though we reaped what we ourselves sowed, whereas so often we reap what another has sown. You and I, dear one, are not reaping the harvest of our sowing. There are tares in the wheat. My happiness, your happiness, is marred not by any act of our own, but because my father happens to be heartless, and Pink Kirby possessed of a legion of evil spirits. Tell me the answer to that."

"I cannot, Bronwen. There comes a point when man's reason stops. Then all one can do is to walk by faith."

"Have you faith, Nigel?"

"Yes. I have faith. I do what I believe to be right, and good must come of it."

"I have no faith," the sadness returned to her eyes. "I believe nothing save that you and I shall be parted. And if you go out of my life, Nigel, I shall know then whether the human heart can break."

"I shall not go out of your life, sweet."

"You would not go of your own accord, that I know. But something tells me that we shall not meet again. That our dreams, glorious as they are, have been sent only as a mockery; to remind us of what we have lost and what we have missed."

"I would not be without my dreams."

"No. It has been worth while." She stood up. "I must go home. I must not stay. Father may return. I must not be missed."

"If matters get too hard for you, Bronwen; if you grow desperate, tell me and we will fly to a far country. I will get more gold to add to our store. Remember it is there for you in an emergency. That thought reassures me—gives me fresh courage."

She smiled and kissed him fondly. "I know I must lose you. I know I must let you go. But we will always be one in spirit. Remember that when you are far away. Perhaps, after all, the things that are not seen are greater than the things that are seen. They may part our bodies but they will never part my love from yours, Nigel, never. Till the fires of life burn low, I shall remember."

They looked into each others eyes. No word was spoken. Never before had Nigel seen a look so expressive, ethereal. He felt spiritual. Transported.

And hidden amid the leafy boughs the birds whispered a benediction.

CHAPTER XVIII

I⊤ was a time of mental confusion for Nigel Preece. He felt the need for clearer thinking, yet at the time when he required it most, clarity was denied him. He, whose cool brain had brought him an honours' degree, was incapable of concentration. The meeting at the ruined castle in the wood had left an impression on his mind, an indelible impression. There was something sacred about it; the plighting of a troth; the fusing of two personalities. He was conscious of an influence almost supernatural in the atmosphere. Then suddenly he recollected that Anglesey, Mona, was the mother of Wales. That it was here the druids had their sacred groves; practised their secret rites. Perhaps on that very spot! It was not far from there, surely, that the druids had encouraged their warriors to withstand the Roman legions who, under Suetonius Paulinus, were endeavouring to effect the passage of the straits.

He felt that the meeting under the trees had been ritualistic, sacramental. If, as Bronwen implied, they were to be parted; if, as she feared, they were not to see one another again; then that meeting stood for the forging of a link; it was a uniting. He felt that they were wed as much as though they had stood before an altar in a Christian church instead of looking into one another's eyes in the silence of a secluded wood; a wood where once, perhaps, a druid had been priest.

Nigel felt older. He speculated upon time. What was time? What did it signify? Why was it that one could live longer in a minute under certain conditions than one could live in a year under others?

The snatch of a familiar line ran through his brain like the lilt of an ancient rune—"what therefore God hath joined together, let not man put asunder." What did it mean: "God hath joined?" To most persons it signified a marriage performed in a church. Nigel, possessed of a touch of mysticism, prone as he was to metaphysics, sought to find a deeper meaning. Did it refer to what was known as affinity? Were certain persons so fashioned that each was the counterpart of the other? That neither, alone, was complete? It was no mere physical attraction which would fade with the decline of vigour, but something more profound, more spiritual. The blending of personalities. The ability to understand the other's point of view. A feeling of unity, of one-ness. There was no gainsaying the fact that there were times when kindred spirits did encounter, but the occasions appeared to be rare. Most marriages seemed to be boring affairs. He thought of married couples he knew who went through life like a team of horses in double-harness, plodding stolidly, pulling because they were linked together, devoid of interest or enthusiasm, thinking only of the end of the day when they could eat and rest and forget.

It seemed to him that persons who were truly joined together by a unity of body, mind, and spirit, were comparatively rare. Yet this mystic union appeared to have been vouchsafed to him and Bronwen. If they were joined together as he felt that they were, who was to put them asunder? Her father? A likely person, thought Nigel grimly!

As though he intruded on his thought Squire Vaughan rode down the street. Nigel, head held high, stared at him fearlessly.

He wondered what to expect; was ready for any eventuality. The squire seemed completely at his ease. He looked coolly towards the schoolmaster and raised his whip in a formal salute. Nigel thought he detected a grim, sardonic twist to the thin-lipped mouth. The inclination of the head was courteous but possibly a trifle more pronounced than etiquette demanded. It savoured of satire, cynicism. Nigel was rigidly polite in acknowledging the salutation. The sound of the roan's hoofs faded down the street. The squire was homeward bound from the Bangor ferry. Bronwen would be home well in advance. For this Nigel was thankful. He did not wish her to suffer unnecessarily.

A feeling of intense irritation took hold of him. Why was it that life was so confused; that there were no clear-cut issues? He had been brought up to believe in a guiding hand, a benevolent providence, which helped and steered one through trial and tribulation. He wanted to believe, but if one looked about for proofs there seemed little indication of its effect on the affairs of men. Perhaps that was where faith came in. Marriage was an honourable estate into which he desired to enter. He was deterred because he had no money; or insufficient money. If one had money one could marry. If one was poor one had to go without. It seemed to him that the estate instead of being sacred was a condition reserved for the rich or the improvident. He was neither. Therefore he had to stand idle while the woman he loved, the woman he desired to serve, lived in misery imposed by those who, by ties of blood, should be most dear. And he could do nothing about it! Nigel felt savage. He felt reckless. If money was the solution to the problem, money he would have. Bronwen came first in his life. Bronwen meant more than ethics or custom or convention. He had worked hard, saved what little he could, but it availed nothing. The race was not to the deserving, the conscientious, the worthy, but to the rich, the unscrupulous, the lucky.

He went in search of Piers, who greeted him gaily.

"Where have you been? Puah has been looking for you. We wanted you to come out fishing." Piers grinned. "I mean fishing, this time, Nigel. If you are to be much in our company, the more often you are seen with us right under the noses of the townspeople, the more natural it will look when you slip away for a couple of nights."

"I suppose so," said Nigel abstractedly. "Piers, I mean to cast in my lot with you, if you will have me. Neck or nothing."

"Oh, I'll have you, and gladly. Why this sudden zeal? Weary of teaching the three R's?"

"May I ask you a personal question, Piers?"

"Lord, yes, so long as you don't mind a personal answer."

"Have you plenty of money?"

"I don't call that personal. I thought you were going to refer to my looks, or the number of wenches I have in tow. Yes, Nigel, I've plenty. Do you want some?"

"Yes. Is it here? To hand?"

"It's here, there, and everywhere, Nigel. I never keep all my eggs in one basket. I have a dozen little hoards scattered about the country. No banks for me, my lad. But I know where the gold is hidden. And so does Puah. If ever things get too hot for me in Beaumaris and I have to get out in a hurry, I shall not have to beg my bread."

"It is hard to know what one means by much money. What might be much to me might be little to you. Would you think I wanted too much if I asked you to lend me a hundred pounds?"

"Lord, no. I'd lend a friend more than that."

"At once?"

"If necessary. But why the rush, Nigel? If I'm to lend the money I must take over the questioning. That's fair, isn't it? What do you want if for?"

"What I tell you will be treated with confidence, Piers?"

"My oath on it."

"I want the money so that I can marry Miss Vaughan."

"Hell!" exclaimed Piers, his face flushing darkly. He pulled out his pipe and began to fill the bowl. Nigel noticed that his finger trembled so that some of the tobacco fell to the floor. "Damn it man, you're mad. Old Vaughan would be raving. He'd cut her off with a penny. . . ."

"That's why I want the money, Piers."

"Then you shan't have it."

"What?"

"Not from me. Not for that purpose. Hell, man, you ought to have more sense than to ask me. What will Puah think? Gad, you must not let Puah know you've got this bee in your bonnet."

"It is more (I use your phrase, Piers) more than a bee in my bonnet. It is the most serious step I have ever contemplated. And I must have the money. Will you lend it? You may name your own interest."

"No."

"Is there any risky work you want undertaken? I'll do it. Anything so that I get the money. I'm desperate."

"No. Damme if I'll let a penny of mine go for such a purpose. I'll tell you what! How much do you want?"

"I asked for a hundred pounds."

"To marry Bronwen Vaughan?"

"So I have informed you."

"A hundred pounds! To marry Bronwen Vaughan. I'll give you a thousand pounds—a thousand golden guineas, cash down, if you marry Puah."

Piers leaned forward, his chin thrust out, a trifle pugnaciously, his dark eyes fixed on Nigel's with piercing intensity.

"Thank you, Piers, but my affections are not for auction; neither is my body that of a slave to be bought and sold."

"Damn it, Nigel, take that haughty look off your face or I'll hit you. If you are personal there is no reason why I should not be. You ask for my money; I give you my offer."

Nigel bit his lip. When he had calmed down he said in a restrained voice. "I know you were not intentionally offensive, Piers. I will say no more except that I cannot entertain your offer, generous though it may appear to you."

"I wish you would. It would be better for you." Piers leaned back, fumbling with his pipe. "I always thought you'd marry Puah. She thinks the world of you, Nigel. I hate like the devil to see her suffer. When she suffers, I suffer. Because we're twins, maybe. I'd never let anything stand in the way of that kid's happiness. You don't care for Puah? I thought you did. She thought you did."

"I care for her greatly, Piers, but only as a comrade, as a sister."

"Yes, I dare say. But that doesn't go far enough. And, if I know Puah, she's expecting to marry you one fine day."

"I have never given her occasion to cherish that hope. Piers, I have the greatest regard, the greatest respect for Puah. I assure you that nothing I have ever said or done could be construed to indicate that I held any feeling for her other than tha 1which one bestows on a highly valued friend."

"Ay, ay! I dare say that's so. I'm making no complaints, Nigel. It's just that Puah's welfare is near my heart. I'm a rough devil, and I've not much tender sentiment in me, as folks will tell you quick enough, but what there is belongs to Puah."

"I'm sorry, Piers."

"Ay!" He frowned moodily. "Ay! I dare say. Well, it's a pity. A damned pity. I don't know what Puah will think. I don't know how she'll take it. Women are queer creatures." He got up and began to pace the room. "Now, see here, Nigel. Let's talk this over sensibly as man to man. No offence meant."

"I think it would be well to clear the air. Once and for all."

"And whatever is said—no offence taken? Not that I care a damn if it comes to that."

"No offence will be taken, Piers. Put all your cards on the table."

"Well, Nigel, this is how I look at it. You're a damn fine fellow, straight as they make 'em; clever too. Too clever to be in a sleepy place like this. But you are poor. Bronwen Vaughan is as pretty a bit of goods as I've seen for a long time. But she's been used to luxury, lad. Fine clothes, fine horses. Best of everything. They spend more on one meal than you would in a week. She won't like having to live on shornbugs. She's lonely, now, and she's fallen for you. There's no doubt about that. I don't blame her. But what will happen if you go on with this mad scheme of yours? Her father will either lock her indoors, send her to another part of the country, or turn her on the streets without a penny. I suppose you hope he will do the latter. Well, love in a cottage is all very well for a woman who has been used to living in a cottage. She doesn't know what she's missing. But you'd lose your job. The squire would damn soon see to that, and he'd do all in his power to prevent you getting another."

"Why should he?"

"Spite, you fool. He's got gall in him, has that man. Don't think most people have your silly notions about honour, Nigel, because they haven't. They are out to get what they want and if any man crosses them they hate him like hell and do all in their power to revenge themselves. Well, let that pass. If you marry Bronwen, she will be turned out. You have no home, no job, no food. Where will it land you? And all for a bit of emotion called love. Hell, man, a score of women have made me feel that way, but I've damn soon got over it."

"I am afraid my temperament is not so adaptable, Piers."

"Now, on the other hand, Puah is a good girl; healthy as you make 'em; loyal as you make 'em. Doesn't mind roughing it. She's got a bit of gold put away. Damn good figure. And she's not bad to look at, either—even if she does resemble me."

A mischievous grin flashed for a second across his swarthy face. But it vanished as quickly as it came. "Now, Nigel, there's something in what I say. You see my point? Sound common sense. And all intended for your own good, my lad."

"I am sure you mean it kindly, Piers, and I honour you for your loyalty to that sister of yours. But I cannot change my mind. Bronwen and I are destined for each other. My love for her cannot change; neither can her love for me. If I married Puah I should do her an injustice for my heart would be else-where. I could not give her my love."

"Oh, love isn't all it's made out to be, Nigel. One nice girl is pretty much like another, especially in the dark."

"You cannot make me change my mind. I'm sorry. So you will not lend me the money?"

"Not a penny. Not a damned penny."

"You have no objection to my earning more, the same way as I earned the last?"

Piers bit thoughtfully on his pipe stem. "No, of course not. The more you come out with us the sooner you'll get this silly notion out of your head. Nigel, say nothing to Puah about this. It may never come off, you know, and we don't want her hurt for nothing, do we?"

"The last thing I desire is to hurt her at all."

"Well, say nothing about this. It's a good thing she is out at the moment. I'm expecting word any day now that the French lugger has been sighted. The wind is set right."

"Try and arrange for a week-end, Piers. It is difficult to get away from the school otherwise."

"That's the worst of education. Well, we'll see. But keep clear of old Vaughan, Nigel. Don't go crossing his bows needlessly. He's an ugly customer and likely to open fire without warning.

And watch out for squalls. That slimy little swine of a son of his is hand in glove with that navy chap who knocked you out. Watch 'em, lad. That's my advice."

"Thank you, Piers. I will be on my guard."

"Good night, Nigel. I'll let you know when the *Marie* is sighted off Holy Island. And not a word of this to Puah. You understand?"

It was dark when Nigel reached the cottage. He lit the candles and endeavoured to copy out some of the thesis. It was no use. He made mistake after mistake. His pen-knife was busy erasing word after word. In disgust he flung away the spoiled sheet, put down his quill, cast himself into the winged-chair and gave himself up to reverie. He thought of Vaughan and wondered how he could outwit him; of Piers and his refusal to loan the money; of Puah and how it grieved him to hurt her feelings. He thought of Bronwen, of her dearness, and her understanding, and her sadness and her fears. But most he recalled the look in her eyes when they stood together in the green solitude and heard the gentle whisper of the birds. It had been a tiring day; tiring because it took its toll of his spirit. In thinking of the birds he fell asleep.

CHAPTER XIX

T H E days began to pass. Days of monotony. Days of anxiety.
There was no word of Bronwen, only a silence which was ominous.
Nigel fretted at the inactivity. He made several attempts to
resume his fair copying of the thesis and then, in despair, laid
it aside in a cupboard. He hoped that Piers would send him
word. To be out at sea in the *Four Winds* again would prove a
happy release from the tension. But no word came from Piers.
The wind had set foul. The French lugger was held up. Perhaps
she had been snapped up by a revenue-cutter, or a naval cruiser,
prowling off the Welsh coast. The suspense, the waiting, the
wondering, took their toll of Nigel's spirits. He walked much.
One evening it would be to the disused quarry in the woods.
Another would take him to the ruined keep. But there was never
a sign of Bronwen. He would stand amid the silence of the trees,
alone with his thoughts, and for a while she would seem near
to him in spirit and he would be content, almost exalted. Then
the tide of desolation would engulf him, and he would be conscious
only of his loneliness, his perplexity, the greatness of his need.

One day the wind veered and blew steadily from the south-
west. There was activity in the straits. Vessels which had been
held up for days shook loose their canvas. A large barquentine
from Sweden which had anchored off Bangor unfolded her wings
and came gaily down with wind and tide, a thing of beauty.
After her stretched an irregular line of sailing craft, brigs and
coasting-schooners laden with slates from Port Dinorwic, fishing
smacks eager for their long-delayed catch, a yacht or two,
and, most ominous of all to Nigel, a sturdy, well-gunned, heavily
manned revenue-cutter. He had not seen her before. She seemed
a bird of ill omen. She did not pause at Beaumaris, a thing for
which he, slightly smitten by a guilty conscience, felt thankful.
He watched her heeling, her great mainsail drawing, as she passed
smaller craft heading for the channel off Puffin Island on her way
to the open sea. Nigel wondered what had become of Piers. He
went in search of the *Four Winds* but she was not at her moorings.
Her dinghy was missing from the shingle at Gallows Point.
Piers and Puah were away somewhere. They had gone without
telling him. There was no reason why they should have told
him. They came and went as the spirit moved them. They always
had done, probably always would do, but their absence and their

silence made Nigel more conscious than ever of his loneliness. He was known in the town; he was respected; but he had no friends. His air of aloofness prevented many who would have befriended him from becoming intimate. Nigel was probably unaware of this. It was not his deliberate intention to be aloof, to stand apart from his fellow men. It was because he lived in a world of his own. A world in which the thoughts of dead Greeks spoke more clearly than the voice of the man in the street. If he was lonely, he must turn to his silent friends for solace. He made his way back to his rooms, sat himself down in his comfortable winged-chair beside an empty grate, and took down a volume of Horace. Here was poetry; here was philosophy. He absorbed it, but not all of it. Bronwen's face persisted in intruding between his eyes and the printed page. He wished he knew what was happening. He felt he could endure anything except not knowing.

Someone was coming up the path. He heard the crunch on the shingle. He looked up quickly, eagerly, anticipating Bronwen. Yet even as he looked he knew that it was not Bronwen's step. It was a man, a young exquisite, vaguely familiar. The face would have been handsome save for the thick, sensual lips and the rings of dissipation around the eyes. He had evidently ridden into town for he carried a riding-crop and wore breeches and tops. The boots were highly polished and a bunch of seals dangled somewhat ostentatiously from the fob which hung below the sprigged waistcoat.

Mrs. Evans tapped discreetly at the door. "A gentleman to see you, sir."

Nigel was on his feet, curious, a little on his guard. "How d'y' do, my dear sir," said the new-comer. He placed a fawn-coloured beaver hat on the table, and bowed. His demeanour seemed a trifle effusive. "Mr. Preece, I believe! Know you by sight, sir. Glad to make your closer acquaintance."

"And I address, whom?" Nigel spoke quietly. The answer did not surprise him.

"Rhys Vaughan, at your service. Heard of me, I dare say?"

"I have heard of you, Mr. Vaughan. May I offer you a seat?"

"Ah, don't mind if I do. Quarters a bit cramped here, Mr. Preece. Demme, more books than furniture. I've heard what a plaguy clever fellow you were. As for me, I'm an ignoramus, and proud of it, so you must excuse me. Regular barbarian. A Corinthian. Wine, wenches and sport are more in my line, you know."

"I am afraid I was not aware of your predilections, Mr. Vaughan. Have you come here to inform me of your tastes?"

"Not at all. I've a notion they would not interest you vastly. I come, sir, on behalf of my sister."

"Indeed. And how is your sister?"

"Not too perky, one might say. Attack of the megrims, or some such feminine fuss. Must keep to her room. Blinds drawn. No noise. No bright lights. Demme, worst thing she could do in my estimation. Hair of the dog good for the bite, eh? That's my motto, Mr. Preece. You get me?"

"I am afraid I do not, Mr. Vaughan."

"She's fretting, sir, fretting. There's been a little dissension in our fair abode. A clash of wills, you might call it. Daughter not so dutiful as irate parent might expect."

"I am sorry."

"I'll wager you are. Parent firm, adamant. Daughter retaliates by refusing to leave her room. Friction and discord. It's the very devil, believe me, Mr. Preece. I find it plaguy trying to my nerves."

"You have my sympathy, Mr. Vaughan. Was it to solicit that which prompted you to call."

"Devil a bit, Mr. Preece. It seems—demme, no offence, this is a delicate matter—it seems that you and my parent do not see eye to eye."

"It is my misfortune apparently, not to find favour in your father's sight."

"So I gathered, my dear sir, though demme, he did not phrase it quite so delicately, 'pon my oath. Called you a . . . but there. No use raking these matters up. Between ourselves I can't understand his attitude. You're a demmed fine, well-set fellow, Mr. Preece, if I may so observe. Man of presence, and what's more, a man of brains. Fancy that's what rubs the old man up the wrong way. Feels he's in the presence of a better man than himself, and it plagues him mightily."

"It is regrettable if anything I have said should cause your father to form an impression which it was not my intention to convey."

"You conveyed it mighty forcible I'm told, sir. Told him you'd murder him if he used a whip to you. Hell's delight! I wish I could have been there. Better than a cock-fighting main any day. Sir, you have courage. It takes a man to stand up to Squire Vaughan. Yes, sir, a man. I take off my hat, so to speak. Now, hark 'ee. I'm on your side."

"On my side, Mr. Vaughan?"

"Just that. Fellow has to take sides, one way or another. And I'm a bit sorry for Bron. Has a devil of a time, between ourselves. Shouldn't like to be a girl. Not in our household. She's all gone on you. I can feel and sympathise, 'pon my oath, sir. This frustration of true love wrings my heart. She's pining, sir, pining. And my sympathies are all with you."

"Indeed, Mr. Vaughan. I have misjudged you. I imagined that your sympathies were all with Lieutenant Kirby, the incomparable dispenser of ale and tale."

A slight expression of surprise, consternation, flitted across the face of Rhys Vaughan. "Oh! Pink? Not a bit, my dear sir. He's a good fellow to crack a bottle with, take it from me, but when it comes to the hand of my only sister, demme, my dear sir, as if I could trust her happiness to a rake-helly lad like Pink Kirby. Not on your life. And he's here now and gone to-morrow. You know the way with these sailors? Eh? He's a good fellow to drink with, is Pink. Never say a word against him there. And some of his stories—gad, man, you'd split your sides. The things that go on in these foreign ports. Demme, I was in half a mind to join the Navy myself. But when it comes to Bron. No, no, my dear sir, she's too good a sister for the like of Pink."

"I am pleased to hear you say so, Mr. Vaughan. The happiness of an only sister must be a matter of concern to a man of honour."

"It is, sir, it is. You are a man of understanding. Now, when I saw Bron get so washed out—quite off her oats, take it from me—I summed matters up, and last night, when the proud parent was out, we had a heart-to-heart talk, my little sister and I. Yes, my dear sir, she took me into her confidence."

"Indeed?" Nigel's tone was icy.

"Well, slightly. Not to any great extent, but I can put two and two together. She did confess that you and she were, let us say, a bit matey. And she was missing her friend. The outcome of it was that she asked me if I would act as her messenger, her go-between, her Hermes! Demme, Mr. Preece, your presence, your influence, makes me quite classical. It is Hermes, the johnny with wings on his feet? So if you have a letter for your love, a *billet-doux*, I am at your service, sir."

"I am afraid that I have not written to Miss Vaughan, nor do I intend to do so."

"You surprise me, Mr. Preece. Lud, you are a laggard in love. She bade me say to you that if you could come to the house to-night it would be safe to have a word with you. The fierce dragon is away, the princess is unguarded. Your chance has come, my bold lover of distressed damsels. To-night is the night, and the hour is ten of the clock. Come by way of the servants' quarters. You will be admitted. A double knock. And all is well. Your love will be in your arms. Lud, man, I positively glow with virtue to think that I have been the unworthy medium for arranging this happy reunion."

He picked up his hat and bowed with some elaboration. Nigel opened the door with precise formality and watched his unexpected visitor swagger down the path.

Then he went back to his chair and sat a while in thought. Dusk was at hand when he bestirred himself. Slowly picking up a quill he penned a note to Piers.

Dear Piers,

In case my disappearance should mystify you this will explain much. Young Rhys Vaughan, a nauseating specimen, has been here this evening posing as a messenger from his sister. She is in distress (which I can well believe) and I am to call at the house at ten to-night. It is so obviously a plot that I have hesitated. But it is a challenge. If I stay away they will think I fear them. So I shall go. There is, also, always a remote chance that I may be able to aid Bronwen. Something strange has happened. So this is to bid you and Puah good-bye. I doubt whether I shall ever see you again. I thank you both for the happy hours of companionship with which you have brightened my life. You think me a fool, Piers; I may as well be an egregious one while I am about it. Take care of that dear sister of yours.

Believe me, your appreciative friend,

Nigel Preece.

He left the note at Piers' home. With a loaded pistol in his pocket, and a fierce determination in his heart, Nigel took the road which led to the squire's home.

*   *   *   *   *

Soft summer night had fallen. There was a hush over the land. The trees were silent silhouettes; not a leaf stirred. The riding-lights of vessels in the roads glowed like fallen stars, throwing their reflections on the dark water. A curlew passed overhead, invisible, revealing its presence by moving cries which sounded eerily in the night, like the voice of a wandering spirit in distress.

Having crossed the meadows and scaled the wall of loose stone which marked the end of the paddock, Nigel took the beaten footpath which led to the house of Squire Vaughan. He could see the chimneys and gables stand out sharply against the star-sprinkled sky. The chimneys, he thought, looked graceful. Never before had he considered the possibilities of gracefulness in anything so prosaic as a chimney. The building seemed in darkness. There was no sign of life. Not a dog barked. A chink of light showed through a thick curtain. He paused at the postern gate which led to the servants' quarters. As he stood there in the stillness a sudden revulsion stole over him that he should creep thus stealthily, like a thief in the night. It was humiliating to enter by the servants' way. He had the blood of a de Loryinge in his veins. Recklessness took possession of him. It was hardly ten o'clock but he would not wait. He strode resolutely around the bordering wall, crossed the broad gravel drive which led to the front portico and, catching the iron bell-pull, sent an imperious peal clanging through the silent house.

He heard a man's footsteps approach. A bolt was shot back. A chain clattered and fell. The door swung open. Outlined against the light of the hall lantern stood Squire Vaughan himself.

"The devil!" ejaculated the squire in unconcealed surprise.

"Not at all, sir. Nigel Preece, at your service."

The squire looked at him from beneath heavy brows, stared curiously, suspiciously, inquiringly. When he spoke his voice was hard, expressionless.

"And what does Nigel Preece require of me at this hour of the night?"

"I wish to speak to you regarding your daughter."

A grandfather clock stood in the hall. Nigel could hear its slow and solemn ticking in the stillness as he awaited the squire's reply. The man turned his head slowly, and glanced at the clock. It lacked five minutes to ten o'clock.

"Ah!" he said slowly. "You had better step inside, Mr. Schoolmaster. I play my own butler to-night, as you see. The servants have been given a holiday. Come this way."

He stepped back to allow Nigel to enter the hall. The door shut behind him. A side door was flung open by the squire. It led to a room full of light and warmth for a small fire burnt in the broad hearth. There was a heavy table with a decanter and glasses upon it; several glasses, but only one used. The walls were decorated with sporting prints, a fox's mask, deer's head, antique weapons. A churchwarden pipe lay on the table beside

an easy chair. Vaughan picked up the pipe but did not fill it,
He did not ask Nigel to sit down but left him standing, haughtily,
in the centre of the carpet. The squire put down the pipe
impatiently and crossed to the hearth-rug where he stood, legs
apart, his back to the fire.

"Well, sir. I am waiting the reason for your presence. You
mentioned my daughter's name, if I heard aright."

"I did, sir. I came here to say that I wished to marry her.
I felt it a matter of honour that you should be acquainted with
my intentions."

He saw the squire's thin mouth twist in a grim smile. "Very
honourable of you, sir. I am sure. So you call—at a somewhat
peculiar hour, it is true—to ask my permission, I assume?"

"The hour was not of my choosing, but what you say is
correct. I come to ask your permission."

"And might I ask, sir, whether you for a moment imagined
I should give my permission?"

"Not for a moment, sir."

"I have heard that you were a man of more than usual
intelligence. The brilliance of your brain does not, in this instance,
play you false. You assume correctly that I shall not countenance
such a preposterous idea. I have other plans for my daughter
than that she should be thrown away on a penniless dominie."

"Might I inquire, sir, whether the other plans of which you
spoke commend themselves to your daughter?"

"You may inquire as much as you like, but I'll be damned
eternally if I shall answer you."

"In that case there is no reason why I should remain. I have
acted in a fit and proper manner. I now feel free to marry your
daughter with or without your consent."

The squire's face flushed. His brows contracted. Before he
could speak a small gilt French clock on the mantelpiece struck
ten. Ere it had finished the more ponderous chime of the hall
clock testified to the passing of time. As though unwilling to
interrupt so solemn an occasion both men remained silent until
the last note had died away.

"I give you good night, sir," said Nigel bowing stiffly.

"Stay!" The squire spoke abruptly. Almost eagerly.

"And why, sir?"

"A glass of wine before you go, Mr. Schoolmaster."

"I thank you but I cannot accept."

"Now, now, let there be no ill feeling. We have had words,
and a difference of opinion. It is regrettable, but there you are.

These things happen. You want my daughter's hand in marriage. It was gracious of you. Your intentions, doubtless are honourable, even though they should not coincide with mine. Let bygones be bygones, sir. Come, as I request, stay for a glass of wine."

Nigel hesitated as the squire picked up the decanter. His natural courtesy first responded to the change of tone. Some intuition cried out that it was not genuine. The ruby wine gurgled. Nigel watched, fascinated. No, he would not drink. The squire's hand suddenly shook so that some red spots of wine spilled on the polished table. From somewhere up the house sounded a crash, the splintering of glass, a shrill cry, a shriek.

"Nigel! Nigel! Fly! The press-gang are here!"

Nigel wheeled in time to see the squire making for the door. From the front of the house came the sound of heavy boots hurrying across the gravel.

"Stand back!" yelled Nigel, and as the squire turned on him he whipped out his pistol. "Back!" He snatched the glass of wine and flung it in Vaughan's face, and as the squire, half-blinded, drew his sleeve across his eyes, Nigel rushed to the door, slammed it behind him, and turned the key in the lock.

"To the back, Nigel. Quick!" He glanced up the stairs to see Bronwen's dishevelled face over the banister rail as she wrestled with her brother. His first impulse was to rush to her aid but she read his thoughts.

"Escape, Nigel. You cannot help me. Save yourself. The sailors are surrounding the house. Run or you are doomed."

Something within his tortured brain revealed the wisdom of her words. A captive, he would be powerless to aid her; free, there would still be a chance. The front door burst open and several burly sailors headed by Lieutenant Kirby forced their way in.

Nigel sped down the passage-way. As he passed a high-backed chair his right hand instinctively caught it and spun it into the passage behind him. His ruse succeeded almost before he realized what he had done. With a crash and a curse Kirby tripped over the chair and measured his length. Two of the seamen piled on top of him.

Nigel burst through a door, rushed across the darkened kitchen and flung open the door which led to the yard. A sailor, armed with a cudgel was on guard. He aimed a blow at Nigel's head. Nigel took the blow on his arm, and leaped forward. A second seaman sprang at him, Nigel fired his pistol at short range. He missed, but the shot made the man pause. He was through the postern gate, now, and running across the meadows. He could hear the panting and cursing of hurrying men who laboured in his wake. He leaped into a lane. A stout brier caught his coat and momentarily delayed him. He tore himself free to find several seamen crashing into the ditch alongside. One touched his shoulder, but Nigel drove his fist into the perspiring face and dragged himself clear. Light of foot he sprinted towards the town. A pistol shot was fired after him. Then another. He did not know whether he was hit or not. A cudgel came whirling through the air and caught him between the shoulders. It made him stagger and gasp. It felt, so far as he could imagine, as if his back were broken. He was running blindly now, staggering, half-blinded by sweat. His breath was broken by the blow. His pursuers were gaining on him. There came a crashing in the hedges on either side. His retreat was cut off. Dark figures leaped into the roadway. He was doomed . . . doomed . . . no! He was safe. The command yelled in Welsh came from the lips of burly Madoc Morris. Piers was there, black of face, club in hand.

Piers . . . how came he there! Nigel did not know. . . . All his reeling brain realized was that the pursuit was over. That the darkness resounded to the thud of blows, and the yells and cries and curses of those who suffered. Then his trembling legs played him false and he pitched forward into the ditch and was conscious of little save that the touch of the dewy grass was refreshing on his face.

CHAPTER XX

IN the small cabin of the *Four Winds* was a locker which served as a seat by day and bunk by night. Nigel lay on this and idly gazed through the open door to the sunlit deck and the blue sky which showed beyond the edge of the brown sail. The gentle heave of the waves seemed soothing. He felt curiously limp, and his body ached from head to foot. In the excitement of the chase he had not realized the extent of his injuries. He had a cut on the head, his arm was so swollen that it seemed a miracle that it was not broken, his back where the cudgel had struck him was so sore that Piers had strapped him and was keeping him quiet lest a rib had been fractured. Nigel required very little persuasion to remain still.

He lay and thought, He had not liked running away. He felt as though he had abandoned Bronwen to her fate. Yet what could he have done—one man against so many? And she had saved him. Her warning had been in the nick of time.

On the whole he felt well pleased with himself. He had lost an excellent pistol and a good hat. On the other hand he had showed his contempt for Squire Vaughan and his fawning son, had outwitted Pink Kirby, and had escaped from a trap which had been carefully set for his downfall.

A shadow fell across the sunlit doorway. He saw Puah approaching. Puah in her snug-fitting blue guernsey and her boat-skirt which swirled from her hips like a kilt. Tanned and rosy and healthy she came into the cabin bringing a breath of the sea with her. She sat beside Nigel on the blanket and put her small, rough, hand on his brow.

"You look better," she assured him.

"There's little the matter with me beyond laziness, Puah."

"You are so knocked about it's a miracle you are alive. Nigel, for goodness sake stop getting hit on the head. You'll lose all your good looks."

"I don't suppose I should notice their loss."

"Well, I should, so keep out of harm's way for my sake. You bring trouble on yourself. I warned you!"

"Warned me, Puah?"

"Yes. I warned you to leave that stupid girl alone. She's not for you, Nigel. There's been nothing but trouble, trouble,

trouble, ever since you started bothering about her. Her and her silly poetry!"

Nigel was silent. Puah had turned her head and was staring out of the open door. He could see her profile clearly, finely chiselled, swarthy, virile. A daughter of the sea. Self-reliant. Almost boyish in her independence. She gave orders to the crew like a second Piers. It was only when she looked upon him that she became tender, thought Nigel. She seemed to regard him as one who was unable to care for himself despite the fact that he was older than she was. Nigel smiled at the thought.

In a flash she turned and caught the laughter in his eyes. "What are you laughing at?" she demanded.

"The way you mother me, Puah. Anyone would think I was a child."

"So you are. A great, soft, overgrown, boy who needs some-one to look after him. Bothering about poetry and squire's daughters, and getting into trouble with press-gangs! It's time you stopped."

"What a little tyrant you are, Puah. You just gloat at having me powerless, at your mercy. You can order me about to your heart's content, tyrannize over me, mould me to your way of thinking. You like me quiescent. It's the blood of old Piers Griffith in your veins, I suppose, which makes you so masterful, so imperious."

"You are wrong," she said almost fiercely. "It is because you are so stupid, so silly. I do not want to be a tyrant. I want to do your bidding. I want you to be the stronger, to force me to your will, to master me. . . ."

She sprang to her feet so suddenly that she nearly hit her head on the cabin roof and before Nigel realized what she was doing she had hurried out on deck.

He lay back a little bewildered by this unexpected ebullition. A few minutes later Piers joined him.

"Well, old lad, how's the skull? For a peace-loving fellow you have a great knack of getting into scrapes."

"I would not have got out of this last one but for your help. Piers. I am grateful. Accept my thanks."

"Bah! I haven't enjoyed myself so much for ages. I've been dying to have a crack at those Revenue swine. The King's spoil-sports! But what a clown you were to go walking into the trap with your eyes open."

"It was a matter of honour, Piers."

"Well, thank goodness I never bother about honour. Sooner have common sense any day."

"What puzzles me is how you made an appearance so opportunely."

"You can thank yourself for that. We got home and found your note waiting. It was so obviously a trap, especially with that blasted revenue-cutter in the offing. It's been a plot from start to finish to do away with you. That Kirby fellow has got special leave, so I'm told, and is co-operating with the cutter's crew. I fancy the squire's at the back of it. Save a lot of unpleasantness if you were impressed and taken on a cruise for a couple of years. Give his daughter time to get over the heartache. And if I'm any judge of Kirby he'd have made your life such a hell afloat that you never would have come back. Well, Puah rounded up the lads and we set off across the meadows. Heard the pistol shot and the shouts, and ran like the devil across country. Got there just in time. Easily beat 'em back. They were winded, and the odds in our favour. It was a damn sight harder lugging your carcass across to the boat. Puah joined us. She's got her head screwed on right has that kid."

"Yes," agreed Nigel. "And her heart's in the right place."

"Taken you long enough to find out, Nigel. While we were off to your rescue she went to your rooms and explained to Mrs. Evans what had taken place. They both agreed that the Excise men would probably search your rooms, so Puah gathered up all your things that she could find and crammed them into a dunnage-bag and lugged 'em to our dinghy and brought 'em aboard. Damn, Nigel, I never thought books could be such a weight."

"How good of her. I must thank her. But Piers, I must get back to Beaumaris, my friend. There's the school, you know."

"The school will have to wait," said Piers grimly.

"But I must get back."

"Sorry, Nigel, not even to please you. Hang it all, this is a business venture, and I'm due at the Isle of Man to-night."

"I am sorry, Piers. You are quite right. You have indeed done much for me. Do not think me ungrateful. I suppose I shall have to wait, though what the outcome will be, heaven only knows."

"The wind's against you for one thing. Even if I could spare the time there's no turning back!"

"No," said Nigel softly. "There's no turning back." He lay staring out of the door watching the sharp edge of the brown sail against the white clouds. He sat up so quickly and spoke so vehemently that Piers turned in amazement.

"You are right, Piers! You are right! There's no turning back. Why should I? Damn the school. I wanted to be a scholar. I wanted to be a respectable member of society. But I will not be subjected to insults by a stiff-necked autocrat like Vaughan. If he turns his hand against me, I'll turn mine against him. If society persecutes me, I shall wage war on society. You say my effects are on board, my clothes, my books?"

"Everything Puah could lay hands on."

"Including my thesis?"

"Ah, I don't know a thing about that."

"No matter, I can write another. Yet why should I?"

"Yes, why should you? Lot of damn nonsense to my mind. See where it has landed you."

"A Master of Arts degree is not necessary for successful smuggling, Piers, I take it. Ha! My dreams and my visions and my ideals have all gone overboard. Crashed in one fell swoop. So be it. Your hand, Piers. Your hand, lad. I'm with you now. Neck or nothing. As you say—the wind of Fate has set foul. There's no turning back!"

*　　*　　*　　*　　*

So clearly was the island sculptured it looked almost artificial when lit by the westering sun. Nigel had grown weary of inactivity and when the wind dropped, he came on deck and stood drinking in the cool, calm, beauty of the scene. The Isle of Man seemed to be suspended on a mirror, and the Calf floated nearby, a quaint imitation of the parent isle. A window caught the sun's ray and glowed like a flashing beacon. In the mellow light the grass on the cliff tops gleamed a more emerald green, and the fissures and crevices of the rocks were outlined a darker black. Somewhere inland a lone field of corn spread a golden carpet amid the verdure. On the western side several fishing smacks, homeward bound for Peel, lay becalmed, too. It was a picture for an artist, a subject for a poet.

Piers was neither. "Blast the wind," he complained. "Another half-hour's breeze would have seen us about in. If we don't get some wind by nightfall I shall get out the sweeps. I'm not idling here when there's good ale to be had so near at hand." He stared resentfully at the placid sky.

"Sit on this locker, Nigel," said Puah solicitously. "Does your arm hurt very much?"

"I had forgotten about it. Tell me, what are those little places right ahead?'

"Have you not been to the Isle of Man before? I am surprised. I have been here so often that I think that everyone else knows the place as well as I do. That's Port St. Mary; and that is Castletown at the east of the bay."

"And the magnificent, bold promontory at the tip?"

"Spanish Head."

They fell silent. Puah seated herself on the locker, and picking up a rope-end began to make an eye-splice. Nigel watched her nimble fingers. "You must teach me to splice, Puah," he said.

"When your arm is better." Silence again. The splice was completed.

"Puah, it was good of you to collect my belongings; my books especially."

"You need someone to look after you."

"But do you think it was really necessary? They would not dare to have taken my goods."

"Huh!"

She took a sheath-knife from her belt and carefully finished off the splicing. It seemed to occupy her whole attention. "You never want to leave any odd bits showing, Nigel. Make a neat job of it. It looks better and lasts longer. There. Even Piers could not find fault with that."

"What are you going to do with it? What's it for?"

"I don't know."

"Then why go to all that trouble?"

"Because I wanted to. Let's go for'ard. A little moving about will do you good. You'll be getting stiff."

Piers was stirring up Madoc and Tom and an elderly man who comprised the *Four Winds*' crew. "Get those sweeps out. I'm not hanging about out here all day for anybody."

"We're not going to row to Peel," muttered Madoc mutinously.

"Who said we were, you fool? Let's get to Castletown and have a drink."

They dropped anchor in the bay. Piers and Puah assisted Nigel into the dinghy. Piers knew the way to a tavern. It was dark when they finished their meal.

"Do you feel like a walk to the bay, Nigel?" asked Puah. "Piers will spend the night drinking. He'll be no fit company for respectable folks like you and me. Piers is too fond of his glass.''

"It's been plaguy hot to-day,'' explained Piers apologetically.

They walked slowly down the narrow street until they came to the waterfront. Here they stood in the cool of the evening listening to the almost imperceptible murmur of the wavelets that lapped the shingle. It was one of those nights when Nature cast a spell. There was a tranquil beauty which seemed almost not of this world. It was dark but stars were bright, like diamonds on velvet. Lights from cottage windows cast rippling reflections across the bay.

"It is very beautiful,'' said Puah softly. Nigel did not answer. Nature invariably stirred his emotions and his imagination. His mind drifted off to the green seclusion of the woods. How still it had been when he looked into Bronwen's eyes! He wondered how she was. Where she was. Had she been ill-treated? Was she a prisoner in a locked room? Was she being forced into matrimony with that brutal beast Pink Kirby? He could see her now—her flushed face, dishevelled hair, disarranged dress, as she leaned over the banisters to shout a warning to him. Why had he run away? Why hadn't he dashed up the stairs to her rescue—hopeless though it would have been? That execrable brother of hers—the fatuous fool who tried to lure him into the trap! He would like to have wrung his neck and flung him from an upper window. Then perhaps it might have been possible to have fought his way through with Bronwen. . . .

"You are thinking about that damned woman again!'' Nigel became aware that Puah was staring up into his set face. Her voice was crisp. Curt. Like Piers' orders when he battled with a gale. "Stop it, Nigel!'' she cried, almost fiercely. "Put her out of your mind. She's not for you. There's been nothing but trouble since she set her cap at you. You are with me now, and you shall stay with me. I'm not having you dreaming about that cat. Do you hear?''

Her hand closed on his right arm in passionate protest. He winced.

"Oh, my dear, I've hurt you! Nigel, I've hurt your arm!'' It was a cry almost of anguish. Gone was the hard light from Puah's eyes; they brimmed with tenderness and contrition. "I'm sorry. I've hurt you.''

"It is nothing. I have hurt you, Puah. I am sorry.''

They both fell silent. There was so much to be said that there were no words with which to say it.

"Puah, do you think they could put me up at the inn? I—I think I will turn in early. I still feel somewhat knocked-about."

"Yes, Nigel." Her voice was curiously restrained, modulated, gentle. They turned their back on the bay and made their way slowly back to the tavern. Nigel never broke the silence; Puah's head was bowed.

And all the while Nigel was thinking. What could he do? He did not want to hurt Puah. He could not prevent her caring for him. She was so splendid in every way. Too good for him, in a sense. He wished he could put Bronwen out of his thoughts. But he could not. These matters seemed beyond human control. But, he reasoned, if they were arranged, why were they not arranged sensibly, logically? If he had never met Bronwen he would have been well content with Puah. But he *had* met Bronwen.

He had never intended to fall in love with her. Nothing was farther from his thoughts. It had just happened. He could no more help loving her than Puah could help loving him. Yet he could not marry Bronwen whom he wished to marry, and he could marry Puah whom he did not wish to marry. It was all too absurd, ridiculous, nonsensical. He felt exasperated with life that it should cause such confusion. He could see no way out; nothing but strain and suffering. Unnecessary suffering. Everybody suffered, and what good did it do? That was the worst about the thing called life. It could hit you brutal blows like some coward concealed in ambush, and you could not hit back. It was like grasping at a cloud, smiting at a shadow. There was nothing to hit.

And he, whose great intent was never to cause pain or harm to anyone, must always have the knowledge that whichever way he moved he must wound one who was dear to him.

"Oh, damn!" he exclaimed viciously.

Puah looked up in surprise.

"I mean it," he said, in a tone wholly unlike the scholarly graduate. "Damn life, damn the muddle, damn everything!"

He flung into the inn and stamped up the narrow stairs in search of a lonely cot.

CHAPTER XXI

FOR days they lingered at the Isle of Man. At first Nigel was impatient, feeling that he ought to get back to his duties, finding it difficult to comprehend that he had finished with the past. Piers assured him solemnly that Vaughan would break him for his participation in that night's affair, but Nigel was slow of comprehension. It was not until a smack arrived from Beaumaris that the truth was brought home to him. There had been trouble at the school, the fishermen said. The governors and some of the magistrates had been there looking for him. It was given out that he had been dismissed from his post for some misconduct and the fact that no particular charge was specified made the gossips speculate all the more wildly. The unfortunate curate had been again installed as shepherd of the flock pending the appointment of a new schoolmaster. So there was, as Nigel had already resolved, no going back. All the same he wished he could have returned to find things out for himself, and he chafed at not being able to do so until Puah pointed out, quite logically, that even if he had wished to go it would have been difficult with the wind right in their teeth. It was impressed upon Nigel how dependent a vessel was on the vagaries of the wind. So he resigned himself to the inevitable and made the most of his time. Piers was busy with his cronies arranging for a shipload of merchandise for France. This was stored in the stone cellars of a large house which fronted the sea, and they only awaited a convenient night and a north wind, to hurry it aboard. Nigel with Puah at his side, explored the island, visiting ruined castles which filled him with delight, and examining traces of the long-departed civilization which filled him with speculation. The Tynwald fascinated him. The Manx laws were so different from those of England that the island was the resort of many who, for political or economic reasons, desired greater freedom. He encountered men from Scotland and Ireland, men who were obviously smugglers, men who might well have been Bonaparte spies. They mingled freely with the throng. There was no dread of the press-gang, and Nigel no longer walked apprehensively. His bruised body mended, and the change and the sunshine and the freedom hastened his recovery. He and Puah roved like two schoolboys starting the vacation. There was no hint by either of the tense moment beside the bay at Castletown; it might never have taken place.

Nigel, in fairness to Puah, controlled his mind when in her company. His images of Bronwen were restricted to the night watches. On one occasion Piers took him in hand and made him spend some hours in the cool darkness of the stone warehouse. It was explained to him how the bales were packed; the most convenient size and weight; the commodities which were sent from Britain to France in return for those fetched from France to Britain. Each country found a ready market in supplying those things which the other lacked. Piers saw nothing unpatriotic about the transactions. They merely appealed to his commercial instincts. It seemed, so he assured Nigel, only common sense.

"You'd be surprised, Nigel, if you knew how many ladies encourage us. Some of those high-born dames have no scruples whatever. Lace or scent means more to them than patriotism, my lad. There's the wife of an army officer on this very island who will pay any price for a length of silk from Italy. And believe me, I name my own price. That silk has to come by way of Smyrna and sometimes takes a year to get into these waters. It is only right that she should pay, eh?"

"What else do you get from the French luggers, Piers, in addition to the kegs of brandy, and the tobacco which you smoke so freely?"

"There's a fair amount of tea, and there's silk and lace and scent. The French are more broad-minded than our folks. They encourage smuggling. And they'd sell their souls—if they have any—for good, solid, English guineas. Guineas and cotton-twist, seem to be most in demand at present. They're glad of sugar, too. The chances of their getting any from the West Indies are pretty remote now that we have control of the seas. Sugar's not easy to handle. Apt to get damp. But it's profitable if we can get across quick. It will fetch as much as six-and-six a pound on the continent."

Nigel soon lost interest. He supposed that he would have to force his mind to wrestle with these matters, but actually the construction of Peel Castle appealed to him far more—even if there was no money attached to it. He wished he could have completed his thesis. If only he had stuck at the copying, if only he had disciplined his mind, instead of day-dreaming of Bronwen, the work would have been done. The Master of Arts degree which he had so long coveted, would have been his. Suddenly he laughed.

"What is it, Nigel?" asked Puah, who dangled her feet from a bale of cotton-twist beside the hidden wharf.

"I suddenly wondered what use a degree would be to a smuggler."

For a while Puah sat silent. Nigel had laughed a trifle bitterly when he spoke. There was no laugh of response from Puah. When she spoke her voice was quiet, almost dreamy. "You have suffered disappointment, Nigel. I am sorry. It maybe that you must suffer now in order to get a reward later on. You will get the degree you want. I am sure of that. We will trade just now until you have plenty of money. Then you shall have a quiet cottage somewhere where you will not be disturbed and you will write more treaties or whatever you call them. And you will be happy."

"Bless you, Puah! One thesis is enough, thanks. But I should like to write books. Books about old castles; books, perhaps, about smugglers."

"And people would say: 'Wherever did he get all his information?'"

"And it would remain a complete mystery, because, of course, a person so respectable as Nigel Preece would not even speak to smugglers!"

She raised her eyebrows mischievously as she glanced up at him. "I like you when you talk like that. You are always serious; so serious these days. You will learn to laugh again, won't you, Nigel?"

"I will try." He made a valiant attempt, but watching, she felt that it was only his lips which smiled and that his eyes were still sad.

That night they worked in the darkness, loading the bales into small boats and rowing with muffled oars to the *Four Winds*. Tired and hot they lay down on deck and snatched an hour's sleep before dawn. When the morn wind blew, the anchor was hauled dripping aboard, the brown sails stretched themselves to the breeze, and the *Four Winds* stole out to sea before the good folk of the island were awake.

It was a brisk breeze and the ketch made good headway. At first Nigel imagined that they were returning to Beaumaris. He had taken his share of hoisting the sails and, under Puah's guidance, learned to distinguish the peak-halliard from the throat-halliard.

Once they were well away and everything snug and shipshape they reclined on one of the lockers. Nigel was thinking that if Piers had wanted to bring the two of them together he could not have done better than to take them a cruise in the *Four Winds*.

As Nigel sat watching the morning sun sparkle on the tossing wave-crests he was silent. Talking to Puah was not easy. That was one of the differences he had already discovered. It was not her fault. Their minds had little in common, that was the reason. A seemingly irrelevant matter to a superficial observer, perhaps, but much, very much, to a man who had grown accustomed to dwelling within the kingdom of the mind. In Bronwen's company, thought led to thought. With Puah he often fell silent because he abominated platitudes, and he could think of nothing which would interest the girl. The surprising thing to him was that these long silences did not apparently embarrass Puah in the least. She seemed well content to be at his side. Whatever Piers might think it was asking much to expect two people to traverse the long highway of life so ill-equipped for the journey.

Nigel glanced up at the sun and looked puzzled. "I do not understand a thing about navigation, Puah, but I should have thought that Beaumaris lay more to the left."

"You mean more to larboard, Nigel. We are not going to Beaumaris."

"Indeed? Then where? Amlwch?"

"Farther. Much farther."

"Not France, surely?"

"You sound quite horrified. No, not France. Only South Wales. You see, we have different store places, depots they call them, where we leave the cargoes. It is not always possible to meet at a rendezvous, sometimes on account of the weather, sometimes because of the frigates which are cruising in the channel. No one wants to run a longer distance with contraband in his hold than is absolutely necessary. So usually we do it in stages. We take this cargo to South Wales. A smack from Ilfracombe will pick it up and carry it to Fowey. The Cornishmen will run it across to Roscoff in Brittany."

"Is there risk on these long voyages?"

"Of course there's risk. That's why the pay is so high. The revenue-cutters are always on the look out, but we are usually more than a match for them. The *Four Winds* has been chosen for this run because of her speed. Not many small craft can touch her, though Piers never shows her paces when she is near Beaumaris. Have you noticed he nearly always has her under easy sail?"

"No, I hadn't noticed, Puah."

"You take notice. You don't often see Piers with more than jib and mizzen set when we're near home. He waits until we are well clear of land before he lets the li+tle lady have her head. We are moving quite nicely now. I hope the breeze holds."

Nigel hoped so, too. It was rather like sitting on a powder barrel, to be out in the open sea with scores of bales of contraband below deck. Yet he felt strangely unconcerned. The only emotion he experienced was a feeling of unreality. A craving for the real world which to him was the realm of literature took hold of him. He made his way to the cabin and rummaged in the kitbag into which Puah had flung his cherished books. He was soon stretched full length on the bunk with his favourite edition of Horace in his hand. He loved that master of polished phrases. Nigel wondered if he, too, would retire one day to his Sabine farm there to cultivate the verse and prose which meant so much to his cultured mind. He hoped he would be able to write so worthily that he might leave behind him something more tangible than a name on a tombstone.

Immersed in his reading he lost track of time. He became oblivious that he was taking his ease in a speedy ketch, because his mind roved the verdant hills of Tivoli. The ketch seemed to be heeling more, plunging more. It inconvenienced him. In his endeavour to retain his equilibrium, the tilting of the vessel produced a sense of irritation. He became conscious of movement on deck, crisp orders, the creak of blocks, the shuffling of bare feet. He glanced from the page interrogatively when Puah appeared at the entrance.

"I think you had better come on deck, Nigel," she said, and her voice was curiously expressionless and calm.

"Certainly." Nigel placed a marker between the pages and closed the worn leather covers of his favourite book. He got to his feet—and lost his balance. "Confound it," he cried, half laughing, half vexed, for the lurch had sacrificed the dignity which was part of Nigel's being. "The *Four Winds* behaves inconsiderately. Have we struck bad weather or something?"

"Come on deck," said Puah succinctly and vanished. Nigel grasped the side of the doorway and worked his way outside. He paused for a moment and then, with an undignified lurch, clasped a mizzen stay and clung precariously to the weather bulwark.

Piers was at the tiller, his face set hard. His feet were braced. It was taking him all his time to hold the kicking rudder. Nigel followed Piers' gaze aloft. He saw that the topmasts had been run up and the topsails set. He had never before seen so much canvas on the *Four Winds*. Little wonder she heeled and slanted and plunged. The spray was whipping his face. Puah swung herself across by means of a rope and joined him. She linked her arms through the shrouds.

"Look astern," she shouted.

Nigel turned. A large vessel under full sail was following. He could see a pennon rippling to leeward from her main truck. The white foam was flung from her bows, and as she heeled Nigel could see a yellow band along her black hull. A thing of beauty, and yet an ominous sight.

"A ship of war?" he asked.

Puah nodded. "Your old friend the *Unique*. She has been chasing us this last hour or more."

Nigel looked about him. There was no sight of land. Sea, sea, everywhere, right to the horizon which was fretted by the crests of tossing waves. He stared thoughtfully at the corvette.

"Are we holding our own?" he asked, and to his surprise he found that he was more curious than anxious.

"No. She has gained steadily."

"What are our chances of escape?"

Puah did not reply. Instead she cupped her hands and shouted to her brother. "What are our chances of escape, Piers?"

Piers took his eyes from the sails for a moment and Nigel saw his teeth showing in a reckless grin. "Damn poor! We may just do it if the sticks hold." He glanced astern, sizing up the distance with appraising eye. They saw him shake his head. "We'll have to jettison the goods. Curse! There goes our profit for a couple of runs at least. Ah well. It's the first time we have lost a cargo so I must not complain. Madoc, start passing the bales up. Drop 'em overboard. Lee bow. Keep under cover of the sails. We don't want their look-out to guess what we are doing. If they overhaul us it will take us all our time to bluff our way out of this mess."

They saw Madoc disappear from sight and then his brawny arms reappeared as he handed bale after bale to Tom.

"Puah, take the helm," ordered Piers. "And Nigel, you'd better lend a hand. There's the devil of a kick. Too much for her. But Puah will hold her steady if you just do as she says. I must give a hand with those bales. We don't want 'em making a splash, and Tom is too small to wrestle with them. Especially in a wind like this."

Puah grasped the tiller and Nigel, bracing himself, helped her to hold the strain. They saw Piers glance over his shoulder and then pause as he moved forward.

"Ah!" he said and posed like a statue. Nigel turned in time to see a white cloud of smoke obscure the bows of the corvette. It looked curiously like cotton wool. He noticed a fountain of foam leap into the air a hundred yards astern. The hollow rumble of a gun came to his ears.

"If that is supposed to be shot across our bows it's damn bad shooting," said Piers coolly.

"It was good shooting, Piers," retorted Puah. "Short range, only. The sighting was right on the mark. And they'll soon lessen the distance."

"You're right. And they're getting out stun's'ls, blast them."

As he hurried forward, Nigel saw strips of additional canvas appear on the corvette's yardarms. Nigel was working furiously now. Bale after bale was hurled over the rail and disappeared with a hollow splash into the tossing sea.

The tiller engrossed Nigel's attention. He was almost surprised when a fountain of white spray leaped into the air on the starboard bow. The report which came down the wind told him that the corvette's bowchaser was busy again.

"They are getting the range," observed Puah. "Lie down, Nigel. You are not so likely to get hit."

Instead he shifted his position on the tiller so that he stood behind Puah, his body covering hers.

"That is typical of you, Nigel, but quite unnecessary," said Puah composedly. "If a roundshot is to hit me, your body will not shield me."

"Perhaps not, Puah, but if it comes we'll go together."

She did not speak. Instead, she turned her head and looked at him. Nigel never forgot that look. The breeze had set her curls streaming, leaving her forehead free and smooth. Her eyes met his. They were eloquent. There was a look in them which he had never seen before. An unspoken thanks. Thanks—and adoration.

The bowchaser spoke again. A hole appeared in the mainsail's brown expanse. Nigel looked with fascinated eyes as severed halliards and shrouds whipped the air. Piers heaved the last bale overboard and yelled to his sister.

"Luff! Luff! Take the strain off the topmast. . . ."

It was too late. Even as the *Four Winds'* nose fell away, the maintopmast bent. With a crackle of splintering wood down it crashed, and the great sail crumpled as the gaff sagged forlornly across the mast. The *Four Winds* came to an even keel, and lay helpless as a gull with a broken wing.

Piers stood, feet apart, and cursed the corvette which came crowding up behind. Then he looked about him with a quick, eager glance. "Is there anything which will give us away?" he asked. "Slip into the cabin, Puah, and if you see anything, heave it overboard quick."

"The name," called Puah, as she disappeared.

Piers opened a locker and took out the *Moonraker* name-board, cracked it into three with two quick stamps of his foot, then whipping out his gully he splintered it ere he flung the fragments over the side.

Puah returned to say that so far as she knew the vessel was clear. They waited. No one spoke. Puah had come close to Nigel and stood with her arm touching his. They watched the corvette, counting the black gunports in the yellow band. She was abreast of them now and shortening sail with the rapidity of a ship which carries a large and well-trained crew. A longboat splashed from the booms. They saw the oarsmen bending to their task, keeping unison with a precision which would have aroused their admiration under more pleasurable circumstances. A blue-coated officer stood in the sternsheets. Even at a distance they could recognize the red face and hair of Lieutenant Kirby.

"You're in for trouble, Nigel!" said Piers grimly. "Sorry I brought you into this."

"My dear fellow. It was none of your doing. It is one of those delightful ironies tossed out to mankind by the Fates. It is decreed that when that fellow and I encounter the odds are always in his favour."

He spoke calmly. He felt Puah's hand slipped beneath his arm. She gave a reassuring squeeze. He looked down and smiled. An undramatic conclusion to a dramatic incident, thought Nigel. But the end was not yet!

The ship's boat was alongside. The bowman had his boathook fast, the men came swarming over the sides. Lieutenant Kirby stepped on to the rail and dropped on deck. Madoc and the elderly man, were standing near the wreck of the mainsail. Little Tom had dived out of sight. Nigel and Piers and Puah were grouped near the tiller.

The lieutenant stalked towards them. There was an aggressive swagger about his walk.

"What ship is this?"

"*Four Winds*. Beaumaris. I am the skipper," said Piers curtly.

"Why the hell didn't you heave to when we fired across your bows?"

"Because your shooting is so damn bad you never came near our bows."

"Don't cheek me, or I'll make you rue the day."

"You have already made a wreck of my ship. Why can't you keep your shots for the enemy? You haven't the guts to fire at a Frenchman! Hell of a Navy we've got these days."

"Ay! Ay! Room for improvement, I've no doubt. A smart young fellow like you would bring about many changes. Well, you shall have the privilege of showing us what you can do. Seize him, lads."

Before Piers could protest, three burly tars had him in their grasp.

Lieutenant Kirby turned his attention to Nigel. He stared, his eyes narrowing, into the calm, haughty features of the former schoolmaster.

"What I have to say to you, my fine fellow, will keep!" he said with an ominous calm. "We shall have plenty of opportunity for making better acquaintance."

He nodded and two sailors grasped Nigel's arms.

"You are the personification of discretion, sir," observed Nigel, with mock civility. "Now your men hold my arms I have no doubt you feel safe to insult me with impunity."

Kirby scowled and turned to Puah. "Lord, here's a damn pretty little pirate," he said and he stared her up and down. "My dear, it wrings my heart, 'pon my oath, not to be able to impress you, likewise. Let me console you for the loss of your friends."

He caught her in his arms and kissed her fiercely on the mouth. Piers struggled furiously, flung off two of the seamen. The third held him fast. In a flash, Piers whipped out his gully and plunged the blade into the man's arm. The fellow let go with an oath. The next instant a pistol-butt descended on Piers' uncovered head and stretched him on the deck.

Nigel, too, had endeavoured to move but the men held him tight. His injuries were still tender and he could not withstand their grip. Instead he could only look miserably at Puah. She had gone very white. Her eyes sparkled as he had never seen them before. She reminded him of Piers when he was in a temper. But Puah did not seem to be in a temper. She seemed frigidly cool.

"How nice of you, sir, thus to honour me," she said, picking her words with care. "Will you not kiss me again?"

"Gad, I've made a conquest!" roared Kirby, and he bent towards her. The next instant he screamed a curse and sprang back with blood pouring from his mouth. Puah's strong white teeth had met in his lower lip. She spat in his face.

His great red fist crashed into her tender mouth. As she rolled stunned into the scupper, Nigel saw red. It was not merely the blood which had spurted from her shattered face. It was a primitive red which must have smouldered in his veins, bequeathed by some long forgotten cave-man ancestor. Oblivious of his injuries he tore himself free from the seamen and hurled Kirby to the deck. He flung himself upon his enemy with hands which groped for his throat, but before his furious fingers could close their clutch, a boat's stretcher descended on his head and he fell limp across the body of his enemy.

Lieutenant Kirby rose unsteadily to his feet and applied a handkerchief to his mouth.

"Search the ship, Bo'sun. Let her go if there's no contraband aboard. I doubt if you'll find a stick. They've had time to jettison it. Then heave these two into the boat. To-morrow we'll give them a taste of discipline aboard a man-o'-war."

The boat pulled slowly back to the *Unique*. The *Four Winds* drooped forlornly on the tossing sea, her booms banging with every surge of the rudder.

For Madoc Morris and the elderly seaman sat captives in the longboat with the unconscious forms of Nigel and Piers across their feet.

In the scupper of the *Four Winds* the diminutive Tom crouched anxiously over the prostrate form of his young mistress as he endeavoured to wipe the blood from her still face.

CHAPTER XXII

NIGEL lay face down on a pile of canvas in the heaving fore-castle of the *Unique*. He was conscious, but in that stage of physical exhaustion when he was scarcely conscious that he was conscious. His back, lacerated by the flogging he had received, caused him such excruciating pain that he shunned the slightest movement lest the caked blood should crack and set a thousand fierce agonies in motion. Yet it was his spirit which suffered more than his wracked body. The vicious, brutal, sadistic ceremony which accompanied the flogging was degrading and humiliating. And there was no redress. With the exception of one seaman, more human than his fellows, the crew ignored him, leaving him without a passing glance as they would have passed a dead dog on the roadside. Piers was in little better state but he did not experience Nigel's agony of soul. Instead he was obsessed by a smouldering, murderous hatred for the author of their misery.

It all came back to Nigel as he lay with his cheek on his naked arm, his eyes closed. The mockery of a trial before Lieutenant Kirby, who, during the absence of the captain, was in temporary command of the corvette.

"Thirty-nine lashes! I'll teach you mutinous dogs to assault an officer of his Majesty's Navy. Another attempt, and you'll swing from the yard-arm for striking a superior officer. The only thing that saves your necks is that you were, at the time of the assault, not impressed. B'sun, get the gratings rigged. Have the crew parade to witness the flogging, and get your cat ready."

Nigel could picture how he and Piers, stripped to the waist, had stood with a guard of Royal Marines at their side, watching the preparations. The grating was up-ended and lashed to the main shrouds with another grating underneath on which the victim was to stand. The crew formed a hollow square. The men, inured to hardship and brutality, waited for the spectacle with something akin to grim pleasure: just as they awaited a brush with the enemy—it was something to break the monotony of life aboard ship. The burly boatswain ran the lashes of the cat through his fingers, and then made it whistle through the air to ensure that the thongs were all free. Piers was led out first and his wrists lashed to the upper corners of the grating. Nigel had to watch. His first reaction was to close his eyes, but he saw the baleful gaze of Lieutenant Kirby fixed on him, and his pride refused to allow him to flinch. The lash came across the smooth tanned skin of Piers' naked back, and the red weals glowed as if a gigantic cat had drawn its talons there. Swish! The lash clawed a second time. There was a faint trickle of blood. Again and again the scourge descended, the bo's'n changing sides as each stroke of ten was called by the master-at-arms, in order to criss-cross the pattern. The blood dripped into the belted waist. Piers, white of face, his lips set, endured without a groan.

"Thirty-nine!" The ordeal was over. The wrist lashings were cut free. Piers staggered, head bent, towards the forecastle, the seamen parting their ranks to let him through.

The bo's'n drew the blood-stained thongs through his fingers. "Next!"

It was Nigel's turn.

He had not taken the thirty-nine strokes. Or at least he had no recollection of so doing, for after the twentieth cut Nature administered her merciful opiate. Nigel had been cut down, swooning. Someone must have dragged him to the canvas on which he lay for he had no remembrance of how he got there. All he knew was that he never wished to move again. He must have slept. His next conscious realization was that someone was close beside him, bending over him, a big, dark form which seemed vaguely familiar.

"How d'yer feel?" came a low voice. "Can you take a sip of grog?" It was Madoc. He had a tin pannikin in his great fist. Nigel looked at it. The mere sight of the liquid was comforting for his mouth was parched. But he could not drink without moving, and any movement sent those spasms of agony through his wracked body. His back was not merely cut, it was bruised. The craving for drink became irresistible and with a stifled groan he wriggled on to one elbow, and Madoc held the cup to his lips. The liquor was strong and it made him gasp, but as his throat glowed and burnt he felt a slight return of vigour.

"I could not come before, mate," said Madoc. "It would not have done, nohow. They ain't for much use for pity in these floating hells. I know. I've had a taste."

"You've—what?"

"Ay. People don't know, but I done three years before the mast. I never wanted no more so I just kept out of the way. And I kept my mouth shut. You're the first I've told, so don't go for giving the game away."

"That's not likely, Madoc, after your kindness to me. But what of Piers? You must give some to him."

"Finish that up. Piers has had his grog. I give him some long since whilst you was sleeping. Now I must go. Keep quiet, and don't go letting them know as you care a damn."

The burly man stole softly from the forecastle, leaving Nigel alone. He felt slightly better. Less exhausted. Cheered somewhat by Madoc's solicitude. He put his head back on his naked arm and again tried to sleep. He was aroused by stentorian tones "All hands shorten sail!" The ship was heeling so that he was flung against the bulkhead. He was aware that Piers was on his feet staggering towards the deck. There was a fierce, indomitable glare in his dark eyes. He was going aloft. Piers, hardy, tough, resolute, his fighting-blood roused, would not admit the infirmities of the flesh.

Nigel experienced a glow of admiration. It stimulated his own flagging spirit. He sat up painfully and groped for his shirt. If Piers could go he would, too. His legs shook, his head reeled. Cautiously, gently, he pulled the shirt over his lacerated shoulders. As he rocked with the swaying vessel, he was conscious of a form shutting out the light.

A voice yelled, "No skulking here! Bo'sun, get a rope-end to this waster. Up aloft, you dog, and furl sail."

It was Lieutenant Kirby, working himself into a fury. "Get aloft, d'y' hear?"

He shook Nigel roughly by the shoulder, causing him to catch his breath.

"Easy, there, Pink," came a smoother voice. "The poor devil's not recovered yet."

"Recovered? He's slacking, I tell you. I'll have no wasters aboard this ship. Up aloft with you!"

Nigel gamely rose to his feet but a lurch of the vessel made him stagger and he measured his length on the deck. Lieutenant Kirby drove a boot into his ribs. "Up, you lazy devil," he stormed.

"Stop it, Pink," protested Lieutenant Moir. "He's scuppered. Can't you see? The poor devil's done for!"

"Done for be damned. I'll have every man aboard this ship obey orders."

"When orders are given it is assumed that the person to whom they are given is in a fit state to perform them. You would not order a man whose leg has been shot off to climb to the mizzentop."

"This man has not had his leg shot off; he's malingering, I tell you."

"Don't be a fool, Pink. Your prejudice has blinded your sense of proportion. I shall not allow this man to be ordered aloft to-day."

"*You* won't permit; you? Hell and damnation, who are you to countermand my orders? Answer me."

"I'll trouble you to keep a civil tongue in your head when you address me."

"Damnation. This is intolerable, Moir. I have been left in charge of this ship. I am acting as captain."

"You are acting as an idiot. Let me remind you that we are out to get fresh hands for the fleet off Toulon. Dead men are of no use to Nelson. Your personal grudges are prejudicial to the interests of the service. This man shall be examined by the ship's surgeon. If he is passed fit, I will say no more. If he is not you may send him aloft if you choose, but if he falls overboard I shall prefer a charge of manslaughter. So now you know."

"Moir, you shall answer to me for this!" Kirby stalked away, but after a couple of strides he paused and scowled at Nigel. "You malingering dog, you may escape now, but I'll see you do your duty once you are on your feet again."

*　　*　　*　　*　　*

It was a mixed crowd that inhabited the forecastle. There were seamen who had served in every part of the globe; men who had been in actions of which the world had talked. There were men from inland villages who never succeeded wholly in dragging their bucolic feet from the loam; there were married men snatched by the press-gang from their homes; sullen, morose men; reckless, careless men; heart-sick, home-sick men; vicious, evil men; sturdy, stalwart men. Piers and Nigel began to drift apart. They were in different watches. Their temperaments were even more remote. Piers was drawn to the reckless spirits who made mock of misfortune. They drank and diced and cursed, accepted punishment with a reckless bravado, vied with one another in daring as they swarmed over the futtock-shrouds, or worked their way out along the swaying yardarms to reef sail in a gale. Nigel became introspective. He undertook his duties with a thoroughness which won the approbation of the men in charge and gave Pink Kirby little opportunity to discipline him. But he rarely spoke. His one companion was the little leather-bound volume of Horace which he had inadvertently slipped into his pocket before joining Puah on the *Four Winds'* deck. His silence proved his best friend. He left others alone so others left him alone. Madoc Morris had tried to cheer him but his efforts failed. Nigel was quietly polite; indicated that Madoc's well-intentioned efforts were appreciated. But they were not encouraged. Madoc was in Piers' watch and bit by bit he, too, drifted away and left Nigel to his solitary existence.

A chance incident brought about an improvement in his lot. He had a pencil in his pocket and having come across a sheet of blank paper he was spending an idle half-hour during his watch below in sketching. Jack Doyle, the captain of the foretop, happened to be leaning against the bulwarks smoking a short clay pipe and Nigel saw in his rugged profile an excellent study. He sketched rapidly, and then proceeded to touch up the features. Engrossed in his shading he did not notice that his model had become interested in what he was doing. Before he knew it Doyle was bending over his shoulder. "Well, blast my eyes, if I hadn't seen it myself I would never have thought it possible." His large fist took the paper from Nigel's hands and held it admiringly at arm's length. "Well, if it ain't drawed as pretty as any artist could have done it. Look here, lad, do me another, and I'll give you a florin. If I can send this home to Molly, she won't half be pleased. Could you do another, do you think?"

"As many as you like if you will provide the paper. And there is no occasion to waste your money. I do not need it."

"You're the first seaman as ever I heard utter words like them," said Doyle grinning. "However, I'll take this, and thank 'ee."

Nigel thought no more about the matter, but presently he began to see that his work became less arduous. He drew two more sketches of the captain of the foretop, one full length; the other a torso, Doyle insisting that the details of his tattooing were duly emphasized. Before many days had passed Nigel found himself fully occupied. Horace lay neglected in his pocket. There was hardly a man in the forecastle who did not want himself sketched; the more so as Nigel steadfastly refused to accept payment for his labours. All he asked was that paper should be provided. By the end of the week the bulkheads were adorned with his sketches, so that Doyle observed the place began to look like a junk shop.

The occupation did Nigel good. It cured, to an extent, his

brooding. Yet he could not wholly escape from the past. He was given to reverie, especially at night. When he stood on deck watching the tracery of the rigging moving against the starry heavens, listening to the swish of the waves, his mind would go back to the old scenes. He visited again the quarry in the greenwood and looked into Bronwen's eyes. He was out in the ketch again with Piers and Puah, carefree. He wondered whether Bevan had left Beaumaris. He wondered who was the new schoolmaster; what had become of Bronwen. Often he saw Puah go down before that cruel blow, and he would bite his lip. To recall it usually worked him into a fury which was all the worse because he was denied the means of outlet. If only he could meet his enemy on land. But here he was powerless. The rigid discipline of the Navy prevented his showing resentment. Doyle had stood his friend.

"See here, my lad," said the captain of the foretop as they leaned together over the bulwark, watching the phosphorus one quiet night, "that damned officer has got his knife into you, so watch your step. Now, don't show as you care. If you does you plays right into his hands. And remember he's always got the last word, and maybe that last word is the cat. He can make your life a hell, so do whatever he says and do it prompt. Don't give him no chance for complaint. The skipper's back aboard now, and he's a fair-minded man. If you does your duty, you don't need to fear—much. But Kirby is a mean swine. He's got influence because he's the son of a lord, d'y' see? And he's out to break you. So just lie low. Your time will come, lad, your time will come. At present you can't do nothing about it so just make the best of it. But mark my words, your time will come."

*   *   *   *   *

It was a strange contrast, this life aboard a man-of-war. Something which Nigel had never contemplated, or if he had given it a thought, it was different from anything he had imagined. Nothing fashioned by the hand of man could have been more glorious than a ship under full press of sail; living, graceful, human. But within the stately shell there was rottenness. When battened down in bad weather the fetid atmosphere was nauseating; the smell of unwashed humanity, sour food, bilge water, assaulted not merely Nigel's nostrils but clung like slime to his throat and stomach so that he was glad to get up the rigging and take deep breaths of the ozone-laden air to purify his polluted system. The food was coarse, and the salted beef was almost more than he could swallow. He craved for vegetables and fruit. But worse than smells or salted food was the company he had to endure. In their cramped and crowded quarters there was no privacy. It was a state of affairs which had to be tolerated without respite. Sometimes he would listen wonderingly to the conversation. The blasphemy and obscenity did not strike him so forcibly as the restricted limits of topics and vocabulary— the paucity of imagination. He concluded that expletives were freely used, not because the heart of the speaker was full of sin, but because his mind was void of adjectives. Fortunately the crew left him much alone. This was largely the result of an impulse on Nigel's part. . . .

He was sitting with his well-thumbed Horace in his hand, endeavouring in the dim light to find solace in a favourite ode, when a lanky fellow, intent on provoking trouble, knocked the book out of Nigel's hand. A page ripped as it fell.

Nigel's impulse was to hit the man. He did it so effectively that he knocked him out completely. As the seaman lay like a log in a corner Nigel picked up his volume, smoothed the torn page and resumed his reading. So trivial an incident attracted little outward attention. It was too commonplace. One seaman, more loquacious than his fellows, removed his pipe to observe, with embellishments, that it served the beggar right. A companion squirted a stream of tobacco juice across the prostrate form and agreed that it did serve the beggar right.

There the matter ended, but Nigel's studious habits were thereafter tolerated.

Sometimes when seated on deck he would be joined by Piers. Their conversation was restricted. One thought seemed to run in Piers' mind; it recurred again and again.

"Wonder what's happened to Puah!" He would suck moodily at his pipe. "Nigel, if ever I get a chance. . . ." Then he would clench his teeth.

"I know, Piers. If only we could get word, somehow. If only we could get into some port. Could we send a letter to Beaumaris?"

"Maybe, if we'd the money to frank it with. But we could not get a reply, so what's the use. No, Nigel, we've got to put up with it. Nothing else for it, but if ever I get a chance to desert——!"

The strange thing was that Lieutenant Kirby left them both

F

severely alone. Why, they could not determine, unless he had been reprimanded after the captain's return. If the occasion demanded Lieutenant Kirby would give a curt order. Nigel invariably obeyed with a promptitude which would have satisfied the most punctilious martinet. Otherwise the officer passed them by with a blank stare as though he were unaware of their identity.

Nigel began to take pride in his work. The activity in the fresh air kept him fit and served to counteract the atmosphere between decks. There was a spice of risk which served as a tonic to his jaded mind. He could outpace almost every man in climbing the rigging, and could work his way along a weather yard-arm to wrestle with a refractory fore-top-gallant in a manner which elicited praise from the critical Jack Doyle.

But within himself the fight was not against wind and tide, but against life itself. He kept trying to puzzle out the reason for the strange course he was compelled to take. He, who could have filled a useful place in the community, was forced to herd with humans whose mentality was little above that of the brute beast. There was bitterness in the cup from which he had to drink. But he fought to acquire a resilience of character which would prove as armour against the slings and arrows of outrageous fortune. Life had not broken the sword of his spirit but it had undoubtedly dulled the finely tempered edge.

Horace was his constant solace. He was reading, as usual, in a corner of the forecastle, which was almost deserted, when Piers put in his head.

"Better come on deck, Nigel," he said, "there's a sail to the so'west and the lads swear she's a Frenchman."

CHAPTER XXIII

THE *Unique* was cruising under easy sail half-way between the Lizard and Ushant, hoping to snap up a few prizes before returning to Portsmouth. Her captain, Commander Gardner, a comparatively young man, was ambitious. He was a disciplinarian who, while being firm, was not unjust. The presence of the stranger whose topsails showed plainly was the subject of considerable speculation. From the number of glasses turned in her direction by the officers on the quarterdeck, Nigel could tell that their suspicions were aroused. There was a change in the atmosphere throughout the entire ship. The men appeared to hang listlessly about but a discerning eye could have told that they were ready to rush to their respective stations the instant the word was given.

Then he heard the captain's crisp: "Clear decks for action!"

Even before the boatswain's stentorian voice had bellowed the order forward, the effect was electric. Indolent seamen became active. The decks were alive with hurrying, heaving figures. Ports were triced up and the gun-tackles cast free as the captain of each gun took charge. There was a hammering below as the bulkheads were removed. Hammocks were stowed in the nettings as a precaution against splinters and a barrier against boarders. Powder-monkeys rushed to the magazine for supplies. The marines looked to their muskets. In the waist the master-at-arms was issuing small-arms. Nigel, as he belted on a cutlass, experienced a thrill of expectancy. A transformation was in process. The foul-mouthed loungers of the forecastle had disappeared, and in their place were eager-faced fighting men, grumblings subdued, hardships forgotten, eager only for a brush with the foe.

The gun-crews, stripped to the waist, stood by expectantly. They had loaded the guns, ten to a broadside, and awaited orders. Nigel was conscious of magic in the air. It was infectious. His fingers closed about the heavy finger-grip of his cutlass. He drew the blade and tested it. Something within him stirred; some throw-back in his blood linking him to the long-dead Nigel who rode behind the Black Prince at Poictiers. The pattern of the sword differed, but the urge for action remained unchanged by the passing centuries.

Jack Doyle came down the ratlines with long, clean, sure strides. He grinned at Nigel. "Well, lad, how d' y' feel? You'll be having your first crack at a Frenchie before long."

"A bit tense," replied Nigel with a quiet smile, "extremely curious, and happier, I must confess, than I have been since I left the Isle of Man."

"We're going to have our work cut out," confided the captain of the foretop. "She's got heavier metal. A small frigate by the look of her. Twenty-six guns; perhaps twenty-eight. It might be wiser to give her wide berth, but the Old Man is a bit of a fire-eater in spite of his quiet looks."

It was obvious that the corvette's captain was quite unimpressed by the superior weight of the enemy. The ships drew together steadily. Nigel could discern signs of activity aboard the Frenchman. There was no doubt about her nationality. He could detect the tricolour streaming to leeward. And there was a smartness of design which, even to a landsman, was noticeable; a smartness absent from most English ships of war. Nigel could see Piers standing by a gun on the starboard side. Lieutenant Kirby had strapped on a sword, and thrust a brace of pistols in his belt. His pugnacious face now seemed more in its right setting.

It was a time of waiting. A time of manœuvring. Both vessels were intent on securing the weather gage. Nigel heard the captain tell the gunner to try the range, and the crew of the bow-chaser ran out their gun. The foemen forestalled them. A cloud of smoke obscured the Frenchman's figure-head and a column of water rose a few yards away from the *Unique*. As if in reply the corvette's bow-chaser was fired. The smoke which drifted to leeward prevented Nigel from seeing the effects of the shot. The deadly game had started.

There was little opportunity for Nigel to be an idle observer. He was allowed for a short while to stand beside the gun he was to serve, the gun which was soon to become a leaping, living creature bellowing forth death. At the crash of the first broadside Nigel's ear-drums seemed to split, but he had no time to pay heed. The gun sprang back to the extent of its breechings, and had to be sponged and loaded and run out again. The smoke partly hid the enemy from his view. He was conscious of their roundshot tearing gaps through the bulwarks. There was the thud of shots biting into the hull: the crash of blocks falling from aloft as the cordage was cut adrift. It was, to him, pandemonium. The acrid smoke made his eyes smart; his throat was parched. He saw men fall screaming on deck, the red of the scuppers was dyed a deeper crimson from the life blood which flowed. As a gust of wind parted the smoke cloud he was aware of the topsails of the French frigate looming darkly against the sky almost alongside. The marines were exchanging musket shots with their opponents. But there was little time to observe or to speculate. The gun had to be sponged and loaded again. He assumed, in a vague manner, that the officers knew what they were doing; that some one was looking after the steering of the corvette. So far as he was concerned the gun occupied his whole attention.

With a crash which shook the entire gun a roundshot ripped through the porthole and carried away a trunnion, shattering the gun-carriage and killing two of the crew. Nigel was hurled to the deck where he lay stunned. When he recovered consciousness—some unknown person had stumbled across his body—he sat up and slowly got to his feet. He looked about him in bewilderment. The wrecked gun lay useless and deserted. Several others were also out of action. The gun-crews were grouped about the guns which were still in commission. The firing from both sides was less severe. The smoke was thinning. He saw the jib-boom of the French ship come thrusting like a gigantic spear between the main and mizzen masts.

"Repel boarders!" The boatswain's bellow rose above the crash of the guns. He saw the marines fix bayonets; seamen seize cutlass and pike. There were Frenchmen swarming along the bowsprit and dropping to the *Unique's* deck where they were struck down ere their feet touched the planks. Nigel drew his cutlass and flung himself into the mêlée. Suddenly he felt complete self-assurance. The broadside had bewildered him, dazed him, but this was straightforward fighting, primitive fighting, and the blood in his veins responded. Almost without his knowing it he found himself in front of the press, plying his cutlass, clearing a way. The Frenchmen were beaten back. The gun-crews ran again to their guns and fired furiously into the Frenchman's bows.

"Lash her bowsprit to the mast," yelled Captain Gardner. "Now, my lads. It is our turn. Carry her by boarding."

There was a rush for the side, a rush so vigorous that Nigel was swept off his feet as the yelling cursing crowd of seamen surged towards the enemy. He could see Lieutenant Kirby sword in hand, striving to get his foot on the Frenchman's figurehead. Nigel saw Piers dash towards a musket which had been dropped by a wounded marine: saw him look to the priming and bring the weapon to his shoulder. At the crack of the piece Nigel turned—intuitively—he knew not why. Lieutenant Kirby let go his hold, straightened up, clutched at his right shoulder, toppled slowly backward and vanished from sight.

Nigel was on the hammock-netting. As he glanced down he saw the blue and white figure strike the water and disappear with a splash of foam. He never knew why he acted as he did. It was without volition or intent. The cutlass fell from his fingers as he raised his hands and dived. There was the shock of the cold sea; the struggle with the moving body; the fight to the surface; the horror of the grinding hulls close above his head; the belching of cannon; the never-ceasing din; the consciousness, as strength was leaving him, that a spar was hanging over the side of the corvette, that trailing shrouds were entangling his feet.

He got a grip on the spar, hoisted the unconscious officer across it, and clung, clung desperately, with hands that grew numb, until he became aware of the French vessel drifting away. . . . The gap was widening . . . the firing had almost faded . . . and he saw the great, red, heavy face of Madoc Morris looking down on him, and then friendly arms dragged him upwards towards a shattered porthole.

*   *   *   *   *

It was a grim night, dark, the littered decks picked out in the glow of battle-lanterns. The corvette was shattered. Her three topmasts had gone by the board. The carpenter and his mates were busy plugging shot-holes. The seamen were improvising a jury rig. The main yard had been lashed to the stump of the foremast, and sufficient sail was hoisted to keep the vessel under way. A guard was continuously on duty lest the Frenchman should attempt to board during the hours of darkness. In the cock-pit the surgeon was over-worked. Nigel, as soon as he recovered from the effects of his immersion, joined the riggers who were splicing the severed cordage. There was no time for idling. Every fit man had a task to perform. Captain Gardner saw to that. He meant to resume the action at dawn. Lieutenant Moir found time to pause to compliment Nigel.

"You have done well, my man," he said in his crisp way. "You have the makings of a swordsman. And the manner in which you dived overboard to save Mr. Kirby is commendable. I shall see that his lordship is duly notified."

"If I am permitted to ask a favour, sir, it is that no further mention be made of the matter. I acted entirely without thought."

"Nevertheless, it was a fine gesture."

"I think, sir, it was a gesture of contempt."

"Ah!" Lieutenant Moir was succinct. He passed on his way and Nigel heard no more. At least not from his officer. Piers was less restrained.

In round nautical terms he told Nigel that he was a fool. The world would have been rid of a dirty scoundrel had Lieutenant Pink Kirby fed the fishes. Nigel did not reply.

"Perhaps you've forgotten how he treated Puah?" said Piers in bellicose mood.

"No, Piers, I have not forgotten; I shall not forget. As soon as I get out of the Navy I shall meet the rascal and thrash him."

"You'll wait a long time, my lad," said Piers grimly as he selected a fresh rope for splicing. "It's not going to be easy getting away from these devils once they get their claws into you. But I mean to have a shot at it when we get to port. Are you game to try?"

"I . . . don't . . . know !" Nigel hesitated.

"I wouldn't mind so much, Nigel, if only I knew what had happened to Puah."

"Could they have got the *Four Winds* back to port?"

"Oh, lord, yes, under jib and mizzen. Tom would cut away the wreckage and he could manage that. I keep wondering whether Puah is dead."

"I don't think so."

"What makes you say that?"

"I don't know. I have a feeling that if she were dead I would somehow feel it."

"I think you are right. Maybe I should, as her twin. But that's the devil of it. I keep wondering. Isn't that a sign?"

Nigel could not answer. Piers blazed up again. "When I think of the way that swine treated her I'd like to——"

"I know, Piers. I saw you do it. I think that's partly why I dived overboard. I didn't have time to think. Somehow I can't picture you living happily if you always had the realization that you had shot a man in the back."

Piers thrust his marlinespike savagely under a strand. "Huh! I would prefer to meet him face to face; that's a fact. But the chance came my way and I took it."

"Suppose someone else had seen you?"

"It was worth the risk. In any case all the men hate him like fury."

"Piers, don't think I'm soft-hearted. I mean to make him

pay for what he has done to Puah. But it must be in fair fight."

"Then you'll have to wait a long time. I hear that the swine is likely to lose his right arm. Hope he dies under the knife!" added Piers savagely.

They both fell silent and worked intently. Slowly the confusion on deck lessened. The guns which were undamaged were loaded and run out. The ship's one remaining boat was manned and hovered a short distance away from the corvette, vigilant lest the enemy made an attempt to board. There was an ominous silence from the Frenchman. When the faint green light in the eastern skies heralded the coming of day the crew of the *Unique* stood to arms.

Anxious eyes peered into the dim dawn. There was no sign of their opponent. As the light improved a hail from the look-out brought everyone alert.

"Sail to the so'west, sir."

Captain Gardner himself climbed the foretop and subjected the suspect to a long scrutiny from his glass. He descended slowly and walked grimly to the quarterdeck.

"Gentlemen, we may go home. The Frenchman has had enough. He has called off the fight."

CHAPTER XXIV

THE jury-rigged *Unique* limped into Plymouth. The lack of
prize money was disappointing, but the fighting spirit inherent
in the British sailor found consolation in the realization that
a superior vessel had been fought to a standstill, and the *Unique*
had not come off second-best in the encounter. The wounded
were taken ashore. Nigel did not see Lieutenant Kirby, there
was no word of him or from him. For this Nigel was glad. He
and Piers had their heads together plotting an escape but there
were thought-readers on the *Unique's* quarter-deck. Their
every movement was watched and they, with a number of other
impressed men, were speedily transferred from the shot-shattered
corvette to a seventy-four, the *Colossus*, refitting after months
of arduous blockade work off Ferrol. Madoc Morris, less con-
spicuous or more fortunate, managed to get ashore, and was
seen no more. The *Colossus* put to sea, and many months passed
before Nigel saw the green pastures of England again. He found
life on the *Colossus* more tolerable. Though the crew was larger,
there was a compensating increase in space. Moreover she was
a renowned fighting ship with the aura of The Nile still on her
brows; well-officered, well-manned. There was no Lieutenant
Pink Kirby to be a perpetual thorn in the flesh to Nigel or
Piers. With a resignation born of necessity they adapted themselves to the routine of a British ship of the line. Nigel found
each fresh experience of interest. A believer in education he
automatically availed himself of each new source of knowledge.
He grew to know the long heavy swell of the Bay of Biscay;
watched while the *Colossus*, under reefed topsails, rode out an
Atlantic gale; saw the famous peak of the Rock of Gibraltar
cutting a sky of rarest blue; gazed for the first time upon Africa;
mused upon the Pillars of Hercules. He found much time for
meditation. Sometimes he dwelt lingeringly on the pleasure
of the past; at other times he tried to pierce the veil of the future.
Above all he endeavoured to find some definite pattern in life.
He could not regard life, somehow, as a haphazard affair.
Somewhere in it there must be some scheme, some plan, if
only it could be found. He felt that the truest form of worship
was a diligent searching after that plan, coupled with a willingness
to comply with its demands as they became plain. It was
sufficiently intricate for his cultured and cultivated mind. One
day, while looking at a group of seamen who listened open-

mouthed to a narrator expatiating on the night charms of Casablanca, it struck Nigel that these men did not appear to be unduly concerning themselves with the problem of the universe. Were they, perhaps, by accepting life as they found it, falling in with some scheme? He wondered if they had immortal souls. And if so, why? He could not picture them deriving delight in a celestial existence. They were different from him. Vastly different. Intellectually he was their superior. As fighting seamen they were immeasurably better than he. England was at war. Therefore a sturdy man who could wield a cutlass or fire an eighteen-pounder was a greater asset to his country than a student who possessed a Bachelor of Arts' degree and indulged in a taste for metaphysics. Life, he decided for the thousandth time, was undoubtedly involved. One had to pay for one's culture.

Then his mind turned to his thesis, and he mourned once again that he had not completed it. His Master of Arts degree would not benefit him now. It might never do so. But there was something irritating about not being able to complete the task to which one had set one's hand.

Mostly his mind dwelt on Bronwen. He would concentrate on her until the mental images became so vivid that it was hard to realize that the presence which seemed to be so near to him was but the product of his imagination. He wondered just how powerful and effective was the power of thought. Whether it was possible for his thoughts of her to be transmitted to her brain. He trusted so. There were times when she seemed so near to him that he felt convinced that she must be thinking of him with as great intensity as he thought of her. Never before had he encountered anyone whose mental outlook so nearly coincided with his own. It was as though he had found a precious treasure —only to have to relinquish it. There were times when he almost regretted having met her, so acutely did he miss her. And then he thought how barren life would have been if he had not known her. Their minds were wedded. Her mind was rare, indeed. And, to make everything perfect, so was her physical attraction. It was perhaps, typical of Nigel that he put the mind first. Hour after hour during the hot stillness of the Mediterranean night Nigel would meditate thus as he stood on deck under the stars, looking sometimes at the tracery of the rigging and sails; at other times at the line of two-deckers stretching ahead, inexorably pursuing their blockade night and day. Sometimes Piers would join him. His meditation was ever the same. "I wonder what's happened to Puah?" More than once Nigel, at his request, penned letters to Puah, addressed them to Beaumaris, and had them sent to the mail-packet. But there was no means of ascertaining whether they ever reached their destination. They could only wait—and hope.

The following spring the *Colossus* dropped anchor at Plymouth again. Piers promptly deserted. Nigel, he knew not why, would not accompany him. Perhaps it was his pride which prevented him. He could not visualize himself as a fugitive for the rest of his days.

He looked older. He was bronzed and in fine physical condition, but given to introspection. Remembering his success at sketching in the *Unique* he bribed his messmates into leaving him alone by a generous distribution of their portraits. It pleased them. They decided he was not a bad sort but weak in the head. Nigel found increasing solace in his leather-bound Horace. Had it been lost he might almost have recited the odes from memory so often had he read them. They were a perennial joy.

He was sitting on a grassy bank overlooking the Sound one sunny afternoon when a longshoreman approached.

"I say, mate, there's a pretty little bit o' goods across yonder as wants a word with yer."

Nigel raised his eyes from his book. "Tell her to go to hell," he said curtly. "And you have my permission to accompany her." He resumed his reading. The longshoreman, discouraged by the eyes as much as the tone, withdrew. It was not long before he was back again.

"See here, mate, no offence now, but that there young woman is mighty pressing. Says I was to tell you she was pure."

"I am gratified, though sceptical!" Nigel was more succinct than ever. He discouraged further conversation and his eyes returned to the page. Suddenly the book was closed with a snap which startled the longshoreman like a pistol shot. Nigel leaped to his feet and the man drew hastily back.

"No offence, mate——" he began, but Nigel had brushed him aside. He almost ran in the direction indicated. He saw a trim, familiar figure, dark eyes which brimmed with welcome.

"Puah!" he cried. "My dear girl. Is it really you?"

"Oh, Nigel," Puah was smiling, smiling through tears. Nigel caught her by the shoulders and looked into her face. She looked up with a shy smile, longingly, wonderingly.

She saw his eyes dilate. They were piercing. Intense. His face grew grim.

"Nigel!" she cried almost in alarm. "What is it?"

He touched a little white scar which ran from the corner of her lip to her chin.

"That!" His word was clipped.

"Oh, yes, it disfigures me. I'm so sorry. . . ."

"Puah! Don't! Don't talk like that. Disfigures you? Transfigures you! It makes you dearer than ever because you suffered so cruelly. It was the thought of what that devil did; how he struck you, that stirred me. I shall revere that scar to the end of my days. It shall be to me something sacred, something precious. You shall never regard it as a disfiguration. Never."

She smiled, a happy little smile. "Then I shall not mind it any more, if you feel like that, Nigel. I thought you would consider that it spoilt my beauty, and I was almost afraid to see you."

"How little you know me. But Puah, how came you here?"

"You could not come to me, so I came to you. I thought you might like to see someone from Beaumaris."

"But how did you know I was here?"

She looked about her. "Piers told me, of course."

"He's been home? How did he get home?"

"Yes, he's been home. By night, of course. Madoc Morris came back long since and told us all the news. And I had a letter from you. And we have had the smugglers watching for the ship to return, and Madoc was waiting in South Wales with a cutter to cross to Ilfracombe. And we came across the moors on ponies by a bridle-track the smugglers use. And—here I am."

"You are good, Puah."

"Do you think it good of me to come to see you, Nigel?"

"Indeed I do."

"I had no idea that being good was so easy—or so nice."

Nigel permitted himself to smile. It was many months since he smiled. He only just realized it. They sat down on the grassy bank, hand in hand like two children, oblivious of the eyes of the longshoreman who watched them surreptitiously for a while and then shuffled away. They talked. There seemed so much to talk about. First, of course, Nigel must learn how the *Four Winds* got back to port. And Puah told him how Tom had brought her round, and bandaged her wounded face, and helped her to the bunk before he set about cutting away the wreckage of the wrecked mainsail. And how he had finally got the ketch in sailing order and steered her for Beaumaris, Puah joining him at the tiller as soon as she felt strong enough to stand. She had been ill for a while, she confessed for the first time in her life.

She did not like being ill. She thought it was the upset as much as anything, especially not knowing what had happened.

"I know," Nigel assured her. "I always feel that I can endure anything except not knowing."

She told him that a new schoolmaster had been appointed. She said that Lieutenant Kirby had been brought to the Vaughan's home, pale and ill and without an arm. "Serve him right," she added vindictively. "I kept out of the way while he was about. I hope when he was shot it hurt him as much as his blow hurt me."

Then she saw the expression on Nigel's face and became all contrition. "Oh, what a little beast I am, Nigel. I have upset you. I should not have brought it back to your mind. I am a fool. I won't mention that devil again. Let's forget him. Nigel, let's talk of something nice."

She looked about her quickly, her dark eyes bright like those of an excited child. "Shall I tell you a secret?"

"Rather. It's tantalizing not being allowed to participate in a secret."

"Well, you know that Piers has plenty of gold hidden away in various places?"

"So he has assured me."

"Now that he has deserted from the Royal Navy there can be no going back to a district where he is known—at least, not till it's blown over—so we have left Beaumaris, and we have bought a cottage in Gower."

"In Gower?"

"Yes, where Worms Head is. It's near Swansea if you want a port, but Gower itself is a lovely secret place, full of sandy coves and rocky headlands where there are caves. We smugglers know it well. There's a toll-road down the middle of the peninsula and everybody to the north is Welsh and everybody to the south is English, and they say that a person on one side of the road does not know what a person on the other says."

"Just the place for keeping a secret, Puah!"

"Piers has bought the cottage. It is only a little place but it has a field or two, and is quite near the shore. And we have furnished it. And. . . ."

"Well, Puah. I can see you are anxious to tell me something more?"

"It's all ready and waiting for—you." She dropped her voice impressively.

"For me?"

"Yes. It is all arranged. There is a house down the road where, if you go in, they will show you to a room in the back. There is a complete change of clothes there for you. As soon as it is dark a man with a horse and wagon will call and you will get in with some goods he will load. And he will bring you out into the country where Piers and I will be waiting with the horses and then—off we go to our little home and those cruel wretches in the Navy will never flog you again."

Nigel took a deep breath. "But, Puah! It is so good of you but really I could not."

"Don't be such a fool, Nigel."

"I can't desert."

"Of course you can. Piers did."

"Yes, but Piers is——"

"Not so high and mighty as you. No, he's not, and I'm glad of it. He's got common sense. He knows that his sister means more to him than a silly king he has never seen. They never asked you to go to the war. They took you—took you brutally. You don't owe them anything. Get out of it while you can."

"Puah, there is much in what you say. But before I was allowed on shore I gave my word that I would rejoin the ship."

"And just because of that you will go back. Go back when we have been to all this trouble to save you?"

"I must, Puah. It is a point of honour."

"Oh, Nigel, Nigel." He saw that she was crying and tried to comfort her.

"Leave me alone! You don't care for me. You will go away and I shall never see you again. There'll be a big battle with the French and you will be killed. I know you will. Oh, you are a fool, and I'm so fond of you, and I shined all the brasses, and I have scrubbed the table till my arms ached, and I've polished the oak settle, and the little garden is looking so nice with gillyflowers and Sweet Williams and London Pride, and—and you'll never set eyes on it after all my trouble."

Nigel stared moodily out across the water. "I don't mind how much I hurt myself," he said slowly, "but I grieve to hurt you."

"Well, you are hurting me, and that's telling you plain. Come on, Nigel."

He shook his head. "I will tell you what I will do. I will see the captain and ask his leave to come with you to visit the place."

"That's not good enough. You must stay. We'll be so happy. You and me and Piers."

"It sounds ideal. Listen, Puah. I have been told that the ship will be paid-off at the end of the next cruise, and then I shall be free to come with an easy conscience. Free to come, and free to stay."

"You will be killed," she said sullenly. "I know you will."

"Don't think of such a thing. Meet me here to-morrow afternoon, and I shall, in the meantime, ask the captain's leave, and then I'll join you and we'll go and see this wonderful little cottage in Gower."

"He won't give you leave. Mark my words."

"Of course he will. I am in his good books."

"He won't. He will refuse."

"He will certainly give his consent."

"What if he doesn't?"

"If he doesn't Puah, I wil allow myself to be tempted after all!"

"You mean if he doesn't give you leave, you will desert?"

"Yes, Puah. I will."

"Promise?"

"Doesn't my word suffice?"

"Yes it does, Nigel. You need not promise. Oh, I hope now that the fool refuses."

It was with reluctance that Nigel finally went to the boat which was to bear him back to the two-decker riding at anchor in stately majesty in mid-stream.

He was alone on deck that night, but unlike other nights on watch, it was not spent in idle speculation. He was elated, more excited than he had been for many a month. Life had ceased to be something to be endured and had become something to be enjoyed. So much can be achieved by the presence, the physical nearness, of a slip of a girl.

Thoughts raced through his brain. He wondered how Bronwen was. He had wanted to ask Puah, but a sense of delicacy prevented him. It would have hurt Puah's feelings; provoked an outburst. He knew that. And he would never hurt Puah if he could help it. What a dear child she was! How solicitous for his well-being.

She was at the rendezvous when he went ashore the next day. He saw her in the distance as she walked to meet him. How well she walked. Straight and easy and lissom. She radiated health and spirits.

"Well, Nigel?" she greeted him. "He refused, of course?" Now you can desert!"

"Not at all, Puah. There was no difficulty. I can come to see your cottage. I have obtained my leave."

"Damn!" said Puah.

CHAPTER XXV

T H E blessed relief of freedom! Nigel was tempted to break his word and never return to the cramped confines of a line-of-battle now that he had felt the turf beneath his feet and the gorse-scented breeze of the uplands in his face. It had been good to be with Puah again after so many months of the companionship of men. The overland route across Devon by moor tracks known to the smugglers had been a time of delight. The sturdy ponies bore Piers and Puah and Nigel at a pace which, if slow, was dogged. Nigel did not care about speed. He was happy. He was free. The larks sang in the sky. He was in England. They found a cutter awaiting them in a cove, and when the wind set fair they beat their way across the Bristol Channel to where the shores of Wales showed green against the northern sky. Nigel did not talk much. The thoughts which hurried tumultuously through his mind never reached his lips. But he was well content. Puah said little. She, too, seemed well content. Piers was reserved but, unlike the other two, he was morose. He seemed to be changing somewhat; no longer the reckless, carefree young man who climbed for seagulls' eggs on the rocks of Puffin Island. Perhaps it was only natural that a man who had endured the hardship of tempest and battle should mature, yet he seemed much older than his years. He brightened somewhat when the cutter dropped anchor close inland in a sandy bay about which the high, green-crested cliffs rose as though to shelter it from prying eyes. Through a gully a path rose precipitously to wind across a sloping meadow which appeared invitingly between the cliffs.

"You cannot quite see the cottage from here," Puah explained, "It is hidden by that tiny copse, but we can look through this gap and see the blue ocean from the end of the garden."

They were rowed ashore and made their way up the path, Piers carrying the kit-bag which contained Nigel's scanty possessions. It savoured of a home coming. Puah appeared to think so. Her eyes were bright, and it was something more than the steepness of the cliff which had flushed her cheeks. "Look!" She pointed. Through a gap in the trees Nigel could see the white-washed walls of a cottage, a squat chimney rising from the thatch. Puah glowed with the pride of possession. Nigel strode ahead and swung open the small, green-painted, wicket gate which led to the path and Puah passed in. Piers was nowhere to be seen. For some reason he had lagged behind. Puah fumbled beneath a large round stone and produced a heavy key which she inserted in the lock. There was a click, and she flung back the door. She looked almost shy as she glanced back at Nigel.

"Welcome—home, Nigel."

He stepped inside and looked about him. The little room was spotless. A ray of sunshine percolating through the chintz curtains which flanked the small square window danced on the polished brass and oak. Puah was standing demurely in the centre of the room. It never occurred to Nigel that she was waiting to be kissed. Somehow he felt that she was expecting something so he praised her handiwork. complimenting her with a fulsomeness which was almost alien to his style of talk.

"Thank you, Nigel, I hope you will be happy here during your—your brief holiday. Sit down. I will get some tea."

Nigel sat down. It was a comfortable chair, not unlike the chair with the high back and wings which had so often received him in Mrs. Evans' parlour. He felt the pressure of a book in his pocket. He drew out the Horace. How tattered and worn it had become. But all the more prized on that account. He opened it, and glanced at an ode. He could hear Puah in the kitchen. She seemed to be lighting a fire. Nigel's conscience smote him and he threw the book on the little round table with the pink-checkered table-cloth and strode to the door. Fancy his sitting idle while that dear child waited on him.

"Let me help you, Puah."

"It's all right, Nigel, I'm better at this than you are. You don't have to light fires on board a ship, do you? Pass the bellows. Now, if you really want to make yourself useful, take the kettle and fill it from the spring. You will see the path leading from the back door just across the field."

It was a pleasant meal. Piers had been across to a neighbour's and came in with milk and butter and eggs and a home-made loaf. Nigel thought he would never stop eating. Fare aboard ship was something to keep life in one's body, not ambrosia which fed, also, the spirit of man.

Piers filled his pipe and strolled out to the cliffs. Puah cleared the table. Nigel moved restlessly. Just to sit back and enjoy life seemed too wonderful to be true. He felt that he ought to be doing something.

When Puah had washed up, she took off her apron and walked into the room where Nigel sat. She had a letter in her hands, a somewhat imposing-looking letter, Nigel thought. She placed it on the table close to his elbow and said in a manner which was unusually restrained: "The last time Madoc was at Beaumaris he called at your old rooms and Mrs. Evans gave him this."

"I wonder who could be writing to me!" Nigel turned the missive curiously in his hands. Its fold was secured by a large green seal on which was embossed a crest which was familiar indeed to him.

"It's from the University," he cried. Puah was studying the garden from the window.

"Is it, Nigel?"

"Yes. I wonder why they are writing to me."

"Why don't you open it, Nigel, then you could find out."

He laughed. "You always were practical, Puah." He broke the seal and read. He read slowly. He re-read uncomprehendingly. Then he sat back and the letter hung almost listlessly from his fingers. He lay back in his chair with his eyes closed. He was so still that Puah turned quickly, a look almost of alarm in her eyes.

"Nigel," she said sharply. "What is it? Is it bad news?"

"Eh? Bad news? No, not bad news. News that's so good that I feel almost stunned."

"And you are glad?"

"Glad? It's incomprehensible. I'm so glad that as yet I am incapable of any emotion but bewilderment."

"What does it say, Nigel?"

"Ah, of course, you don't know what I'm talking about. Here, read it for yourself."

"I'd rather you told me, Nigel. I'm not good at reading— much."

"It's from the Dean and he informs me that the degree of Master of Arts has been conferred upon me. He compliments me on serving my country and trusts that I shall be spared to return to the University which is proud to honour me, and that when the war is over I can attend in person to receive my hood. My thesis, he says, was an outstanding contribution. But how the devil did he get it, Puah? I never finished copying it. Many a time when I was at sea I used to wonder what had happened to it. Not that a degree is likely to be of use to me now."

"Then it doesn't please you, if it is no use?"

"Of course it pleases me, Puah. I hardly know what I am saying. It means more to me than people have any idea. It means that my life ambition has come true."

"I'm glad, Nigel."

"Thank you, Puah. I—I will take a walk along the cliffs I think. It may clear my brain. I'm still bewildered."

"Yes, Nigel." Her head was bent. He crossed to the door, bowing his head because of the lowness of the lintel.

"Nigel!" she called after him, a trifle anxiously, "You are quite sure you are pleased?"

"Pleased? I could sing for joy. I feel that I ought to thank somebody but don't know whom to thank."

Nigel walked on air. A dream of his life had come true. He could see himself, an honoured veteran of the war, obtaining a position of consequence. He could see printed on the fly-leaf of some book which he had written.

"Nigel Preece, A.M. (Oxon)"

It still savoured of the miraculous. More than once he drew the letter from his pocket as though for confirmation: as though he feared that it was only a phantasy of an excited imagination. But the letter was real, in very truth.

He saw Piers and hailed him.

"Give me your hand, Piers. Congratulate me, my lad. I have my Master of Arts degree. It's here, here, as large as life."

"Lord, man, how excited you get about a degree. I'd sooner have a good drink."

"This is drink to my soul, lad. The nectar of the gods."

"Well, I'm glad that it brings you happiness. Now the next thing is to get away from the damned Service and set up on your own. See here, Nigel, have done with this nonsense of going back."

"I gave my word."

"Well, so did I. They weren't so particular when they carried us off against our will. Why should we be?"

"I'm not built that way, Piers."

"Hell! It's a marvel to me that I like you, Nigel, for you're the most awkward devil to deal with that I've ever met. Yet somehow I do. That's why I've bought the cottage for you."

"For me?"

"For you and Puah. It's not much but it's a start."

"I don't quite understand, Piers."

"You are going to marry Puah, aren't you?"

"Marry her? Such a thought never entered my head."

"Then it's damn well time it did. What's the matter with her? Isn't she good enough for you?"

"Good enough? Of course she is. I think the world of her."

"Then why the devil don't you marry her? You can see the kid's in love with you. Hell, man, she dotes on you so much that I'm fair jealous at times, even though she is only my sister."

"You distress me, Piers. I—I am so fond of Puah, as a friend, that there is little I would not do for her happiness."

"Rot. You have a chance to make her happy and you don't take it."

"But, my dear fellow, one cannot make love to order. To marry it is necessary to love."

"Not necessary."

"Then, let us say, customary. If I were free I should feel honoured at the suggestion."

"So you damn well ought to be. I think a lot of Puah and believe me, I wouldn't go throwing her at any fellow's head. Let's get this settled once and for all, Nigel. Are you going to marry Puah?"

"No."

"Why not?"

"I am not free to do so."

"You mean you are married?"

"No."

"Betrothed?"

Nigel was silent. It was a difficult question to answer. In his heart he was pledged to Bronwen; unalterably pledged. But it was not formal. It was not recognized. Piers seemed to read what was passing in his mind. "You are not still hankering after that Bronwen Vaughan are you?"

"I thought I had already explained the situation to you, Piers. Many months ago at Beaumaris when I asked you to lend me some money."

"But hell, that was months ago. You've got over it by now, surely?"

"I have not got over it, to use your expression. I am pledged to Bronwen and nothing will make me change. I must wait until I am in a position to marry her."

"Ay," said Piers darkly, "but supposing she is not willing to wait? Women like to wed and they don't like waiting too long. They're made different from us men from what I can make out."

"Bronwen will wait for me. I know it."

"I'm not so sure."

There was an awkward silence, and then Piers said. "Well, you may as well make the most of your holiday. Go and talk

to Puah. But if you break her heart I'll break your neck. . . .
You don't think her good enough for you, that's what it is.
You're so damned high and mighty, Nigel. And when I think
of all the poor kid did to get you that cursed degree that you set
such store on. . . ."

"Get me my degree?"

"Didn't she tell you? That's like Puah! She found the papers
in a cupboard in your room and tried to copy them out. But she
could not manage it. Do you know what she did? Went all the
way to Oxford—footed it part of the way until she could get
a coach—carrying your papers. And saw the big man at the
University. I don't know what you call him. And told him everything. I'll say this. He was a gentleman. Treated her like a lady
and told her she could leave everything to him. Well, Puah
got you what you wanted, and you don't think her good enough
for you. Hell!"

Nigel barely heard him. He had turned towards the house.
He walked fast. He broke into a run.

Puah was in the chair, listless. She did not glance up when he
came in. Nigel dropped on his knees at her feet. "Puah, Puah!
What a blind fool I have been. Piers has just told me what you
did. Oh, my dear, how can I thank you, for making that journey?"

She turned her head away. "I knew that your treaty meant
a lot to you, Nigel, and I tried so hard to copy it. I sat up at
night, but the big words were too hard. I did not know what
they meant. I—I'm not clever like you. So I just took it there
and—and told them all."

"My dear. You are crying."

"I'm *not* crying! I'm *not!* Oh, I'm a fool, Nigel. I *am* crying,
and I can't help myself. It's because I'm so happy, I think.
Happy that I have been able to do something for you. Something
that gives you pleasure and makes you happy. I don't often cry,
Nigel, but don't be cross with me because it's been such a long
time waiting for you, and I thought you might be killed at sea,
and that I should never see you again."

Her head went of its own accord against his shoulder. He
put his arm tenderly about the slender shoulders which were
shaken by sobs.

"Puah! My dear! What can I do to make you happy?"

The only response was a sob. Nigel was silent. He knew how
he could make her happy; he knew that he could not make her
happy. Truly life was involved.

CHAPTER XXVI

THE days began to slip away quickly. It was pleasant at the cottage. Fine weather added to their joys. It was good to be among the bracken. It was good to bathe from the sandy cove. It was good to have wholesome food in abundance. It was good to fetch drift wood from the shore, or dead boughs from the woods, and chop them into kindling for the kitchen fire. Everything seemed good. And yet across the content there fell a shadow, the shadow of a past remembered, the shadow of a future unknown. At times Nigel would stand bareheaded in the sunshine with the sea breeze blowing through his hair, and stare out to the far-off line where sky and sea were one. At times there was shipping to watch, a barque outward bound with ore from Swansea, an East-Indiaman beating up channel towards the port of Cardiff, topsail schooners engaged in the coasting trade. But often enough there was nothing to see but the gulls which wheeled above the cliffs. Nigel saw them not for his eyes were full of images. He beheld on the screen of his mind a disused quarry in a greenwood. Or it might be a ruined keep. And he recalled the tryst which once he kept there, and the gold he buried. He wondered whether it was still there or whether Bronwen had been forced to have recourse to it. At other times he would live over again the hectic night at the squire's house. He was sorry that he had dropped his pistol in the skirmish. Still, Puah had salvaged his other belongings. They were all there in his room in the cottage. She had even obtained shelves for his books. Everything had been arranged waiting for his arrival. There was even a posy of flowers in a vase on the table in his room.

These evidences of her care for him touched him, stirred him deeply. He almost wished that she would not do these things. It placed him so irrevocably in her debt. She did so much for him; he could do so little for her, because Bronwen was for ever in his mind. He would stand day-dreaming, wondering where she was, wondering how he could find out, wondering how he could let her know that he was alive. He had hesitated to write to her lest her father should intercept the letter. He began to toy with the idea. It was worth the risk. But suppose she was no longer there! He wished he knew.

And Puah, watching from behind the chintz curtains, would

remain motionless until his thoughts came back to earth. Then she would bustle about the house when he moved towards the door, and she would keep her face averted lest he should ask her why she felt sad.

Piers was restless; more restless than usual. He had found some men among the local fishermen whom he had met on smuggling excursions and he frequently consorted with them. Nigel wondered whether Piers was embarking on fresh adventures or whether he deliberately absented himself in order that Nigel and Puah might be thrown more together. Sometimes they rambled the cliffs; they rarely stayed in the house. They were outdoor folk. They liked the feel of the cropped turf beneath their feet, the breeze on their cheeks, the sight of the gulls, and rooks cawing above the elms, or rabbits scurrying under the gorse. Puah pointed out some of the smugglers' haunts—for Gower had its smugglers—and named some of the caves. Culver Hole was one. Nigel remembered it long after. It was one of those names which stuck in the memory. He wished he could talk more to Puah. Often he tried but his mind and hers followed different paths. If only it had been Bronwen. . . ! The thought came to him so often that he reproached himself. One day he tackled Piers.

"Do you ever go to Beaumaris, Piers?"

"I have been there, and I shall go again some day I suppose. I can always get about safely after dark. I know the ropes. But I'm not courting trouble—not at the moment. Why? What do you want? Something fetched? I could arrange for that."

"Nothing fetched, thank you, Piers. Just some information."

"What sort?"

"I should like to know what has happened to Miss Vaughan."

"Damn! I thought you were forgetting about her. Why can't you put her out of your head?"

"She refuses to be put out. I may never see her again, but it would be a relief to me to know that she was safe. That she was well. If possible, that she was happy."

"What do you mean; that you will never see her again?"

"It hardly looks as though it were possible, does it, Piers? Let's look facts in the face."

"I'm damn glad to hear you talk like that. Well, let's look facts in the face. Is it only this woman who stands between you and Puah? Would you marry Puah if it were not for her?"

"I do not love Puah; not in that sense, Piers, but if it were not for Bronwen, I—I am inclined to think that the least I could do would be to ask Puah to become my wife. She has been so good to me."

Piers fumbled for his pipe, and began to fill the bowl with deliberation. "Nigel," he said. "Nigel, there's something I want to say." He paused, and concentrated on his pipe. He pressed the tobacco in so firmly and persistently that Nigel, watching, decided that the pipe could never possibly draw.

"Well, Piers, what is it?"

"Don't quite know how to begin. I never told you, Nigel, but there's been queer things happening in Beaumaris since we went away."

"Queer things?"

"Ay! Folks say—mind you, I don't know myself, I'm only telling you what a fellow told me. He said that Bronwen Vaughan had made it up with that naval officer from the corvette, and that either they was married or were about to be."

"What!" Nigel started back in amazement. "What? Marry Kirby! Bronwen would die first. I know her father wishes it, but she hates him like poison. Marry Kirby? Make it up with Kirby?" He laughed harshly. "You don't know Bronwen, Piers."

"Kirby?" Piers looked up sharply. "Who said anything about Kirby? I never mentioned his name. Never thought of him. No, it's the other fellow I'm thinking of. It's him; so I'm told."

"What? Lieutenant Moir?"

"Ay. That's the name. Better sort of chap, now, isn't he?"

"Yes. Moir is a better sort." Nigel began to pace restlessly. "Piers. I wish you could be more definite. If—if what you say is true—! But I can't believe it. Bronwen is the sort of girl who would stay true as long as life would last."

"That's just it, Nigel! Suppose she was told as you were dead? That might alter her views, now, mightn't it?"

"Yes, Piers. I had not thought of that. I wish I could be certain."

"See here, Nigel. I'll do something for you. I'll go to Beaumaris and find out for certain. If it will set your mind at rest."

"You are a good fellow, Piers. Yes, it would set my mind at rest. If she is married, well, that's the end of it. I shall just keep out of her way and let her think me dead. Keep away from Beaumaris—and try to forget."

"I'll start right away, Nigel," said Piers, looking out to sea. "I know a fellow who will lend me a cutter. If this wind holds. . . ."

It will take me all my time if I am to bring the news before your leave is up."

"You are a good fellow, Piers."

"Rot. I want to see you happy. Well, I'll get started right away. You and Puah will be all right."

"Piers! I can't stay at the cottage if you are not there."

"Lord. What does it matter? Go and sleep at the farm if it makes you happier."

He walked briskly in the direction of the cove.

* * * * *

The shadow of Nigel's departure fell across every walk and every conversation. Rarely was any mention made of it but both Puah and Nigel were conscious of it creeping softly but sombrely nearer and nearer. How could it be otherwise? Nigel was beset by restlessness. He had imagined that, given a quiet place in the country with his books about him, he would have settled to undisturbed study. Each day he resorted to the table which Puah had prepared for him. On it were his favourite books, his pen and paper, but though he toyed with one idea and another, nothing came of it. The urge to write was not with him; nor, for that matter, was the urge to read. He wondered how one got into the mood for writing. What produced the afflatus? How could one coax the muse? What was the stimulus called for by nature to produce the children of a man's brain? He knew this, that unless one had peace of mind, good, solid, worthy work was all but impossible. And Nigel had no peace of mind. Constantly he gazed up at the sky, reading the direction of the wind. Wondering how it was with Piers. One day he started a letter to Bronwen but he tore it up. What use writing until he *knew!*

The sudden disappearance of her brother perplexed Puah, though it did not cause her concern. She was too accustomed to Piers' coming and going. You could no more chain him down than you could the wind.

"Still, I wonder what made him go off back to Beaumaris like that," she remarked thoughtfully. "He's up to something. There was a time when Piers and I shared everything. But he's different now. He's never been quite the same since he went off in that warship. What did you do to him, Nigel?"

"You mustn't blame me, Puah!"

"No, I don't blame you, Nigel. I was teasing; that was all. I wonder what took him to Beaumaris."

Nigel did not enlighten her. It was a subject which experience had shown him was best left alone. As he lay reading on the turf one sunny morning, a shout from Puah caused him to glance up. Coming up the steep path from the cove was Piers. Nigel rose and went to greet him. Piers was uncommunicative. After he had eaten, he lit his pipe and walked into the meadow. Nigel followed.

"Well, Piers?"

"Can you stand a shock?"

"I can stand anything except not knowing. I have told you that before."

"Well, it is right enough. She is married."

"Bronwen married!" The words reached Nigel's ears but his mind refused to accept them. They persisted in echoing but they were not convincing. What were words? Mere sounds. They meant nothing. Bronwen married? The very idea was farcical. He was conscious of Piers speaking. His voice seemed indistinct, as though he were a long way off.

"She thought you were dead. She still thinks you were killed in action at sea."

Of course, reasoned Nigel. It would make all the difference. After all it was the only sensible thing to do. He hoped that she would be happy. She would escape from her father and that fatuous fool of a brother, and have a home of her own. Babies perhaps. Yes, he hoped that she would be happy. He was not hurt. Not exactly hurt. After all he could not be much more lonely than he had been for many months, now. He had grown used to being without her, but somehow he always felt that she was with him in spirit. And now that could not be. At least it did not appear feasible. Not logical. Not that anything was logical.

"I think I'll just take a stroll along the cliffs, Piers. I—I would like to be alone with my thoughts for a while."

"All right, Nigel. Only don't go doing anything silly. It's been a bit of a blow for you, I dare say, though it looks to me as if it was all for the best. You and she would not have got on together for long, not to my way of thinking. Well, if you're lonely, you know that there's a home here for you, and—Puah. You'd go a long way to find a better lass than Puah."

"I know, Piers!" Nigel sighed. "Puah has been very good to me. Goodness itself. I am grateful."

He moved away. He walked along the grassy path which cut diagonally across the meadow. He looked down at the wild flowers in the grass. They seemed close at hand and yet he felt as though he floated through space. His mind was disconnected. He wanted to think sensibly, clearly, but all the while his thoughts were confused. He wished to collect them all together in a heap so that he could grasp them: have something solid on to which he could hold. Bronwen was married!

She had been married for some time. She must have been married when he was dreaming about her; conscious of her presence so close to him that she seemed always with him in spirit. He knew now that it was but the product of his imagination. She would have no thought for him now, save remembrance. Thoughts of a lover killed at sea! He wondered if, in the midst of her happiness, she felt overcome with sadness as she recalled the past, remembering that moment near the ruined keep when they looked into one another's eyes and felt that a bond existed between them that not even death could shatter.

And now it was severed. It all seemed unreal. Nigel felt resentful. Why had he been so convinced that he and Bronwen were meant for each other? That they were natural affinities, destined from birth, so it seemed, to be mated? Surely the encounter had not been arranged as a mockery? The very thought was abhorrent. There must be something finer, grander, nobler in life than that. Man's sensitive perceptions were given to enable him to climb higher, to aspire to greater achievements, not as something to be deliberately lacerated, wounded . . . killed! No, his feelings had not been killed. He wished they had been. Stunned, perhaps, but still alive. When the numbness departed they would probably hurt more. . . .

The main thing was—what was he to do? Rejoin his ship, of course. Perhaps he would be killed in action—in very truth, the next time. That would solve a good many difficulties. But people who wanted to get killed did not get killed. It was usually those who desired most earnestly to live; those who had something to live for.

Perhaps Piers was right after all. The best thing he could do would be to marry Puah. He was fond of her, Certainly he could never be happy with anyone else. He could not imagine himself becoming even friendly with another woman. If he followed his own inclinations he would turn recluse, and spend his life dwelling with his thoughts of the past. They, at least, were more real than reality. And these things having happened, could not be undone. They were part of his life. Woven into the very woof and the warp of the fabric of his being. He did not regret having known Bronwen. He gloried in it. Fate could not deprive him of memory. What had been, had been. It could not be undone.

And Puah? Would she make him happy? He supposed so. Would he make her happy? He would do his best. What a dear girl she was. So easily satisfied. He seemed to give her so little yet she was content just to have him near her. He wished he could give her more. He must try. He had never really tried. Always he had been true to Bronwen, even in his thoughts. But there was no need for that, now. The great thing was that Puah must never suspect that he did not love her. He must try to make himself love her. Could one do that? At least one could try.

He made his way sadly towards the cottage. Twilight was settling over the land. The rhythmical breaking of the waves in the cove came not unmelodiously to his ears. He liked to be within sound of the sea. A thrush was singing, repeating each assertion, as though intent on making himself thoroughly understood. Was it a love song? Nigel wondered. A faint curl of smoke rose lazily from the cottage chimney. There was a yellow glow from the window. Puah had lighted the candles. She was waiting at the wicket gate. Waiting for him. He thought she seemed anxious. He forced a smile. He paused, looked long and earnestly into the deep brown eyes upturned to his. With something akin to a sob he bent suddenly and kissed her.

CHAPTER XXVII

THERE was no time to spare. This was impressed upon Nigel
and Puah when they walked across the fields to the little church
at Oxwych which stood, like an ecclesiastical Canute, forbidding
the tide to encroach—and with little more success. The Vicar
looked grave. These matters could not be rushed. There were
stipulations, conditions. How long had they resided in the parish?
What of the banns? Special licence? Nigel grew dismayed. The
mere thought of marriage terrified him and he had not expected
to encounter obstacles in a path which should have been made
smooth and easy. A man should be encouraged, he felt, not called
upon to face additional worries and unexpected burdens. For
a brief moment a faint hope leaped within his heart. If time were
so short perhaps the affair might be postponed. He would marry
Puah when next his ship returned to port. That might give him
a year's respite! Somewhat timidly he suggested that the marriage
be left over. Puah's mouth was set in a firm line; her eyes were
bright. Looking down at her Nigel thought that she had never
appeared so beautiful. He was vaguely surprised. None of the
books over which he had pored had informed him that a woman
looks her best when she is loved.

"I am not going to have my wedding spoilt by a lot of silly
rules," complained Puah. "I don't care where I am married so
long as I am married. Do you?"

Nigel lacked her enthusiasm but he made a tactful reply.

"There's a Methody preacher over at Horton, Nigel. Let's
get him to marry us. They won't be so fussy. You wouldn't mind
being married in a dissenters' place of worship would you?"

"I am afraid it is a matter I have never deliberated." Nigel
was inclined to be docile. He was on unfamiliar ground, uneasy,
apprehensive. He was content to leave all the arrangements to Puah. And Puah was equally content to take charge.
She seemed in her element. The Methodist minister was found.
Arrangements for a wedding breakfast made. A few neighbours
came to Puah's assistance, the women folk glad of the excitement
to break the monotony of their rural lives. Puah appeared in
new gowns; stylish, well-cut gowns, of a rich quality which
even Nigel could recognize.

Piers, it seemed, had been in the habit of bringing his sister
choice lengths of silk from France. Lace, too. Piers kept in the

background, but he had told Nigel that he was looking out for a house for them and intended to purchase it as a wedding present. He had his eye on one at the Mumbles—a well-built, double-fronted house which faced the bay. A building of some dignity worthy of the scholar who was to inhabit it. For the first time Nigel began to take interest in the proceedings. Perhaps, after all, it might be worth while getting married. If he was to have a house of his own, a spacious house, he would be able to have a study, something for which he had longed all his life! A study lined with books, and a table in the window where he could write in summer, or a cosy fireplace before which he could read in winter. Assuredly there might be something to be said for matrimony, after all. It did not occur to him that, so far, he had forgotten to spare a thought for the bride.

To his surprise Puah seemed comparatively indifferent about the new house. "The cottage will do nicely until you come back from sea, Nigel," she said. "Though some day we will have to move to a bigger place. There won't be room to bring up a family in that little place."

A family! This, assuredly, was something which had not occurred to Nigel. He walked out into the meadows and stood staring out to sea. It all seemed so unreal, unnatural. He supposed that it was normal and natural to get married. So many people did. And there was usually laughter and good wishes, also silly customs which he devoutly trusted he would succeed in avoiding. The whole thing seemed farcical. Yet he had not always thought of marriage as being farcical. The truth was that he was not marrying Puah. In his heart he knew that. There was only one marriage for him and that had taken place when he and Bronwen had looked into each other's eyes when they stood amid the green tranquillity of the ruined keep and there had plighted troth. He felt, somehow that he was breaking faith; being disloyal. Yet it was none of his choosing. Fate—circumstance—life—he knew not what to call the force at work, had taken matters out of their hands, played strange, mad, unkind pranks with them, made mock of their affections. Bronwen would never have married had she not thought him dead. Of that he was convinced. He would never marry Puah if he could claim Bronwen. He might marry Puah with his body but never with his mind, and he was more and more persuaded that marriage of the minds was the more essential, the more abiding element.

He felt sad, ineffably sad. With a sigh he turned towards the cottage. He pulled himself together. The past was past. He must close the door on it—if he could. It was not fair to Puah. He must give her of his best. She was standing at the wicket-gate watching him. He noticed that the hollyhocks were growing tall as a background. Her eyes were upon him, dark, deep, a trifle anxious.

"You have been thinking!" There was accusation in her voice.

He shrugged his shoulders and essayed a smile.

"Nigel," she slipped a hand through his arm and looked pleadingly into his face. "Nigel, when—when we are married you won't go *thinking*, will you? I could not bear it."

He patted her cheek. "When we are married, Puah, my one great resolve will be to make you as happy as it is humanly possible. I ask you to believe that, my dear."

He bent and kissed her lightly. She caught her breath and with unexpected suddenness her arms went about Nigel's neck pulling his head down with a fierceness which surprised him. She kissed him again and again, all the pent up passion in her warm nature overflowing. "Nigel, you must love me; you shall love me. I do love you so, my man. I will be a good wife to you; far, far better than any other woman could be. I will work for you, care for you, bear your babies, manage your home, be true to you. I just love you, Nigel, until I feel as if my heart would burst, and you must love me back. You will won't you, darling, darling?"

Nigel was conscious of a feeling akin to panic. This tenderly fierce outburst was something the like of which his phlegmatic nature had never before visualized. Instead of experiencing elation he was conscious only of embarrassment. Some instinct told him, however, that this was an occasion when he must set aside his scholarly reserve, and he endeavoured to return her kisses with what was, for him, demonstrative affection. It was, actually, a poor attempt, but Puah who had never been accorded so much before, accepted his caresses thankfully.

"I worry when you *think*," she confided with her head against his shoulder. "You won't ever, ever *think* when we are married?"

He knew what she meant. He was not to think of Bronwen. His heart sighed. His lips lied. "I promise that I will endeavour to discipline myself not to think," he assured her gravely, not wishing to wound her feelings. In his heart he knew that he could never put Bronwen from his mind. Whether he would or no, she was there, there for all time, for eternity.

That night, instead of undressing, he stood looking through the tiny window of his bedroom into the starlit night. And, despite his promise—he *thought!* The roof was so low that he had

to bend his shoulders to see through the window. His eyes traced
the outline of trees and wall against the night sky. How vast the
heavens seemed . . . star beyond star . . . and what force was
at the back of it all? Was there a guiding power which concerned
itself with the destiny of humans? Could this power, so mighty,
so vast, that it could hold the myriad stars in the firmament,
find time to interest itself in the perplexities and the heartaches of
infinitesimal mortals who must surely appear as insignificant
as insects crawling in the dust? If only he could answer that
question! Was the power a spiritual power? Did the very thoughts
which disturbed him emanate from some great source of love?
What was conscience? He wanted so desperately to do what was
right. Was he doing right in marrying Puah—just because she
wanted him to—when he could not, no matter how he tried, give
her a heart which belonged to another? Should he tell her; and
ask her to cancel the marriage? If he did that, it would wound
Puah terribly. He did not want to hurt her. Rather he would
sacrifice his own feelings, his own freedom, in order to try to
repay a little of the debt which he owed her. Only (and this was
going to be the hard part) he must never let her suspect he did
not love her.

He must strive to deceive her all his life; deceive her into
believing that he loved her. Could a woman be so deceived?
He undressed and lay on his bed but not to sleep. His brain
would not cease its puzzling. Why, why, why, was life so confused?

*   *   *   *   *

For better or for worse they were married. Nigel was struck
by the solemnity of the vows. He set store on his word. And here
he was vowing to love until death parted them . . . as though
love was something which could be achieved by an effort of the
will. He still felt it was all unreal, unnatural. The homely little
chapel seemed incongruous. The farmer from the near-by farm
on whose land the chapel was built, gripped his hand and gave
his blessing. Curious villagers came crowding round. All the
while Nigel was forcing himself to smile. Puah, on his arm, was
smiling. Never had she looked so radiant. Her dreams had come
true.

Piers, looking unnaturally respectable in a trimly cut suit, was
grimly quiet. His dark eyes were inscrutable. He paid for everything, giving lavishly.

The *Four Winds* had been brought south and lay anchored in
the bay. Piers was arranging another of his smuggling trips to
France. As he stood beside Nigel while the people chaffed or

blessed the bride, he made a last attempt to persuade Nigel to break from the Navy and come with him. Nigel was adamant. His code was peculiar, perhaps, but rigid. He had said he would go back to the Navy—the Navy which had pressed him—and go back he would. In two days he would have to return. Two days of married life!

Perhaps he could endure it! But Puah was happy. Her cheeks were flushed, her eyes were bright, her white teeth gleamed in smiles. The villagers all vowed, and with reason, that they had never seen a more lovely bride.

And then, after a breakfast in the old kitchen of a white-washed farm, they had walked across the fields to the cottage, which, somehow, now seemed of different aspect. The villagers followed them thus far across the footpath way, but they paused at the cottage wall and Nigel and Puah walked up the narrow flower-fringed path unescorted. Nigel solemnly produced a key, unlocked the door and flung it wide.

"You must lift me across the threshold, Nigel." Puah was emphatic.

Nigel's strong arms, muscled by months of rigging-climbing, picked up his warm and shapely bride and lifted her over the threshold of her home. Their home.

"Kiss the bride! Kiss the bride!" There were insistent shouts from the people at the gate. Nigel overcame his reserve and, smiling, delivered a hearty kiss on Puah's cheek, a kiss given with such goodwill that even the exacting critics were satisfied, and burst into good-natured applause.

Puah waved her hand happily to their smiling faces. Then the door was shut.

*   *   *   *   *

Two days later Nigel made his way down the cliff path. He wore his seaman's uniform and had a bundle slung over his shoulder. A cutter was waiting in the bay to carry him across to the Devon coast. Puah accompanied him. They made their way by the packhorse track over the moors until they came to Plymouth where, riding at anchor on the placid waters of the Sound, there lay the great two-decker, the white ensign drooping lazily from the ensign-staff. There was bustle aboard. Boats were pulling between ship and shore. Other war vessels were close at hand, active also. For the French fleet was out and Vice-Admiral Nelson was resolved to make one last stupendous effort to chase it from the seas, and to see that for all time the island home he loved was freed from the menace of foreign invasion.

G

NIGEL PREECE was weary to the verge of collapse. A battle had been fought and won. The naval might of France and Spain was broken. As he leaned wearily against the shot-torn side of the *Colossus*, and stared over the heaving water from red-rimmed eyes, he was barely conscious of a victory having been gained. His head still ached from the crash of the broadsides, his eyes still smarted from the acrid smoke, he was weak from lack of food yet he could not have swallowed a morsel. His mouth was so dry that he could not speak. Dimly he marvelled that he was still alive. Death had been round about him. His arms were still red with blood; not his own blood, but that of comrades, whose shattered bodies he had heaved, without ceremony, into the tossing waves, in order to clear, as far as possible, the ship's littered deck. He had fought throughout that momentous day; he had striven throughout the night. For when the fight was done their troubles seemed to increase.

Away on the starboard bow lay the *Victory*, dismasted, unmanageable, a parody of her name, seemingly, and from her shattered frame the white ensign whipped at half-mast, for Nelson was dead: dead in the hour of triumph. Some of the near-by vessels wore their ensigns at half-mast; others had matters of greater moment to think about, for the gale from the south had caught them when they were least prepared. Perilously near lay the shoals about Cape Trafalgar.

The stout seventy-four which had survived the ordeal of battle seemed now at the mercy of the storm. The *Colossus*, top-masts shot way, hull riddled with French shot, was making bad weather of it. She wallowed in the trough of a wave until it seemed as though the next comber would engulf her. Then shaking her heaving body free she would rise in ponderous majesty on a wave crest—up, up, only to plunge heavily down again, as though to her doom.

Nigel, clutching a stay to preserve his balance on the swaying deck, looked across the wind-whipped waters to other vessels in even more perilous plight. Eighteen prizes taken, so one of the seamen had heard Captain Morris report. Eighteen prizes taken! But where were they? England was to have little show for her victory. Nigel had seen the captured *Redoubtable* go down with most of her men, and, doubtless, some of the British prize crew

aboard as well. He had seen the captured *Fougueux* driven
ashore to become a total wreck. The fierce glare from another
ship cast a lurid light on the tempestuous scene—some French
vessel set on fire by her captors to prevent her being retaken by
the enemy. The *Algesiras* and the *Bucentaure* had been recaptured
by their crews, and the former had got away safely into Cadiz.
That sort of thing must not happen again; better to burn a vessel
and have done with it.

The wind was moaning through the shot-torn rigging, a
weird, eerie, soul-chilling sound, as though demons of the air
rejoiced in this scene of desolation and death. Away to port a
fresh orange light leaped up, throwing its ominous hue over the
grey sea. Another ship was on fire. Victor and vanquished
were alike at the mercy of the storm. Seamen who had laboured
at their guns; men who had boarded an enemy ship, using a fallen
mast as a bridge to victory; men who the day before were valiant,
and dauntless, and indomitable, drooped listless, spiritless, weary
nigh unto death.

A reefed main-topsail and two or three staysails were as
much canvas as a ship could carry in such a gale. There was
nothing more the dispirited men could do but watch that nothing
was carried away, and wait for the storm to abate. More ships,
out of control, were driving towards the lee shore, their fate
inevitable amid the angry breakers ahead.

Nigel, watching with languid, almost uncomprehending eyes,
saw the drama and the tragedy enacted before him and yet
absorbed it not. Life had become completely unreal. He had
reached that stage of physical exhaustion when the body ceased
to ache because it had ceased to feel. The nerves, so tense a few
hours before, had been so overworked that they had become
numb. A floating mast with a corpse woven into the futtock-
shrouds went heaving past like some angry sea monster. The
ungainly motions of the dead seaman entangled in the rigging
appeared almost grotesque. Nigel watched. Not that he was
interested. It was just something new to look at and he was tired
of looking at sinking ships, ships on fire, ships battling with the
gale, ships driven ashore. He wished devoutly that he might
get ashore and never look at a ship again. He experienced no
sense of glory. He did not experience even a sense of thankfulness.
Almost he felt irritation. Irritation that he was still alive. Jack
Doyle, the pleasant foretop captain, was dead—and Jack had
his Molly waiting for him at home. He had something to go home
for. Nigel had—what? An obligation to Puah. He had almost

forgotten her. Poor Puah. She was so devoted to him he wished
he could give her more in return. But his heart was with Bronwen
Vaughan. She was always with him—at least in his imagination.
She had been with him all through the battle.

More than once during the action he had been roundly cursed
for not obeying orders but really he had not heard them. His mind
was so fully occupied with Bronwen that he was not conscious of
what was happening about him. When the guns of the *Colossus*
had been almost touching the side of the Frenchman they had
engaged when Collingwood's column opened the action, Nigel
had not experienced a trace of fear. Neither, for that matter,
had he experienced any interest in what was going on. He worked
mechanically and all the while he knew that Bronwen was near
him. Her presence was so real, so close, so vital, that he was
as much aware of her existence as though he could have seen or
touched her. He carried on endless imaginary conversations with
her. He wondered all manner of strange things: whether it was
possible, by an effort of the mind, to detach the soul from the
body and to travel through space at will. Whether the soul had
a freedom which was denied the physical frame. Whether it was
possible for persons possessing affinity to communicate their
thoughts and their emotions to one another despite distance and
circumstances. Bronwen, in some mysterious way, had been at
his side during the fierceness of the sea-fight. A scoffer might
ridicule the suggestion but to Nigel it was so real that he never
thought of doubting it. Never once had he thought of Puah. As
the realization came to him he looked about him uncomfortably
as though he had been detected in doing something shameful
and dishonourable. The men at the shattered wheel, a wounded
marine who lay still in a sheltered corner of the deck, a group of
men engaged in splicing the cut rigging; these met his eyes but
they seemed oblivious of his presence. Life was too involved he
decided for the hundredth time. If there was a scheme of things
at the back of life, what was the use of it to mortals when they
could not understand the workings? There seemed no set pattern,
and man, from sheer desperation, was driven back on his own
resourcefulness. Perhaps that was the best thing that could
happen. A man might, at least, depend upon himself. Or could
he? Nigel gave a cynical smile. Almost mechanically he fumbled
in his pocket and brought out his worn leather-bound volume of
Horace. He did not attempt to read. The gale would have whipped
the pages loose had he essayed to open the book, but he smoothed
the cover fondly. A contrast from the Sabine farm, this. He would

always associate Horace, thereafter, with the great sea-fight in which Lord Nelson was killed. He wondered what they would call the battle in years to come. The Battle of Cadiz, perhaps, or it might be they would select Cape Trafalgar. It would be interesting to notice what was recorded about the fight. He himself, could have written scarcely a word. He had seen little for smoke. All was noise and turmoil and confusion. Until it was well-nigh over it was difficult for anyone to tell how the struggle was going. Yet, somehow, it had never occurred to him or to his companions to doubt for an instant that the battle could have ended in anything but a British victory. Nelson's presence seemed to assure that. And now Nelson was dead! And as though his death had broken a spell the charm had departed and a gale was robbing him of his fruits of victory.

A terrific explosion was borne down the bellowing wind. Nigel turned to see the leaping flames and the uplifting masts and spars of a French vessel. The *Achille*, another captured seventy-four, had blown up. He stared in amazement at the terrifying spectacle. Would there never be an end to killing and suffering and death and loss? He could see the survivors of her crew struggling in the heaving waves.

Instinctively the jaded seamen on the deck of the *Colossus* moved as though to go to the aid of the unfortunates; equally instinctively they paused at second thought—the *Colossus* had not a boat which was not splintered or riddled. In any case, could any boat live in such a sea? Apparently the men of the *Conqueror* close by, thought so. Nigel could see their one remaining boat being swung from the yards. A volunteer crew were clambering in, each man waiting his opportunity as the passing waves heaved on their way. Boathooks and oars and hands were used to keep the fragile craft from being crushed against the side of the parent ship. It seemed madness. It was madness. Yet Nigel felt his heart grow warm at the very sublimity of the madness; that glorious trait so characteristic of the British sailor which blinds his eyes to risk when fellow seamen, even though they be his enemies, face death by drowning. The *Conqueror* was not far distant—as near, in fact, as sea room would permit—and Nigel could see distinctly the tall slender figure of the officer in charge as he balanced in the stern of the tossing boat. The wind whipped his long, dark hair clear of his high forehead, and set the tails of his blue jacket streaming. The boat was thrust off from the *Conqueror's* side. The men bent to their task. The stout ash oars literally curved at the pressure exerted. Trained oarsmen

who, in fine weather, would have rowed with mechanical precision,
now thrust and tugged with irregular force. The little craft heaved
and rocked erratically. A wave crest would hurl a shower of
spray over the crew, well-nigh hiding them from sight. More than
once the boat appeared to have been engulfed, but she shook
herself free. A man in the stern was baling out water furiously.
She drew nearer, slowly, very slowly, scarcely seeming to make
headway despite the herculean efforts expended.

The bulwarks of the *Colossus* were lined with spectators.
No word was spoken but the seamen watched the progress of
the boat anxiously, apprehensively. Nigel saw a leadsman climb
into the forechains of the *Colossus*, lash himself securely into
position, and lean forward with a coil of light rope swinging from
his right hand. It was obvious, now, that it would be impossible for
the *Conqueror's* boat to reach the crew of the ship which had
blown up. If the venturesome boat's crew could only attain the
side of a friendly vessel it was as much as they could hope to
achieve. The waves were washing remorselessly over the sides;
the boat was water-logged and going heavily. More and more
of the *Colossus's* men picked up ropes as the doomed boat crept
nearer. The leadsman's arm circled and his line, thrown with
perfect precision, snaked out into the wind and was carried in
a graceful curve across the labouring boat. The bowman caught
the line and made fast. Another and another rope followed.
They were none too soon. The boat was awash. It was sinking.
Going down . . . down. . . . ! In another instant the crew were
at the mercy of the waves. It was well for them that the stout
timbers of the *Colossus* were close at hand. They were hauled
dripping and exhausted aboard. Every man was safe. A few oars
tossing on the angry grey waves alone proclaimed their valiant
but unavailing effort. A quartermaster, followed by men with
pannikins, was dishing out rum. Nigel saw the officer in charge
being helped to the quarter-deck. His dark, dank hair was
plastered grotesquely about his saturnine head; his clothing
oozed sea-water. But he was recognizable. It was Lieutenant
Moir.

Her husband! Nigel again drifted into a world apart; a world
of speculation. Had his hand cast the rope which saved his
fortunate rival? He did not know; there was such confusion.
But the very irony of it appealed to him, for by now Nigel detected
in life a strong vein of irony. And it would have been typical if
he had been instrumental in saving Bronwen's husband. Giving
back to her the one man who stood between him and his happiness

. . . perhaps (he wondered) her happiness. It was equally ironical that he, who had no desire to live, should have survived the battle while Jack Doyle, who yearned to get home to the woman he loved, should have had his shattered body cast overboard to the insatiable waves. Yet Nigel could not help feeling glad that Lieutenant Moir had been saved. He was a brave man. God knew! Chivalrous. Perhaps he was, after all, a more suitable husband for Bronwen than an impecunious schoolmaster—a man before the mast—a man with a stubborn pride and no prospects. Yes, assuredly Lieutenant Moir was a husband more in keeping with Bronwen's position, and yet, and yet. . . .

His mind went back to that ruined keep in the greenwood, that silent, sacred tryst, when all that was real and vital and abiding in his nature had gone out to claim the one woman he wanted, the one woman he desired, the one woman he was convinced was made for him, intended for him, and for him alone. Life had struck him a staggering blow. It was not merely that it had robbed him of his love, it had robbed him of his faith. Surely, a love as great as his had never been allowed to develop merely as a mockery! And what of Bronwen? He felt that he could have resigned himself to his loneliness, if he could only be assured of her happiness. He would remain "dead" to her, just a memory, and glory in the sacrifice if he could be assured of her happiness. How long he stood dreaming he never knew. The day dragged on. The waves heaved and tossed. The wind howled. The ships were never still an instant. His world seemed composed of restless, creaking timber. The vessels all about him were perpetually restless. Their masts, their bowsprits, their spars, never stopped moving. The *Royal Sovereign*, dismasted, looked like a huge, ungainly, black and yellow striped log rather than a first-rate ship.

He saw Lieutenant Moir, clad in borrowed clothes, walk across the main deck, solicitously inquiring after the welfare of his boat's crew. A sudden impulse took hold of Nigel. He stepped forward and saluted smartly.

"I am glad that you are safe, sir."

"Thank you, my lad." Lieutenant Moir spoke calmly, and then paused as his eyes met those of Nigel. His gaze grew more intense.

"We have met before, I think?"

"Yes, sir. At Beaumaris."

"At Beaumaris, yes. I recollect. And you have survived the battle. I am glad. Let us hope that it will not be long before you are able to return to Beaumaris."

"Thank you, sir. I shall not return to Beaumaris. You think there is a likelihood of our being paid-off?"

"Every likelihood, I should say. You lads have done well. We have swept the French from off the seas. Four ships have escaped but Strachan is sure to catch them. The French have a dozen ships of the line at Brest, but they are not likely to cause us much concern. I think you may count on being paid-off next year. I am glad. You have done well. You deserve well."

"Thank you, sir!"

Lieutenant Moir gave a slight nod of acknowledgment. Nigel spoke again. "Sir!"

"What is it?"

"I trust you will not think it out of place if I offer my felicitations on your marriage."

Lieutenant Moir raised his eyebrows slightly. "I was not aware that you knew of my marriage. Still, I thank you."

"I trust, sir, that Mrs. Moir is well and happy."

"Thank you. She is well, and I trust as happy as a sailor's wife can be in time of war."

Lieutenant Moir turned and walked slowly away. Nigel stared after his retreating back. Bronwen's husband! It all seemed unreal. He was not jealous. Only puzzled. Mystified. His brain could not take it in. For Bronwen belonged to him. To him. Now and always. He was married to her mind, her spirit, no matter who was the legal possessor of her body. And what had Moir said—she was "as happy as a sailor's wife could be in time of war."

It must be terrible to be a wife waiting at home for news of a battle. He was thankful that he had no wife watching and waiting on his account. Suddenly he recollected Puah.

CHAPTER XXIX

NIGEL long remembered his home-coming. It was, perhaps naturally, a day destined to stand out in his memory. The year had crept into summer before the long-awaited day of his liberation was reached. After Trafalgar he had been transferred to the fleet under Vice-Admiral Sir Thomas Duckworth and set off across the Atlantic in search of the French fleet under Willaumez. He had been in action again off San Domingo, and had again survived.

The long summer day was drawing to a close when, bundle in hand, he toiled up the cliff path which led to his cottage home. He paused more than once, not from breathlessness but because the world was so full of beauty, and the soil so good to feel beneath the feet. The fields were yellow with corn, and amid the ears the poppies were bright as blood. The slanting rays of the westering sun turned the harvest fields to a rich gold. How green were the meadows of Gower. The curl of grey smoke from the cottage chimney, which rose lazily in the still air had a wholesome, homelike look about it. Homelike. And this was his home-coming. He felt strangely sad; not pleased, or elated, but sad. Sad with that deep, sublime sadness which comes, often at close of day, when the eye rests on peace too great to comprehend.

He was through with the sea. No more for him the swaying yardarm in a gale. No more for him the leaping eighteen-pounder. The thunder of the broadside. Instead, a quiet cottage, his books, leisure, tranquillity. And of course—Puah. She would be excited to see him. He must try to appear pleased. Indeed, he would be pleased. He was fond of Puah. It would be good to see her dark eyes and glossy hair again, her rich tanned skin. To be conscious of her radiant health. It would not be unpleasant, either, to feel that he was wanted. To know that, in a lonely world, someone cared. He paused for a while, half-hidden by a clump of furze, to look at the cottage. It was much as when he had seen it more than a year ago. More colourful, perhaps, as though Puah had spent much of her time in tending the garden. He wondered whether his sudden appearance would startle her. How ought he to approach? He walked hesitatingly forward, wondering. His dilemma received an unexpected solution. The front door opened and Puah, bare of head, came slowly out. She was singing softly to herself. Some clothes were in her hands, and, engaged in spreading these over the clipped bushes she used for drying, she never gave so much as a glance in his direction. Nigel was conscious of a slight increase in his heart-beat. So this was his wife. He had hardly grown accustomed to think of Puah as his wife. How lovely she looked. So healthy. So vital. A little more mature than when he went away. Even to his untrained mind this was apparent. He let his eyes rest on her kindly, tenderly. And then she looked up. He saw the expression change on her face. Her eyes grew intent. The colour flooded her cheeks. Her mouth opened in an inaudible exclamation. She ran towards the gate, and wrenched it open. Suddenly she paused, turned right about and ran, not towards him but towards the house. He could hear, in the stillness of the evening air, the quick crunch of her little shoes upon the gravel of the path. Nigel quickened his pace. What was wrong? Was she frightened? Was she ill? Perhaps he ought to have sent someone to warn her of his approach!

By the time he was at the gate Puah was at the cottage door. Assuredly she was not ill. Her cheeks were pink and her eyes were bright.

In her arms she held a bundle in a shawl. At the sight of this Nigel stood stock still. A feeling akin to panic stole over him. He had never had anything to do with babies. Puah was coming towards him. Never had she appeared so radiant. Her warm face was upturned to his. Dutifully he bent and kissed her soft lips. He did not embrace her.

"Nigel," she whispered. "Oh, my man. You have come back to us. At last. You have come back to us."

"To—us!" Nigel looked at the bundle a trifle apprehensively.

"Oh, it has seemed long waiting. Isn't this a pleasant surprise for you? Don't you want to look at your little son."

"Son?"

Puah laughed. A spontaneous, happy, buoyant, girlish laugh which caused the baby to stir in her arms. "Isn't it a lovely surprise? I have longed and longed for this moment. Yes, you really have a son and he is four months old. You may peep, but you mustn't take him in your arms or you will wake him. He had just gone off. Isn't he big for his age?"

"I presume so." Nigel was guarded. Never before had he seen a baby so close at hand. The very minuteness of the features almost terrified him. Puah had a baby. Puah always wanted a baby. He was not surprised that Puah had a baby. It seemed natural. That he should have a son was less easy to comprehend.

"Darling, aren't you pleased? Say you're pleased, Nigel. I

have given you a son and you stare as if you did not know what to make of it."

"Of course I'm pleased. It's just that I find it difficult to accustom myself to the fact that I'm a father. This has burst on me. *You* had warning!"

"Oh, Nigel, how adorably funny you are."

"Lord, Puah, let's go in and sit down. This is more devastating than the Battle of Trafalgar."

"The idea!" Puah laughed happily. "You look positively scared, Nigel, and you a veteran of great sea fights. I'm ashamed of you being frightened by your own son. Kiss him good-night. No, you'd better not. You'll wake him. I'll put him back in his cradle."

In an instant Nigel was forgotten. Puah was bending over her treasure. He was placed gently and the bed clothes tucked in firmly, lovingly, with sundry pats and touches to ensure that everything was just as it should be.

Nigel had seated himself on a chair. He watched wonderingly. This was his son. He was not merely a married man. He was a father. Other men had been fathers but somehow in his wildest dreams he had never pictured himself as one. He felt a little puzzled, almost irritated, as though Puah should have consulted him before springing this tremendous surprise upon him.

He looked about him. The little room, growing dim now that twilight was falling, was as neat as ever. The brasses gleamed like gold. The chintz curtains were colourful as of yore. Only a pile of diminutive garments gave a slightly untidy and certainly unfamiliar appearance to the room. His son was asleep—it occurred to him that he had not yet so much as asked the child's name— and Puah was coming towards him. Undoubtedly she was more matronly; yet she seemed the more attractive on that account, She came softly behind his chair, and, bending, kissed the top of his head.

"It has been so lonely without you, Nigel. It has been such a long time. Such a very, very long time. Are you pleased to be back, my darling?"

Before he could answer, with an impulsive gesture, she pulled his head against her breast and strained him to her. "Nigel," she said, and there was a catch in her voice. "Oh, my man, my man. You shall never, never go away again. We will be happy here—you and me and little Kit. I'll make you very happy, my darling. You shall have all your books and you can write another treaty, and we'll be very happy always, won't we?"

Her warm, soft arms were close about him. Almost they seemed to be suffocating him. Nigel moved a trifle restlessly. He did not reply.

"Nigel, why don't you speak? We will be happy won't we, darling, always?"

He nodded his head. It was what he had always wanted, and yet it was not what he wanted.

"And you won't go—*thinking*, never no more?" Puah's voice seemed far away, breaking in upon his reverie.

He mustn't think! No assuredly, he must not think. To think of Bronwen now would be double disloyalty. He must forget. God help him, how could he forget? He must not compare, contrast.

This was his home, his wife, his child. They were his first charge. His only charge. He stood up so that his head almost touched the cottage rafters. He bent forward and gathered Puah's unresisting form in his muscular arms.

"We shall be very happy, Puah," he said. "I intend to do my utmost to make you very happy, always."

With a sigh of happiness which was almost a sob she turned impulsively in his arms and held up her face. He saw that there were tears in her eyes.

*   *   *   *   *

Nigel's life at the cottage was not what he had imagined it would be. Life, he decided, rarely was. To his amazement he found that he had changed. Three years before the mast had made a different man of him. Puah had set aside a little bedroom as a study for him, placing a table under the window where he could obtain the best view and the most light, and arranging shelves of books within reach. He appreciated this thoughtfulness of hers. Kissed her and told her so, which pleased Puah mightily. Morning after morning he went to his study after the breakfast-things were cleared away and Kit had been bathed and fed, but though he took down book after book, many of them old favourites, he had lost the art of reading. He could not concentrate. He would read a few lines, perhaps a page or two, and then his thoughts would drift away. He, who had been a student, was a student no longer. Instead of studying, he would sit staring across the meadows to the cliffs with their bracken and gorse, and beyond them the blue sea, and he would think and think. But it was aimless, unprofitable thinking. He spent his time in reverie. He conjured up mental images. And Bronwen was always with him. He grew a little ashamed. Puah released him from her presence so willingly because she wanted to encourage him in his studies, and this was what he did. It was positively dishonest. It disturbed his peace of mind. Again and again he tried to drive his mind to the printed page. But it was no use. Something had happened to his brain. When Puah, excited as a child, spoke of the house at the Mumbles which Piers was to purchase for their wedding present, Nigel distressed her by his apparent indifference. As Puah became more ambitious—she had a son to think of now—Nigel became less so. He no longer wanted to go to Oxford to receive his degree. The things he had wanted all his life were coming to him, but they were coming too late. He no longer wanted them. To think of them was a mockery! He, who had set his heart on writing, no longer desired to write. The fire had gone out. The inspiration was dead. The source from which it sprang was dried up. His whole being cried out for Bronwen, Bronwen, Bronwen. She it was who fired his enthusiasm, stirred his ardour, roused his ambition. The brain would not work, at least, not adequately, without stimulus, and the stimulus was no more. He tried to work without Bronwen's influence. Reminded himself of his wife and his child. It was no use. There was no other stimulus. He could not write.

As the days passed by he spent more and more time on the beach with the fishermen. Day after day he would put out in one of their boats, sharing in their work, holding aloof from them and yet willing to be one of them. As time passed they accepted him. The fact that he had fought at Trafalgar wreathed a halo of romance around his head. They were proud to associate with him for that reason alone. They knew that he was a scholar, and somehow it flattered them that a man of learning should associate with humble fisherfolk and oyster-dredgers. Nigel's pride was a peculiar thing. It was never in evidence where humble folk were concerned. To them he was kindly and courteous. It was the rich and the patronizing who kindled his ire. The fishing pleased him. Sometimes he would cruise for days. It occupied his hands and gave his mind freedom to meditate— to think. He who vowed that he would never set foot on a deck again once he left the Navy, found an irresistible attraction in the little vessels which plied along the rocky coast.

As Kit grew bigger Nigel began to take an increasing interest in his child. At the start he regarded the baby as Puah's possession —a possession in which he held a nominal share only. He would watch, with something akin to nervous awe, while Puah bathed the warm, soft, glistening body in the tin bath on the hearthrug, but he steadfastly refused to hold the child. He was afraid that if he held him too tightly he might hurt him, and if he did not hold him sufficiently tightly he might let him drop. Puah was highly amused, and never missed an opportunity of teasing him, but Nigel was adamant.

And then one day Kit's diminutive fist closed on one of Nigel's fingers. With the gentleness of a strong man, Nigel made no attempt to release himself from the baby clutch. He marvelled at the strength in the tiny fingers. Their pressure sent a strange new thrill through him. It was impressed upon him for the first time that this miniature man was his own flesh and blood. When Kit finally released his hold Nigel experienced a feeling of regret. He missed the pressure of those baby fingers. Puah noticed, though with the wisdom of a woman she made no comment, that thereafter Nigel made shy but determined efforts to coax Kit into holding his finger on every possible occasion.

October passed uneventfully, though on several nights Nigel had to get up to light a fire when his son had croup. On these occasions he was devotion itself. Puah was the braver, and fought to secure her baby's breath. Nigel, fearful lest he should lose the child, could only stand in dumb misery and watch. Morning brought Kit a return of health.

"I wish Piers would come," said Puah one day. "He has not been here for months."

"Is he still interested in smuggling, Puah?"

"I suppose so."

"I think I will join him if he will let me."

"Oh, no, no. I don't want you to."

"But why not, Puah? It was you who enticed me into being a smuggler in the first instance."

"But things are different now."

"I fail to see it. Then, I had a responsible position which I jeopardized. Now, I have nothing to occupy my time and I could do with the money."

It was a false move. "If it is money you want, Nigel, I have plenty put away."

"No, my dear. I cannot touch your money."

"You are too proud?"

"Yes, I am too proud."

"You will have to earn some money soon, then, Nigel. And I don't know how you are going to do it. I thought you were writing a book in your study, but I never see a word of writing when I dust."

"You are too observant, Puah. No, I spend my time reading. I fear I have lost the desire to write."

"Why?"

"I don't know. Inspiration is like the wind. It bloweth where it listeth. Possibly the long years of life aboard a warship have driven all inspiration out of me." He spoke lightly.

"I am sorry, Nigel." Puah sounded wistful. "I wanted you to become famous. You are so clever. But most of all I want you to be happy."

"I am happy, my dear," said Nigel tenderly. But in his heart he knew that he lied.

CHAPTER XXX

E A C H week as Kit grew older Nigel's interest in his son increased. So long as he was a baby in arms Nigel fought shy of him, but when he commenced to scramble about the cottage floor or to clutch flowers in the grass, uttering, as he did so, strange sounds which were intelligible only to a mother's ears, Nigel began to find him companionable. One day, greatly daring, Nigel picked up his son and the two looked into one another's eyes. Evidently Kit approved of his high position in the world. He gave vent to an excited chuckle and grabbed a handful of his father's hair.

"Here, my lad, slacken off! I have no wish to be scalped yet!" Nigel made a humorous protest and endeavoured to free himself from the determined clutch. His efforts were unavailing and he had to submit. Puah, watching, smiled fondly. She felt that her husband's education was beginning. She was glad to see Kit in his arms. It meant the strengthening of ties.

Puah made a point of walking each day to the beach when Nigel went fishing. Sometimes, if the day was cool, they merely watched the launching of the boat and stood upon the shingle waving farewell. At other times if the sun shone Nigel and Puah would sit on the dry sands while Kit searched for coloured shells and tumbled drunkenly over almost imaginary mounds. One day, when Nigel was busy mending a net, he turned to Puah who was assisting him. "Why is it, Puah, that Piers never comes to see us?"

Puah looked troubled. "I do not know, Nigel. I have often wondered that myself."

"He used to come regularly when I was at sea?"

"Yes. He was very good to me."

"It is strange he never comes now that I am back."

"Maybe he thinks that we are so happy that there is no need for him to come."

"All the same he might drop in just occasionally."

Nigel resumed his patching of the net. Puah stole a look at him. She was proud of her handsome husband. The outdoor life had tanned his skin so that, with his fair hair, he looked more like a Swede than an Englishman. Despite his rough guernsey there was a certain refinement about his broad intellectual forehead which set him apart from the other fisherfolk. Yet he seemed one of them. The days and the weeks and the months had slipped by and Nigel seemed well content to be just one of them. He appeared to have no ambition beyond earning a precarious living by fishing. He was under the impression that his takings provided for their needs. Puah never let him suspect that often she had to draw upon her own savings to pay the bills. She would never let him know that. Knowing him as she did, she understood how it would have wounded his pride. To please her he had started what she termed a school. Three or four boys, sons of better-class farmers, came of an evening to receive tuition at his hands. The fees he charged were slight but the work interested him. Puah encouraged him. She felt that, in time, this might develop into something worth while. She was very happy; happier than she had ever been so far as she could recollect, and yet she was a little disappointed though she would only admit it to her secret heart. She was so proud of Nigel, proud of his brilliant brain. She wanted him to do great things, not for her sake but for his own. She was content to stay in the background if only men would accord him his due. She had tried so hard to take his thesis to the University, yet he had not made an effort to go to claim the degree which once seemed to mean so much. She sighed.

Nigel looked up from his work. "That was a big sigh, Puah! Is anything troubling you, my dear? I thought you were happy."

"I am happy, Nigel. So happy, now you are back home with me again. But all the while a nameless dread keeps clutching at my heart. I sometimes feel that though I have you with me, though you sleep beside me every night, I have not got you. Not the real you. Tell, me, you are mine, aren't you, Nigel? You are my man?"

"What a quaint child you are, Puah. Of course I am."

"I am afraid that you will go away and leave me."

"Where should I go? Have I not settled down to a fisherman's life. I am scarcely out of your sight save when I am across the bay."

"I know. I know. It isn't that. Nigel—you don't do any—*thinking*—these days, do you?"

Nigel did not answer. His eyes stared out to sea. A brig outward bound was tacking. He watched her intently as she came about, seemingly absorbed in the vessel. Actually he was wondering what answer he could give. He hated to tell a lie. He put down his net and seating himself in the sand beside Puah put a strong arm about her and pulled her head against his shoulders. "What's come over you, Puah?" he asked gently. "You were not like this when we came out. Has anything upset you?"

"No, Nigel. The mood just came upon me. Silly of me."

"Very silly, dear. Very silly." He kissed her on the cheek. "Let us talk of something else."

"You are satisfied with me, Nigel?"

"Satisfied with you? You are a wonderful wife, and mother. I should just think I *am* satisfied with you, Puah. No man could have a more devoted wife. As a matter of fact, you are too good to me. Too good for me. More than I merit."

"I get sad at times, Nigel. I feel that somehow I have spoiled your life."

He gave a start of surprise, but he answered gently. "Now, what a ridiculous thought. How could you spoil my life when you are so kind to me? I know that you would do anything for me."

"How true that is, Nigel. I would do anything—anything. But I cannot help seeing the change in you."

"The change?"

"Yes. You are so different from when I first knew you. Then you were so proud and haughty and clever and ambitious, and now it has all gone from you. You are content to work with fishermen. Content to dwell in a little cot. How you have changed."

"Possibly it was the life in the Navy which has altered me. A man cannot serve for several years in the forecastle without it leaving some scars on his soul"

But she shook her head. "That may have had something to do with it, but not all. It is something more than that." She turned to him quickly. "Tell me, Nigel. Why was it you wanted so much to see Piers?"

"I told you. I want to try my hand at smuggling again."

"But I don't want you to. The press-gang might get you again. Or there might be a clash with the Excise men and you might be taken or killed. Why should you want to go?"

"Oh, excitement, I suppose. I am very happy here with you and Kit, my dear, but you must admit that it is a little uneventful for a man who has been taught—against his wishes—to roam."

Puah sat staring dreamily out to sea—the sea which called and beckoned. The sea which tempted and destroyed. "I know I shall lose you," she said huskily. "Oh, Nigel, and I love you so."

He saw a tear steal down her tanned cheek and his heart smote him. He grew unreasonable, irritable almost. "Puah, I don't know what I have done to upset you like this. There is not a word I have uttered or a single action of mine which should have caused you unhappiness. To make you happy I have denied myself. . . ." He paused abruptly.

"Denied yourself—what? What is it? That's what I want to know Nigel. You are right. There is no *word* you have said, nothing you have done, which could hurt me. But you never said '*no thought*' that you have had in your mind, your heart? Something tells me that even when you take me in your arms, even when you kiss me, your heart is elsewhere. You still—*think*. Am I not right?"

"Puah, Puah, Puah, please! This is like the Inquisition. Who can control the thoughts of the mind or the emotions of the heart? Do not press me too far. I am your husband. Loyal and devoted. The father of your child. I give my life to your service. I try with my utmost endeavour to make you happy. If I fail it is through no fault of mine. Truly I want to see you happy, my dear. Believe me."

But she turned away her head. "I have spoilt your life," she said with a sob. "I do not know how, but I have spoilt your life. You will never write books. You will never be clever again. You will never be a great man. I have spoilt your life. I, who would die to serve you, have spoilt your life."

She sprang to her feet, snatched Kit from his castle and ran stumbling across the soft sand to where the cliff path led to their little home. Nigel stood in mute misery watching her form until the grass hid her from sight.

*   *   *   *   *

Nigel was late returning home that evening. It was exceptionally mild. He sat on a boulder near the cliff edge watching the night sky, the lights of the ships in the channel, the yellow square of candlelight which indicated that Puah was waiting up for him, and in the stillness of the silent night he communed with himself, analysing his motives, his conduct, asking himself how he could prevent himself from wounding Puah when his great desire was to make her happy. He, himself, would never be happy. He knew that. There was only one woman in the world who could make him happy. He had not chosen her. She had come into his life and some unseen force had drawn them together. Some force which impressed itself upon both of them. A force which proclaimed that their minds were alike. That they understood one another. That each was incomplete without the other. He knew that it was a mistake to have married Puah. Yet he had done it for the best. He had not been unfaithful to her save in his innermost heart, save in the wanderings of his mind, and how could he control those strange, variable unaccountable happenings? What were thoughts? Who or what put them into the mind? Could one pick and choose? No, assuredly not. If he could pick he would prefer to forget Bronwen and live wholly for Puah. Truly he desired it. It was not wantonness which filled his whole being with a yearning for Bronwen. It was something completely out of his control. He only knew that her presence was with him wheresoever he went. His thoughts went out to her every moment of the day when he was free to think at will. It had become an ingrained habit of which he could never hope to be cured. As for it not being fair to Puah, there seemed to be no answer. One thing which disturbed him most was what had become of Bronwen. It was the uncertainty which stabbed and hurt and nearly killed. He could bear anything but not knowing. Let him know the worst and perhaps he could accept it, face up to life. Should he make the plunge? Make a desperate attempt? See Bronwen face to face for the last time. Talk the matter out. Thrash out every detail. Settle it once and for all. Then cut adrift. Say farewell. Have done with this mad infatuation for ever and ever and ever. He sighed and rose to his feet. He turned his heated face to the cool night zephyr and lifted his eyes to the stars.

Oh, the myriad worlds up there, each looking no bigger than a point of light! Each bigger than the world on which he dwelt! In all the vast universe, was there a mind so great that it understood, a heart so tender that it cared for the perplexities and bewilderments and sorrows of tiny mortals who loved and hated and grieved their way through the existence men called life? He wished he knew! How he wished he knew. He would like to turn to that providence as a tired child to its father, crying out: "Help me, for I can do no more."

And then a great conviction came upon him. So potent was it that it seemed like a message from the unseen. He must see Bronwen again. He MUST see Bronwen again! There could be no peace until he had seen Bronwen again.

With that thought ringing in his mind, repeated, reiterated, again and again and again, he turned his steps slowly to the cottage which was his home.

How could he break the news to Puah? How could he? But no answering voice came to him from out of the stillness of the night. Nothing but the eternal murmur of the unresting waves which persisted in their rhythmic beating against the lonely silent shore.

*   *   *   *   *

The next morning he pushed aside his breakfast plate after a pretence at eating. "I must see Piers," he said, and there was a firm and determined ring in his voice.

"Yes, Nigel." Puah was paler than usual. She spoke quietly. Nigel was surprised at her calm. Perhaps Puah was changing, too. The Puah he knew of old had been quick, vital, electric, high-spirited.

"I wish I knew where I could find him."

"He is at Conway." Puah's voice was low. She would not meet his eyes.

"At Conway? You knew? You must have known before. Why do you tell me now?"

"There will be no peace until you go." She spoke with quiet emphasis. Suddenly she rose to her feet. He could see her lower lip quiver, but she controlled her emotion.

"Nigel," she began bravely but her voice broke and she had to pause to regain her control. "Nigel, you must go. There is nothing else for it, my man. I could keep your body here, but I cannot hold your mind. My love, great though it is, cannot do that. It breaks my heart to let you go but I would not keep you in bondage against your will. I want you to be great. I want you to be happy. I cannot make you either. I love you, Nigel. I love you so much that I will give you up—if it means your happiness."

For the first time since he had married her a wave of genuine emotion swept through Nigel. He dropped at his wife's feet kissing her work-worn hands, and hiding his face in the folds of her skirt. He shook his head dumbly. He was conscious of one of her hands being withdrawn. Her fingers caressed his hair.

He looked up but she would not meet his gaze. Her eyes, large, eloquent, bright with unshed tears, were looking out of the open door, looking at the garden, looking at the meadows and the cliffs and the far blue sea.

"I will not go, Puah. I will never leave you. You break my heart with your goodness."

She shook her head. "Please be sensible, Nigel. I wish you to go. You will never know peace of mind until you have gone."

"I will not go. I will never leave you now."

"You must go. You shall go. I have had it all out with myself. Listen to me, Nigel. Nothing can bind a man and woman together but love. The marriage vows cannot bind them. The law cannot bind them. What people think and say cannot bind them. Nothing else can truly bind them. And if there is love, nothing can come between them. Not other folk. Not distance. Not even death. I do not want to hold you to me by ties or vows. I want you to be free. Free. If you love me as I love you, you will come back to me. You will come back to Kit and me if you love us. And if you don't. . . . I am putting it all to the test. Nothing can bind us but love, Nigel, my man, my own dear man. Go, go. I send you. Oh, for God's sake *go*, Nigel, before I weaken! If you love me you will come back. If you love us you will come back. This is the test! There is no other tie."

CHAPTER XXXI

I T was one thing to resolve to go to North Wales. The getting there was quite a different matter. The fishermen were not prepared to make so long a voyage, particularly as fishing, at the moment, was good close at hand. The roads which ran north were bad, and passed through some of the hilliest country in Britain. Nigel could not afford a nag and to traverse so long a journey on foot made him pause. He determined to go as far as Swansea to see whether the port contained any vessels which might be bound for Liverpool.

Winter was at hand when he bade farewell to Puah, and sadness was in the very air. The sere and shrivelled leaves seemed in keeping with his sombre thoughts. Puah came to the gate with Kit in her arms. She did not kiss him. Never had he seen her so calm, so restrained, so resigned. Knowing her, Nigel appreciated the tremendous emotion which must lurk beneath the placid surface, and he honoured her the more for her courage. He took Kit's small, warm, grubby fist in his hand and pressed it to his lips. Otherwise there was no sign of sentiment, no indication of parting on either side. Few words were spoken. Nigel felt numb. He felt, too, that the parting was inevitable. There was no ill-feeling—just a realization that it had to be. More than once, as he took the pathway across the field to the old toll road, he turned to look back at the home he was leaving—a wistful look. Puah was still at the gate with the boy in her arms. She did not appear to have moved. As he crossed the last stone stile he paused with his foot on the worn and polished top and waved farewell. Puah must have seen him but she did not reply. She must, however, have told Kit to wave for the child raised his arm obediently, With anguish in his heart Nigel turned away and a hedge of hawthorn on which the haws glowed red hid them from his blurred eyes. He felt bitter. Not with Puah, not even with himself, but with life. The situation was none of his choosing— that was what irritated him. He had imagined that, once married, he could have turned his thoughts from Bronwen. He had tried. But it was no use. He made the amazing discovery that one cannot turn love off and on as one would a tap. He had been a devoted husband; never an unkind word had passed his lips. He had been true to Puah in his body. His mind was beyond his control, and his mind was with Bronwen, night and day. He asked

himself whether he was to blame for his inability to control his
mind. He could only say that he had tried and failed. Thus he
mused as he went his way along the long white road which
wound like a ribbon across the common. It was a good day for
walking. On either side of him stretched close-cropped grass
land broken by patches of bracken, (tinted russet now) and clumps
of gorse. Shaggy moor ponies and occasional sheep grazed, half
hidden by the wild green sea. A gipsy encampment with tents
stretched on hoops provided a break in the scene. Nigel was lucky.
A farmer, bound for Swansea in a yellow-wheeled trap, drawn
by a stout bay cob, drew up and offered to give him a lift.

Once in the town Nigel descended at the market and made his
way to the docks. Something stirred within him as he saw the
tracery of the rigging of countless ships. The thrusting bowsprits,
the towering topmasts, the branching yards, afforded a sight to
delight an artist. Stepping over mooring ropes he sat himself
on a worn wood bollard and surveyed the scene. There were
full-rigged ships, barques, brigs, coasting schooners, vessels of
almost every rig. He spoke to some of the sailors, telling them that
he had served before the mast. He found them friendly but not
helpful. Not a vessel was, apparently, going Liverpool-wards.
Most of the ships which were laden were outward bound. One
coasting brig was about to sail for Bristol; on her he took a passage,
the skipper being glad to pocket the money, and the fare was
moderate on the understanding that Nigel gave a hand with the
work. He scarcely knew why he chose Bristol. Perhaps it was
because that, now he was really free of home ties, a wanderlust
beset him. Or it might have been that, now it had come to the test,
he dreaded to meet Bronwen face to face. Had she been free he
would not have hesitated. But she was married and some sense
of chivalry made him reluctant to intrude on her new life. Almost
he regretted his decision. It was bound to prove an ordeal to
both of them. Perhaps it would have been better had he been
content with his dreams. Yet Puah had forced the issue. He had
thought it noble of her, but perhaps she had only been wise.
There could be no rest, let alone contentment, in his mind until
he had seen Bronwen again.

There was no vessel in Bristol docks bound for the north, but
at one of the inns he learned that a coach was about to leave for
London. The longest way might prove the quickest, he mused.
A coach to London; another to Chester. He consulted his purse.
He might just manage it. But assuredly he would have to walk
from Chester. He had an outside seat and the wind proved cold,

but years of exposure at sea had hardened him. He suffered less from the elements than from boredom. He was impatient, he knew not why, and it was irksome to sit hour by hour listening to the clatter of hoofs, the jingle of bit-ring and chain, the crack of the whip, and, as they entered a town, the bright, brazen tooting of the guard's horn. The new country through which he passed was interesting. In contrast to the whitewashed farms of Wales were the mellow brick and half-timber dwellings or the buildings of neat Cotswold stone. But his interest was merely casual. For the most part he was absorbed only in his thoughts. He grew more introspective. London made him more lonely than ever. He made a point of finding his way to St. Paul's to gaze at the place where Nelson lay buried. He felt he owed that much homage to his dead Admiral. Apart from that he had no interest in the bustling crowds, and he was glad to escape from the dust and smell. Once again the clatter of hoofs sounded like a soporific as he sat, morose, brooding, heavy-browed, while the London coach clattered up the long diagonal road which once the Romans had traversed on their way to Deva, the gateway of North Wales. He climbed down stiffly from the coach top at Chester, lightened his purse to obtain a warming drink of rum at the inn, and then sauntered through the rows. Already the place had a familiar aspect. Across the Dee he could see the land of Gwynedd, the North Wales he had grown to look upon as his own. He made his way across the bridge and walked upon Welsh soil again. The adventure was beginning to take shape. But there could be no more coach rides. He must husband his money. And already the weather was worsening. The clouds were grey, the hill tops shrouded in mist. He felt a spot of rain. By the time he reached Northop the shower had developed into a steady downfall and he was glad to take shelter for the night.

The next day he made St. Asaph. Under the shadow of the squat square tower of the ancient cathedral which still bore the marks of Owain Glendwr's burning, he found a cheap lodging for the night. He was not hurrying. He made the journey by easy stages. Something held him back. He who had been so eager for so long to see Bronwen, to hear her voice, was now beset by misgivings as the time drew near. And yet some stubbornness within him kept him pressing forward. Having come so far he would not turn back. Indeed, in all matters, Nigel was not of a nature which took kindly to turning back. He would go on. But there was no need to hurry. He went along the old, narrow, hedge-fringed coach road which rose and dipped as it made its

tortuous way to Bettws-yn-Rhos, to Dolwen, and then on to the
ferry at Conway. On the hill above Mochdre he drew to one side,
backing against the prickly quickset to stand clear as the great
coach with its wheels almost locked and the horses straining
back, came precariously down the precipitous road—the worst
coach road in Britain, an old guide book deplores. The coach had
long since made the crossing of the river when Nigel came to the
ferry and sat in the gloaming awaiting the ferryman's convenience
to cross the broad river to the venerable borough which lay, with
the river washing its feet, under the protection of the towered
and turreted castle which Edward the First had built so many
centuries before to overawe the turbulent Welsh he had set himself
out to conquer. That night Nigel slept within the gates of the
old walled town, but he did not take to a bed until he had gone
from inn to inn, in search of Piers. It was a futile search. From the
Old Bull he went to the Black Lion, thence to the Mail Coach,
and so he made the rounds but of Piers there was no sign. Everyone knew Piers, but Piers himself was absent. Courting a lass
in St. Asaph, folks said. Nigel cursed softly. He had passed
through St. Asaph, but a day before. When would Piers return?
No one knew. No one ever knew what Piers was likely to do next.
Nigel smiled grimly. Piers had not changed with the changing
years. The next morning he went down to the quay, through the
Lower Gate which he remembered of old. There lay the fishing
smacks, their nets drying, some alongside, others at anchor in
mid-stream. And there, too, were the mussel-dredgers with their
long-handled rakes, about to put off in their boats for the mussel-
beds at the bar, down near the perch-buoy which marked the
river's right-angled bend to the west. It all looked familiar.
Nigel asked if he might earn some money by a few days' fishing.
He was not unknown to one of the men—Griffith Owen, who was
aboard the *Conqueror* at Trafalgar—and he was taken on. Three
days later, as the wind dropped with the going down of the sun,
the little vessel lay becalmed off the mouth of the Straits. At
Nigel's request he was rowed ashore. His feet touched the soil
of Anglesey after several years' absence. He was nearing his
journey's end.

He walked towards Beaumaris quietly, unobtrusively. In the
dusk he trusted that no one would see him. He had no wish to be
recognized. He knew not why. Something prompted him to
return stealthily as though he had done wrong. He would go to
the old town, not openly, but like a thief in the night. Lights
were agleam in the stately house of the Vaughans as he paused

at the park wall. He stared, a little enviously. A little sadly. Squire Vaughan had despised him, patronized him, when he was a schoolmaster; what would he think of him now? A penniless fisherman. Nigel was aghast at his own effrontery as he thought that he had raised his eyes to a woman of good estate. Ruefully he looked down at his stained clothing, ill cut, worn by hard usage. A pretty scarecrow, he, to go seeking a fair lady. Yet some stubborn pride forbade him dress for the occasion. Bronwen should see him as he was. It would be a test. He would learn whether this marriage of minds on which his thoughts had so long dwelled outweighed convention. He had, for the moment, forgotten that such things had ceased to matter; that she had a husband and that he had a wife. Life had lost all sense of values.

In the darkness he walked up the once-familiar path to Mrs. Evans' cottage, knocked with diffidence, and waited as though some great issue rested upon the opening of the door. He had undergone so much change during the years he had been away that, not unnaturally, he expected to find alteration elsewhere too. But Mrs. Evans, as the lamplight fell on her face, appeared as though it had been but yesterday that he left her presence.

"Why, bless you, Mr. Preece, *anwyl*, it is come back you are!" She was plainly excited. "Come inside, bless your heart. There, it is glad to see you I am." She almost dragged him within, and closed the door as though to prevent his escape. "It is the kitchen we are in, Mr. Preece, isn't it? You do not mind? No? You will have a seat by the fire and sup with us? Humble fare, sir, but I have no doubt you tasted worse away in foreign climes."

She bustled about him, fussing over him as though he were a long lost son. He felt like a returning prodigal. And as she set a place for him and put an egg on to boil, she chattered. Her questions came fast. Where had he been? Had he been wounded in the great battle? Where was he now? Was he coming back to Beaumaris? To the school? Would he want his old rooms again? They were empty, ready for him if he cared to come to her again. He let her talk, fell to with gusto, making inroads into the home-made bread and the good farm butter. He had eaten sparingly on his journey to save expense and he was ravenous. Also, this savoured of a home-coming. He pushed back his chair and held his hands to the comforting blaze. He told her, to her regret, that his was only a passing visit. He could not stay long. He was here to wind up a few affairs, left in disorder when the press-gang had brought about his ignominious departure. Would she oblige him by not talking about his presence until he had gone away?

He would not impose a strain upon her tongue for a longer period than that. He led her to believe that he held a comfortable position down south, referred casually to his pupils until the four farmers' sons who came to him for their three R's appeared magnified into a school of some pretensions. He slept that night in the little bed he had occupied when he lodged with her—slept as one who had reached a haven after stormy seas—slept heavily as though stunned. He was up at dawn, coaxed a parcel of food from his good-natured hostess, and was away from the streets before most folk were astir. Nigel made for the woods. He knew not why, except that it savoured of a pilgrimage. He had no plans. He was conscious of nothing save a madness in his veins. The woods were different now. Not verdant. The trees were all but bare though a few russet leaves clung to some beeches. The fallen leaves which strewed the woodland paths were sodden; they did not rustle as he walked. He could see the graceful, lacelike tracery of bough and twig against the wintry sky. His first visit was to the disused quarry. There he sat long on the lichen-covered stone, oblivious of the chill, so deep in thought was he. He looked about him expecting to see Bronwen's form approach, but only her ghost was at his side. For an hour or two he waited and then, suddenly conscious of the cold, he turned his back regretfully on the hallowed place and began to walk briskly. He would go to the ruined keep in the glade. A figure moving among the trees ahead gave him pause. He stopped with wildly beating heart. Were his prayers answered? Was his dream coming true? Had the message of his mind communicated itself to hers? Was Bronwen coming in very truth?

But his hopes were dashed to the ground. It was only a boy who carried a pail containing his father's dinner. Nigel recognized the lad as the son of one of Squire Vaughan's stablemen. Nigel was frankly disappointed. But he stopped the lad. If metaphysics were of no avail he would try more mundane procedure. He held out a groat.

"Tell me, my boy, is Miss Bronwen at home?" He used the name almost instinctively. The boy was not surprised. His mistress would always be "Miss Bronwen" to her servants. He nodded. "Then go to her and do not let anyone see you. Say to her that—that Ulysses has returned and waits her at the keep."

The boy looked puzzled. Nigel, with the instinct of a school-master, made him repeat the words until he had them by rote. With lighter step Nigel pursued his way through the woods. It was well past noon when he reached the keep. The world was very still. The ivy which clung to the ruined walls seemed to hold secrets in its grasp. He became conscious of hunger and undid the parcel which Mrs. Evans had prepared. He sat upon the fallen trunk and ate. A robin hopped towards him and regarded him with beady, appraising eyes. Nigel tossed it a crumb. The bird flew back a yard, but recovered from its fright and darted forward to peck the bread. More crumbs followed. Finally it flew away satisfied. Nigel was left alone with his thoughts. The hours dragged. The sun, showing pale and wintry through the tree boughs, sank low. A hush fell over the world. Soon he would have to go. His message had failed. So near and yet so far. He would have to wait still longer. He stood up, sighed, and began to trace his way back to the woodland path. A sound caused him to turn. Someone was coming through the undergrowth towards the keep. He nerved himself for possible disappointment. It could not be Bronwen. But it was. She stopped and gazed at him. Gazed and gazed and gazed. Her cheeks were flushed from exertion or excitement. Nigel stared, too. The carefully prepared speeches which he had rehearsed, refused to come to his lips. He was conscious only of a great longing, a great impatience.

"Nigel!"

"Bronwen!"

Just that. Before they realized it they were in each other's arms.

CHAPTER XXXII

THE past was forgotten. The future did not exist. There was only the present. Only the realization that after years of anguish, of frustration, of longing, of despair, they were together again. There, in the green and silent woods where they had plighted their troth they were reunited. Nigel was aware of an emotional intoxication of a nature he had never hitherto experienced, or even so much as imagined existed. All barriers were beaten down. Nothing mattered save that Bronwen was with him again. He was blind. He was mad. He strained her to him as though he would have hurt her, and she revelled in the hurt. It was a fierce reaction after years of privation, renunciation, denial. It was inevitable, It was nature. It was life. The moment for which they had lived, and prayed, and longed, and hoped had come at length, and it was so incredible that it was hard to imagine that it was really so.

"Nigel! I thought you were dead. Oh, my dear, I cannot believe that this is true. That it is really you. I have grown so accustomed to think of you in the past tense that I cannot accustom myself to you in the present. It is like a miracle. You have come back from the tomb."

"I have come back," he whispered huskily. "I had to come back. I could not stay away. It has been a living death to me, these years without you. These interminable years."

She put up her hands and took his face between her palms, staring into his eyes. "It still seems unreal. I have to keep reminding myself that it is really you, in the flesh, and not in the spirit. Not a product of my imagination. So often you have seemed beside me."

"You have never left my side. Wherever I have been your presence has been with me. I have been conscious of it. In the night watches under the Mediterranean stars; when the Atlantic gale has howled in the cordage; when the ship has been in action, amid the thunder of the guns, always I have been conscious of your presence. You have been like a guardian angel to me. You must have been. I have been face to face with death and have come through unscathed."

"If prayers avail, then you have been surrounded with a protective love, Nigel."

He kissed her again. Kissed her with an intensity, a passion which would have amazed Puah, so unlike the phlegmatic Nigel was this outburst of emotion.

"And you still care for me, Bronwen?"

"You ask that!" There was reproach in her tone.

"I am nothing but a humble fisherman, now. Not even a schoolmaster. I come to you as I am. My clothes are old and worn."

"I cannot see them. I am looking into your eyes."

"Bronwen?"

"May I ask you something?"

"Of course. Anything."

"Are you happy—at home?"

"How could I be with you absent?"

"I mean—apart from that."

"No. I am not happy."

"I meant to look to see if you had taken the money we buried. You have not run away?"

"Where could I run? And why should I, if you had gone from my life of what avail? No, the money is still there. Often on my rambles I have come to this place and looked down at the spot. I could see you burying the gold so plainly."

"Your gold."

"Our gold." She took his hand. "Come, I will show you the exact spot where it lies. In case you have forgotten."

"I have not forgotten, my beloved. I have lived over and over again everything we ever did or said. It is imprinted indelibly on my mind. I believe that every word you have uttered is recorded on my brain. I have had so much time for thinking. I have gone over and over these incidents, these conversations, until I have them by rote like a scholar memorizing his piece. No, beloved, I have forgotten nothing."

He paused, and pointed to the base of the ivy-covered wall. "There is the exact spot. You can see, the soil has bedded down."

"It has not been disturbed during these years," said Bronwen, "Shall we dig it up, now?"

"Of course not. It remains there for an emergency."

"But this is an emergency. You have come back from the wars; you have no employment. You need money. It is yours. I shall not require it. Come, Nigel, let us dig it up."

But he put his arm about her, restraining her, shaking his head emphatically, and though he smiled while he looked down at her, she knew his stubborn disposition of old and did not dispute with him.

"Very well, we will leave it untouched for the present. Some day we may need it, then we shall dig it up. Our hidden hoard."

He nodded. "Yes, some day we shall dig it up."

"Nigel, where are you staying?"

"At my old lodgings."

"Then I shall see you to-morrow?"

"If you wish."

"What a perfectly stupid remark, darling. Strange as it may appear, I do wish. Unless you are tired of me already!"

"Not yet, Bronwen. I believe I could endure your company for approximately a million years."

"Is that all? I could tolerate you for eternity! Oh, Nigel, what nonsense we talk. I think it is because if I got serious I should weep. I am almost on the verge of tears, dear one. If I do suddenly burst into tears do not be alarmed. It will be from sheer happiness. The relief from the tension of the years is almost unendurable. I must leave you, now. I shall see you to-morrow, but I must leave you. Just a few hours away from you will seem an eternity."

"Must you go?"

"I had better. I just slipped out of the house and I may be missed. Not that it matters. I am mad enough to do anything; dare anything, now that I have seen you again. But we must plan for the future. We must not make any false moves. We are entitled to our happiness."

"Yes!" Nigel's face was set. His tone was hard, almost bitter. "Yes. We are entitled to our happiness. And—we are going to have it. Have we not suffered enough?"

She put her arms about his neck. "We are going to be happy, Nigel. Come what may. We are going to be happy. Gloriously happy. How can it be wrong to be happy? There is nothing in the world so precious as happiness."

*   *   *   *   *

They met the next afternoon as they had arranged. In the morning it rained and Nigel was consumed with impatience for he had not taken the weather into consideration. But he meant to go, wet or fine. He vowed that there was not a storm which Nature was capable of sending which could have prevented him. But there was no occasion for his concern. By noon a wintry sun was drying out the paths, and he strode, almost dry-footed, over the short-cropped sward, along the forest way which led to the ruined keep. It was a primrose-path for Nigel. His heart was glad. And his conscience? It was asleep. He was deaf and blind to everything save the urgency of his need. He had seen Bronwen again. Heard her voice, touched her. She was coming to him, coming with love in her eyes and love on her lips and love in her heart, and he cared for nothing else.

Of course he was there first. An hour ahead of time. He had no watch but sailor-like he took his time from the heavens, and his eyes travelled frequently from woodland to sky as he paced impatiently until the well-loved form came in sight. He walked to meet her. Walked briskly, as though every second away from her side was precious time wasted. He had never seen her look so pretty, so radiant. Her cheeks were flushed, her eyes were bright, her expression animated. The strain of the long years of waiting had rolled away. He had his boatcloak with him and this he spread upon the fallen log on which they sat—how many years ago was it? It seemed so long ago. Yet he could have sworn that Bronwen looked no older. He told her so. But he looked older, and she told him so. "My dear, you have suffered," she said gently. "I shall help you to forget all those anxious days; those times of danger and privation and suffering."

He took her in his arms and kissed her, not passionately as he had done the day before, but tenderly, as though she was infinitely precious.

He sat staring into the depths of the woods. The robin, bright of eye, hopped close to them hopefully, but there were no crumbs forthcoming this time.

"You are thoughtful, Nigel."

"Yes. It is a bad habit of mine, this drifting off into abstract speculation. The result, I suppose of too much of my own company. The years at sea have made me introspective."

"I should imagine the company was not the most intellectual."

"They were good fellows at heart, but their ways were not my ways."

"I could tell that your mind had drifted away. Of what were you thinking, Nigel?"

He gave an embarrassed laugh. "You are too observant, Bronwen."

"My dear, I know you, and your ways. I know so well."

"I was thinking how confoundedly involved life was. It would be so much easier to live if everything was plain sailing."

"It might grow boring—insipid."

"You are right; it might. At least our lives have been saved from that. With a vengeance."

They fell silent. The robin was hopping along the far end

H

of the log now. Still curious. Still hopeful. Nigel flicked a twig at the bird and it flew away.

"Of what were you thinking, Nigel, when you said that life was involved?"

"Our own case, of course. The personal element creeps into most speculations."

"It has been involved, but now that you are back again, it seems all clear and bright. I can think of nothing else. The clouds are rolled away. I have you by me. Nothing else matters."

Nigel glanced at her quickly. She seemed so happy, so carefree. There was almost a girlish ingenuousness about her. He, himself, was not feeling quite so light-hearted. The fierce ecstasy of their meeting had burnt itself out. He was happy to be at her side; sublimely happy. But during the wakeful hours of the night he had thought, more than once, about Puah. It was a recollection of this which had prompted him to observe that life was involved. How involved it was not even Nigel then guessed.

"Does nothing else matter, at all, Bronwen, save being with me?"

She glanced at him happily. "Nothing in the wide world, darling. As for my parent, he can turn me out of doors if he wishes; I care not one straw. I care not what people say or think. I have suffered so much during the past few years that I would not go through it again for all the gold in the world. This has given me a new sense of values. I know now what I want. I am prepared to pay the price for what I want. And I want you, Nigel. You mean all the world to me, my dear, and I can say so to you without restraint, because I know, in my very heart, that I mean as much to you."

"God knows you do," he cried passionately and he turned impulsively and kissed her lips. "You mean everything! Everything!"

And the echoes in the old keep—or was it in his mind? reiterated softly . . . mockingly. . . . "Everything? Everything?"

His jaw set hard. Resolute. Remorseless. Yes, Bronwen meant everything to him. Puah was—an obligation. No more. There was no love. No affinity. He did not want to hurt Puah but if the choice had to be made; if he had to decide which of these two women he must hurt—and assuredly he must hurt one—then, he vowed mightily to himself, it would not be Bronwen. The cruel years had inflicted hurt enough already. He would not add to their score.

He saw Bronwen glancing at him and realized that again his mind had wandered. How far had it wandered? How long had he been day-dreaming? He did not know. He lost all track of time. Only he was conscious of a feeling of utter content—just to be at her side. Just to be near her.

"Why cannot we be happy like this, always?" he exclaimed passionately. "Are we not entitled to happiness? We ask so little and yet it seems so much."

"So little, yet it is everything," she said softly. "We might be too happy. Perhaps that is why it is denied us. I should not give heaven a thought if you were with me."

Nigel looked about him at the silent woods which encircled them. "This is my human heaven," he said, and then they fell silent. He was wondering how he should tell her about Puah. and then. . . .

"The last time I was in Conway," said Bronwen casually, "I saw that dark fisherman you used to be so friendly with. Was not he captured along with you by the press-gang? I haven't seen him for years. He seems to have left the district."

"Yes." Said Nigel awkwardly. "Yes."

"And his pretty sister," added Bronwen. "I wonder what has become of her. Have you heard?"

"I married her." It was typical of Nigel to come straight to the point. He was conscious of Bronwen shrinking from him. When he glanced at her, anxiously, he saw that she had gone very white. Her eyes were large, as though with horror.

"You—married—her?" The words were almost inaudible.

Nigel nodded his head. He tried to speak but no words would come.

"Oh, Nigel!" That was all. But it was like a sword driven into his heart.

"But, my dear——" He put out his arm but she drew away from him. A gesture which hurt like a blow in the face.

"Oh, Nigel, and I believed that we were meant for each other. Have you forgotten? Why, here, in this very place, this spot which has been as sacred to me as any cathedral, we plighted our troth. Through the long, anxious, heart-breaking years I have waited . . . waited, hoping against hope, knowing in my heart that if you were still alive, you would come back again to me, someday. And you come back—married!"

"But Bronwen—you——"

"Please do not interrupt, Nigel. It is hard enough to speak these words. I scarce know what I am saying. I believed in you so utterly. And you took me in your arms, you kissed me, and all the time you belonged to another woman——"

"Never, Bronwen, never. I do not love her. I never loved her. I have been yours, heart and soul, all the while. It never so much as entered my head until I felt there was nothing else to live for."

"You had me to live for! Or so I thought. Why did you not come back to me if I was all you say?"

"How could I? I renounced you. The news that you were married nearly killed me—made me desperate!"

"Married, Nigel? I am not married. I waited for you as I said. I would never marry anyone but you."

He leaped to his feet. "Not married? Not married? But—but Lieutenant Moir is married. I—I asked him."

"Lieutenant Moir? I hardly know him, Nigel. He is married to some woman in London. Nigel, what is it? Your eyes frighten me."

"He lied to me!" The words came with difficulty. "He lied to me!"

"Lieutenant Moir?"

"Moir? No, that damnable dog Piers Penryn. He wanted me to marry his sister. Tried to persuade me. But I told him frankly that I was pledged to you. He told me you were married —and my world collapsed."

Suddenly he laughed. "So this is marriage! Trickery and lies! They think to tie me by vows to their treachery. They have mistaken their man. I'm not caught so easily. Bronwen, Bronwen, woman I love. The only woman in the world for me. The gold we hid is at hand. Come away with me. I shall never go back to that treacherous crew. Let us go away and live our lives as we want to live them; as we are entitled to live them. I am yours, beloved, for ever. I love you."

He caught her in his arms but she struggled from his grasp.

"Nigel, you are mad. I would never contemplate such a course. It is dishonourable. Dishonourable of you to mention it. Suggest it. I thought better of you. You must be mad."

"I am mad. Mad with disappointment. I have been tricked. You are mine. I shall have you."

"Never, Nigel, never."

He crushed her to him, kissing her passionately. "Now will you come with me?"

She burst into tears. He drew back, contrite. "Forgive me.

I have hurt you. I think I must be mad. But once and for all, I want you to answer. You are mine and I am yours. Will you come away with me? Once and for all, answer."

"No, Nigel. Never."

He drew himself up proudly and gave a stiff bow.

"I shall kill him!" he said fiercely. "He has killed my happiness. He has killed my soul. I shall kill him."

"No, no," she cried, frightened by the look in his eyes, but he flung off her restraining hands and strode resolutely down the woodland path—the path which led from his human heaven.

CHAPTER XXXIII

W H A T hurt Nigel, what cut him to the quick, was that Bronwen should have misjudged him. He, who had always imagined that because of their affinity she would always understand his motives, was staggered by the realization that she misunderstood him. She had spoken and acted as though it were some light thing that he had done, taking her in his arms and kissing her when he was married to Puah; she failed to see that it was the most momentous move, the most tremendous resolution that he had ever made.

For her sake he had swept away principle; he, who prided himself on his code of honour, had put honour on one side. He had not done it lightly. It had meant months of anguish of soul to arrive at his decision. He had been placed in a position where he had to choose, and he had chosen. Rightly or wrongly he had chosen. He had put her happiness before Puah's—and she had misjudged him. That was what stabbed so deep. That was what rankled. His breath came fast as he strode along the grassy path through the lonely woods, woods that seemed eerily silent now that the shades of approaching night were lurking beneath their boughs. He had been aware of Bronwen calling his name, but he would not hearken. He seemed conscious of her having risen from the log to follow him, but he would not look back. He had finished with her. She, for whom he had made so great a sacrifice had not understood his motive. Affinity! There could be no affinity. Love! There was no such thing as love. It was just a disturbing, primitive emotion. The sooner it was uprooted the better.

He was suffering. He had never known such suffering. He did not think it possible for a human to experience such suffering. And wherever he went he left a trail of suffering. He, who would not have caused pain to any human being, was forced to inflict agony on those who were nearest and dearest. Puah, he knew, was suffering. Bronwen was suffering. And the fault was not his. He denied that the fault was his. He had been placed in a dilemma for which it would have baffled the best man in the world to find a solution. And it was none of his making. The fault was Piers. Damn him! Piers who had posed as a friend. A modern Judas Iscariot! Piers had betrayed him. He knew now why it was that Piers had avoided him; why he had kept away. He could not meet him face to face after his treachery. But he would have to one day. Nigel's eyes narrowed at the thought. There was a time when he wished to meet Pink Kirby, to wipe off the insults and indignities he had sustained. But Pink Kirby was brushed aside by this vaster, deeper hatred. Kirby's lashing and insults were but trivial. They had wounded Nigel's body, injured his pride. This villainy of Piers' had, so he imagined, cost him his very soul. He would kill Piers. It was no idle threat he had made. He meant to kill him. He had spoken those words in Bronwen's presence in the heat of passion. Now, in cool deliberation, he repeated them as unemotionally as a judge would pass the death sentence on a condemned felon.

One pistol had been saved. He remembered well where he hid the duelling case. He had placed it, with the one remaining weapon, underneath the boards of his bedroom. And with it was the bag of bullets and the little canister of powder. It would be dry beneath the floor of that upper room; the powder would have come to no harm. He would load the pistol and cross to Conway and wait for the coming of Piers. And then. . . .

He would have to find out more about Piers' movements. He could soon find out. That man who had fought at Trafalgar aboard the *Conqueror* would tell him. What was his name? Griffith Owen, yes, that was it. A good fellow. And there was a bond of brotherhood among seamen who had survived that great sea-fight. Owen would give him information. Of course he would not tell Owen why he wanted it! Nigel smiled grimly at the thought.

It was dark when he entered the house. Mrs. Evans came to the door of her room to tell him that his tea was ready; that the toast was on the hob. But he went upstairs.

"Thank you, Mrs. Evans. I do not feel hungry. You may clear the things away."

How calmly he had spoken. His voice was so even that he himself noticed it, not without pride at his self-control. He shut the door of his bedroom and threw back the square of worn carpet. His fingers found the loose board. He sat back on his heels and, drawing his jack-knife, opened it deliberately and prized up the board. His hands groped along the cavity but they encountered nothing. He paused thoughtfully. Could anyone have found the case? It was dark. What a fool he was to go blundering about in the blackness. He went down the stairs and borrowed a candle in a brass candlestick. Once more he closed the door. He placed the candle on the floor beside him and bending forward he thrust his hand once again between the joists. This time his finger tips touched the polished mahogany of the case. He drew it out slowly, firmly, deliberately. With fingers that did not tremble he clicked open the catch and lifted the lid. There lay the pistol, neat, business-like, richly chased, a fine specimen of the gunsmith's art. Only the impression on the velvet beside it told of its companion—dropped on the occasion of the visit to Squire Vaughan's. Nigel picked up the pistol, examining it with care, admiration, almost affection. His fingers closed on the grip and he sighted at the corner of the window.

He heard steps in the hallway, a step on the stairs. Quickly he flung a corner of the carpet over the aperture. A knock sounded.

"Mr. Preece, sir. There is a lady wishing to see you."

"I am sorry, Mrs. Evans. I am busy."

"If you please, sir, it's Miss Vaughan and she says it is important."

"I regret I cannot see her. Tell her to go away."

There was a hesitant shuffling of feet but Nigel's tone was emphatic. Mrs. Evans went reluctantly down the stairs. Nigel picked up the pistol. He toyed with it, but his mind was elsewhere. Why couldn't Bronwen keep away? He was not going to let her interfere with his plans. He had made up his mind. He was adamant. Let her keep away and leave him to—to . . . to what? His brain would not work. It seemed to be balking. There were footsteps on the stairs again. Mrs. Evans was coming back to pester him. Damn the woman!

There was no knock. The handle was grasped firmly. The door opened. Nigel leaped to his feet, the pistol hanging limply at his side.

"Bronwen! Really, this is too much! How dare you enter my room? Are you mad?"

"I am not mad, but you are. Give me that pistol."

"Never. Leave my room."

"Not until you give me that weapon. I will not have you commit murder. Give it to me."

"Never. I'll kill him, I tell you, and not even you shall prevent me."

"Nigel, be quiet. The woman will hear you. Come downstairs and let us talk this matter out. It has gone too far."

"What is that to you?"

"Everything. You know what you mean to me, Nigel."

"I thought I knew what I used to mean."

"You still mean it; I love you. You mean more than life itself. There is nothing I will not do for you."

"Words!"

"True words. Give me that pistol."

"Never."

"Then put it away and come downstairs where we can talk."

Almost sullenly he replaced the weapon in the case, snapped the lid, and concealed it beneath the flooring. When he had straightened the carpet he picked up the candle and lit the way downstairs. No word was spoken.

In the parlour they looked at each other. "Let us go out," he said huskily. "Under the stars."

"Yes. She may overhear."

They closed the door and walked towards the woods. There was a gibbous moon. It picked out the open path, but the shadow beneath the trees was black as the darkest night. They knew the way. When they came to an ancient beech they paused. Nigel leant his shoulders against the broad bole, and placed a foot upon an arching root. For a while there was silence.

Bronwen broke it. She came close to him, and took the lapels of his coat in her fingers. It was as though she held him, fearful that he might escape.

"I love you, Nigel," she said. He did not reply.

She put her head against his shoulder. He was conscious of her hair touching his face. He thought she was crying but she was not. She seemed weary. He stood motionless, waiting, he knew not for what.

"Oh, Nigel," she said softly. "What is this you have done for me? You, who hold your honour so dear, are prepared to sacrifice it for my sake! You, who are legally bound to another woman, are prepared to leave her for my sake!"

"You understand—that?" he asked in a low, unbelieving voice.

"I understand everything you say or do, my dear one. The shock of your words distracted me. When you said that you were married my whole world crashed. As soon as you had gone I knew that I had wounded you; you, whom I would never hurt. I am sorry, Nigel."

He sighed. His eyes were staring into the woods, seeing nothing.

"Because I love you," she went on in a low, tense voice, "love you utterly, I ask you not to do this thing. Oh, my dear, to think of you as a murderer. . . ." She shuddered. He felt the shudder pass through her frame.

"It is but justice," he said harshly. "He has wrecked your life and mine. Nothing he can ever do can make amends. We go through life, blighted, damned, because of him. And his sister? She may be privy to the plot for all I know. Like as not; tarred with the same brush. There is a wild strain in their blood. Damn him! Because of his treachery, his lies, his trickery, I have lost the woman I love . . . lost her for ever."

"No, Nigel."

"Yes, Bronwen. I am a married man. I cannot forget that. You cannot forget that. The fact that I was basely tricked into matrimony does not count for a straw in the eyes of the law or the church. I have your good name to think about. I will go away and you must try to forget me."

"Could I, Nigel?"

"No. You couldn't. What am I saying. But I must go away, and you will never see me again. Only—Piers Penryn shall not live to gloat over the evil his cunning, scheming mind has wrought. I shall kill him."

"You shall not, Nigel. Never! Never! Never!"

He took her face fondly in his hands. "Go, my darling. Go home and leave me to my fate. Words cannot tell you the grief I feel at having to wound you so. If I had my way I would never let a hair of your precious head be harmed, but I have no option but to hurt you."

"You must go back to your wife."

"Never. She is no wife of mine now. I renounce her. If I cannot have you, I vow I shall never go to her. Never. Come what may."

"But Nigel, what will you do? How will you live?"

"I shall not live. There is nothing left for me to live for. Life has become a mockery. I meant well of life, and this is how I am requited. I intend to shoot Piers Penryn through his sinful heart. He is away at present, but he will return for the Christmas celebrations at Conway I have no doubt."

He gave a low laugh. "Gad, this appeals to my sense of humour. I will greet him and tell him that I have a Christmas present for him. It will provide a touch of irony which ought to amuse all the devils of hell."

"Nigel, dear one, don't! Don't! You frighten me. You terrify me."

"And then, Bronwen, I shall give myself up to the authorities and pay the price of my—whim."

"They will hang you."

"My dear. I wish to die. The manner of it does not concern me. I have nothing to live for."

"You have me."

"That's just it, Bronwen, I have not you. I never shall have you."

"You have me, now and for ever if you want me. Listen, my dear one. When you left your home and came to me, it was because you placed me first. Before obligation. Before honour. Before pride. I came first. Now, I reply. I place you first. Give me your word that you will put this evil thought out of your mind. Say to me that you will not harm Piers Penryn, and I will leave my home and my people for ever more, I will come with you wheresoever you wish to go, live with you, love you and serve you, until I die with your precious name on my lips. That is how much I love you, Nigel."

He was breathing hard. He was silent for so long a time that Bronwen grew nervous.

"Do you love me, Nigel?" she whispered.

"You know I do."

"Do you want me, Nigel?"

"You know I do."

"What is your answer, then?"

He did not answer in words, but his lips told her what she wished to know.

CHAPTER XXXIV

I T was a new experience for Nigel—and presumably for Bronwen also though being more emotional than he by nature she was more conscious of satisfaction than surprise. Nigel experienced bewilderment. He was happy to a sublime degree; happy to an extent that he had never imagined possible. Some instinct had told him that life held such pleasure, such delight, but he had never tasted it, never sampled it, knew nothing of the wild ecstasy of requited love. Bronwen's nearness, the soft, warm, curving yield of her body intoxicated his senses. He felt that he wanted to hold her to him for ever; never to let her go. For long enough they did not speak. It was as though words, even words of endearment, would have broken a magic spell. A fine rain began to fall softly. They scarcely heeded it. The great broad boughs of the beech were some protection, but Nigel moved sufficiently to open his coat. Bronwen, as though obeying an unspoken command, slid her arms about his body while he enfolded her. The coat may not have added greatly to her preservation from the damp but the gesture itself was warming, comforting. As Nigel felt her glowing shape strained close to his he was aware, for the first time in his life, of that sense of one-ness which, surely, must be the essence, the very heart, of all true union. For years they had been one spirit—of that he was sure. What was meant, then, by that ancient expression—to be of one flesh? He caught his breath at the thought. Here was a mystery. A new discovery. Puah had never been so much part of him, not in their most intimate moments, as had this woman whom he had but enfolded within the warmth of his coat. A fierce exultation took possession of him.

"You are mine!" he said, almost fiercely. "Not all the devils of hell shall render us apart. You are mine, Bronwen. I love you. I love you as I never thought it possible for a man to love a woman."

"I feel married to you," she whispered.

"You are married to me. You have been married to me from the first moment our lips touched. You are more married to me than the woman with whom I went through a formal ceremony into which I was tricked. You are mine, mine, mine, until death us do part."

"No!" she exclaimed. "No!"

"What do you mean?" He drew back slightly, pained, hurt, surprised. "You mean you are not mine?"

"Not that. I mean I resent 'until death us do part,' Nigel! It is for ever and ever, all through eternity."

He kissed her. "Do not mention death with those cherished lips. You make me want to be immortal. You make me want to live for ever. Who would ever wish to die when loved by you?"

"Oh, Nigel! This is glorious. It is not the Nigel the world knows. It is not the Nigel you yourself know. It is a new Nigel who I have discovered . . . created by my love."

He gave a slight laugh. "Yes, the words come from my lips, but they do not seem to be uttered by me."

"They do not come from your lips, beloved. They come from your heart. Nigel, cannot you see? In the past you have been guided solely by that brain of yours. To-night for the first time, I have broken down barriers, I have unloosed the floods of emotion which for years have been pent up in your hungry heart."

"This is love," he said slowly. "It has been nothing but a name to me until you revealed it. I had no idea of the meaning of love. A fiery flame. A rushing torrent. What power there is within human emotion. I feel exalted. You have put new life into me. I could remove mountains."

Bronwen laughed. "Darling! There is no other stimulus!"

"Wise woman!" said Nigel, touching her cheek. "You have discovered qualities in me which I did not suspect existed. You have a magic key which has unlocked secret doors in my mind. You have made me utter words which have never before passed my lips, or so much as entered my brain. You are an enchantress. You have bewitched me. I never want to leave you. I never want to let you go."

"I never want to leave you. I never want to go. All my life I have dreamed of a mating with a man who understood me and whom I understood. To live with him would be a terrestrial paradise of our own creating."

"A terrestrial paradise! Dear heart, you turn an apt phrase."

"If I do, it is because you inspire me."

He bent close to her ear. "Come," he whispered. "Let us go. Let us run away from the world and lose ourselves. Let us prolong this perfect bliss."

"To-morrow!" she said. "Darling, much as I want to come, it is not arranged quite so quickly, my impetuous lover. I must gather a few clothes to wear. I must attend to a few matters at home. And I want to collect the jewels my mother left me.

They are valuable. Sold profitably they would keep us in comfort for years."

"I shall obtain my degree," he said proudly. "I shall get a post of consequence so that I shall at least be able to support you with some semblance of comfort if not in the state to which you are accustomed to live."

"Darling, you are returning to your old, precise, dignified self. I like you best when you are a lover, Nigel."

"You can soon transform me into one again."

"I know it. I revel in the realization. But not to-night. Do not tempt me. To-morrow I will come to you and we will go—? Whither? I scarce know, and care less, so long as I am with you. To-morrow, darling, we will meet at the ruined keep in the glade. Together we will dig up your gold—our gold—for now is the time we shall need it. It will be the start of the great adventure! Our great adventure."

He kissed her tenderly as she stirred in his embrace. "The great adventure," he repeated. "The road of life stretches broad and straight before us. We will venture down it, you and I, side by side, until we come to the sunset where lie the Isles of the Blessed."

"I must go," she protested, as though he detained her. "I must go. I don't want to go. I want to stay with you for ever. But they may miss me. What shall I say? Where have I been? I do not know. I do not care. Oh, hasten to-morrow! To-morrow!"

His arm was about her as they began to walk down the mossy path. It was dark now in the wood under the trees, but Nigel kept a hand outstretched in front lest they should crash into a trunk. So long as they had the soft, smooth sward beneath their shoes they knew they had not strayed from the pathway. Presently the trees thinned and the way grew lighter. They were nearing the open meadow and the way to the boundary wall.

When they reached it, Nigel rested against the stones, oblivious of the wetness of the grass or the wall. Bronwen leant against him but this time there was no passion in their embrace. Only the sadness of farewell. Suddenly she sighed.

"What is it, dear?" asked Nigel tenderly.

"I was thinking of Puah," she said. "Poor Puah. She is bound to miss you terribly. Oh, Nigel, I have been blind. Is what we are about to do right or fair?"

"Of course it is——" he began. He paused. "No," he said hardly. "It is not right, and it is not fair. But I have been placed in this position. Life has struck me a cowardly blow, in the dark, from behind. This is how I strike back. I do not want to hurt anyone. I do not want to hurt Puah. The reason I married her was because I did not want to hurt her. But I was basely tricked into this marriage, and that wipes out everything so far as I am concerned."

"Do you think Puah was a party to the deception?" Bronwen spoke softly.

Nigel started. "I never gave it a thought. She might have been. She and her brother were as thick as thieves." He stood thoughtful. Then: "That was not generous of me," he said soberly. "I do not know. I do not think so. At least I should give her the benefit of the doubt. She was generous to me, at least I must be generous to her. It is the least I can do for her. No, I will not believe that she knew anything about it. I know now why Piers kept out of my way. He was afraid. . . ."

He put his hand across his brow. "Poor Puah! I feel for her. She has done her best for me. I have nothing but kind thoughts of her. Gratitude. But, I do not love her, and, God help me, God forgive me, try as I will I cannot make myself love her."

"How was she generous to you, Nigel?"

"How? She sent me to find you. She *sent* me. She could see that you were always with me in my thoughts. Your presence never left me. She said that she knew that I would never know happiness or peace of mind until I had seen you and settled the matter one way or another once and for all."

"That was very wise of her. I think she does understand you, Nigel, probably better than you think."

"She has been good to me," he said softly and sadly. "I can see her now standing at the gate as I went away. She would not wave farewell—but she made Kit wave his hand to me."

Nigel was conscious of Bronwen drawing away from him. She seemed to be shrinking.

"Kit?" The word was almost inaudible.

"My little son."

"Your son. She bore you a son. Dear God! It might have been mine!" The words were so softly spoken that he scarcely caught them. "Nigel! You never told me you had a son, a child."

"Did I not, sweet? If I neglected to do so it was because I had so much else on my mind. I did not withhold it deliberately."

Bronwen's head was turned away.

"Darling," he protested, "I did not withhold it deliberately. Say you belive me. What is it? I feel as if I had hurt you; struck you. I did not mean to. What have I done, Bronwen, my dear?"

"Nothing. I—I must go in, now, Nigel."

"Darling, say you are not cross."

"I am not cross. Why should I be cross?"

"But you are strange. Different. What is it?"

"I am sad, Nigel. And bewildered. And upset."

"Because I did not tell you I had a little son?"

"No. Just because you happen to have a little son."

"But darling, it makes no difference to my love for you. It makes no difference to your love. Nothing can alter that, can it?"

"No!" she spoke almost defiantly. "Come what may nothing can alter that. Thank God nothing can alter that. I thought there would be a primrose path for us but already it is beset with thorns. I thought the way lay clear ahead but already I flounder in the dark. Nigel, before I go, take me in your arms for a moment. Hold me close, close to your heart. Oh, God, my heart is breaking! Tell me, promise me, that you'll never doubt my love for you. Never! Never! Never! And oh, Nigel, it never was greater than it is this very moment. Promise me you will never doubt my love. It is yours for ever. Promise."

Nigel promised.

* * * * *

Nigel knew not sleep that night. Through the hours of darkness he lay listening to the thudding of his fast-beating heart. His brain seemed on fire. Like wheels revolving, thought after thought turned, never ceasing. He lived the past, he tried to penetrate the veil of the future. He was devoured by remorse, tortured by the wildest yearnings, fired by the bitterest resentment . . . against life. He did not know what life was. It was invisible, intangible. Life could hit you, but you could not hit back. But Piers was tangible. Piers was the author of this misery, these hellish complications. Ever since Kit had been mentioned something had stirred within him. Something primitive. An emotion which, like his love for Bronwen, had lain latent. And now it stirred. Kit. His little son. His precious little son with his funny ways. How quaintly he crawled sideways across the floor—like a crab. Nigel could feel dirty, warm, chubby hands slapping his cheeks. Could hear the inflection in the baby voice as he shouted, "Daddy!" He would miss Kit. But he would sacrifice even his first-born for Bronwen, so great was his love. It nearly broke his heart to make the decision, but his stubborn jaw set firmly. He had set his hand to the plough! He had not deliberately withheld

Kit's name. He was sincere in that. It had been a trick of the brain. He could not bring himself to face the issue of leaving his baby son and so he had put it from his mind. But the problem remained unsolved. There was no solution! Oh, curse Piers for bringing such a state of things to pass!

Once he found temporary relief by groping under the floor-boards for the pistol. He fingered it grimly; then put it back in its case and replaced the carpet. There would be no need! He had promised Bronwen.

He was up early, before Mrs. Evans was astir. He could not eat but he took a copious drink of milk and felt refreshed. His throat was on fire. He put his few belongings into a parcel, left some money on the table, a note thanking Mrs. Evans for her care. Then he let himself into the dark street.

There were lights in some of the houses. The church was lit. The coloured glow from its graceful windows cut the morning darkness pleasantly. There must be some special service. With a shock he realized that it was Christmas Day.

He went into the woods, awaiting the lifting of the curtain of the dawn. A drab day. Some rooks winged by, black against the grey sky. But the rain had stopped. Slowly he walked to the disused quarry. There was no hurry and he would like to visit the place just once again. A place of happy memories; of hallowed memories. It was a pilgrimage.

It was broad daylight now. He could hear some children shouting happily in their gardens afar off. It was a great day for them. . . .

He reached the ruined keep ahead of time. That was but natural. He was impatient. That, too, was natural.

He paced the sward. His eyes kept turning to the pale sun which vainly struggled to pierce the eastern clouds as though in honour of the day. He frowned. It was the hour of meeting. Bronwen was late. . . . His restlessness increased. His eyes never left the woodland track. Would her beloved form never appear? The minutes slipped away. The robin hopped towards him. He paid no heed. Instead he made his way into the interior of the keep. She might be waiting there! Foolish hope. Vain hope. As though she would not have been equally alert for his arrival.

He walked towards the ivied wall where the gold was hidden, glanced fondly at the spot. He stopped with a sudden fear. The soil was loose! Newly turned! Someone had been there. Had the gold gone?

He thrust his hands recklessly into the moist soil. Yes!

The gold had gone. The white of paper caught his eyes. His soil-stained fingers fumbled until the note was open, spread before his eyes, his burning eyes, his tear-blinded eyes, his incredulous eyes.

Darling,

I want you to believe that I never, NEVER loved you so much as I do this instant. You promised last night. Never forget that promise. When you read this I shall have gone. Gone for good. Gone for ever. Do not try to follow me for I shall leave no trace. I have the jewels and I have the gold. Your gold. Our gold. I felt justified in taking it. It was little Kit that decided me. Oh, Nigel, I have wept and prayed the whole night long and my way seems clear. I cannot take you from your baby son. He means so much to you. You mean so much to him. I know that—I who love you better than life itself. So I am forcing your hand. Making a decision for you which you could not make for yourself because of your great love for me. You could hurt yourself but you could not hurt me. Soon I shall know whether the human heart can break for I shall never, never see your dear face again Nigel, man I love more than life itself.

Beloved, do you remember telling me how, during the night watches at sea you were conscious of my presence beside you? I believe that my spirit truly was there because, somehow, my thoughts, my soul, seemed to go out to you with every waking breath. It will be so during the lonely days ahead. Every hour of every day my spirit shall be with you, my thoughts and my love shall be with you. Someday perhaps we shall learn the reason for this suffering, this misery, this mystery. But all I know now is that my heart is aching, breaking, and that I must never see you again. Do not forget your promise, I love you now more than I have ever done—I love you so much that I go out of your life for ever.

Bronwen.

*   *   *   *   *

As Mrs. Evans opened the door of her cottage she saw Nigel Preece standing there.

"A merry Christmas, Mr. Preece," she greeted him. "So you have come back, sir? I am glad."

"I have come back Mrs. Evans!" He smiled. It was a strange smile. She long remembered that white face with the lips which smiled and the eyes which were concentrated in a fierce intensity. "I had to come back. I must go to my room to fetch something I overlooked."

CHAPTER XXXV

THE weather had broken. The pale, watery sun which showed yellow above the cloud banks at break of day bore an ominous look; obvious to anyone less engrossed in affairs of the heart than was Nigel Preece. The wind, coming in unexpected gusts, bore with it flurries of hail or stinging rain. Nigel had experienced difficulty in persuading a boatman to risk the passage to the Conway, but he was prodigal now with what money remained. He thought, grimly, that he would soon be past the need of money. It so happened that it suited Madoc Morris's own ends to make the passage, and, reckless by disposition, he closed with Nigel's offer on the understanding that his former comrade aboard the *Unique* would take his share in the sailing of the boat. Under reefed sails they butted their way through the white crested waves which carried with them an angry swell. Penmaenmawr's giant headland was all but lost in the gathering cloud mist. The Ormeshead was invisible. Nigel cared nothing for the risk. A strange indifference took possession of him. With the wind-whipped spray stinging his face he was conscious of a curious elation of spirit. He had long been subjected to tension. All that was now gone because everything was gone—or at least as good as gone. He became aware of the barrel of the pistol pressing against his ribs. The weapon was within his shirt breast well hidden from sight.

Madoc Morris, hand on tiller, looked anxiously at the grey sky. "The damned wind keeps backing," he complained. "It's going to be risky work when we get near the bar.

"Sorry you came?" Nigel spoke calmly, there was almost contempt in his tone. Madoc spat to leeward.

"No. I'm not sorry I came. I like a bit o' risk, within reason. What beats me is why you should be so damned anxious, Nigel Preece, to risk your life. Fleeing from somebody, eh?"

"Not in the least, Morris. Why should I? It is just that it pleases a whim of mine to celebrate Christmas with my old acquaintance Piers Penryn."

"Ay. What of Piers? Time was when you and him was cronies. He don't see much of you these days. Is there bad blood between you?"

"Lord, no. I'm married to his sister."

"I know it. I thought as he was jealous, maybe."

"It was Piers who arranged it. He was most anxious that I should marry his sister." Nigel was smiling at Madoc Morris; a grim smile. He moved slightly. The pistol was slipping. He buttoned his jacket tighter. "It is on account of this marriage of mine that I am so anxious to see Piers. It is not good that there should be any misunderstanding at Christmas."

"You are right. Not at Christmas 'specially. It is a time of good will."

"I have a present for him, Morris."

"From his sister?"

"From myself alone. He will be at Conway, you think?"

"Last I heard of him he had gone to St. Asaph. But he's sure to come home for Christmas. Courting Nancy Hughes he is, and I heard him say last time as I was over that they'd Christmas together. If he's not there already he will come by the coach."

Come by the coach. The words rang in Nigel's ears. They drummed in his brain. He could picture the coach, the four horses straining up and down the narrow, hedge-girt road through the picturesque hamlet at Bettws, by way of Dolwen, Mochdre, to the ferry of the Conway. The worst coach road in Britain. That was its reputation. And Piers would be there. His black eyes bright with anticipation of his Christmas revel. He would not know what lay in store for him. What a pity, thought Nigel, that he could not lure him to some lonely spot and there put him through a period of mental torture first. But it would have to be done swiftly or there might be some miscarriage. He wondered where he should shoot him. In the head? Or through his black heart?

"What are you thinking of, Nigel Preece? Your face is working with rage." Madoc Morris's voice broke in on his reverie. Nigel forced a smile.

"Was it? I was thinking how this accursed storm is going to spoil all the holiday plans. The wind's backing nor'-east now, which means that it will be sweeping right up the estuary. It will be an uneasy anchorage."

"Ay. You're right. But once there we'll be safe enough." Nigel fell silent again. He would have to be more careful. Exercise more self-control. What a good thing people were not thought-readers. He was sorry that Madoc Morris had noticed his expression. But the fellow was a dolt. He would never suspect. It would be easy to fool him. All the same Nigel was more careful, more on his guard.

They were in the channel, now, and there was more to do; more to keep his mind occupied. They dropped anchor off the quay, and ran their small boat on to the shingle, pulling it well up out of reach of the washing wavelets. The wind was sweeping up river and the tide was rising. Nigel could see the white waves breaking against the rocks of the islet which lay beneath the old castle. The boats were heaving and straining at their cables as though they were live animals, anxious to be free. The curtain wall sheltered them from the blast. Nigel paid his boatman, but kept back a few coins. He must have enough for some drinks. At the Lower Gate they parted. Nigel made his way along Castle Street until he came to the Black Lion—that little low-eaved tavern which had dispensed hospitality since Queen Elizabeth's days. It was a favourite haunt of Griffith Owen who had fought aboard the *Conqueror* at Trafalgar. That mariner was on a settle near the fire, cosy, tankard in hand. There were plenty of free drinks for a man who had fought at Trafalgar. And it was Christmas. The lads of the old town were in a mood for yarns and drinks, and a cosy fire. Especially the latter. The wind moaned down the chimney. The rain pattered against the small-paned window. It made the room seem more snug. Nigel got a seat on a bench because of his having been at Trafalgar. The glory reflected from Griffith Owen was his in some measure. But he was not to be induced to talk. His mind was elsewhere.

"Better take your boat-cloak off," suggested Owen, but Nigel shook his head.

"I must not stay," he said. "I am to meet the coach. When is it expected?"

"She's overdue. Lord, I don't envy Enoch Jones his drive on a day like this."

"Maybe he's stopped for shelter?" suggested a youth.

"Stopped for shelter? You don't know Enoch Jones. The devil wouldn't daunt Enoch, my lad, and him with his Majesty's mails to deliver. No, the coach'll be here, come wind come weather."

"Maybe she's the other side already, and old Parry is fearful of bringing the ferry across."

"Enoch'll make him."

"I think I'll go and see," remarked Nigel, rising.

A fiercer gust rattled the window. "Sit down, man," protested Griffith Owen. "It's not a day for a dog to be out. You'll hear when the coach arrives, never you fear."

Nigel smiled and shook his head. The pistol in his shirt breast was pressing against him. A reminder.

Griffith Owen was right. It was not a day for a dog to be out.

But it was a day for a murderer. . . . A line tucked away in the back of his brain stirred. An unseen voice seemed to whisper . . . *"for without are dogs and murderers. . . ."*

Yet there were no dogs about in the deserted streets of Conway. It was not four o'clock but the light was failing. In every house there were lights. They looked cheery in the gloom. They spoke of comfort, and hospitality, and revelry, and good will.

Nigel Preece had no good will in his heart. Only bitterness and hatred. He made his way up the street. How high the castle towers loomed! He could see the merlons outlined sharply against the darkening sky. As he turned through the postern gate—the Porth Bach —a sudden gust almost knocked him off his feet. It wrapped his wet cloak about him and made him stagger against the aged stones of the town wall. His hat had been whipped off and had vanished over the house roofs. He barely noticed its loss. The wind, and the driving rain, were cooling to his heated brow. He heard a crash behind him. Slates, ripped from a roof, had clattered into the roadway.

He looked across the tossing, heaving, waters of the river. The eastern bank was lost in mist. He could faintly discern the outline. The fishing boats were tugging and jerking at their anchors. On the shingle near the curtain wall he could see a group of excited fishermen endeavouring to save one small craft which had dragged her anchor and had been washed ashore. Nature was in one of her wildest moods. So, for that matter, was Nigel. The elements seemed in keeping with his own tumultuous emotions. Dimly, through the deepening dusk, he could discern a dark shape on the distant bank. The coach had reached the ferry. It seemed sheer madness to put off on such a day. But the first bridge crossing was at Llanrwst, and hours would be lost if the mails were to be taken that way. Enoch Jones was proud of the responsible task entrusted to him. His Majesty's mails must be on time. He was not a man to turn back. Storm or no storm he would finish his run, fulfil his obligation. The ferry put forth. Nigel could see the white waves slapping against the side, flinging up showers of spray. His hour approached!

He put his hand into his breast and gripped the pistol-butt. Sudden apprehension seized him. Suppose the powder had become wet! He must look to the priming. A shed stood nearby; a shed in which some fishermen stored his goods, for Nigel could see a small anchor with its coil of rope, a bundle of nets, some oars. He could see them easily for the door had been blown off its hinges and lay against the curve of a wall tower some distance away. He put his head down and forced his way against the blast until he climbed within the shelter of the shed. When he had regained his breath he took out his pistol and made sure that it was loaded to his satisfaction. A worn, wooden chest stood against one wall. On this he sat, waiting, pistol in hand. He felt strangely calm. It was as though his brain would stand no more strain and had become numb. He was not conscious of remorse. Not conscious of loss. Not conscious of heart-break. Not even conscious now of hatred. He had a task to perform; one which he would carry out dispassionately. And then? He would just give himself up. Pay the price. He was sorry for Puah. She would feel distraught, robbed of both brother and husband. But she would always have Kit. For one brief second feeling returned to him. Kit! That dear child. Innocent. And he had brought him into the world, only to——. With an effort of will he drove thoughts of his child from his mind. He would not weaken now. Now that he had gone so far. These wrecked lives were all Piers' fault. Through Piers he had been robbed of Bronwen. Through Piers he had been forced to hurt Puah. Through Piers he had no longer any desire to live. Assuredly Piers should pay the price.

Cautiously he peered forth around the corner of the shed. So fierce was the gale that he had to wrinkle his eyes to stare towards the wave-whipped river. The ferry was drawing near. He could see the passengers huddled together, seeking shelter from the flying spume. The coach was rocking and heaving perilously on the inadequate craft. He could detect the shape of the horses. There was a white one among them. Poor creatures. They swayed miserably with the tossing ferry.

The time had come. With deliberation he placed the loaded pistol under his arm, shielding it with his coat. His boat-cloak was whipped about his form. Before he had gone a few yards the rain had drenched his uncovered head, plastering his hair about his white strained face. He marked the place where the ferry would land. Already several hardy men were on the spot awaiting it. He drew nigh, a fierce resolve in his heart. He would, he decided, clap the pistol to Piers head and blow out his brains.

He saw one of the watchers fling up his arms. There was something in the gesture which more eloquently than words bespoke terror, despair! Nigel turned his gaze to the river. He saw the ferry balanced precariously on the crest of a mighty breaker, saw several dark figures hurled screaming into the torrent,

saw the unwieldly coach topple, crash, splash into the waves.
Then, amid yells of terror which came down the wind like the
cries of lost souls, the doomed ferry lurched and slid from sight
in a swirl of spray and foam.

*   *   *   *   *

Nigel knew that he would find Piers' body. It seemed but
fitting he should. He fully expected he should. That was why he
searched all through the night. Other horrified Conway men did
too. They had dragged ashore one man alive. That was all. They
continued to search. Nigel was still seeking when the dawn came
slowly to his aid. And with it came the calm which follows storm.
The wind dropped. The tide ebbed. He could see the yellow sand-
banks. A cormorant was perched on one sandy spit, black,
ominous, like Nature's mute. And the gulls were lamenting in
the sky. Nigel could see the wreck of the ferry with the painted
coach sticking grotesquely above the water's surface. He could
see, too, the dark mass which indicated where the drowned horses
lay. Their rounded flanks were visible (the haunches of the grey
showed particularly clearly) but their heads were held down by
the weight of the harness. The fate of the horses touched Nigel
more than the fate of the passengers. He knew not why. Somehow
it seemed more pathetic.

He went on seeking. And then, stretched on the shingle, he
saw a dark form. He broke into a run. A slim man in blue clothing
lay face downward. He turned the body over. It was Piers. His
face was marble and calm and white, marred only by a patch
of sand which had collected in one of the eye-sockets. Nigel bent
to wipe the stain away. As he did so something clattered to the
stones at his feet. The pistol had slipped from the breast of his
coat. He picked it up and with sudden revulsion hurled it far
into the placid river. Its black shape struck the water with a
fountain of spray and plunged from sight. The eddies circled
and faded.

Piers was dead! As Nigel looked down on the still face a sudden
compassion swept over him. In the presence of death all rancour
fled. What was death? What lay beyond? That mystery of
mysteries! Confronted by it, face to face, how petty and
insignificant seemed the strivings and even the wrongs of man.
Puah would be desolate. She loved Piers.

And Piers had loved her. Suddenly the thought came to Nigel
that Piers must have loved his sister very dearly to have acted
as he did. Bronwen was nothing to him. Puah was everything.

Nigel could see now why Piers had avoided him. He was ashamed! How he must have loved Puah. To have betrayed his best friend in order to secure her happiness. Nigel sighed. He would have to tell Puah. How could he tell Puah? Yet he must. No other than he could break such sad news. Piers was dead!

He dropped on one knee and, inserting his arms under the body, he raised it. The head fell back awkwardly, striking a stone.

"I'm sorry!" he said spontaneously. Then he laughed. It was so incongruous. Fancy apologizing to a corpse! Piers was beyond any human hurt. Nigel came to himself.

"Yes, Piers," he said aloud. "I repeat—this time deliberately —I am sorry. You cannot hear me—but I am."

Then he gathered the dead man in his arms.

CHAPTER XXXVI

T H E way south was long, it was dangerous, it was hard. Hard not merely by reason of the mountains and the passes, but because it was the road which led to Puah. To home.

Nigel stood on the hill up which he had toiled and looked down upon Conway. He could see the old town so clearly. The stately castle. The triangular walls with their numerous round-towers. The protected gates. The cluster of houses within. The stepped gables and watch-tower of stately Plas Mawr. And round about lay the woods, bare now, like a cluster of witches' brooms, save where a conifer grew or ivy clung to a dying trunk. And there stretched the river. The tide had ebbed. The yellow sand-banks glowed smooth and warm in the pale morning sun, outlining the winding grey-blue channel which showed where the Conway made its way to the sea. Gone was the horror of the night. All was peace. But there were more people than usual on the quay, and two boats had been driven ashore, and men with a rope were hauling on the overturned coach. They looked like toy figures.

He turned away sadly. Would he ever look upon the scene again? The vale wound inland. Sloping fields, patterned by hedge-rows. Whitewashed farms. And then the steeper sides of the hills. And far off, cutting the skyline, the austere outlines of the peaks.

There was snow on the peaks. There would be snow in the passes. Of a truth the way would prove hard. But then the way of the transgressor was hard! Or was it? Nigel grew critical. The transgressor often appeared to thrive. His way was made easy. Was the way made for one, of did one make one's own way? He wished that he knew. Almost he felt that, though he had devised and desired and planned, some greater power, invisible but invincible, had been too powerful for him, and that nothing remained but for him to conform to its will. He walked slowly up the valley. There was no hurry. He dreaded having to meet Puah; he would put off the evil day. He gave a short laugh at the expression. Why should he think of the hour of his return to a home and a wife and a child as an "evil day"?

He wondered whether he ought to go home. He wondered why he resolved to go home. It was due to no inclination. His inclination was to die; to have done with the mockery of life. It was due to no sense of honour, of obligation, of duty—at least, not to Puah. No. He was going because it was what Bronwen would have wished him to do. She had made the sacrifice—and well he knew how great was that sacrifice because his own heart was well nigh broken—she had made the sacrifice which drove him from her because he must go back to Kit. Kit was his flesh and blood, his child, his boy, his son. Henceforth there would be little left in life but to care for Kit. To guide him. Encourage him. Instruct him. He could picture the child's sandy hands patting his cheeks even as he thought.

How was he to get home? He did not know. Nor care. He had no money. He gave a grim smile at the thought. Yes, he had. Some big, heavy pennies were weighing down his pocket. He put in his hand and solemnly surveyed the coins. There were seven. He had seven pence to carry him on his pilgrim way. The smile deepened. Solemnly he placed them in a row on a smooth stone which jutted from the hedge-side grasses. Some child would be sure to find them. It would be a hoard of wealth. Fancy being able to bring happiness into some unknown life so easily. And at such little cost!

Now he was literally penniless. He would have to work for his food. Or beg. Or steal. He neither knew nor cared. A sense of complete and utter indifference had taken possession of him. He had reached that point at which, after long and unrelieved strain, something snapped. He was not dead, but he had undergone a spiritual amputation. He wondered what good had been accomplished, if there was a plan at the back of life. What good had it done to anybody or to any cause to have a man who was honourable and gifted and capable and of good intent, bludgeoned by fate until he was rendered numb and impotent. An encumbrance. A creature without ambition or drive or purpose or desire. One might as well be a cow and lie chewing the cud. And this was life!

His mind reverted to Bronwen. Almost instinctively his mind drifted to her when he had nothing tangible on which to concentrate. Now she had left him she seemed more with him than ever. The presence of which he was aware when he was at sea had returned. Her love enfolded him like a cloak. He was warm and content so long as he thought about her, and did not try to unravel the mystery of life. How dear she was; how indescribably dear. One could not measure time. Those moments under the shade of the beech meant more than all the rest of his life put together.

It had been a revelation to him . . . the sublime heights to which human emotions could ascend. He knew that he would never know the like again. Almost he regretted the experience, he would miss it so. He knew that he would spend the rest of his life craving for a repetition. But would he have willingly for gone it? No, a thousand times no. Despite the suffering, despite, if so it must be, the sin, he would glory in it. He asked no higher heaven than to love and be loved like that. If love, of a truth, were the greatest thing in the world then he had tasted it. His one regret, his one everlasting regret, was that he had not drunk of the cup to the lees. Still, it was better to have the glorious memory which he retained than to live as so many mortals did, unawakened and unhallowed.

So, dwelling within his memory, his mind wedded to Bronwen, he walked on, unconscious of hunger or cold. Snow was frosting the grasses as he climbed higher. Snow sprinkled the roadway. His footprints left a trail to show where he had walked. The snow grew thicker. It interested him to see the tracks which crossed it; where a thrush had hopped or a mouse had scurried. Snow was so white and pure and chaste. Was it symbolical? Yet how cold, how chilling! Why was it, he mused, that there was no warmth in chastity? A fire was fierce, and could be devouring, but at least there was comfort in the glow.

He was amid the upland passes now, and the snow lay thicker. He paused awhile to gaze into a black tarn. Its still depths seemed to hold awesome secrets as though dead men lay there. Men drowned. He stood leaning on a great smooth glacial boulder which thrust its dark shape from out of a carpet of untrodden snow. Piers was dead. At least his body was dead. When he picked up the corpse Piers was cold and hard and stiff. Like marble. But where was Piers himself? He would have given much to know. He thought so long about it that he felt a kind of remorse, as though he had been guilty of his death. He had been so obsessed with the idea of shooting Piers that it was difficult to rid his mind of the idea that it was not an accomplished fact. Nigel passed his hand wearily over his head. It was bare and it was burning. Perhaps he was feverish. He hadn't killed Piers. Piers was drowned. And no one would know what had been intended. He had thrown the pistol into the river. No one would ever know. But had he (Nigel asked himself, as he resumed his laboured way along the path), had he been as guilty as though he had performed the deed? After all, motive was everything. Or almost everything, and assuredly he had meant to kill Piers. He decided solemnly that he would regard himself as a murderer for the remainder of his life, and with the decision he found strange consolation, as though he had settled a knotty point.

How was he going to tell Puah? What was he going to tell Puah? That was even more to the point. He slipped on a patch of ice and rose with his boat-cloak covered with snow. He scarcely heeded the fall. There was Puah to be considered. Puah, it suddenly came to him, was an even greater problem than Piers. Even greater than Kit, for where his son was concerned the way was plain.

He tried to analyse his feelings towards Puah. She had been a good wife to him: considerate, loyal, helpful, loving. He had an idea that she would prove even more loving if he gave her any encouragement. But he did not want her to be more loving. He would live with her. Do his duty by her. He was fond of her in his way, appreciated her. But she was not Bronwen. Bronwen would never leave him. Now she had left him she would always be with him. A paradox! An anomaly! But nevertheless truth. What was truth? Had people got the wrong conception of life? He slipped again and staggered to his feet. It was heavenly to think that Bronwen was with him. He was very conscious of her presence now. He could speak to her. Yes, there in the snowy pass, amid the tarn and the rocks, with the lowering sky and the chill frosty air, he could speak to her. "Dear heart," he said aloud. "You are with me always. Right to the end of the journey. Bronwen, I know now that you will never leave me. Never forsake me. Your presence shall go with me, not only through this world but through the worlds to come. You are mine, beloved, and I am yours, wedded in mind as well as body. Wedded now and through eternity. A love like ours can never pause for death. . . ."

* * * * *

Some sheep-farmers scouring the mountain side found him lying face downwards in the snow. As they picked him up they saw his cheeks were flushed, but he smiled gently in his sleep as though his dreams were sweet.

* * * * *

The snowdrops were out when Nigel, lean from fever, made his way slowly along the Gower lanes. In sheltered spots the early primroses were already peeping from their nests of curly green. He stopped to caress them tenderly. What mighty hand had wrought the miracle of their simple, homely beauty? He picked one and meditated as he walked. He walked slowly. Reluctantly. He was at his journey's end. The cottage was just around the corner of the hawthorn hedge. The cottage where Puah lived. Where Kit lived. Where he must henceforth live. He would never leave it now. Gone was his ambition. He cared nothing for his hood which awaited him at Oxford. Cared nothing for his books. He would go out day by day with the fishermen. And in the evenings he would play with Kit. And he would be very tender to Puah and never let her know what he had suffered. He could keep silence about his Gethsemane. He must grow to love Puah. Perhaps it would not be hard. It would be a different kind of love, of course. A second best. Not the grand, glorious experience which Bronwen had given him, leaving him exalted in spirit, emotionally uplifted, but a homely, placid, affection which might grow and strengthen with the coming years. Dreams! Dreams! Yet how could man ever ascend the heights without his dreams?

He had had his dreams, his ideals, and they had been taken from him. And yet he had striven so hard to bring them to pass.

A sense of the futility of human endeavour swept over him. He had tried to do what seemed to him to be right and it had come to naught. He had planned and he had suffered. He had striven and he had endured. And all to no purpose. To his finite mind the way had seemed clear. From the very start he was persuaded that he and Bronwen were one; that they were made for one another; that they understood one another. But apparently it was not to be.

As a floating leaf is swirled remorselessly along by a stream in spate so he had been carried by the current, against his will and against his desires, down the river of life. It was no use striving further. He must learn to accept. Perhaps, after all, this life was not the end but the beginning. That things which were obscure now would be seen more clearly later on. In the meantime he must take life not as he desired it to be but as he found it.

Sadly he turned towards the cottage which was now his home, his humble home. Puah was in the doorway. She had been watching for him. She was watching him . . . wistfully. She always looked wistful when he was a prey to his thoughts.

He was conscious of little fists thumping against a window. And a high, excited voice. . . . "Daddy. Daddy come home!" Nigel's eyes grew blurred. He had his boy. His precious boy. And Puah had given this priceless treasure to him. Puah. His wife.

How pretty she looked with her dark eyes and hair and tanned skin. Sad but still pretty. And how warm was her form now that she was more mature. Life did hold much, after all. He must cease to kick against the pricks. He must learn to accept. It was no use fighting against destiny. Life was more powerful than puny man.

He could only hope that at the back of it was some kindly force, which understood human frailties. A father who pitied his erring, wayward, heart-sick children.

And Nigel prayed that his mental conflict would henceforth cease, and that he would come to know that peace which passeth understanding.

Puah was regarding him steadfastly. Her dark, eloquent searching eyes never left his. He quickened his step. He moved towards her—his wife—his patient, tender, understanding wife, though now he only saw her through a mist. She ran to meet him. "Oh, Nigel, you have come back to us!"

It was the "us" which broke him down completely.

"You have stopped *thinking*! You will never *think* any more; will you Nigel? You have come back, my man! You have come back!"

She was in his arms, sobbing. He strained her to his breast. Gently he lifted her across the threshold and closed the door of their home.

THE END